ELIZABETH HEITER

HUNTED

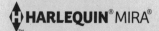

HARLEQUIN® MIRA®

D0053210

Recycling programs
for this product may
not exist in your area.

ISBN-13: 978-0-7783-1584-1

HUNTED

Copyright © 2014 by Elizabeth Heiter

For questions and comments about the quality of this book, please contact us at
CustomerService@Harlequin.com.

Printed in U.S.A.

First printing: January 2014
10 9 8 7 6 5 4 3 2 1

Look for Elizabeth Heiter's next novel

Vanished

available soon from Harlequin MIRA

For my mom,
who made up stories for me as a child and who always
supported me in my pursuit to tell my own stories.

And for Robbie Terman, who has walked this
writing journey with me, and made every step better.

HUNTED

ELIZABETH HEITER

PROLOGUE

HE SHOULD HAVE KILLED THE OLD MAN.

The second he'd realized Harris had spotted him trespassing, he should've flanked the old man. Just crept around behind him and snapped his neck. Instead, he'd disappeared. Blended right into the woods and slipped away.

And while he'd huddled in his car, cursing himself for getting distracted enough to let Harris spot him, the old man had kept looking. And the old man had found something.

An angry tirade screamed in his mind as he watched another police car swing into Harris's driveway, sirens blaring. All those months of scouting out the woods wasted. All that time finding the perfect place, making sure not even Harris would discover it, squandered. It'd been his secret hideaway, where he could display his trophies, revel in his triumphs.

And Harris was ruining everything. Damn it! Why hadn't he stopped the old man when he'd had the chance?

By now, the cops were digging out his women, taking them away. By now, the cops were calling the FBI. Same way they had three years ago.

Unease surfaced, mingling with the anger, blurring with guilt. Three years ago, he'd made one mistake. Made just one kill he regretted.

But besides Diana, no one had ever suspected. And here in Virginia, no one knew him. The cops could call whoever they wanted; he'd taken precautions. They weren't going to catch him.

And he wasn't finished yet.

1

"BAINE. MY OFFICE. NOW!"

FBI Special Agent Evelyn Baine spun the chair in her tiny cubicle, but her boss was already slamming the door to his office.

She shrugged back into her suit jacket, buttoned it to cover the weapon at her hip and straightened her spine. Dan Moore's tone didn't bother her; the ASAC—Special Agent in Charge—was always curt with her. In fact, getting called into his office this early was a good thing. It meant she was getting a new case to profile.

Her anticipation grew as she wove around cubicles in the unmarked office building in Aquia, Virginia, where the FBI's Behavioral Analysis Unit (BAU) was housed. This was her favorite time, early in the morning before most agents arrived, before the smell of burned coffee and stale air-conditioning permeated everything, when it was just her and her cases.

She entered Dan's office and found him settled at his oversize desk. The head of BAU was, as usual, surrounded by an aura of stress that gave his skin a grayish hue and constantly slanted his eyebrows toward his nose. Today, he also looked frazzled.

"Take a seat." Dan popped three antacids into his mouth and took a swig of coffee. "Ever been to Bakersville?"

"No, but it's north of here, right? Small and rural?" She leaned forward, ready for another chance to take on one of society's worst predators. Ready for another chance to give someone else the closure she'd never had. "What happened there?"

Dan frowned, maybe because he hadn't warmed to her in the past year despite her high success rate. Then again, maybe the antacids had gotten stuck in his throat.

Evelyn didn't need to hear the answer to her question to know there were sleepless nights and more long hours in her future. When police had a problem so terrible they couldn't handle it themselves, they came to BAU. Given the number of profile requests faxed into the office every day, to actually get a profiler assigned meant a police department's problem was both unusual and deadly.

"Earlier this morning, two murdered women were discovered in the woods," Dan said. "There are a few preliminaries in the file I emailed you, though not much. I took a lot of it over the phone, but I think it's better if you go straight to the crime scene and get the specifics firsthand. Bakersville wants you on-site now."

"Now? For only two murders?" The question might have sounded insensitive to her a year ago, but she'd been here long enough to understand that time was a commodity BAU agents didn't have. Normally, the police would have to strike out big before BAU swooped in.

"It's a weird one. The Bakersville police are leading the investigation and they've asked us to consult. Police Chief Caulfield wants a preliminary criminal personality profile immediately."

Dan turned back to his computer, effectively dismissing her. "If you need help, ask Greg to go with you."

Evelyn hid her annoyance. A year ago, Greg Ibsen had initiated her into the world of behavioral analysis. But she wasn't a rookie anymore. She didn't need anyone checking her work simply because she was the youngest agent in the office, the one with the least field experience. She'd earned her spot at BAU. And she worked her ass off every day to prove it.

"Is there anything else?"

"Just get to work. Bakersville's never seen anything like this. They're not equipped to handle this killer."

She nodded and stood. "I'm on it." As she left his office, she couldn't stop herself from glancing at the partition near the coffeepot serving as a bulletin board for anything the agents found of interest. Next to an article on a new brain-mapping technique and a list of the Most Wanted, someone had thumb-tacked a sheet with the heading Predator Still at Large. Underneath was a computer-generated sketch of Dan.

The spot-on sketch had everything from the dome-shaped head that was only bald on top to the thin, pinched lips, but Dan hadn't yet figured out who it was. Evelyn wasn't going to be the one to enlighten him.

As soon as she was ensconced in her cubicle again, she quickly skimmed through the meager file in her email, then grabbed her briefcase. When she turned around, she almost slammed into Greg.

He yanked his mug out of her way, sloshing coffee onto his shoes.

She grimaced. "Sorry, Greg."

He shrugged, setting his coffee down as he slipped out of his suit coat to reveal his standard dress shirt and some cartoon-character tie. "No worries. I'll spill it on myself later, anyway."

Greg Ibsen had been at BAU seven years longer than she

had, logging thousands more hours profiling complicated cases. Somehow, he was still the most easygoing guy in the office—even after he'd gotten stuck training the newbie Dan didn't want.

Dropping into his chair, he said, "One of these days maybe you could sleep in a little. Stop making everyone else look lazy." The smile in his tone told her he was at least partly kidding.

Evelyn fiddled with the thin gold band topped with a small diamond—once her grandma's—that she never took off. If her grandma realized how much time she spent working, she would've told her the same thing Greg often did: to get a hobby.

But her grandma would have understood why she didn't. She'd been the one to pull Evelyn's life back together when her best friend, Cassie Byers, had been abducted. She was the only one who truly understood Evelyn's drive to find her, even seventeen years later.

Pushing back memories of the woman who'd raised her and now needed extensive care herself, she peered at Greg around their shared cubicle wall. Unlike her blank one, his was filled with pictures of his wife, Marnie, and their adopted children, Lucy and Josh. "Dan just gave me a new case. I'm heading out the door."

"Really? What did you get?"

"Serial killer."

Greg's eyebrows reached for each other. "Really? And you're going to the site now?"

Serial killers were what the unit was best known for profiling, but between evaluating terrorist threats and interpreting the behavior of arsonists, bomb-makers and child predators, they didn't always get priority.

"Dan said it was weird." And considering the cases they dealt with regularly, that was saying a lot.

"Weird, huh? Tell me about it when you get back."

"Sure. Dan thinks I should ask for your help, anyway."

"What? The little lady can't handle the big, scary serial killer alone?" Greg joked. "Didn't you hear that BAU has a no-women-allowed rule?"

Evelyn wished Dan's attitude didn't bother her. "You know what a rule-breaker I am."

He snorted, because that was just as much of a joke as her being unfit to work as a profiler. "Good luck with the case."

"Thanks," she said. But luck had nothing to do with it.

She'd worked toward this for most of her life and she was a damn good profiler. Whatever the case, however wily the criminal, she'd write a profile that would bring him to justice.

The Bakersville, Virginia, police station squatted on a bare patch of land. The faded brick building with weathered windows seemed out of place amid the hundred-year-old pine trees bracketing it on three sides. It was off the main road through town, beside a mom-and-pop coffee shop and a neighborhood of starter homes.

Evelyn slung her briefcase over her shoulder and trudged up the steps into the station. Inside, it was abuzz with uniformed officers. Two had a cuffed prisoner between them, obviously brought in on a drunk and disorderly charge. Others wore nervous, uncertain expressions, probably because of the murders.

Evelyn walked up to the desk, where a young officer sat. "Evelyn Baine. I'm the criminal investigative analyst. Chief Caulfield is expecting me."

The officer's gaze shifted over her questioningly, and Evelyn tried not to let it get her hackles up. Bakersville was rural, and despite the diversity surrounding it, almost entirely white.

With the mocha-colored skin she'd inherited from her Zimbabwean father and the sea-green eyes she'd gotten from her Irish-English mother, she stood out.

When she added, "I'm with the FBI," the officer's gaze traveled skeptically from her tidy bun, over her well-tailored suit to her sturdy heels, then squinted at the credentials she held up.

Finally, he nodded and she tucked them back in her pocket, tugging down the hem of her blazer on the side where she wore her gun. The expensive clothes sometimes raised eyebrows, but they helped bolster her self-confidence when she arrived at a crime scene and had to establish credibility immediately.

"It's this way," the officer told her, leading her through a bullpen packed with cops.

There were a few civilians, too, most demanding to know about rumors of a killer. One, a heavyset, bearded man, was asking about ViCAP.

Surprised at the mention of the Violent Criminal Apprehension Program, the database the Bureau used to match unsolved cases of violent crime, Evelyn glanced back.

The blue-eyed civilian was talking to an officer whose uncertain stance and red face labeled him a rookie. "I don't think we do that," the officer said with a shrug.

Evelyn made a mental note that no one had cross-checked the murders. Most small towns weren't plugged into ViCAP. Once she saw the crime scene, she'd try to determine whether these were the killer's first crimes; if not, she'd access the database herself and see if she could track him before he'd come to Bakersville.

The officer escorting her knocked on a door marked Police Chief Tanner Caulfield, then left her alone.

"Come in," a distinctly Southern voice barked.

The man inside was young for a police chief. When he

stood, he looked as if he had more than a foot on her five feet two inches and a past as a high school linebacker without quite enough bulk to make it into college ball.

Evelyn thrust out her hand. "I'm Evelyn Baine, from the FBI's Behavioral Analysis Unit. I'm here to consult on your murder investigation."

His thick eyebrows furrowed. He stared at her dainty hand with its short, unpolished nails, then took it carefully, as though he was afraid he'd break it. As he shook her hand, he was also shaking his head. "Sorry. You don't look like an agent."

"Really?" Evelyn replied, frustrated by the too-common reaction. "What does an agent look like?"

"Bigger. But yours is a desk job, right?"

His assumption annoyed her, but a year of consulting with outside law enforcement had shown her the best way to respond. He wasn't going to respect her unless he thought she could hold her own in the field. "I was a field agent for five years before transferring to BAU. I worked violent crime."

Tanner's eyebrows jerked up, and he studied her a little more closely as he settled in his chair. "You're going to give me a profile of the killer, right? Something that'll tell us how to catch this bastard?"

"That's right. It's my job to study behavioral evidence the UNSUB doesn't know he left at the crime scene." That was what had always fascinated her about her job—turning an unknown subject (UNSUB) into an identified killer from clues he didn't even realize he was leaving behind. "From that, I can tell you how to locate him and how to interrogate him once he's in custody."

"Okay," Tanner said slowly. "What exactly do you mean by behavioral evidence?"

"What I find at the crime scene helps me see how he thinks, what he's looking for in his victims, why he kills."

"Uh-huh." Tanner sounded as if he didn't quite understand profiling, but that didn't matter.

Because she understood Tanner. Her job wasn't just about profiling the perpetrators. It was also about profiling the people who called her onto their turf. Most of them only came to the FBI if they were desperate, and many of them resented it. She'd learned fast that sizing up whoever was in charge made her job easier.

Five minutes in Tanner's office was all she needed to figure out that his position was a major source of pride and that he'd felt underqualified *before* he'd been tested with a serial killer. As long as she was careful with his ego, he'd be eager to listen to her.

"Let's get started." Energy hummed in Evelyn's veins. Time to nail another predator to the wall. And he'd never see her coming.

"Do you have the profile for me now?"

Without knowing anything other than that there'd been two murders? Did Tanner think she was a psychic? "I'm afraid it doesn't work that way."

"How does it work?"

"You have cops at the scene? Let's start there. I want to join them."

Tanner frowned. "It's ugly, Agent Baine."

Evelyn nodded. As a woman, she got this reaction a lot. "Trust me, I've probably seen worse."

"Okay." He stood. "I'll take you."

Evelyn followed him out to a patrol car and, ten minutes later, they were talking to Jack Harris to tell him they'd be joining the other cops on his property.

"I wanted him to know I was back. We wouldn't want him

to think we were trespassing and shoot at us," Tanner told her as they returned to the car.

Evelyn glanced at the elderly man watching them from his doorway. He looked as if he shouldn't be able to walk without assistance, let alone fire a weapon.

"Why are we driving? How far into his property are we going?"

Tanner gunned the engine. "Pretty far."

He pulled out of the driveway and headed back the way they'd come, then unexpectedly swung left onto a dirt trail. The police car slowed as it bounced over the uneven ground, and branches scratched both sides.

Finally, he pulled to a stop behind several other patrol cars and the medical examiner's van. The forest seemed to have swallowed them. Tall oak, hickory and pine trees blocked out most of the sun as Evelyn followed Tanner deeper into the woods.

"Does this area get much traffic?"

"The woods?" Tanner grunted. "None. Harris has a hundred acres back here and he guards it with his shotgun. He's the one who found the bodies, and only because he thought he spotted someone trespassing."

"So where you parked, that was the closest place to bring a vehicle to the crime scene?"

"Yes."

"Then the killer knows the area. And he's not looking for attention."

"He's not?"

Evelyn had no idea how deep into the woods they were going, but she couldn't hear the cops yet. "He didn't expect these bodies to be found. So he's not looking for press coverage."

"You might change your mind when you see the bodies," Tanner muttered.

Evelyn held back her rebuttal. It didn't matter what state the bodies were in, the drop site told its own story. And this one was already telling her they had a killer who liked his privacy, who was careful and even-tempered. Someone who'd be hard to track down

"There it is," Tanner finally said, pointing.

Up ahead, crime scene tape had been strung around trees, and cops were working inside it. Two men in black coats with the words *Medical Examiner's Office* stenciled on the pockets were carrying a gurney.

Evelyn picked up her pace, her heels sinking into ground that was still damp from last week's rain, still littered with decaying leaves even as the first day of spring beckoned. She wanted to see the crime scene intact.

But the closer she got, the more she realized that would be impossible. The cops were trampling the scene. Reminding herself that these particular cops didn't get many murders didn't help.

Frustration bubbled to the surface. "Your officers are stepping on potential evidence."

"We're not incompetent." Tanner caught up to her. "We took pictures before I sent my officers in to dig them out."

The case file had mentioned partial burial of the victims, as well as knife marks so specific they suggested a killer's signature. Evelyn had hoped to see at least one victim the way she'd been left by the killer. "Have both bodies been pulled out yet?"

Tanner gestured to the crime scene. "See for yourself."

And when two cops moved aside, she did. "Shit," she breathed.

There was a skull sticking out of the ground. Nothing but

a skull, the long brown hair still partially attached. The killer had dug a vertical hole some five feet deep and put his victim in it, then shoveled dirt back over her until her chin rested on the ground. Animals and the elements had violated her after the killer had.

They'd pulled the second victim out, which was one reason Evelyn knew there was a body underneath the head. The victim was laid out on the bag she'd be zipped inside to transport her to autopsy.

And being buried up to their heads wasn't the only indignity these women had suffered. The one who'd been dug up had been tightly wrapped in plastic sheeting, but the medical examiner had peeled it back. The woman was nude, her skin discolored and slipping from the bones. She was covered in circular bruises that had never healed because she'd been murdered before they could. In the center of her chest, slicing over both breasts, the killer had carved a circle into her now-rotting flesh.

The fact that Evelyn's immediate reaction wasn't to bring up her breakfast, but to step closer and study the details for what they said about the killer, suggested that she'd seen too many crime scenes in the past year. Still, like every other case, it put a familiar twinge in her heart, made her remember what it had felt like when she'd lost someone she loved.

But at least these bodies had been found. At least these families had closure. It was something she and Cassie's family might never get.

Tanner came up beside her and gulped, trying not to gag. "What does it mean?"

She didn't know. But Dan was right. This case was weird. Why display the victims if the killer wasn't showing off? The heads above the ground were shocking, the sort of action she'd expect from a killer who called the press and bragged about what he'd accomplished.

But this killer had done it for himself. Which meant he was nearby. And that he came back to visit.

"Who's the medical examiner?" she asked Tanner instead of replying.

He pointed to a heavyset man wearing rubber boots and a scowl.

"How long have they been dead?" she called, making several cops with green-tinged faces look her way. Their curious gazes lingered, skipping over her from the top of her bun to her mud-caked heels.

"The one here, probably a month. The one in the ground, likely a week or two. Hard to be exact, given the unusually warm weather we've had in the past month, which would speed up decomp. I'll know more when I get them back to my lab."

"Have they been in the ground that long or were they moved here recently?"

He nodded at the victim still in the ground. "My guess is they've been here since they were killed."

She turned back to Tanner. "Any evidence they were killed here?"

"None that we've found."

"So just a drop site." She edged a little closer to the body on the bag. This one wasn't smeared with dried blood from the circle carved in her chest. There was only dirt around her neck, where the plastic hadn't quite covered her. "And he cleaned them before he brought them here."

"But do you know why?"

"Why he's killing? To create an accurate profile, I need victim information, too. But I can tell you that this—" she gestured to the skull resting on the packed dirt "—is really unusual."

She squinted at the skull, considering the killer's intended symbolism. Studying serial killers for a living had shown her depravity she'd never dreamed existed, but there was something singularly creepy about this.

An ominous feeling rushed over her, sending ice up her spine. She tried to shake it off, put confidence in her voice. "Typically, you'd see this sort of thing if the body was left in a public place. Since it's not, we aren't looking at showmanship. He's not trying to shock or disgust anyone. This display is personal. It has some meaning for him."

"What?" Tanner pressed.

"I don't know." She'd never seen anything like this before. "But once I figure it out, it'll tell me how he thinks."

She stepped closer to the body still packed in the dirt, knelt down next to it and felt her nose pinch at the stench of decay wafting up from the ground. Anger at the callousness of the murder knotted in her chest. She already knew the killer had gotten off on holding this woman's life in his hands, liked hearing her beg even though nothing she said would change the fact that she was about to die.

Behind her, she heard Tanner mutter under his breath, "How he *thinks?* He's a fucking head case who likes to hide in the woods and carve up women."

Studying the brunette, Evelyn replied, "If you're assuming he's insane, he's not. These crime scenes are neat, not disorganized the way they would be if the perpetrator was clinically insane. He does have an antisocial personality disorder, though."

Tanner let out an ugly snort. "Yeah, I figured anyone who could do *this* wouldn't have tons of friends."

"He can probably make friends," she corrected. "He has no

empathy for others, but he can fake it. He's smart. I don't need the autopsy results to tell you this is a sexually motivated serial killer. He's intelligent, adaptable and extremely methodical. He enjoys outwitting the police and his victims."

Goose bumps prickled her skin as she stared at what was left of the victim in front of her, knowing if she didn't move fast there'd be another one. "He won't be easy to catch."

"Isn't that your job? To make him easier to catch?"

Evelyn stayed perched next to the victim in the ground, but looked up at him. "It is. And to do it, I need to get inside his head, see the world through his eyes. So, tell me about the victims. Have you identified them?"

Tanner's whole face hardened and a cold, determined sheen fell over his eyes. "Yes. The one in the ground is probably Barbara Jensen. The blonde victim on the autopsy bag is definitely Mary Ann Pollak—we identified a tattoo on her ankle. They both disappeared in the past month. They've lived in Bakersville for years. Mary Ann got married a few months ago."

"What do they have in common?"

Tanner's massive shoulders rolled. "Nothing as far as I can tell. They had totally different jobs and different interests. Friends and families said they didn't know each other, except maybe in passing. The only thing I can see they had in common was getting grabbed by a psycho."

"Did they look alike?"

"Well, they were about the same age. They were both white."

The same age and race from one victim to another was normal, but a serial killer would be seeking a more specific quality. He'd have a type. "What about eye color or stature? Or anything else?"

Tanner frowned, shook his head.

Evelyn frowned, too. If this killer wasn't searching for a

physical attribute, there was something else. Something she couldn't see.

"They were taken pretty close to when the M.E. says they were probably killed," Tanner added.

Evelyn looked back at the brunette in the ground. So, the killer didn't hold on to them for long. And that told her displaying the bodies was as important to him as the kill, perhaps more so.

But she didn't know what to make of the display. Tension weighed down on her shoulders as she said, "Tell me about the abductions."

"Like I mentioned, we're pretty sure the one still buried in the ground is Barbara. She was last seen at a supermarket. A few hours later, her husband called to say she was missing. We found her car at the supermarket with a flat tire, but no sign of her. Mary Ann was last seen leaving a friend's house around eleven at night. We found her car around the corner."

She glanced at him. "Flat tire?"

"No."

"What else can you tell me?"

"We couldn't find any enemies. No one with a reason to hurt Mary Ann or Barbara."

Of course not. Because these murders weren't based on any typical motive, like revenge. If they had been, solving them would be a simple matter of solid police work. Looking at who had a reason to hurt the women and digging into that person until he broke. If the motive was typical, a profile would be a waste of time.

Serial murders were a whole different crime. Normal motivations didn't apply and normal investigative methods didn't work. That was why she had a job. Profilers saw crime scenes differently.

"You're not going to find the killer by investigating people in the victims' lives who held grudges," Evelyn told him. "They didn't know him, at least not more than superficially."

"So I was wasting manpower?" Tanner's face broadcasted anger, but beneath it, she saw the regret.

"When they went missing, it was the right thing to do. Now that we're convinced we've got a serial killer, we go a different route."

"I'm sorry," he said, so low she barely heard him.

She wasn't sure if he was talking to her or Barbara, but she answered, "It's not your fault." He was a cop, not a profiler, so there was no reason for him to know how serial killers thought. Sometimes, late at night when she couldn't get a case out of her head, she wished she didn't know, either.

But she'd picked this job when she was twelve years old, when the world had been falling apart around her. And now, it was the one thing she excelled at, the one place where she could make a difference.

She dusted off her hands and stood, letting the cops with shovels move past her to dig Barbara out. She'd wait and see for herself, but she already expected Barbara to be covered in strange bruises, with a circle carved into her chest.

"I don't suppose we know cause of death yet?"

"The M.E. suspects blunt force trauma to the head on Mary Ann, but there's no evidence of that with Barbara. He won't be sure until he does the autopsies."

"What about the bruising? Any idea what caused it?"

"No." The medical examiner fixed his penetrating gaze on her. "But it wasn't fists. And it was multiple objects, because the bruises aren't the same size or shape."

Evelyn took a closer look at Mary Ann. The bruising on her body was mostly circular, but the M.E. was right. The circles weren't consistent. They suggested the killer was inflicting pain for his own pleasure, that he was a sadist. But something about that felt wrong.

As the cops started working, Evelyn moved farther back, taking in the sheer vastness of the woods, the isolation. Thinking about the two victims who'd been left here. "Two weeks apart," she mused.

"What?" Tanner asked.

"Mary Ann and Barbara went missing two weeks apart. Assuming, of course, that this is Barbara. And now it's been another two weeks."

Tanner's face had gone ghost-white and he rocked back on his heels. "Serial killers stick to that kind of pattern?"

"Usually. But two weeks between murders is short." Evelyn scanned the scene around her, the killer's playground. "Not a lot of time to find a potential victim, then stalk and kill her."

Red flooded Tanner's cheeks, creeping up his ears to his hairline. "Another woman went missing two days ago."

"What?"

He shuffled his feet. "We don't think she's connected. She's not from Bakersville, either. She's from Kensington. Her husband told Kensington police she took off after an argument."

Evelyn tried to keep the frustration out of her voice. "And you think she isn't connected, why? Because you didn't find her buried here, too?"

"No, because apparently this is a repeat performance for her. The husband didn't even report it until twenty-four hours later."

"What do you mean 'repeat performance'?"

"Apparently, after she argues with her husband, she leaves town with a friend. That friend is off on vacation and not answering her cell phone, but her husband says chances are this woman is with her."

With a serial killer on the loose, Evelyn didn't like to take chances. "You should coordinate with the Kensington cops. Make sure they follow up."

Tanner looked ready to snap at what had probably sounded like an order, so she asked quickly, "How far did we walk to get here from the car?"

He seemed surprised by the change of topic, but replied, "About a quarter mile."

"And there's no other way to get in?"

Tanner shrugged, letting out a heavy breath. "If there is, even Harris doesn't know it. And he's lived here his whole life, right on this property. It belonged to his parents before him."

"A quarter of a mile is a long way to transport two bodies. Did you see any ruts from wheels in this mud?"

"No. Definitely nothing like that."

"That rules out a wheelbarrow to transport the bodies."

"I guess that's true. But does it really matter how he got them here?" Tanner demanded. "Shouldn't we be more worried about finding him now?"

"If the UNSUB carried his victims a quarter of a mile, then he's really strong. Carrying a grown woman's dead weight would be unwieldy, especially if rigor mortis had set in."

Interest sparked in Tanner's eyes. "And?"

"And he'd have to be taller than his victims and weigh more. He had to know it was unlikely he'd be interrupted when he buried his victims, because if he was seen a quarter mile into the woods and the cops showed up, he'd be in trouble. How would he get away? And imagine how long this took him." She gestured to Barbara, only partially dug out, even with three cops working.

When Tanner opened his mouth, she knew exactly what he was going to say, so she preempted him. "He *did* want to get away. People sometimes say serial killers try to get caught, but it's usually bullshit. This guy is having fun. He doesn't want to end up in handcuffs or with a bullet through his brain. He wants to get away with it. To keep killing."

"Do you think he's targeting the women in Bakersville exclusively?"

"I think he's hunting where he lives."

Tanner swayed, his expression queasy. "Bakersville is a small town, Agent Baine. I know pretty well everyone here."

Bakersville was never going to be the same. She'd been to other small towns where the residents thought all serial killers looked like monsters, that no member of their community could hide such dark desires. Once upon a time, she'd lived in one.

And the monster there had ripped her life apart.

"The killer seems normal to everyone around him. He's not a stranger. And he's not an amateur. These aren't his first murders." Evelyn gave Tanner her profiler stare, the one that warned things were going to get worse before they got better. "This killer is not going to stop until we stop him."

2

"GREG!" YELLED A DEEP VOICE, BORDERING ON obnoxious in the otherwise quiet room full of BAU agents.

Greg's head popped up over the cubicle partition, his eyes slightly unfocused, as though he was still inside his own head.

Evelyn recognized the voice as that of Greg's cousin, Gabe Fontaine, who worked a city over in Quantico.

"How come you're early?" Greg asked when Gabe reached his cubicle.

As always, when they stood next to each other, Evelyn got a sense of what Greg must have looked like a decade ago. Gabe was taller, broader and blonder, but there was no denying the family resemblance.

"Chopper rappelling got cut short because of a helicopter malfunction," Gabe replied.

Gabe was a member of the FBI's Hostage Rescue Team. Along with BAU, HRT was part of the Critical Incident Response Group, formed to react to crises around the country. While BAU agents usually worked from their desks, getting into the disturbed minds of killers, HRT agents strapped on Kevlar and went out to face hostage takers and terrorists directly.

"For some reason, when Mac heard I was going to the BAU office, he suddenly wanted to come for lunch," Gabe said.

Evelyn spun her chair around and bumped into a pair of muscular legs. Sure enough, while Gabe had gone into Greg's cubicle, his teammate Kyle McKenzie had snuck up behind her. She was surprised she hadn't felt his presence. She worked in an all-male office, but when the HRT agents stopped by, the testosterone levels seemed to increase tenfold.

"Hey, Evelyn," Kyle said with a flash of his dimples and a wink. "You trying to knock me over?"

Heat rushed to Evelyn's cheeks at Kyle's teasing. No doubt it was his standard M.O. with women. With those piercing blue eyes and easy, flirtatious grin, the man probably had more dates in a week than she'd had in years.

She tried for a glib smile. "I need to work on my spin."

Kyle let out a snort of laughter. Like Gabe, he was dressed in what she thought of as ass-kicking gear. While suits were practically the only thing in her closet, HRT agents went to work in cargo pants and T-shirts.

As he moved closer, she looked into his probing gaze, the one that locked on hers and held a little too long, and she cursed herself for egging him on. He was already too tempting when he was just teasing her. If she encouraged him and he took it up a notch, could she still resist him? She shifted her eyes. "Hi, McKenzie."

"Everyone calls me Mac." He reminded her every time he came to the BAU office.

But Evelyn never did. His constant flirting left her off balance. And unlike the average guy who hit on her, the fact that she wore a gun on her hip and had a stare that could break hardened killers didn't deter him. Using his full last name gave her a bit of distance.

Because, also unlike the average guy who hit on her, this

one made her want to toss away caution. But she valued her career too much. Dating another agent was cause for reassignment and she'd worked too damn hard for too damn long to let that happen.

She slid her chair a little closer to her desk.

"Mac never wants to go out to lunch unless I'm coming here," Gabe continued. "I think he has a crush on you, *Greg*."

Evelyn didn't have to look to know Greg was rolling his eyes. Being serious was about as alien to Gabe as joking was to her.

"Maybe Evelyn should join us." There was humor in Gabe's tone, although Evelyn wasn't sure why.

"Okay" was on the tip of her tongue. But then she glanced at the BAKBURY case file on her computer —FBI shorthand for Bakersville Burial Killer. She thought about the killer's fast pace and said instead, "I've got—"

Kyle cut her off. "Too much work." He pointed at her computer. "It'll still be here when you get back from lunch. You need to go out, have some fun."

Gabe was making a face at Kyle, and Evelyn wondered if it was because he figured her personal dictionary didn't include the word *fun*.

He was probably right. She couldn't afford to screw up on a case, and this one was extremely time-sensitive. Besides, she had her eye on Dan's job. It might take her a decade or more, but being the boss meant having control over the jobs the unit took on, even the very few cold cases they tackled. Every case mattered, but she'd joined BAU to solve one particular crime.

So she shrugged apologetically and said, "I do have too much work." She'd even skipped her usual early morning run today to get a jump start, which had turned out to be a good idea, since the Bakersville case seemed as if it was going to be complex.

Kyle looked like he might argue, but Dan appeared at her desk. "How did the meeting at Bakersville go?"

"Fine." Knowing Dan wanted her to elaborate, she added, "I'm working on the profile now."

Dan nodded, then scowled at Greg's companions. He'd never made any secret of the fact that he didn't like non-BAU personnel at Aquia.

And Evelyn suspected every time the HRT agents visited, he went back to his office and doubled up on his antacids.

"If you want to go over your profile with me, I'll be available later in the day."

As Dan disappeared inside his office, Evelyn tried to unclench her jaw. Why was Dan always suggesting she get help with her profiles, a full year after she'd joined the unit? What was it going to take to prove she was qualified?

"You still the FNG here, Evelyn?" Kyle asked, using Bureau-speak for Fucking New Guy. It technically referred to agents at their first field office, but the term was sometimes used to describe agents new to a particular specialization.

"I guess so."

"Dan just doesn't like that Evelyn had a reputation as being a natural profiler before she started working for him," Greg piped up.

"Really?" Gabe stuck his head over Greg's cubicle wall and grinned at her. "How did that happen?"

Evelyn tried for a flippant reply. "It's a mystery."

"Aw, come on," Gabe wheedled in the same tone she'd heard him use on Greg when he wanted to know something Greg didn't particularly want to tell him. "I love a good mystery."

"I got lucky," she lied. Talking about her past was hard. Even thinking about her past was hard.

She was at BAU because she'd worked most of her life to

get here. She wasn't really a natural at profiling; she'd been studying the techniques since she was twelve, since her best friend was abducted. But she'd never been able to talk to Greg or anyone else at BAU about Cassie.

Maybe because if she didn't talk about it, she wouldn't have to admit the truth—that there was a damn good chance Cassie's abduction would always be a cold case.

"All the mystery surrounding Evelyn is part of her charm." Kyle winked at her.

Evelyn fidgeted, avoiding his too-perceptive eyes. She could sit across from convicted killers and hide her fear, her disgust, get them to believe she admired their cunning so they'd tell her the burial location of their victims. Then why could too-attractive-for-his-own-good Kyle McKenzie read—or seem to read—every thought in her head?

But Greg was in storytelling mode, so there was no stopping him. "Evelyn was apparently born with the ability to profile people, while the rest of us had to learn it. So, they let her join BAU younger than anyone else I know. While she was in the Houston field office, she picked a serial rapist out of the police force."

"Really?" Gabe asked, his eyebrows raised comically high. "And BAU came calling?"

"Not exactly. I applied like everyone else." A smile slipped out. "But that case definitely helped my application."

Amusement danced on Kyle's lips. "Come on. If she tells us the whole story, it'll detract from the woman-of-mystery thing she has going."

Evelyn felt the edges of her lips curl, but she held back a full smile before Greg could really get started.

"You sure you won't come to lunch?" he asked as he buttoned his suit coat over a coffee stain.

She longed to say yes, but forced herself to shake her head.

"It's been more than two weeks since the last victim in my new case, which seems to be his timetable. Every minute we don't find him, he's trolling for someone else."

And she was still a long way from creating a real profile of a killer who carved circles in his victims' chests and then buried them up to their necks. She looked at her computer screen again.

"Have fun, Greg. Bye, Gabe. McKenzie."

When he'd left for work that morning, Greg Ibsen hadn't expected to spend his afternoon at a funeral. But here he was, his gray suit coat buttoned up to hide the Mickey Mouse tie his daughter, Lucy, had picked out for him, as well as the usual coffee stain on his shirt.

Beside him, Evelyn stood ramrod straight, surveying her surroundings. Her expensive pantsuit was cut slightly big to hide the gun holstered at her hip and her dark hair was pulled back in its typical neat bun. She was in serious profiler mode, her eyes sharp and her jaw tight.

Barbara Jensen, positively identified as the second victim in the case Evelyn was assigned yesterday, had been buried privately. At Mary Ann Pollak's funeral, the cemetery felt overcrowded. Which meant they could blend into the crowd. And so could a killer.

Evelyn had asked him to come along because she'd stand out less if she wasn't alone. Especially since she stood out, anyway, with her light mocha skin in a sea of mostly paper-white.

"See anything?" Evelyn asked.

"No one who looks like they don't belong." No man who seemed to be alone. No one who had sadness on his face, but enjoyment in his eyes.

Evelyn thought the killer had murdered before he'd come to Bakersville, and if she was right, there was a good chance he'd be here. Initially serial killers tended to stay away from risky things like funerals, but the experienced ones often showed up to relive the thrill they felt dominating and killing their victims.

Still, not all of them liked funerals. Some chose the drop site instead. And some had the restraint to stay away entirely. "Maybe he's not here."

"Maybe." Evelyn sounded unconvinced.

If she'd been any other profiler in the unit, he'd know what she was thinking. That the killer hadn't sent notes to the police or the newspapers. That he hadn't abducted anyone new—as far as they were aware. So the likelihood of his being here was high.

Since it was Evelyn, though, she might have been thinking about anything. Case-related, of course. She seemed to spend every waking hour thinking about her cases. Probably most sleeping hours, too.

He'd seen it before, agents who came into BAU and couldn't separate the job from the rest of their life. It always led to burnout, sometimes even to psychological problems of their own.

A full year after she'd been assigned to BAU and they'd become friends, Greg didn't know much about Evelyn's personal life. But he suspected she'd never had a healthy work/ life balance. She was too driven, too obviously still haunted by some tragedy in her own past. Still, he wondered how long she could go on like this, putting the job first, before it took a toll.

"Are you sure the other one isn't related?" he asked quietly, following Evelyn as she moved closer to where the rabbi was speaking.

She instantly knew what he meant. Despite the fact that no one could read *her,* she could have had a career as a mind reader. It was without a doubt why she was one of the most gifted profilers he'd ever met.

"I talked to her husband. He said he was embarrassed he even called the police," Evelyn whispered.

From what she'd told him, Carla Bridgemoor had disappeared from Kensington, a nearby town, and hadn't been seen again. Since this killer didn't like to advertise his bodies, Greg wondered why she was so sure Carla wasn't the latest victim.

He didn't have to ask, because Evelyn answered, "We're still trying to get hold of Carla's friend, but everyone's positive that Carla's with her. Plus, he buried his first two victims together, like he wanted to come back and visit them both at the same time. I think if he'd grabbed Carla, we would have found her nearby."

As she spoke, Evelyn shifted farther into the crowd, giving them an opportunity to look at more people.

But no one seemed suspicious. Most people had red-rimmed eyes, their heads bent in prayer. Some were openly crying, leaning on their friends or family for support.

As the rabbi stopped speaking, mourners turned to hug and console one another.

"It's terrifying," the woman behind them whimpered. "She was so young. To cross paths with a killer..."

Silently, Greg agreed. In his line of work, he'd seen too many victims who'd crossed paths with killers. What frightened him was that, going by Evelyn's notes, he couldn't grasp anything about this killer. Heads displayed deep in the woods made no sense to him, especially combined with the other behavioral evidence.

He might have thought necrophilia, except the bodies were dumped too soon. And the logical assumption about the heads was that the killer had left them unburied so he could come back and remember his kills. But deep in the woods was a bad place to leave bodies if you wanted them to stay intact. If the killer liked the additional indignity of letting animals get the bodies, why bury most of them?

No, there was something else, something specific about the heads. He was sure of it. Only he didn't know what it was.

He hoped Evelyn had a better understanding of this killer, because with only two weeks between murders, she didn't have much time to find him.

The media had splashed the story across the front page, dubbing the UNSUB the Bakersville Burier. That might scare off the killer—or it could tempt him to keep his name in the headlines.

There were actually reporters in the street outside the cemetery, and he skirted the camera operators as he and Evelyn joined the throng of mourners heading for their cars.

When they reached his Bucar—his Bureau-issued Ford Taurus—Evelyn stood at the door, watching the crowd. He stopped beside her, pretending to be waiting for someone.

But they watched until only immediate family remained, and no one looked as if he didn't belong. As they got into the car, Greg suggested, "Maybe he didn't actually come to the funeral. Maybe he found a perch somewhere nearby and just watched from a distance."

"Maybe." She drew out the word and he knew she didn't believe it. "This guy is *so* careful. There was nothing at the crime scene. Nothing. It makes sense that he wouldn't risk being noticed."

Greg eyed her briefly as he maneuvered through the side streets. "But?"

"But my gut tells me he was there. My gut tells me he likes hiding in plain view. It tells me he's just that good."

Her hands were clenched in her lap, a sure sign that she was struggling with her profile, which almost never happened to her.

"He must have studied police procedure closely," she continued. "And the fact that he went two weeks between those abductions and now there's been nothing and we're going on seventeen days worries me."

"You think he's moved somewhere else?"

"No. But why wouldn't he stick to his pattern?"

"Is that a rhetorical question?" Greg asked. They both knew the reasons a killer would break a time pattern.

He'd gotten scared, was worried someone in his life was on to him or he'd been arrested for something else. Or his trigger—whatever set him off in the first place—had ceased. For now.

"This killer is wily, Greg."

"Well, what's your next step?"

He felt Evelyn look at him as he pulled into the lot at the Bakersville police station, where he was dropping her off. "I've got to give the Bakersville cops a profile soon. They need pro-active ideas to catch this asshole. But Bakersville hasn't had a murder in five years and that case was open-and-shut. The cops are no match for this killer."

Maybe not, but Evelyn was. In her year at BAU, she hadn't caught *every* killer, rapist, arsonist, child molester or terrorist whose case file had been sent to her. But she'd come closer than any other agent there.

"You'll get him," he reassured her.

She rewarded him with a half smile, which for her was like a full-blown grin. "That's the plan."

Slowly, though, her smile shifted until her lips were compressed into a hard line. "The killer may not have struck again, but I have no doubt about one thing. He's picked his next victim. And whoever she is, she doesn't have much time left."

Anger burned in his chest as mourners came forward and said their prayers over the casket. The whore. If they knew the truth, they wouldn't be praying for her now.

He ached to join them, to run his hands along the cold steel encasing her body, instead of just her jewelry, the piece he'd tucked in his pocket that morning.

Mary Ann's husband moved away from the casket, weeping, and the anger intensified. Anger over mistakes he couldn't fixate on now.

He worked to keep his face full of false grief, fought not to pluck at the mustache glue itching his lips. Resisted the urge to step forward and touch the casket.

The urge grew stronger, consuming him, until he had to look away.

That was when he noticed her. She looked so restrained in her pricey suit, probably purchased for her friend's funeral. Her husband was beside her, trying to console her, but she ignored him as he followed her faithfully through the crowd. She was just like all the others. And she deserved to be punished.

His anger shifted, settled deep in his gut and spread outward, turning into something else. Anticipation.

She was the one. Her icy exterior tempted him to snatch away her control, to make her beg for her life and then take it, anyway. He could already imagine her in his woods, her head displayed for him. Only him.

His lips quivered with the desire to smile, but he could be restrained, too. So he watched. Waited. The moment to strike would come, but not yet.

Haggarty's was the sort of place Evelyn generally avoided. The dimly lit, always noisy pub was a notorious singles spot, but one of the friends she was meeting liked to come here when she was on the lookout for a new guy.

Since Evelyn had moved back to the D.C. area, she met up with Audrey Foster and Josephine Carlyle, her roommates from college, once a month. They were the center of her social life and she almost never canceled unless work sent her out of town.

But tonight, with the headache that had started after going to a news conference in Bakersville, Evelyn wished she'd begged off. Just as she was considering calling her friends, Jo arrived.

Her black dress hugged generous curves, stiletto heels added height to her five-foot-six-inch frame and makeup played up big hazel eyes. Chestnut hair swinging, Jo walked with the sort of confidence that made men abandon their conversations and stare as she headed for the booth Evelyn had grabbed.

"Evelyn! How's life?" Jo settled into the booth and signaled for a waiter, ordering a cocktail when he rushed over.

Jo's effect on the male population made Evelyn smile. "It's fine. Same as usual."

Jo's lips twisted with concern. "Too many criminals, too little time?"

"Something like that. I've got a particularly challenging case right now. How about you?"

Jo made a shooing motion with her hand. "Well, work's work." Jo was a speechwriter for a senator, which she liked to say was a waste of a perfectly good English degree. "Dusty and I broke up." She wrinkled her nose. "Did I tell you about Dusty?"

"You were dating someone named Dusty? Maybe that was the problem," Audrey said as she reached their table.

Evelyn choked on her laughter, but Jo nodded thoughtfully. "You're saying my new rule should be never to date a man whose name I wouldn't want to scream out in a fit of passion?"

Audrey's grin always made Evelyn think of how she must have looked as a child, all freckles and slightly crooked teeth, instead of the polished, stylish woman she was now. "*There's* a way to screen your dates," she said, slumping into the seat with a sigh.

"Long day?" Jo asked.

"Accountants aren't used to being on their feet for hours on end." Audrey had traded in her old job for her dream—being the owner of a specialty flower shop—when she'd married Mike Foster, an orthopedic surgeon who came from money.

"I think Evelyn's feeling overstressed, too," Jo said.

"Oh?" Audrey turned to Evelyn.

"Stress is part of the job when you spend your days chasing serial killers," Evelyn quipped.

"Maybe if you went on a date sometime this century, you'd have a chance to relax." Jo grinned to lessen the sting. "Did I tell you my brother and Faith are getting divorced?"

Jo watched her expectantly, but Evelyn had had years of practice hiding her emotions.

During college, she'd fallen for Jo's older brother, Marty, breaking her own rule about getting too invested in a man. But a couple of years later, Marty had traded her in for Faith and never looked back.

Audrey's gaze darted between them. "What happened?"

"I guess he realized he made a mistake." Jo waited until they'd ordered and then added, "He's been asking about you, Evelyn."

Evelyn's stomach started churning, the thought of food suddenly unappealing. "It's been a long time, Jo."

"Yeah, it has. He's changed. He's staying with me while the divorce goes through. When it's all over, he might remain in D.C. instead of going back to New York."

"I don't want to see him." The pounding in Evelyn's head increased with the hurt clamping down on her chest as she remembered how Marty had dropped out of her life. Just like everyone else inevitably did.

Everyone but her grandma. And Jo and Audrey, who'd stuck by her from the moment she'd walked into the dorm room in Georgetown, nervous and overwhelmed. They'd kept in touch as she tackled grad school, then the Bureau Academy and during her stint in the Houston field office. Now that she was back near D.C., they were her lifeline to the world outside BAU.

Jo took a long sip of her drink. "Okay, I… Well, I think he finally gets what an idiot he was for the way he treated you." She shrugged. "I thought I should tell you."

Evelyn put a hand to her temple. "Water under the bridge."

Before Jo could reply, Audrey asked, "Do you know them?"

She was looking at the entrance of the pub, where two men were threading through the mob of patrons toward them.

An assessing smile curved Jo's lips. "*I'd* like to."

"From work," Evelyn told Audrey, feeling self-conscious as she patted her head to make sure her long hair was still twisted neatly into its bun.

When they got to the table, she introduced everyone. "Jo, Audrey, this is Kyle McKenzie and Gabe Fontaine. Guys, meet Jo Carlyle and Audrey Foster."

"Nice to meet you," Kyle said, then glanced over at Evelyn. "You can call me Mac."

As Jo not so subtly eyed the agents, she said, "So, give us the scoop. Evelyn tells us she usually leaves work at a decent hour, but I don't buy it."

Jo was grinning as though she was only teasing, but Evelyn recognized that her friends worried about the number of hours she spent in Aquia.

"We actually work in a different division," Kyle said. But the way his gaze darted quickly to her and then back to Jo told her he didn't buy it, either.

"When we met her, she was even more serious than she is

now," Jo said. "If you can believe it… But she always knew exactly what she wanted to do."

"Born to be FBI," Kyle said. "She could be their poster girl."

The unexpected contact of his hand on her shoulder surprised her, especially when it lingered there. Heat spread outward from his hand, firing nerve endings to life, and she tried to ignore it. "I don't think Dan would agree with you."

"Dan's a fool."

Evelyn blinked a few times. "Thanks."

Kyle winked at her and Evelyn whipped her head back to the others, her heart beating faster.

"So, you guys taking a break from saving the world tonight?" Jo teased.

"We've done it too many times this week," Gabe replied with an easy grin. "It's someone else's turn."

Jo and Gabe continued their banter, Audrey and Kyle joining in periodically, while Evelyn struggled with what to say. Before she'd found a way to jump into the conversation, their food arrived.

As the waiter set down their meals, Kyle said, "You should all come to the Den next week."

The Den was a nearby bar that catered to off-duty cops and FBI agents. Every Tuesday, a group of agents from Aquia and Quantico went there after work.

Kyle, Gabe and even Greg had pushed her to come with them a few times, but Evelyn had never gone. She didn't drink and large crowds made her uncomfortable. And although Jo had tried to cure her of that discomfort during college by constantly dragging her to parties, Evelyn had never mastered the art of small talk.

"We'll get there sometime." One of these days, she'd drag up enough courage to leave her comfort zone, but she had a feeling it wouldn't be this week. Not with the Bakersville killer still on the loose.

"I'll take that as a promise," Kyle said before he and Gabe headed to their own table.

Once they were gone, Jo demanded, "So, you and Mac have something going?"

Evelyn choked on her sip of water and forced herself not to fidget. "Of course not. He's a colleague."

Mischievousness hid in the corners of Audrey's smile. "He sure seemed interested in being more than a colleague."

"I don't have time for dating, anyway." Evelyn gave her standard excuse. It was partly true. This week it was the Bakersville killer keeping her up nights, but too soon there'd be another case. And another one after that.

But work was also safe. She had mastered deconstructing the personality types of serial killers and tracking them down, but understanding the subtleties of dating had never been her strong suit. And trust didn't come easily for her, either.

When she was silent for too long, Jo said in her straightforward way, "Just because my brother burned you once doesn't mean he'd do it again—or that it'll happen with every guy."

When Evelyn opened her mouth to respond, Jo lowered her head sympathetically and added, "And just because your mom brought home one man after another who hit you or—"

She broke off, as Evelyn felt herself tense.

"It doesn't mean you can't try again. I mean, who's going to mess with you now?" She grinned. "You carry a big gun."

Evelyn felt a matching smile twitch on her lips. "My gun is regular size."

"Well, still."

"You want to give dating a try?" Audrey pressed, looking hopeful. "We could set you up with someone nice."

Evelyn managed to nod, even though there was only one

man who made her feel remotely interested in dating. And he was off-limits. "I'll think about it."

An hour later, blaming her headache, she told her friends she was heading home for medicine and sleep.

She waved at Kyle and Gabe as she wove around their table toward the door, tugging on her ring. Virginia had been hit with the beginnings of a heat wave that morning. Her fingers had swollen and the ring had been cutting off her circulation, so she'd moved it to her left hand.

She yanked on it now until it came off and then tried to slip it back on her right ring finger. It got stuck at the joint, so she returned it to her left hand, flipping it over again so the diamond faced her palm and it wouldn't look like an engagement ring.

As she walked outside, the heat and humidity felt like a wall she had to physically push through. Her head throbbed with new intensity, and her lungs complained as they tried to draw more oxygen out of the water-laden air. She started to unbutton her suit jacket, but decided not to take it off until she was in her car. There was no reason to flash the SIG Sauer P228 she wore holstered at her right hip, even if there was no one else in the parking lot to see it.

She squinted, leaning toward her door as she fit the key in the keyhole. Haggarty's really needed to invest in some safety lighting.

With her free hand, she rubbed her temple, briefly closing her eyes to relieve the pressure behind them. When she opened them again, a prickling sensation ran from her neck to her toes. *She wasn't alone.*

Evelyn spun, reaching automatically for her weapon, her feet already shifting into a fighting stance.

She'd only turned partway when a sharp pain pierced her neck. Dizziness hit with blinding intensity and she swayed, trying to take a full breath as the humid air went from D.C. in a heat wave to a sauna on way too high. With one hand she groped for her car to keep herself upright. The other hand shifted up from the butt of her gun to the right side of her neck, where something was protruding.

She tried to grip whatever it was, but her hands weren't working. Then a blurry figure stepped closer, his features swimming in front of eyes that wouldn't focus.

Evelyn swayed again, losing her battle to stay upright, and opened her mouth to scream.

Was this how Cassie had felt just before the end, helpless and terrified and alone?

A hand clamped over Evelyn's mouth, stifling her scream. Then the whole world tilted and big hands hooked under her arms as the man dragged her away from her car, her heels scraping across the concrete. She willed herself to move, to fight back, but her limbs didn't work, and then it didn't matter, because the empty parking lot dimmed into blackness.

3

SOMETHING WAS VERY WRONG.

That certainty slammed through Evelyn as she grasped at consciousness.

Unease crept over her like a thousand insects trying to burrow into her skin. Her mind was fuzzy, as if she'd just woken from a long sleep. But she didn't remember going to sleep. And she didn't know where she was.

Her limbs were heavy and her whole body felt contorted, her chin denting her collarbone. Something pressed against her, holding her upright, but digging into her skin. She felt off balance, as if she were falling in slow motion.

Evelyn forced herself to remain still as awareness hit with the intensity of a lightning bolt. Someone was beside her.

Who had her mother brought home this time? Or was she at her grandparents' house? Her grandma sometimes liked to check on her while she was sleeping.

Evelyn wanted to shake her head to clear it. She wasn't a little girl anymore. There was no one left to hurt her and no one left to check on her.

But where was she? Who was next to her?

Her hands twitched in her lap and she sensed someone's

gaze on her. She kept still as a large hand gripped her forehead and lifted her head.

Blood rushed back to her head, clearing the cobwebs. Someone had ambushed her in the parking lot. She must have become unconscious afterward—but for how long?

The hand on her forehead turned her head to the left and the fingers felt slick and rubbery, not human.

A sudden, senseless urge to scream for help almost overwhelmed her, but she swallowed it back. Finally, the hand released her forehead and she let her head fall against her chest. In response, she heard a satisfied grunt.

Cracking open one eye, Evelyn peered over and saw the blurry outline of a man—a big man—and realized where she was.

The motion she felt was driving and the pressure across her chest was a seat belt.

Head pounding, she looked at her hands resting in her lap. As they slid into focus, Evelyn bit down on her tongue, filling her mouth with the coppery taste of blood.

Her wrists were bound together with her own handcuffs. She focused on her right hip, wedged against the seat belt. She could feel her holster, but there was no doubt about it. Whoever had cuffed her had taken her gun.

Just breathe, Evelyn commanded herself. *Concentrate.*

Breathing normally was hard enough. Concentration was nearly impossible. Her body was telling her to go back to sleep and her head felt as if someone had smashed it with a cast-iron pan.

She glanced to the right without moving her head, but through the window was nothing but darkness. No headlights from other vehicles, just dense woods, rushing past at high speed. They were probably on a country highway, moving farther and farther from civilization. Farther and farther from witnesses.

She opened her other eye and studied the man next to her. Through the darkness and the drugs, he was blurry, but vaguely familiar.

As dizziness washed over her, Evelyn closed her eyes and wiggled her toes, making sure they still worked. She prayed that given the chance, they would obey a command from her mind to run. Once he knew she was awake, she'd get one shot at escape. And drugged, with her hands bound, running was the only option.

In her line of work, she made dangerous enemies. There was no way to know her abductor's agenda.

The faces of those she loved and didn't want to leave flashed through her mind. Her grandma. Her best friends, Jo and Audrey. Her Bureau partner, Greg.

And Kyle. Kyle, who flirted shamelessly with her and managed to break holes in the shield she'd built firmly around her heart.

She didn't want to leave them. She didn't want to die like this.

Sweat slicked her palms, and fear dampened her senses. Now that she needed it most, all the training drilled into her by the FBI seemed useless.

Her heart jackknifed as the vehicle slowed, made several sharp turns and came to a stop.

The man shifted toward her and lifted her head with both hands.

If he looked closely, he would notice her accelerated breathing and realize she was awake. The desire to raise her hands to protect her head was overpowering as she imagined him using those powerful hands to snap her neck.

Instead, his cold, unnatural-feeling fingers traced a line

across her cheek in what might have been a caress. Then he carefully lowered her head back against the seat and she heard him step out of the car and slam the door.

The car vibrated lightly underneath her. It was still running!

Could she get to the driver's seat? Her body felt too heavy to move. Her best chance was now, but fear paralyzed her.

Then it was too late. The door beside her opened and he unhooked her seat belt.

When he slid his hands behind her and under her knees to lift her out of the car, her eyes opened instinctively. She thrust her knees upward, aiming for his head. But the drugs slowed her down and he jerked back, surprise on his face.

Panicked, Evelyn twisted away from him, into the interior of the car.

He moved fast, grabbed her knees before she could get far and wrenched her violently out of the car.

Her head smacked the metal base of the door frame and pain exploded inside her skull. The air whooshed out of her lungs and her vision dimmed, her attacker's face fading behind flashes of light.

Before she could recover, he was leaning over her. She threw her hands up to protect her face, chafing her wrists with her handcuffs, and then kicked hard, connecting with his shin.

Even through her blurry vision, she could tell it wasn't hard enough.

"Bitch!" he snarled, his voice grating on her eardrums as his fingers sank into her bun. With a yank that pulled out a chunk of hair and nearly made her throw up, he forced her onto her feet.

Then he shoved, flat-palmed, against her chest. She flew backward into the open car door and the impact reverberated from her hip to her shoulder as it slammed shut.

The FBI's defensive training hadn't covered what to do if

you got handcuffed with your own cuffs. There was no time to go for her key. But she decided her best option was to use them. She raised her cuffed hands in front of her face as he came for her, holding them as far apart as she could. When she drove her hands forward, the metal hooking the handcuffs together smashed into his nose. There was a loud crack as his chin went skyward, but he didn't fall over, just lurched back.

Metal ripped her skin and sent blood, slick and sticky, dripping down the backs of her clenched hands. Ignoring her throbbing wrists, she kicked, hitting the solid wall of muscle at his stomach.

As he fell, dizziness tilted her off balance. She thrust out her hands, but there was nothing to catch herself on and she stumbled into him, then kept going, falling on top of him.

Arms that bulged with muscle instantly wrapped around her legs like a cobra winding around its prey.

Evelyn jerked backward and fell sideways. He squeezed tighter and she turned her head to see him inches away.

The ferocity in his eyes made her kick blindly, desperately. He lost his grip, but shot his palm high into her cheekbone. A million lights exploded behind her left eye.

As her vision returned, three versions of him shifted, and he started to stand. A whimper escaped as she shot her hands up and out, slamming her palms into his already-damaged nose.

He let out a guttural howl and more blood dripped down her arms. Bracing her hands in the dirt, Evelyn shoved to her feet, but the drugs made her balance as well as her vision unsteady.

She tried to run, but her legs felt disconnected, her movements too slow. When she hit the car, new bruises swelled. She felt her way around the front of the vehicle, desperate to get to the driver's-side door.

A grunt made her look back. Her abductor had gotten up.

Either everything seemed to move in slow motion because of the drugs, or he was hurt, clutching his face.

Frantic, she groped for the door handle with her cuffed hands. It took three attempts to open it and then he was at the hood of the car, coming for her.

She choked on a sob as she tried to get into the car. But he was there, grabbing at her.

Kicking out with her right foot, she connected with something hard, probably his kneecap. His hand slipped off her arm as he staggered backward with a yelp.

Evelyn fell into the driver's seat and pulled the door shut. She swiped her hands across her face, trying to wipe away the blood dripping into her left eye. Agony ripped through her head as the handcuffs scraped a deep cut near her eye.

She went for the keys dangling in the ignition, and then realized the car was still running.

But it didn't matter because he was beside her again, his face framed in the window, those ice-blue eyes promising death, his hand reaching for the door handle.

Her heartbeat drummed inside her ears as she jerked the gearshift and punched the gas. The car raced backward toward the road and she grabbed the right side of the steering wheel.

Struggling to stay upright, Evelyn eased off the gas, glancing over her shoulder. She hit the brake hard as the car slid into the street. Without a seat belt, she banged into the steering column. Her left arm, tethered to her right wrist and twisted in front of her body, took the brunt of it and immediately started throbbing.

She glanced forward again, blinking to clear her vision, and saw a cabin she hadn't noticed earlier. The man who'd abducted her was running toward the car, his hands stretched in front of him, holding something.

A sob ripped free, gagging her as the air whistled through

her dry throat. Shifting into Drive, she yanked the wheel left just as a sound she would recognize anywhere pierced the air.

Instinct made her duck, but not before the bullet hit metal. He'd hit the car—and he was probably shooting with her gun.

Pulling herself back up, she sped away from the cabin, wrenching the wheel sideways as curves came at her too fast.

The gravel road turned to pavement and Evelyn squinted until it looked less blurry. Sucking in shallow gasps of air, she fought to keep the car to the right of the yellow line.

A car rushed past her on the other side of the road, its head-lights blinding her and its horn blaring as she rode the yel-low line.

She swiped at the blood dripping into her left eye and then whipped both hands back to the wheel when the yellow line disappeared under the car again. She swerved right as a tree raced toward her.

Evelyn stomped on the brake and the car slowed, but not fast enough. The front of the car crumpled in around her, the tree engulfing it, as she flew forward.

Pain, blindingly intense and razor-sharp, erupted and then she felt nothing.

4

EVERYTHING HURT. EVELYN COULDN'T FEEL THE individual parts of her body, just unending pain.

She thought she heard someone moving nearby, but it might just have been the pounding inside her own head. She hadn't had a headache this bad in—

Evelyn lurched upright, clenching her fists in front of her as a memory surfaced. She was standing by her car and someone shot her with a dart. Was she still in the parking lot?

A beeping sounded to her left and Evelyn forced her eyes open. Everything was blurry.

A figure loomed across the room, moving toward her, and she screamed.

"Visiting hours don't start for a few more hours," a nurse informed Kyle McKenzie as he raced through the emergency entrance doors into the hospital.

Kyle didn't bother arguing. He just flashed his badge.

She squinted at it and then skeptically at him—probably because of the running pants and T-shirt he'd thrown on when he'd gotten the call from Gabe, who'd heard from Greg. The bedhead didn't help, either.

But he didn't give a damn.

"I'm looking for Evelyn Baine," he said. "She's a federal agent. She was admitted sometime during the night."

The nurse eyed his badge once more, then took her sweet time flipping through charts as his heart thudded a too-fast tempo. All he knew was that someone had abducted Evelyn—from right outside the pub when he'd been sitting in there with Gabe. That she'd somehow gotten away and crashed a car.

Gabe had told him she hadn't regained consciousness.

For the hundredth time since that phone call, he cursed himself for not walking her out. He'd thought about it, too. Not because he'd been worried about her, but because he'd wanted to steal a few minutes alone with her. He hadn't, since he'd figured she'd see right through it.

Instead, he'd gone home, oblivious, where he'd conked out until the call had woken him at 6:00 a.m.

"Room 102. Down the hall." The nurse pointed and Kyle took off at a run.

His feet slowed as he reached her room and he took a deep breath before going inside.

Evelyn looked small and helpless in the stark-white room. A bandage lined her forehead, close to her left eye. Bruises and cuts jockeyed for space on the rest of her face. She looked like something he'd never expected from tough, smart Evelyn— a victim.

His stomach knotted worse than it had before his first mission.

"She's going to be fine," Greg said, but his voice was shaky. "She woke up once."

"Thank God," he breathed. He stepped farther into the room, pulling the other visitor chair up to her bedside.

Under her eyelids, he could see her eyes shifting too fast, as if she was in the middle of a nightmare.

"Evelyn?" Greg leaned close to her. "Evelyn, can you hear me?"

"Greg?" Evelyn croaked, opening her eyes slightly. She squinted in the dimly lit room.

Even though Kyle could only see slivers of her beautiful sea-green eyes, he could clearly read her agony.

"Hey. Welcome back." Greg sounded as if he was pretending not to be upset.

"Huh?" Evelyn's eyes opened wider, confusion in them. "Where've I been?" she slurred.

"You're okay now," Kyle said, his voice as strained as Greg's.

She turned her head, pain flaring in her eyes.

Judging from the huge bruise on her forehead, she had to have one hell of a headache.

He longed to reach for her hand, but he suspected that would make her uncomfortable, so he just kept his own hands clasped tightly together as Evelyn's doctor walked into the room.

"How do you feel?" the doctor asked cheerfully.

Panic flooded Evelyn's face as she jerked her head toward the doctor. Her heart monitor started beeping.

The doctor immediately turned it off. "Try to relax," she said. "You're in the hospital. You were flown here after the car you were driving hit a tree."

Evelyn looked back at Greg, her movements slow, and rasped, "What happened?"

The doctor inclined the bed and handed her a glass of water, holding it as Evelyn took a sip.

"What happened to me?" she asked again, and Kyle glanced at the doctor, too, dreading whatever she was going to say.

"The car you were driving hit a tree. You were going pretty fast and you weren't wearing a seat belt. It's pure luck you didn't go through the windshield."

An image of Evelyn—all one hundred and ten pounds of her—slamming through a windshield into a tree imbedded itself in his brain. His hands began to shake and he realized he was squeezing them so tightly he was cutting off the circulation.

"You didn't look so hot when they brought you in here," the doctor said with a smile that seemed to be ready-made for all her patients, no matter what was wrong with them. When confusion filled Evelyn's eyes, she clarified, "Virginia Hospital Center. We managed to get you patched up nicely."

"You woke up while the firefighters were pulling you out of the car," Greg told her.

Greg had only given Gabe the basics, so that was all Kyle knew. He figured Gabe would arrive soon, although he'd probably break fewer speed limits than Kyle had.

Greg put his hand on Evelyn's arm since both of her hands were tucked under the sheet. "A driver in another car saw you crash. He called 9-1-1 and firefighters were sent. They needed the Jaws of Life to get you out of the car. The firefighters said you were mostly mumbling incoherently, but they did find out that you were a federal agent."

At the mention of the Jaws of Life, Evelyn's face turned ashen.

He wondered if she was thinking what he was. As a federal agent, she was trained in defensive driving. And defensive fighting. Quite possibly, those skills had saved her life.

Without them, he might have been visiting the morgue tonight instead of the hospital. He felt his own face drain of blood, and a tight ache wrap around his lungs.

"Cops at the scene ran the plates on the car you were driving and discovered it wasn't yours," Greg was saying. "You said you'd been attacked, so the car's at the lab being checked out, in case it belongs to your abductor. And there are agents working on your case right now."

"I was attacked?" she asked weakly, then looked over at the doctor, the confusion on her face battling with fear.

"If you're having trouble remembering, that's normal," the doctor said. "You were given an injection of a combination of chlordiazepoxide and buprenorphine by your abductor. From the bruising on your neck, we're pretty sure the drugs were injected into your carotid artery."

"A dart," Evelyn managed, then blinked rapidly, as if she hadn't expected to remember.

The doctor nodded, apparently not surprised. "Lucky shot. With an injection into the carotid artery, you probably lost consciousness within seconds."

So, she hadn't even had the chance to fight the guy off before she was abducted. If only he'd gone with her. Or at least watched out the window as she walked to her car.

"Chlordiazepoxide is a type of benzodiazepine," the doctor continued, "related to flunitrazepam, commonly known as a date rape drug. It causes anterograde amnesia."

Kyle jolted along with Evelyn at the news, and the doctor was quick to reassure them. "There's no evidence you were raped. But the two drugs combined have a synergistic effect— they're more potent when used in conjunction. Chlordiazepoxide is commonly used as an antidepressant or for alcohol addiction withdrawal and buprenorphine is used to treat opiate dependence. Both, when overdosed, cause central nervous system depression, trouble breathing, even unconsciousness."

Kyle's mind swirled with all the information, trying to make sense of who could have abducted her, and the doctor finished with, "We did our best to flush the drugs from your system. You've been here for close to six hours, so the worst of it is over."

She must have arrived at the hospital just as he was getting ready to leave the pub. Kyle knew it had taken the doctors a while to find Evelyn's emergency contact, who turned out to be Greg.

"We've been taking good care of you," the doctor assured her.

When Evelyn pulled her hands out from under the sheet and reached for her head, Kyle saw that her wrists were heavily bandaged.

So did she, because she pulled them back and stared at them. "What happened to my wrists? Did I hurt them in the car accident?"

She looked at Greg, hope in her eyes. "Did I fight him?"

Greg didn't have to answer for Kyle to know. She must have. She'd gotten away, so she must have used those deceptively small fists to pummel him.

Greg's expression was pained. "Your handcuffs were on your wrists. They were cut off before you went into X-ray."

"X-ray?" Kyle and Evelyn asked together.

She looked over at him and, this time, he couldn't help himself. He took her hand.

She blinked at him as though she wasn't sure how to respond. But to his surprise, she didn't withdraw her hand. It even curled slightly into his.

"Where's my stuff?" she asked the doctor before the woman could tell her why she'd needed X-rays. "My ring? Please tell me you have my ring."

"We have your jewelry, some cash, a cell phone and keys," the doctor replied.

"I left my purse in the trunk of my car. What about my creds? My weapon?"

"The agents working your case found your credentials at the scene of your abduction, under your car. Your weapon wasn't recovered. But there were two bullet holes in the car you were driving. They were made by a nine millimeter weapon."

She'd shot at the car, Kyle thought, careful not to squeeze her hand too hard. Hopefully she'd shot at her abductor, too.

Her hand started to go limp in his and her eyelids began drooping. "I'm okay, though?" she asked, her words slowing, too. "What were my injuries?"

"You're going to be fine. You have a concussion and two cracked ribs. Those are painful, but they'll heal themselves."

The asshole who'd abducted her had hurt her so badly she'd cracked ribs? Suddenly Kyle prayed the man wasn't dead—and that he'd have the chance to spend the rest of his life in jail.

"You needed twelve stitches at the corner of your left eye, but you probably won't even have a scar there," the doctor went on. "The handcuffs scraped a couple layers of skin from your wrists, which is why they're wrapped, and you have a lot of cuts and bruises. You didn't suffer any injuries that won't heal."

A hint of a frown curled Evelyn's lips as she blinked and shifted, looking as if she could hardly keep her eyes open.

"We also drew some blood when you came in. Since we suspected you had both your own blood and your assailant's on you, we'll test you to make sure you didn't contract anything. You'll obviously have to be tested again for HIV after six months. Sometimes hepatitis doesn't show up for a couple of months, either."

Shit. Kyle hadn't even thought about the medical dangers. The knots in his stomach twisted until he doubted they'd ever untangle. As an agent, Evelyn would have been vaccinated for hepatitis A and B, so what she had to worry about was hepatitis C. And, of course, HIV.

Focusing instead on what they could control—finding the

bastard who'd done this to her—he asked, "She had his blood on her? Enough for DNA?"

Greg was nodding before he finished the question. "Maybe. A sample was sent to the lab. They should be able to separate Evelyn's blood from her abductor's."

Of course, that would only be useful if they found a suspect to match it.

"Evelyn?" a new voice, laced with worry, interrupted.

Gabe had arrived.

"How are you feeling?" he asked.

A lopsided smile shook on Evelyn's face, but her doctor sounded less than pleased as her eyelids drooped again.

"Your friend just woke up. Don't overtire her."

"I'm 'kay," Evelyn mumbled, but her fingers were starting to go limp in his.

Kyle's gaze met Gabe's and he saw his own worry reflected there. He hoped she was right.

But whatever had happened to her, at least they hadn't lost her. At least she was still alive.

And knowing Evelyn, the minute she was out of the hospital, she'd be on the trail of whoever had abducted her.

When she woke again, Evelyn wasn't sure how much time had passed, but her friends were gone. In their place, an unfamiliar man was sitting on a chair just inside the door.

Evelyn pulled the sheet higher. "Who are you?" came out in a barely audible whisper. She reached for the glass of water that had been left by her bed and drank the rest of it.

Apparently, he had good hearing, because he strode purposefully to her side. "Special Agent Ron Harding. I'm from headquarters in D.C."

Ron's face reminded her of an old bloodhound—droopy and a little bit dopey, but within the folds of his face were

sharp, attentive pale gray eyes. It didn't take training in profiling to see he'd been with the Bureau a long time.

"My partner and I are coordinating with the Kensington
police on your case."

Evelyn tried to focus. "Case?"

"Your abduction."

"Oh." Evelyn nodded, realizing that since she was FBI,
the Assaulting a Federal Officer Statute made the investigation federal.

"My partner is waiting outside. Do you mind if he comes
in and we talk to you?"

Evelyn glanced through her open room door and spotted
a younger agent slouched on a plastic chair, reading a maga-
zine. "Uh, okay."

"Come on in, Jimmy," Ron yelled. "This is my partner,
Jimmy Drescott."

The younger of the pair by probably twenty-five years,
Jimmy seemed better suited to modeling than being an agent.
Evelyn was pretty sure he knew it as he flashed her a smile.
If she'd been asked to profile him just based on meeting him,
she'd say he'd relied on looks and charm for most of his life,
that he'd joined the FBI because it sounded cool and that his
default action around women was to flirt.

"Evelyn, right?" He offered his hand.

Evelyn pushed a button at her right side and her bed inclined so she could sit. Dull pain pulsed through her as she
put her hand limply in Jimmy's.

Ron frowned. "We'll get this guy for you, honey. We're
heading up the investigation and we take care of our own."

Evelyn raised her eyebrows. He had to be old school to use
the endearment *honey* on someone who carried a gun. She
was too exhausted to comment, so she just asked, "What do
you need?"

"We have a few questions." Jimmy flashed her another toothy, practiced grin.

He and his partner proceeded to question her for what felt like hours, but Evelyn knew couldn't have been more than twenty minutes.

No matter what question they asked, she couldn't remember the answer.

"We found your vehicle here," Ron said, showing her an aerial photo.

Evelyn stared at it, transfixed. A black Crown Victoria was wrapped around a tree a few feet off a highway. The windshield had shattered, leaving only jagged pieces of glass around the edges, and the entire front of the car had crumpled inward. The roof had been peeled back and the driver's-side door removed—probably to extract her from the car.

A violent shudder ripped through her. It was astonishing that she'd made it out of that car alive. Another foot forward and she would have been crushed.

Ron removed a map from his briefcase and showed her where the car had been found. "It looks like you were coming from the south. Can you tell us how far you think you drove or where you might've come from?"

Evelyn tried to focus on the map, but her gaze kept straying back to the aerial photo.

Finally, Jimmy took the photo and returned it to his partner's briefcase. Evelyn glanced up. Ron's eyes were locked on hers as if he could read every thought in her head. Even Jimmy's face revealed pity.

Her cheeks heated. It was bad enough that someone had gotten the jump on her, a trained and armed FBI agent. She didn't want to make things worse by acting as if she couldn't handle the investigation.

Trying to keep her face blank, she studied the map, hoping something would come to her, but finally had to admit, "I don't know. I don't remember anything. The car doesn't even look familiar."

She stifled the sob that welled up. "Apparently, I told the firefighters who pulled me out of the car that I was abducted, but I honestly don't remember. I don't remember getting away from him. I don't remember getting on the highway or how long I was driving. I don't remember anything after that dart hit me."

"Do you have any idea where this guy took you?" Ron's voice was filled with frustration.

Evelyn didn't blame him. She felt frustrated herself.

She closed her eyes, straining to recall. Her fists clenched the sheet. "A cabin," she said, surprising herself.

"A cabin." Ron sounded unimpressed. "There are tons of cabins around this area. Vacation spots, hunting lodges. Do you remember anything specific about this cabin?"

"No. Just a cabin." She tried to picture it. "It was wood. A straight drive leading up to it, unpaved."

"What about the guy who did this?" Ron asked, his too-warm, coffee-scented breath hitting her cheek as he leaned closer. "What did he look like?"

Evelyn's breathing came faster and faster as she tried to remember *him*. The man who'd abducted her. The man she'd been lucky to get away from.

Why couldn't she remember him? How could she not remember being abducted and then hitting a tree in her assailant's car? "I don't know," she admitted again as tears gathered behind her eyelids.

She tried to even out her breathing. She wasn't a crier. She definitely wasn't a crier in front of anyone.

"Did you see his face?" Ron prompted. "What color was his hair? Was he tall? Short? Black? White?"

"Uh..." Evelyn tried to remember something, *anything,* about what had happened. But nothing surfaced.

"He drugged me," she explained. "With something that causes amnesia. I think my memory will come back eventually." More quietly, she added, "I hope so."

No matter what had happened, she would rather know than wonder. In her line of work, imagination was far worse than the truth.

"You remembered the cabin, right?" Jimmy pressured. "Try to describe that. What did he do when you got there?"

"I don't know," Evelyn said, her voice breaking. Mortified, she took a calming breath and focused on the cabin.

But her mind kept returning to all the things that *could* have happened to her while she was drugged. She fingered the bandages on her wrists.

"Evelyn," Ron said in a surprisingly gentle voice. "Is there anything? Don't think about what could have happened. Just try to visualize his face. And his size. Was he heavy?"

"He was..." Evelyn conjured up an image of herself, stumbling on top of a man. She'd been fighting him, but she couldn't remember what he looked like.

She did remember turning her head to see him there, inches away, and, staring into his eyes, she'd known. Her voice uneven and hoarse, she said, "He was going to kill me."

No one said anything, but Evelyn could tell the other agents were uncomfortable.

"Blue eyes," she continued quickly. When she licked dry lips, she tasted blood and realized she'd bitten them. "His eyes were so blue. And cold. Evil."

She knew the last part wasn't helpful, but after staring into the eyes of serial killers, child molesters and religious fanatics who used their beliefs as an excuse to kill, *evil* was more of a real adjective to her than *blue*.

"What about his face?" Ron prompted again. "Any facial hair? Tattoos?"

Evelyn tried once more to visualize the face that went with the eyes, but nothing happened. "I don't know." She felt as helpless as she sounded. "All I can remember is his eyes."

Ron nodded and snapped his notebook shut. "Okay. We'll let you rest. Just focus on getting better. We'll focus on finding this guy."

Like hell. No way was she leaving the investigation to someone else.

She managed not to say it out loud as they handed her their cards and left the room. But not knowing what her abductor looked like wasn't going to stop her from finding him. And when she did, *he* was going to be the one in handcuffs.

"Finally," Evelyn sighed as Audrey pulled her SUV into Evelyn's driveway. The hospital hadn't wanted to release her for another day, but she'd signed herself out against medical advice—and against her friends' pleas.

Audrey tried again. "You really should've stayed in the hospital longer."

Jo cut off Evelyn's impending argument by commenting, "I can't believe you drive this monster around D.C."

Audrey looked confused before she seemed to realize that Jo was intentionally changing the subject. "I'm going to need it once Moose gets big." Moose was the Newfoundland puppy she and Mike had recently adopted.

"And when you have those two point five kids," Jo added.

Audrey rolled her eyes and hopped out of the car, opening Evelyn's door before she could do it herself.

When her friend reached for her arm, Evelyn complained, "I'm not an invalid."

"Aren't we grumpy?" Jo asked cheerfully, coming around the side of the car to take her other arm.

"Sorry," Evelyn mumbled, stumbling along between them as they made their way into her house.

They helped her shuffle to the oversize chair in her living room and then Jo said, "I thought you were going couch-hunting last week."

Evelyn shrugged. "I didn't have time."

"Of course not." Jo picked up the book on antisocial personalities Evelyn had been reading in the evenings. "Bringing your work home?"

Evelyn chewed on the inside of her cheek, debating the wisdom of telling Jo that, yes, she regularly brought her work home, but that wasn't work. The book was pleasure reading.

"Maybe we could help you shop for furniture," Audrey suggested, sparing Evelyn from having to answer.

Evelyn glanced around. She was used to it, but she supposed it did look strange with only one chair and a side table in the living room. The other rooms were the same. She didn't spend enough time at home that it mattered.

Not to mention that the house was way too big for her. She'd bought it based on emotion, not practicality. The second she'd seen the cozy wraparound porch and columns out front, it had taken her back to the only stable period of her life. It looked so much like her grandparents' house that she'd decided to buy it before she even stepped inside.

The money her grandparents had put in a trust fund for her meant the house—out of reach on a special agent's salary—had been within her budget.

Since she planned to remain at BAU for the rest of her career, she'd wanted to put down real roots. But once she'd moved in, her plans had stalled. She was too busy at work to spend time on the house. And she found she really had no idea *how* to put down roots.

She'd tried. She'd taken a whole weekend off last month, and Jo and Audrey had helped her start to fix the stairs, which had been a dangerous mess when she'd moved in. They were now partially finished, but Evelyn didn't foresee another open weekend in her near future.

"You've been here for over a year," Audrey said hesitantly. "Maybe it's time to buy some furniture."

"Once you're out of your twenties, you really need to own a couch," Jo teased.

A smile tugged on Evelyn's lips. "I'm not there yet, re-member?"

Jo gave her a mock scowl. "Oh, yeah. I forgot you skipped ahead in school." She held up a finger. "Okay, fine. You have a few more months and *then* you need to buy a couch."

Evelyn's smile faltered. She hadn't so much skipped ahead as worked her ass off to get into college early so she wouldn't have to live with her mother again after her grandma's stroke.

She'd arrived at Georgetown already set on her path. Double major in criminal justice and psychology. Get a job with the FBI. Dedicate her life to something that mattered.

Use her job to find Cassie.

Then she'd met Audrey and Jo, who'd taught her that she didn't have to totally isolate herself to get by. Who'd reminded her she was allowed to have fun. Who'd offered the kind of friendship she hadn't had since she was twelve. Now that they were all living in the same area again, it was as though hardly anything had changed.

"Thanks for bringing me home," Evelyn said, trying not to choke up. It had to be the painkillers she'd been on at the hospital; they were making her emotional.

Jo and Audrey just smiled, probably knowing she was really thanking them for their friendship.

"You want us to hang out here tonight?" Audrey asked. "Mike won't miss me for one night. Moose is convinced he gets to sleep in the bed, anyway."

"A sleepover would be fun. It'd be like we were back in the dorm, only you wouldn't have to spend so much time helping me study," Jo said with what sounded like a great deal of enthusiasm.

Knowing it was for her benefit, Evelyn managed a laugh. "Thanks, but I'll be fine," she insisted, pushing her protesting body to her feet so she could walk them out.

Jo stuck her hands on her hips. "I don't like it. What if this guy knows where you live?"

"So, what? I put you in danger, too?" When Audrey paled, she immediately regretted her hasty response. "He doesn't know where I live."

"How—" Jo started.

"I didn't bring my purse into the bar. And my credentials fell in the parking lot. He doesn't know my name. So how would he know where I live?" She tried to sound as if she believed it.

The worry lines hadn't left Audrey's face. "What if he came after you specifically, Evelyn?"

Evelyn tried not to let her own fear show. As an FBI agent, she had a lot of enemies. If her abductor hadn't picked her on the spot, then he probably did have her address.

"Greg already brought me my replacement weapon." It was a Glock 23, which was what the Bureau was currently issuing the smaller-size agents. It was lighter than the SIG Sauer P228 she normally carried, and a forty caliber. She'd had practice with it, but right now, she wished she had her trusty SIG on her hip.

"And this asshole carries around a dart full of drugs," Jo shot back. Her expression shifted into determined mode. "You have two choices, Evelyn. We stay with you or you stay with one of us."

Evelyn looked to Audrey for help, but Audrey's worry lines had morphed into a locked jaw.

"This was a fluke, a mistake on my part. I wasn't paying attention and I paid for it," Evelyn said, but she could see they weren't convinced. And she was too tired to argue. "Okay. You win. Let me go up and grab my bag and I'll stay at Jo's."

As Jo walked her up to her room, she said, "I appreciate you and Audrey worrying about me, but this is just for tonight. As soon as I get my strength back, I'm coming home. I'm not letting this guy run my life."

Jo didn't respond, but her expression said they'd be arguing about it.

Next time, Evelyn wasn't giving in so easily. She'd spent too much of her life not being in control—first living with her drunken mother and then with her grandparents' constant worry after Cassie had disappeared and they'd been afraid to allow her out of their sight. She couldn't let go of the control she finally had, couldn't let one perp take over her life. Especially when her job was to put criminals like him behind bars to protect others.

Still, she shivered as she grabbed her FBI "Go Bag," already packed for when she had to leave town quickly for a case. It didn't matter which bed she slept in that night. She knew she wouldn't be sleeping.

5

BACK AT WORK.

Evelyn's smile trembled as she flashed her security badge at the guard posted out front and pulled her Bucar into the parking lot. She took a deep breath, meant to be fortifying, but it just sent a sharp ache vibrating through her ribs. She tried not to flinch as one of her colleagues walked past.

Kendall White squinted at her curiously. Kendall was one of the few agents in BAU close to her age. He was a talented profiler, and he knew it. His excessive self-confidence also seemed to spill over into other areas.

When she'd first started at BAU, he'd rushed over to introduce himself and then asked her out. Either he hadn't taken her refusal well or she'd done something else to earn his dislike, because he usually avoided her.

As Kendall disappeared inside the building, Evelyn stepped carefully out of her car. She passed her security card over the cipher lock on the door of the unmarked industrial building in Aquia, Virginia, where she spent too many hours each week.

Inside, she kept her head down and hurried to her cubicle. She'd dressed carefully that morning, in her most professional suit, with a sleeveless white turtleneck underneath to cover the bruise on her neck.

With the help of more makeup than she'd worn in years, the yellow-green bruises and scabbed-over scrapes on her face were mostly hidden. But as she settled into her cubicle, she touched the bandage covering the skin at the corner of her eye. There'd been no way to disguise it.

As she reached for her desk phone to listen to her messages, she sensed someone behind her. When she spun around and saw Kendall leaning against her cubicle, annoyance slithered down her spinal cord. She hadn't taken a day off since she'd started, so she'd known her colleagues would be wondering where she'd been the past few days.

"How are you doing?" he asked, his expression blank, like a good profiler's.

"I'm fine." She tried to discourage more questions by swiveling her chair back toward her desk.

"Really?" Kendall persisted, the word dripping with disbelief.

"Yes, really." *Go away,* she willed. *Leave me alone.*

"Dan told us you were abducted. But you got away, huh?"

Damn her boss. Damn, damn, damn.

Evelyn spun back around. "I'm here, right? Guess I must have gotten away." At least he didn't seem to know she had no idea how.

Kendall's head fell back with a soft grunt.

Before he could ask anything else, Greg arrived. "Kendall," Greg greeted him, his voice unusually subdued.

Kendall nodded at Greg and returned to his desk.

"Thanks."

"So, why *are* you here?" Greg demanded.

Evelyn mustered as close to a real smile as she could manage and some of Jo's attitude. "That's a nice hello."

Greg frowned. "I'm just worried about you." He looked her over. "You're still injured, Evelyn. You shouldn't be here yet."

Her smile faded. He sounded like Dan and some of her other male colleagues who constantly worried she'd faint when interviewing a serial killer or go into maternal mode when profiling a child murderer. Had this soured Greg's opinion of her, too?

Greg pursed his lips, studying her too closely. "How did you talk Dan into letting you come back so soon?"

The smile returned. Greg did indeed know her. Go figure. "I called him over and over until he couldn't stand it anymore and gave in." It had only taken three days.

Greg snorted. "Of course you did. Well, don't work too hard."

"I need to catch up. Then I'm giving the profile in Bakersville this afternoon."

Greg sent her the stern look he used on his kids. "There's no such thing as catching up with this job. And are you going to be ready to give a profile that soon?"

Evelyn shrugged. "I already wrote most of it."

"When?"

Well aware that the answer would get her harassed about taking her recovery seriously, she tried not to squirm. "There was nothing good on TV, so I worked on the profile."

"Like you watch TV."

Evelyn glanced at the rapidly blinking light on her phone and grimaced as she imagined the number of calls that must be waiting. "Did I miss anything important?"

Greg slipped out of his suit jacket and tossed it over the cubicle. "I did pick up a call from a Chief Tanner Caulfield in Bakersville. He said he'd tried calling you a bunch of times."

Dread settled in Evelyn's gut the way it always did when she was about to get bad news on a case. No wonder Dan chewed antacids like breath mints.

"They found another victim?" she guessed.

"No. Nothing like that. He wants advice on what to ask the victims' families."

"I'll call him." She bit her lip. "Greg, you read the file before we went to the funeral. What do you think about how the bodies were buried?" It was the one part of the profile she hadn't been able to pin down—why the killer had left the heads displayed. She looked up at Greg hopefully.

Greg acted surprised, either because she hadn't figured it out herself or because she was asking for help. But then he shook his head and her lungs deflated.

"Honestly, I have no idea. I've thought about it, but combined with the other behavioral evidence, nothing I come up with makes any sense."

"Yeah. It feels like a message, but in the woods, who's listening?"

Greg was nodding before she'd finished her sentence. "That's what I thought. There was probably a better chance of animals taking off with the heads than anyone finding them. Frankly, I'm amazed the bodies stayed intact as long as they did."

"He was there. A lot. Maybe he scared the animals away?"

"I think you got lucky. If Harris hadn't spotted them, this guy could have killed for years before anyone knew what was happening to those women."

Evelyn's lips tightened. "He's smart. I'm worried that I can't figure out his signature."

"You have a usable profile without it?"

Evelyn let out a heavy breath. "As usable as I can make it. I'm going to check the case against ViCAP. Maybe that'll give me something to work with." Police and Bureau agents across the country could enter unsolved crimes into ViCAP. The idea was to help connect cases that involved a perpetrator committing a crime, then moving into a new jurisdiction and doing it again.

"Good luck," Greg said.

I'll need it, Evelyn didn't reply. Finding the killer's previous murders in ViCAP would mean the investigator had time to enter the case—and time was not something most cops had a lot of. Since entering potential serial crimes into ViCAP wasn't required, it was often overlooked.

But hopefully, finding heads sticking out of the dirt would be unusual enough to make an overworked investigator somewhere else in the country add it to the database. Because she knew for certain there had been other bodies. A killer didn't get that good without practice.

Walter Young, the investigative analyst who ran ViCAP searches, was down the hall and Evelyn walked as fast as her injuries would allow.

"Hi, Walt." Walt had been at BAU for almost a decade. He was middle-aged, rarely smiled and tended to come to work at exactly eight and leave at exactly five.

Walt looked up. "Evelyn. I'm glad you're okay."

She blinked. For the normally silent Walt, that was practically a speech. "Thanks."

When she didn't immediately tell him what she needed, he raised his eyebrows and she held back a smile. That was the Walt she recognized.

"I need to do a ViCAP search." She gave him details he could include in the search. After she'd told him about the victims, she moved on to the crime itself while Walt typed, his fingers moving at an unnatural speed.

"Both victims were raped. The perp washed their bodies after death. He took their personal effects. And after they were dead, he cut them."

No emotion crossed Walt's face as he typed. Bad as that was, he'd done searches for worse.

"The cutting on both bodies was on the center of the chest, just under the collarbone, in the shape of a circle. The marks were made with a smooth blade. Their bodies were covered with bruises, though it hasn't been determined what caused them. Then the killer buried them vertically in the ground until only their heads stuck out."

His fingers kept moving, but now Walt's gaze rose to hers.

This, the killer's signature—the thing he was compelled to do—was what would tie his crimes together. The medical examiner had determined that Mary Ann had been killed by blunt force trauma to the head and suspected Barbara's cause of death was internal bleeding, probably from a severe beating. He might have used other methods to kill his earlier victims, but he would've carved circles into their chests and left their heads sticking out of packed dirt. He wouldn't have been able to stop himself.

If the signature showed up on another crime in ViCAP, she would know where her killer had come from. *Please let it be there,* she prayed.

"What else?" Walt asked in a monotone when she paused.

"The victims were placed in a heavily wooded area with minimal foot traffic."

Evelyn waited impatiently as Walt entered the last of her criteria into ViCAP and started the search.

By the time he handed her the list, she'd folded her hands in her lap to keep them from tapping on the nearest surface.

There were plenty of hits—any case that matched any part of the data she'd input. But no case in which investigators had found heads poking out of the ground.

"Damn it," she muttered. There was no other case with the same signature.

Evelyn had a bad feeling that the next time she saw it would be with his next victim.

Evelyn stood stiffly at the front of the Bakersville police station's conference room. The entire police force stared back at her. Every face in the room wore a nearly identical expression. A mix of nerves and expectation, wariness and distrust.

They don't know what happened to you, she reminded herself. They're not going to notice the bandage. They're just going to see a professional who can tell them about their killer. That was pretty damn important since she was about to tell them she knew more about their perpetrator than they did.

She took a deep breath and stepped forward, and the few conversations still going on stopped in midsentence.

"I'm Evelyn Baine, a criminal investigative analyst consulting from the FBI. I've reviewed the double murder case you've been investigating and created a profile to help you find your perpetrator."

As always, she started by telling them about herself. "I've assisted police in serial murder cases for the past year. My job isn't to tell you who the UNSUB is. My job is to tell you *what sort of person* he is."

"*I* could do that," an officer near the back announced. "He's the *sort of person* who's an asshole."

The cops around him stifled their laughter.

It was the same with every profile. There was always at least one loudmouthed officer who disliked her on sight because of her job or her employer. Or both.

A lot of cops didn't believe in profiling. Plus, plenty of them wouldn't want the FBI invading their turf. The FBI had a reputation, deserved or not, for taking over investigations, assigning most of the work to the cops who were doing it, anyway, and then taking all the credit.

In this small, nearly all-white town, she probably had additional strikes against her as a woman and one of mixed race.

And she needed them to take her seriously and pay close attention so they'd know what to look for. She wasn't leaving behind a detailed written list of characteristics, because that would be discoverable if the case went to trial. If one small portion of the profile didn't match the suspect, a defense attorney would go after it. Cops' notes were less formal and harder to get.

Evelyn could see Tanner standing up to reprimand the officer and spoke before he had the chance. Her method for dealing with it was to take control fast and convince them of her worth. "But the question is, what kind of asshole is he?"

Her ribs aching, Evelyn turned to the corkboard behind her and tacked up a picture of the drop site. "The bodies were found just over a quarter of a mile from the nearest spot navigable by car, so we know the suspect is strong."

"No shit, Sherlock," the same officer muttered loudly enough for Evelyn to hear. "This sounds like a bunch of hocus-pocus bullshit."

"If I wanted your opinion, Higgens, I'd have asked *you* to present a profile," Tanner told the officer before she could reply. "Shut up and listen."

Pretending the animosity in the room didn't bother her, she continued. "I'd estimate he's between six feet and six feet five. He's between two hundred and two hundred and forty pounds. He's familiar with this area. In fact, he's probably lived around here for a while. He also has a place he can take his victims where no one will realize what's happening."

The snickering died down and a few of the officers pulled out notepads.

It was progress, but she needed to show them more. "Both of your victims were low-risk—they weren't involved in anything to make them more likely than the average person to be victims of violent crime. Unlike prostitutes, for example, whose job puts them in contact with dangerous people and unpredictable situations. Statistically, these women shouldn't have ended up as murder victims." At least not by a stranger, but Evelyn didn't add that.

"And the abduction sites—a residential street and a supermarket parking lot—were high-risk for the offender. That tells us he's confident in his ability to abduct them without getting caught. And that he enjoys the challenge."

Tanner spoke up. "The sites were well lit," he said. "They're pretty populated, too, even at night."

"But weren't the victims' cars found where they were left?" an officer asked. "If the Bakersville Burier grabbed them when they were walking to their cars, how did he pull it off?"

Even the cops were calling him by the media's moniker. It was the kind of notoriety a lot of serial killers chased after. Evelyn frowned, but focused on the question. "There are two possibilities with serial killers. The first option is the killer abducts the women by using a blitz-style attack—he immediately renders them unconscious or otherwise unable to fight back, often without the women even seeing him." Evelyn had a sudden image of herself reaching for her neck and feeling the end of a dart. The memory made her neck sting as if the dart were still there.

"The second possibility is a ruse, which was clearly what your perpetrator used. The victims were both married, so it's unlikely that they were approached by someone trying to pick them up. My guess is he offered Mary Ann a ride to her car from her friend's house. Barbara's car had a flat tire, so perhaps he offered her a ride home or to a gas station. You'll notice her groceries weren't found—and we know from records at the grocery store that she had several bags. So, they brought the groceries with them, which also suggests she went voluntarily."

"You think these women would just get into the car of some stranger who offered them a ride?" The officer looked skeptical. "Wouldn't it have been easier to knock them out?"

"Different killers choose different approaches to victim abduction. This guy isn't a blitz attacker. We know that because he's too careful, too obsessed with control—you saw that at the drop site. He wouldn't risk giving the victim an opportunity to put up a fight and attract attention. Plus, he likes the challenge of convincing someone he plans to victimize to come with him voluntarily."

"How would he do that?" Tanner asked.

"He made sure his victims didn't view him as a threat." Evelyn ticked off the possibilities on her fingers. "He could have been faking an injury—a broken arm, a pronounced limp, something that would make him seem harmless. Or he was posing as someone in authority, such as a police or security officer."

"So, the Bakersville Burier gets a potential victim in his car," someone said from the back of the room. "What happens when she realizes he's driving the wrong way? How does he keep control of her then?"

"Yeah, I'd jump out of the car," the lone female on Bakersville's police force said.

The bandages on Evelyn's wrists felt heavier at the reminder of her own abduction. "He made sure they wouldn't. Maybe he knocked them unconscious as soon as he got them in the car or as soon as he drove away from the abduction spot. That's risky, so maybe as soon as the door was shut, he threatened them with a weapon. Some serial criminals remove the inside door handle on the passenger's side, so once a victim is in his car, it's more difficult for her to get out."

As she looked around at the officers, most of them stared back expectantly. When a pair of blue eyes met hers, she jerked backward, nearly stumbling at the memory of another, more sinister pair of eyes that same color.

"So, where did he take the women?" the officer with the blue eyes piped up. "To his house?"

Evelyn straightened, tried to get her equilibrium back. "Possibly. Or he has a secondary location where no one will interrupt him. That's important. This isn't somewhere his victims will be able to successfully yell for help. It's where the women are beaten, raped and murdered. Then he carves the circle into their chests and cleans the bodies to remove trace and DNA evidence. Finally, he wraps them in plastic, transports them to the drop site and buries them until only their heads are visible."

Some of the officers started theorizing, so Evelyn continued loudly. "Your perpetrator is an organized killer. He's sane, well-spoken, educated. We know this because his crime scenes are obsessively neat. He doesn't leave evidence behind, so he's researched things like DNA and probably studied other serial killers."

"Come on," someone argued. "The Bakersville Burier is not sane. He's fucking nuts. You saw what he did to those women!"

"Yes," Evelyn agreed. "But this was a planned-out, sophisticated crime. Put it this way—when you catch him and get him on trial, an insanity plea won't fly."

When the officer nodded, Evelyn said, "He's able to have normal relationships with women. He may even have been married at one time, although I doubt he is now. His victims were both white and he is, too. He served in the military, but was discharged for his inability to follow rules."

"Wait," Tanner interrupted. "How do you know he was in the military?"

"He's very consistent. He likes routines. Think about how neat the crime scene was, how well thought out the abductions must have been for no one to notice. This is a man who likes order. He also has an unnatural obsession with violence. The idea of the military would have appealed to him. It's structured and they actually give him a weapon. When he joined, I'm sure he saw it as an opportunity to wield power over others."

Some of the officers in the front row nodded thoughtfully and Evelyn added, "The problem is, this guy enjoys bossing other people around, but he doesn't like it when anyone tells *him* what to do. So, he wouldn't have lasted in the military. Eventually, he would've started talking back, refusing to take orders."

"Can we talk to the military?" someone asked. "See if we can find a match in the area?"

"It's a long shot," Tanner said before Evelyn could answer. "And I'm not sure the military's going to be all that eager to share their records on such a broad scope."

Evelyn agreed, but suggested, "It's worth a try." She glanced around the room. More and more cops were taking notes. "He comes from a dysfunctional family, with a father who doled out inconsistent punishment and a mother who was emotionally unavailable. We can assume this for several reasons. First of all, serial killers don't often come from healthy homes. Statistics say his was abusive."

This fact was something that should have made them sensitive to the pain of others, Evelyn had always thought. That was what it had done to her. But serial killers used the violence done to them as a starting point and turned it on others.

"Beyond that, the UNSUB shows a mixture of extreme caution—the removal of evidence and burying the bodies deep in the woods—with a need to control, shown by the rape and the circle cut in the chest. So we know he's accustomed to being cautious. As a child, he probably never knew what would cause his father to yell at him or beat him and what would get him left alone. At the same time, the abuse accounts for his need to be in total control over his victims, because growing up, he didn't have control over anything."

"What about his mother?" someone asked. "Aren't all serial killers obsessed with their mothers?"

Nervous laughter rippled through the room.

Evelyn ignored the second question. "I can tell you his mother wasn't there for him emotionally and he didn't have any strong female role models. The circle is definitely symbolic to him in some way. But essentially, the fact that he can mutilate these women—carve such precise, careful marks onto them—means he has no empathy for them. He sees them as subhuman."

Looking over at Tanner, who was furiously scribbling notes, Evelyn prayed her profile would work. That it would help catch the killer.

"There were precipitating stressors before the attacks, maybe the loss of a girlfriend or wife or financial problems. He's wanted to do this for quite a while, but something's happened in his life to set him off *now*. He's in his late twenties or early thirties."

When Tanner seemed about to ask how she knew, she preempted him. "He isn't an amateur, but he hasn't been killing for years and years, either. He's had time to let his fantasies evolve—and this kind of murder always starts with lots of elaborate fantasizing. He's had time to research how to carry them out. Still, he's young enough that it's not a struggle to carry these women for a distance. Also, the women he chooses aren't significantly different in age from him."

Shifting to ease the ache in her rib cage, she said, "Either now or in his past, he's had trouble with alcohol. It loosens his inhibitions. It's likely he uses some—not enough to get him drunk, but a little bit to give him courage—before he commits his murders."

"How did you figure that out?" the female cop asked.

"The extreme caution used in disposing of the bodies tells us he's nervous about leaving anything behind. He's not blasé about the possibility of getting caught. It scares him. And the fact that he takes such care not to leave evidence behind after he chooses high-risk abductions tells us he needs to psych himself up before he trolls. That's where the alcohol comes in."

Evelyn flinched as pain sliced through her ribs, then glanced around. But none of the cops seemed to notice. She talked faster, knowing the agony was just going to get worse until she sat. "The killer has probably been in trouble with the law in the past, maybe as a juvenile. But whatever he did was considered minor. My guess would be Peeping Tom offenses, something that's often overlooked as not serious. I suspect this because, as I've indicated, the killer is obviously very careful and has a particular script he follows in his fantasies. So, it's not likely that he committed other major crimes as a young man. They wouldn't interest him. But his fantasies started at an early age and—"

"Fantasies?" someone interrupted. "You keep mentioning that. Do you mean he imagines killing women before he does it?"

"Basically, yes. This guy didn't wake up one day and decide he should stalk a victim, lure her into his car, beat her, rape her, murder her, cut a circle in her chest, remove the evidence, transport her to an isolated location, bury her up to

her head and then search for a new victim. He's been thinking about this for a long time, refining the details. Eventually, imagining wasn't enough. And given the sophistication
of the crimes, these weren't his first murders."

The hum of too many officers whispering almost drowned
out her next words, so she raised her voice. "He holds a job
below his skill level, probably something in a position of some
authority, like a security guard. He also drives a dark-colored
vehicle, in a make commonly used by police. It's a relatively
new model and he keeps it clean, again obsessively so. It's likely
he applied for a job with the police—if not here, then wherever he lived before—but was turned down either because of
his military discharge or his inability to follow rules."

Without giving the assembled officers a chance to ask more
questions, she told them, "I searched for your killer's signature in ViCAP. His M.O., the beatings or blunt force trauma,
might have changed, but his signature won't."

"What's the signature?" Tanner wondered.

"The circular cutting on the body and the unique burial."

"Why won't it change?"

"The signature is an act that's important to him. He's compelled to do it. And the more he kills, the more apparent it
will become."

When she went silent, one of the cops asked, "Okay, the
signature's important, but why does he do it?"

Evelyn grimaced, hating that she couldn't tell them. She'd
hoped to avoid this question. "I don't know. I can tell you it's
the thing that gets him off. The rapes, the murders, he enjoys those, but ultimately this is what he's after—he wants to
cut circles on their chests and then display the heads of the
women he brutalized."

Silence, full of discomfort and disgust at what motivated
the killer, swelled, until Tanner prompted, "How does the

profile help us? We go through all the applications we've had to join the police force in the past few years?"

"That's a good place to begin. The profile is designed to narrow your suspect pool. If you understand what sort of person you're looking for, it'll be easier to find him. You probably haven't interviewed him yet. You would have no reason to suspect him from the initial scene, because he doesn't know the women personally. But now that the bodies have been recovered, he might try to visit their graves. He was definitely visiting the drop site—at least before we found the bodies. So you should keep an eye on these places."

"What else?" Tanner asked, sounding impatient for something more direct. "Can we eliminate anyone over forty?"

"No. The bulk of my profile is right, but little details could be off. Don't fixate on one thing."

Evelyn got ready to explain how a killer's emotional age could differ from his actual age. But she cut herself off. She'd given the officers enough to digest. Now, she just had to pray they'd use it to find the killer before *he* found another victim.

6

"HOW'S SHE DOING TODAY, MELANIE?" EVELYN asked the nurse at the front station of the old-age home where her grandmother had lived for the past year.

Melanie looked up from a pile of paperwork. "She's having a good day. You're sweet to visit so often."

Evelyn didn't say anything. A few times a week—less if a case sent her out of town—was hardly enough time for the woman who'd raised her.

Her grandma having a good day meant she'd recognize Evelyn and would probably know what year it was. Some days, when the dementia had a particularly strong grip, she didn't know where she was, didn't know her husband was gone and her only daughter a drunk neither of them had seen in almost two decades.

"Go on back," Melanie said.

Evelyn's ribs throbbed as she strode down the hallway to her grandma Mabel's room, furnished with a few of her own belongings, the walls covered with photos of her husband, daughter and granddaughter.

Mabel was sitting in her favorite chair, wearing her pink bathrobe, her silvery hair braided and her green eyes sharp.

Her lopsided smile grew as she slowly flipped the pages in a well-loved photo album.

Evelyn felt herself smile, too, seeing the pictures from the first year she'd gone to live with her grandparents. She'd been so withdrawn then, so used to trying to stay invisible to her mother and her mother's latest boyfriend, that she hadn't known how to respond to the attention. Every picture showed her shrinking back and her grandparents grinning widely, as though suddenly having to raise their wayward daughter's child was a dream come true.

A powerful wave of love swept over her. There was no question her grandparents had saved her life. "That was the best thing that ever happened to me—coming to live with you."

Mabel looked up. "Evelyn!" She closed the album and stretched out a frail hand until Evelyn folded her in a careful hug. The rose-scented perfume her grandma had always worn, that she still dabbed on every day, wafted up, and Evelyn closed her eyes and breathed it in.

As she finally sat on the bed, her grandma's gaze skipped to Evelyn's forehead. "What happened?"

Evelyn's fingers itched to cover the bandage there, but she resisted. "Just a bump to the head. I'm okay."

Mabel's eyes narrowed, but before she could say anything, Evelyn insisted, "I am."

She felt guilty about lying, about getting into a situation that could have killed her and left her grandma all alone. It had been just the two of them since her grandpa died when she was fifteen. After her grandma's massive stroke two years later, Evelyn had gone to college early to avoid having to live with her mother again. But she'd brought her grandma with her, finding her a nursing home near each place she lived.

Evelyn handled her grandma's medical care, brought her word puzzles and books to help slow her mental slide and spent hours every week talking to her about Grandpa, about her life at the Bureau and about the past. In return, no matter what kind of day her grandma was having, she was Evelyn's rock—the one person who'd always believed in her and never let her down.

What would have happened if Evelyn had let her grandma down? If she hadn't fought off her abductor? If the car had hit that tree just a little harder?

What would have happened to her grandma then? On her bad days, she would've wondered why Evelyn had stopped visiting. And on her good days, she'd know Evelyn was dead, that there was no one left in the world who cared about her.

Tears rushed forward and Evelyn blinked them back fast, squeezing her grandma's hand. "I'm okay now. Everything's okay."

"Evelyn!"

Her name echoed through the mostly silent room, making Evelyn jump in her seat. Blinking to adjust her eyes after staring at her computer screen all morning, she stood slowly, recognizing Kyle McKenzie's deep, distinctive voice.

Kendall was glaring at her as he got his coffee, as if it were her fault the HRT agents thought everything needed to be done at high volume.

But why were they yelling her name instead of Greg's?

In the cubicle beside hers, Greg stood, looking curious, as Kyle and Gabe approached.

Gabe leaned against her cubicle. "We have something for you."

Evelyn frowned, the movement pulling at the damaged skin next to her left eye. She glanced from him to Kyle. "About a case?"

Kyle grinned, but it lacked his usual charm. No teasing

sparkle lit his eyes and the dimples were nowhere in sight. He hadn't even come into her cubicle the way he usually did.

Was he as disappointed as everyone else that she hadn't been able to fight off her attacker before he grabbed her?

"No." Kyle handed her a small white box closed with a silver ribbon.

A present? She couldn't remember the last time someone other than Audrey or Jo had given her one of those. "What's this for?"

"We wanted to bring you something at the hospital, but you checked yourself out before we could," Gabe said.

Evelyn shifted on the balls of her feet, then recognized the nervous gesture and went still. "Is this a getting-well thing?"

Kyle smiled crookedly, seeming to find her reaction comical, although by now he should've been used to her awkward social skills. "Open it."

Evelyn untied the ribbon and opened the box. Inside was a small Saint Michael's medallion on a delicate chain. Saint Michael was the patron saint of law enforcement officers.

"Gabe and I both have something for luck," Kyle said as she looked up at him, surprised. "We thought you could use one, too."

"What's yours?"

In response, Gabe pulled a chain from under his shirt. A flattened, worn gold cross dangled from the end of it. "It belonged to my mother." Gabe had never told her, but Evelyn knew from Greg that his mother had been killed when Gabe was young.

She nodded soberly, knowing what it was like to lose a parent. Her father had died when she was six. She remembered him just enough to realize how different her life could have been if he'd lived.

"I'm a good Irish Catholic boy," Kyle said with an exaggerated brogue. He pulled his own cross from under his shirt.

"Thanks." A sense of warmth spread through her chest. She knew Jo and Audrey loved her, but after her grandpa's death and her grandma's stroke, they'd been the only ones she'd dared let close to her. And a year into her stint at BAU, she'd started letting Greg in, too. But there was no one else.

It didn't take a degree in psychology to recognize she had abandonment issues, but it was something she didn't like about herself. She needed to make a better effort if she wanted to build friendships with Kyle and Gabe—who were definitely making an effort with her. It wasn't going to be easy to bury her growing attraction to Kyle, but she vowed to try.

Greg took the necklace and fastened it over her turtleneck and Evelyn decided to tuck it under her shirt later when no one would notice her bruised neck.

"Evelyn!"

She looked up from admiring the necklace.

Dan was scowling. As usual, it was aimed at her.

"How's your case load? Do you need anything reassigned?"

Evelyn stiffened, but she tried to keep her voice unaffected. "Nope. I'll be caught up soon."

Dan turned his glower on the HRT agents. "Doesn't the Hostage Rescue Team give you boys anything to do?"

Amusement trembled on the corners of Kyle's lips.

Although they acted as if they had all the time in the world when they visited, the truth was they usually dashed over during a break from running the yellow brick road—the nickname for the marine training course—or keeping their shooting skills sharp before they went back to Quantico to practice rescue scenarios.

"We're in practice mode," Gabe replied. "We're supposed to

take pictures of our subjects without them spotting us. Today, you were our practice targets."

When color started to rise toward the dome of Dan's head and Evelyn tried to figure out if he was serious, a grin broke across Gabe's face.

"He's kidding," Kyle said. "We'd better get going."

Before Dan could warn them not to come back—or he burst an artery—they hurried to the door and sprinted out.

Dan looked furiously at Evelyn, and she immediately turned to Greg, wondering why he didn't get some of the blame. She discovered it was because he'd dropped down below his cubicle wall to hide.

"No fair," she muttered as Dan stalked to his office.

"Move faster next time," Greg shot back.

She could sense his smile as she sank into her own chair and pulled up an active case file on her computer. She didn't have a chance to open the folder because her phone rang. "Evelyn Baine, BAU," she answered.

"Evelyn, it's Ron Harding. How are you?"

"I'm fine," Evelyn lied, her ribs aching either from sitting down too fast or the instant reminder of how she'd hurt them.

"I have some good news for you," he told her unexpectedly.

"You do?"

"We traced the car you crashed."

She wished she could remember crashing the car. Wished she could remember the car at all. But if they'd traced the car, that meant they had a name. Her heart kicked into overdrive.

"It's titled to a man who lives in Boston," Ron said. "We contacted some agents there, who are going to talk to him."

Evelyn clutched the phone tighter. "What do you know about him?"

"Just the basics. But he's probably not your guy, unless the

Bureau's gone soft with training its agents in defensive tactics since I was at the academy."

Evelyn bristled. "What does that mean?"

"The car is registered to a man named David Greene."

David Greene. The name echoed in her head. It didn't mean anything to her. "And? Is he in Boston now?"

"As far as we know. He's also seventy-four years old."

Evelyn's shoulders slumped. "Was his car reported stolen?"

"No. The agents in Boston are talking to him this afternoon. I'll tell you what they find out as soon as I hear." He hung up without saying goodbye.

Evelyn replaced the receiver and stared at her computer screen until it went blurry.

A car stolen from Boston. Drugs used to knock her out so she couldn't fight back.

Shivers racked her in waves. Whoever he was, he'd planned his attack carefully. He'd be hard to find. And she didn't know why he was after her, if he'd given up or if he was planning another try.

When the phone rang, Evelyn's heartbeat instantly surged. She hoped it was Ron calling back with more about the car she'd crashed, but a glance at the phone readout told her it wasn't. "Evelyn Baine, BAU."

"Agent Baine, this is Gilbert Havorth." Gilbert worked for the lab at Quantico. She didn't know him well, but their paths had crossed on previous cases. He fit the stereotype of what a lab agent should look like, with his thick-rimmed glasses, balding head and crooked features.

She knew Gilbert was eligible for retirement, but since he'd stuck around after twenty years instead of trading in the Bureau title for a cushy civilian job, it was obvious he loved it. If you needed an expert in fingerprint analysis, Gilbert was it.

But she hadn't sent him any prints to analyze. "What—"

"I've been dusting the car sent over by the agents working your abduction," Gilbert said, cutting her off.

Ah. Tension locked her shoulders as she realized just how many people knew what had happened to her. She wanted her name known in the Bureau, but not for this reason. Something like this could taint a career.

And all Evelyn had was her career.

"We put a rush on the analysis, considering this bastard went after an agent. But I'm having trouble locating any useful prints. I have a significant number of *your* prints, but so far I haven't found any others. All the emergency workers wore gloves, so I didn't even have to run elimination prints."

"What? How is that possible?"

"I've been told you don't recall anything about your abduction, but could this guy have worn gloves?"

"It must've been almost eighty degrees the day I was abducted. Why would he..." Evelyn broke off as a memory slammed into her consciousness.

Haggarty's parking lot was dark, a mugger's dream. The humidity, so bad she'd moved her grandmother's ring to a smaller finger, had made her headache even worse.

"Evelyn?"

"Hold on," Evelyn said, trying to stay with the memory.

She'd been opening her car door when she'd sensed someone behind her. She'd turned partway around and then... Evelyn touched the side of her neck as she remembered the sudden stabbing pain. She rubbed at the still-bruised spot.

A hand had gripped her mouth so she couldn't scream, but her abductor needn't have bothered. She'd been losing consciousness too quickly.

The hand over her mouth had felt rubbery, she remembered now. It hadn't felt like skin. "Latex gloves," she said aloud.

"What?"

"He was wearing latex gloves." Evelyn waited for more details of that night to surface, but none did.

Damn it. She squeezed her eyes shut, trying to bring the memory back.

There was nothing but darkness.

"Okay," Gilbert finally said into the silence. "That means he planned your abduction in advance and useful prints are unlikely. I'll go over it again, anyway. Even though he wore gloves to abduct you, he probably didn't always wear them. He must've wiped the car down that night, but most people who do that miss prints somewhere. There's still hope."

The reassurance sounded empty, but at least he wasn't giving up. "Thanks, Gilbert."

"I'll call you if I come up with anything."

It wasn't until she heard a dial tone that Evelyn hung up her phone. She shut her eyes and relived what she could recall of her abduction, hoping her subconscious would take over from there.

She remembered reaching for her car door and then panicking as pain pierced her neck and the world shifted beneath her feet. She'd tried to steady herself on her car, prepared to fight or scream and then—

"Evelyn."

She jumped in her chair and spun around.

"Sorry." Dan held her chair, and Evelyn silently cursed herself. Of all people, why did Dan have to be the one to see her act jumpy?

BAU was one of the hardest units in the Bureau to get into, and she didn't want to give Dan any reason to think she couldn't hack it.

"No problem. You startled me."

Dan frowned, obviously skeptical, but replied, "We have a problem."

Damn it, what now? "What is it?"

"A bullet was retrieved from the vehicle you crashed. Ballistics looked at it and they've concluded it came from your Bureau-issued weapon."

"I guess it's not surprising. My weapon wasn't retrieved."

She'd gone to the firing range at Quantico several times, practicing with her new Glock, but she missed the SIG Sauer.

"That may be a problem," Dan said. "You know every time you fire your weapon, it needs to be documented."

Frustration built inside her. "As soon as my memory of that night returns, I'll write up a report."

"From what your doctor told me, it may not return at all."

Deciding not to tell him part of it already had, since the memory hadn't been of much use, Evelyn said definitively, "It will."

"Okay." Dan patted her shoulder. "You just take it easy."

At his patronizing tone, she had a sudden, fierce desire to snap at him. Evelyn bit down on her tongue.

And then she damn near bit through it as her phone rang again.

She swiveled for her desk, grabbing the receiver. "Evelyn Baine, BAU."

"Evelyn, hi, this is Jimmy. Jimmy Drescott. How are you?"

Even on the phone, Jimmy sounded young and flirtatious. It seemed to be taking him longer than most men to realize she was impervious to flirting.

Unless it was Kyle McKenzie doing the flirting. Pushing that errant thought out of her mind, she asked, "Did the agents learn anything new in Boston?"

"Actually, yes. We may have the name of the man who abducted you."

Evelyn's free hand gripped her desk until her knuckles and fingertips went white. She grimaced at the pain that shot through her wrist, but couldn't seem to loosen her grip. "Who?"

"The man whose name was on the title, David Greene, lent the vehicle to his grandson four years ago. Greene stopped driving a few years before that. He relies on a live-in nurse to take him places. The grandson never returned the car."

"Who is this guy?" Possibilities flooded her mind. A relative of someone she'd put away. A killer she'd investigated but hadn't caught. Someone she'd arrested who'd recently been released from prison. "Where does he live? Do you have anything on him?"

"Slow down." Jimmy sounded amused. "They haven't gotten that far. I guess the old guy wasn't used to visitors, so it took the agents a while to get the information. He kept offering them tea and cookies and wanted to talk about his life."

"How far have they gotten?" Annoyance began to seep past her nerves. "What's the grandson's name?"

"Relax, Evelyn. We'll take care of this. Don't worry."

She inhaled a slow, calming breath. "Jimmy, tell me what you know."

"His name is Justin Greene."

Justin Greene. She didn't recognize the name.

"Eighteen years old when the grandfather lent him the car. He'd be twenty-two now," Jimmy continued. "At eighteen, he'd already been in trouble with the law a few times for minor offenses—a couple of burglaries, I think. Apparently, he was often on the outs with his parents, and the grandfather rarely saw him. So, he says when the boy asked to borrow the car, it was the first time he'd seen him in a few years. Justin promised to return it later that week, but never did. Greene said whenever he asks his son about it, he changes the subject. The old man figured the kid crashed it and his son didn't want to tell him."

"Or he took off with it," Evelyn theorized.

"Could be," Jimmy agreed.

"Do you know anything else about Justin Greene?"

"Not a whole lot. Greene showed the agents a picture of the boy, but I haven't seen it. They mentioned he was big, over six feet and around two hundred pounds, so I guess it's not surprising that he was able to overpower you."

Anger bubbled up, red hot and too close to the surface, fed by her fear that one moment of distraction was going to destroy her reputation in the Bureau. Drugging people wasn't the same as overpowering them, but Evelyn managed not to bark that at Jimmy. "What else?"

"That's it so far. Does the name mean anything to you?"

"No." She wished it did. At least then they'd have a starting point, a reason for her abduction.

Instead, she could only wonder. Revenge was the most likely option. An agent at BAU could make a lot of enemies, and most of them were killers.

"We'll find him," Jimmy said, but the certainty in his voice seemed meant to impress rather than reassure.

The question was, would they find him before he found her again?

7

THE ROADS WERE EMPTY AND DARK, THE MOON barely a sliver in the cloudy sky, as Evelyn's feet pounded against the pavement. Her gun bounced awkwardly on her hip, secure in its belt pack.

A shiver of awareness prickled across the back of her neck, her shoulders, and Evelyn picked up her pace. Trying to outrun whoever might be behind her. Trying to outrun the knowledge that someone had attacked her, but having no memory of it.

Then someone else's footsteps joined her own, grew faster, grew closer.

She turned back to look and saw nothing. Stumbling, Evelyn whipped her head around and slammed into someone big, well over two hundred pounds, well over six feet.

Before she could go for her gun, he smiled with predatory glee and slammed his fist into her chin, sending her to the pavement.

A scream was trapped in her throat as he leaned close. There was only a cloak of darkness where his face should have been, but there was a smile in his eyes as he showed her his knife.

Frantic, she struggled, but something held her arms in place as he sliced the knife across her body in one long gash.

Everything seemed to go red, except for his ice-blue eyes. They came closer and closer until she jerked upright, her heart banging in her chest like a metal hammer.

The sheets were twisted around her, confining her arms against her sides. Sweat soaked her pajamas and her body shook with tremors.

The clock radio next to her bed blinked, huge red numerals flashing twelve o'clock. The power must have gone out overnight long enough to reset it.

When she finally untangled herself from the covers, her legs felt wobbly, hardly able to support her weight. Her breathing was still jerky, irregular.

Her gun was in her nightstand and she took it with her into the bathroom. Her hands trembled, making it difficult to shed her pajamas and step into the shower.

As the scalding water sloshed over her, doing nothing to eliminate the chills shaking her body, she thought about Justin Greene. Was it him? The man who'd abducted her and taken her weapon and her sense of security. The killer with the soulless blue eyes who seemed determined to visit her even in sleep.

For the first time in her career as an FBI agent, for one of the first times in her life, Evelyn wished she wasn't alone.

At 4:00 a.m., the BAU office hadn't felt any safer than her house. But three hours later, it had filled with enough agents that Evelyn's pulse didn't spike every time the fax machine beeped to life with another profile request.

Still, she was glad to be on the phone when Greg strolled into the office, because she doubted he'd miss the larger-than-usual circles beneath her eyes. She wasn't pleased with the person on the other end of the phone, however, telling her Tanner wasn't available. Yes, it was early, but there was a serial killer on the loose. Tanner should have rolled out his sleeping bag at the station long ago.

"Please have him call me as soon as he gets in."

The officer's "Sure, ma'am" sounded less than promising, and Evelyn frowned as she hung up.

"Tough case?" Greg asked, leaning against her cubicle.

She looked up, hoping her heavy-handed makeup that morning would fool him.

He squinted at her. "You sleeping okay?"

Evelyn shrugged. "I'm actually a little behind with work." She dodged his question, trusting that he'd assume she'd stayed up late working.

"Did I ever tell you about my training agent? The guy was a legend. I mean, one of the best. He could look at a crime scene and rattle off a nearly complete profile right away."

Evelyn nodded, wondering where Greg was going with this. "I read his book."

"So, you probably read about his last case." Greg lifted his eyebrows expectantly.

"Of course. The pair of killers in Arkansas targeting prostitutes."

"You remember what happened to him while he was chasing those killers?"

Evelyn scowled and the stitches near her eye stretched and stung. "I'm not going to have a heart attack."

"We all have our limits," Greg warned. "Your body can only handle so much stress. Time off never ruined a career." His stern lecturing tone grew worried, almost fatherly. "I take a vacation every summer and I'm still working here."

But Greg had been at BAU for eight years. He had Dan's trust, not skepticism of his skills. And he wasn't trying to prove he was still qualified to be an agent after someone had abducted and almost killed him.

She forced a lightness into her voice. "I get bored on vacations."

Greg's lips twisted in obvious disbelief. "When was the last time you took one?"

The ringing phone on her desk saved her. "Evelyn, this is Gilbert Havorth."

"Did you find anything?"

"Actually, yes. I didn't expect to, after going over the car once and then learning the assailant wore gloves. But I'm thorough. It was a great find, in the trunk, on the right side."

"*In* the trunk?" Evelyn interrupted.

"Interestingly enough, yes. It turned out to be an impressed print, not a latent one—basically someone had stuck a finger in caulk while it was still wet."

"There was caulk in the trunk?"

"Yes. It looks like the person was trying to repair a rust spot that wore a hole in the trunk. At any rate, he left us with a perfect impression. I did some reverse molding and sent the resulting print to Clarksburg."

Clarksburg, West Virginia, was home of the Criminal Justice Information Services Division, and the Integrated Automated Fingerprint Identification System (IAFIS) was located there. If the print was on file, as it would be for a previously convicted felon, IAFIS would tell them whose it was.

"That's great," Evelyn said, although it was hard to muster up a lot of enthusiasm. They already had a probable name for her abductor. But in a courtroom, that fingerprint, if it belonged to Justin Greene, could be his undoing.

"I found something else, too," Gilbert said. "Under the front passenger seat, caught in the mechanism that moves the seat, I found a charm bracelet. It was flattened, but there was

an inscription on one of the charms. You didn't lose a bracelet, did you?"

"No."

"Okay. I didn't figure it was yours. It looked like it'd been
stuck there for a while. I sent it to the agents in charge of the
case."

"Do you remember what the inscription was?"

"Some comment about not needing luck. I can't tell you
word for word. When it arrives, you can talk to the agents on
the case if you want to know."

"Okay," Evelyn said.

It was possible it belonged to a woman in the life of her
abductor, but like the fingerprint, it wouldn't help them find
Justin Greene. It *would* be one more bit of proof when the case
eventually went to court.

Until then, it was just something to fill an evidence bag.

Justin Greene. The name echoed in Evelyn's head with the
intensity of an alarm she couldn't shut off. Who was he? Why
had he come after her?

Maybe he was connected to a case she'd investigated during her five years in Houston. Those files would be a hassle
to get, and Evelyn didn't want to have to explain why she
wanted them.

She'd only been at BAU a year, but that was plenty of time
to make enemies of some of the most dangerous people in the
country. Not all the killers she'd gone after had been caught.
Plus, she had more than a dozen active cases.

Pinpricks jabbed her nerve endings as she thought about
the killer in Bakersville. The man who beat his victims, raped
and cut them, then stuck them in the dirt so he could go back
and stare at their heads, look into their dead eyes.

But it couldn't have been him. Her attacker and the Bakersville killer *couldn't* have been the same man. She didn't remember much about her abduction, but she did know she'd been blitzed. The Bakersville killer was a charmer. It was part of the turn-on for him. He wouldn't resort to a blitz attack.

So, then who?

Focus, she reprimanded herself. There was a backlog of case files on her computer, all begging for her attention. But whenever she looked at her screen, the words went blurry and all she could think of was her abductor and his soulless blue eyes.

A hand landed on her shoulder and Evelyn spun around.

Dan stood just inside her cubicle, crunching on what had to be antacids. The hair on the left side of his head stuck out, as though he'd been running his hands through it. It was a strange contrast to the top of his head, which was bald, and the hair on the right side, still lying flat.

"Evelyn, I have a meeting coming up with the new assistant director. He wants to evaluate our processes and success rate. I'd like you to prepare a list of your closed cases from the past year. Make sure you include the current status of the killers—their sentences and whatever else you feel is pertinent." His lips compressed into a thin line. "Then we'll see what he thinks about our successes."

As Dan headed for the coffee machine, Greg peeked around their cubicle divider. "You still trying to work up to legend status?" he teased.

Evelyn held back a retort about her "legendary" abduction and managed a smile.

Greg shook his head, and she could tell he wasn't fooled.

"You were drugged and handcuffed and you still kicked the guy's ass," Greg said. "That's the part people will remember in the long run. Especially once he's caught. And he *will* be caught."

If by kicking his ass, you mean running away, she wanted to say.

Instead, she directed her gaze at the industrial gray carpeting and muttered, "I hope so." To change the subject, she said, "I need to call Tanner again."

She dialed and got an officer who let out a heavy sigh when she asked for Tanner.

"Ms. Baine," he said, and she could tell he'd intentionally addressed her like a civilian instead of by her Bureau title. "Chief Caulfield isn't available."

"If he's out of the office, patch me through," she demanded in her authoritative BAU voice.

"He'll have to call you later." The officer hung up.

Tanner was avoiding her.

Despite the initial hostility she'd felt in Bakersville, she'd thought her profile had punched through their stereotypes, earned their trust. Apparently not.

Looked as if she'd have to do this the hard way.

Something she'd learned before joining the Bureau was the accessibility of personal information on the internet. Her mom had tracked her down too many times in her first years out of college, locating her phone number or her address online when Evelyn didn't even know it was there. That had taught her to be more careful with the information. But most people weren't.

Tanner was no exception. A public database listed his personal cell phone number and she called it.

"Hello?"

Evelyn recognized Tanner's low Southern drawl immediately. "Tanner, it's Evelyn Baine."

"Evelyn." Tanner's tone deepened with annoyance. "I got your messages. I was going to call you later, when I wasn't busy trying to catch this killer."

"That's why—"

"Your profile isn't helping."

She bristled, but tried to keep her resentment out of her voice. "I wanted to talk about proactive techniques—"

"Evelyn." His voice swelled with anger. "I've got all my officers on longer shifts, looking for the guy you've described, trying to keep the women of this town safe. I haven't slept in three days and we have no strong leads. I just don't have time for any more nonsense that isn't going to work. Especially with the press going crazy, splashing the Bakersville Burier across the front page every day."

She clenched her hands. All profilers faced skepticism; it was the nature of the job. But she seemed to get dismissed more often than most because she was a tiny woman in a profession dominated by big men.

The only time being underestimated had worked to her advantage was in a fight. Back at the academy, during defensive training, her size had actually been an advantage until the other agents learned she was a hell of a lot stronger than she looked.

Now, thanks to a man she couldn't remember, she'd be useless in a fight. And the cracked ribs he'd given her meant she couldn't even run.

Running had always been an outlet for her anger, her frustration, all the emotions triggered by staring at horrifying crime scenes and trying to get into the psyche of the person who'd created them. Right now, the anger was constantly close to the surface, close to erupting at whoever was nearby.

She took a deep breath. "The profile I gave you isn't nonsense. Locking up killers like the one you're searching for is what I do and I'm damn good at it. And this guy *is* going to kill again. You need to get proactive."

"I'll call you when I have time," Tanner snapped.

Evelyn allowed him the parting shot. Mostly because he

hung up on her and she didn't think he'd pick up if she called back.

It was going to take some work to insert herself back into the case. But she had to do it.

Despite what Tanner thought, the women of Bakersville weren't safe. They wouldn't be safe until the killer was caught. And police presence alone wasn't going to do it. That would just force the killer to be more creative.

Whether Tanner knew it or not, he needed her.

Releasing a shaky, frustrated breath, Evelyn pulled up her file on the BAKBURY killer. She'd go through it once more to make sure there was nothing she'd missed.

Greg should've been thinking about his cases. He had more than ten active, and every one was time-sensitive.

Serial killers trolling for another victim while he studied files filled with their latest kills. A serial arsonist who'd eluded capture in three states, but always left the cops taunting notes. A couple of known terrorists he was supposed to profile so someone—probably his cousin's unit—could figure out how to stop them.

But all he could think about was the woman in the cubicle next to him. She'd dropped something ten minutes ago and it had distracted him from his work. He still hadn't gotten back to it.

Instead, he stared at the picture of his son tacked to his cubicle wall. The first year he'd worked at BAU, he'd kept that wall empty. It had seemed wrong to have pictures of his family in the same space where he looked at mutilated, violated victims. Where he crawled into the sick, violent fantasies of rapists and killers.

Then, just before he'd almost bugged out of BAU because of a deep depression, he'd realized how to cope. He'd realized he needed the calming presence of his family to bring him back from the twisted corners of disturbed minds.

He'd tacked up photos of his son, daughter and wife, smiling, enjoying their lives. And it reminded him why he did the job. It kept him focused on the people he could save instead of the victims he was too late to help.

Evelyn had never told him all the details of her life. But he could read the signs. Her unnatural dedication to the job. Her limited social skills, surely a result of having too few people to practice them on. The way she walked through her days as if she was constantly bracing for the next sucker punch.

Something bad had happened to her in the past, something that had torn her life apart. Whatever it was, it had to be the driving force behind her joining the Bureau.

But a horrible incident in the past was a hell of a thing to base the rest your life on.

Greg smoothed the photo of his son. Josh had turned eight last month, marking three years since he'd become a member of the Ibsen family. It felt like much longer. Sometimes it was hard for Greg to believe it was only last year that Josh had stopped having nightmares.

Nightmares about his father, who'd been in jail since the night he'd stabbed Josh's birth mother, killing her. Since he'd stabbed Josh, leaving behind a thin scar on the boy's chest and a much deeper one on his psyche.

He wondered if Evelyn had similar nightmares.

With a sigh, he gave up on his files and wheeled his chair backward out of his cubicle and over to Evelyn's.

The cheery "What are you working on?" died before it passed his throat.

Evelyn was rigid in her chair. On the floor next to her was a notepad. The top read BAKBURY in Evelyn's neat handwriting, which he knew was FBI shorthand for the Bakersville serial killer case.

He got out of his chair. "Evelyn?"

She didn't seem to hear him, so he carefully put a hand on her shoulder.

But not carefully enough, because she jumped, spinning the chair around to face him. She blinked and schooled her face into an impassive expression, but not before he saw the terror that had been there.

Fear overwhelmed him. Very little terrified Evelyn.

"What's wrong?"

Her gaze darted to the notepad on the floor. "I think…"

"What?"

"I have to call someone." She spun back to the desk and dialed a number with hands that shook. Somehow, she sounded composed when she said, "This is Evelyn Baine, with BAU. I'd like to speak to Ron Harding."

Evelyn's foot started tapping a rapid beat under her desk. Finally, she said, "The bracelet that was recovered—can you tell me what the inscription read?" Her voice went too high a minute later when she said, "Thanks," and hung up.

"What's going on?" Greg demanded.

She turned her chair slowly to face him, but her eyes were unfocused. "They found a charm bracelet in the car I crashed."

When she didn't continue, Greg prompted, "And?"

"I was reviewing the BAKBURY case and I realized there was a missing charm bracelet. It was listed as one of the items Mary Ann Pollak might have been wearing the day she was abducted. There was an inscription on one of the charms. It said, 'You don't need luck. You have me.' It had the initials D.P. on it. It was given to her by her husband, Donald."

Evelyn sucked in a breath, but her voice was raw when she

said, "That inscription was on the bracelet from my abduction case."

Dread settled in his gut. "So the guy who abducted you…"

"Is probably the Bakersville serial killer."

8

SEVENTEEN YEARS AGO, EVELYN HAD GOTTEN her first glimpse of true evil.

When she was twelve, living with her grandparents in the only stable home she'd had in years, she'd spent what had seemed like a typical day with her best friend, Cassandra Byers. It was the last time Evelyn had ever seen her.

Since then, Evelyn had purposely surrounded herself with evil.

From the moment she'd met the profiler assigned to Cassie's case, she'd known what she was going to do with her life. Since then, she'd spent too much time learning all the subtle shades of evil, all the different ways criminals tortured and killed and ripped apart lives. One day, she'd vowed, she was going to use that knowledge to find Cassie.

Now a seasoned profiler, intellectually Evelyn knew the little girl with the blond ringlets and the infectious smile wouldn't be coming home alive. But emotionally, she had to believe there was a chance.

A chance to save the first true friend she'd ever had, to ease the pain in the tiny community where her grandparents had lived. Maybe even to change her own path.

She'd spent days searching the marshes with her grandparents, already knowing, that they'd passed the point of searching for Cassie and were searching for her body.

A familiar ache strangled her heart. She thought of Cassie daily, but she'd lost touch with Cassie's family when she'd left Rose Bay. And it had been a long time since she'd lingered on those memories, a long time since she'd let the pain consume her.

But her own abduction seemed to have brought everything to the surface. Every loss, every sorrow, every failure.

Now it all threatened to overflow.

Standing on legs that almost buckled from the weight of those memories, Evelyn shut down her computer. As much as she wanted to deny it, she wasn't still at work because she wanted to finish the profile she'd struggled with all day. She was there because she felt safer in an FBI building and close to a marine base than in her own home.

And that was ironic, when she recalled a case she'd studied before she'd become a criminal investigative analyst. A female marine out for a jog on a marine base had been brutally raped and murdered.

On that thought, Evelyn grabbed her briefcase and rushed for her car.

It only took twenty minutes to drive to the Den. Plenty of time for images of Mary Ann's and Barbara's mutilated bodies and decaying heads to flash through her mind. Plenty of time to wonder how close she'd come to ending up the same way.

The bar's parking lot was packed, so Evelyn had to leave her car at the back. Then she sat there paralyzed as her heart took off at a gallop.

The Den's lot was better lit than Haggarty's. And the place was an FBI hangout.

Before she could change her mind, she stepped out of the

car. With her right hand poised near the gun at her hip, she speed-walked for the door.

She saw only a man and woman staggering drunkenly toward the street. No killers lurking in the corner, no one following her. Still, her shoulders slumped in relief as soon as she walked through the door.

The Den looked as if it was breaking fire code, but she spotted the agents instantly. They were mostly men, crowded along a rectangular table where they barely fit.

Most of the agents she didn't know well, but she did recognize Kendall White. Although he wasn't her favorite BAU agent, at least she wouldn't be at a table full of strangers. But she'd been hoping for Greg; he'd talked about stopping by on his way home. Apparently, she'd missed him.

Her steps slowed. Then she realized Kyle and Gabe were there, and her pace picked up again. Their backs were to her, and they were deep in conversation as she approached.

"How's it going?" Kyle was asking Gabe.

Gabe's shoulders rose. "There're only so many times I can go out with a woman that fixated on my badge. Speaking of women…you've been spending a lot of time at the firing range lately."

He moved his elbow in what was probably meant to be a meaningful nudge, but then his gaze locked with hers. His face reddened, his balance shifted and his elbow caught Kyle in the ribs.

"Watch it," Kyle said.

"Evelyn…"

Kyle whirled around, his eyes widening in apparent shock at seeing her take a night off work.

As they stared, Evelyn gave them a self-conscious smile. "You meet women at the firing range?"

Gabe's lips trembled like he was suppressing laughter and

Kyle's mouth opened and closed a few times. Instead of answering, he leaped to his feet, offering her his bar stool.

"No," she protested. "I can find one…" Her words trailed off as Kyle strode away.

"He'll do it," Gabe assured her, taking her arm and pulling her into Kyle's vacated seat. "I can't believe you finally showed up. I thought it was going to take years of begging," he said with an easy grin.

She tried to grin back, but she suspected it looked half-hearted. She was too antsy to be good company.

She shouldn't have come, but she wasn't going to leave now or Kyle and Gabe would really think she was odd. Not to mention that she didn't want to brave the parking lot alone again.

Frustration built inside her. It had been a long time since she'd lived with constant fear. She'd been so sure she'd left those days behind for good.

She searched for something to say, but then Kyle strode back with a stool he'd somehow procured and set a drink in front of her.

"If you don't want beer, I can get you a glass of wine or whatever."

Evelyn scooted over to make more room for Kyle and eyed the beer uncomfortably. "I don't drink."

The taste of alcohol always brought with it instant flash-backs to her mother, stumbling into the apartment, the sticky sweet scent preceding her so strongly Evelyn could almost taste it. Even now, the smell sometimes reduced her to a ten-year-old, hiding in the bathroom so her mother's latest boyfriend wouldn't attack her.

There was a surprised pause before Kyle responded, "No problem." He moved the beer in front of him, despite having half a drink left. "Want me to grab you a water?"

"What are you doing in a bar if you don't like to drink?" Kendall called from a few seats down.

"I'm here for the great company." It came out sounding snarkier than she'd intended.

She and Kendall had never gotten along. Still, he'd never been outright rude to her. And he hadn't deserved her misplaced wrath.

"Shit," she groaned under her breath, then said a little more loudly, "I'm kidding. Sorry."

Kendall didn't look impressed with her apology, but he didn't get a chance to respond before Gabe said in his typical don't-take-anything-seriously tone, "I think rumors are starting to get out about what you did here last week, Kendall."

"Asshole," Kendall muttered, but tomato red crept up his neck as he turned back to his conversation.

Evelyn tried to ignore the way Kendall leaned in close to the other agent, whispering frantically and shooting periodic glances in her direction.

Next to her, Kyle asked again, "You want me to get you something nonalcoholic?"

"No, thanks. I'm fine. I wasn't even planning to stop by. I just…" Evelyn faltered. She tried to come up with some comment about being bored and wanting to get out, but drew a blank.

They knew she was a workaholic without a life. Would they really buy an excuse like that? Or would they realize her abduction had left her off balance and afraid?

Gabe saved her. "We're glad you did."

"Thanks." Evelyn cleared her throat, trying to figure out how to make small talk. She'd always been bad at it. It was easier to hide behind what she knew—her job. But tonight, with the new knowledge about the BAKBURY killer, her job was the last thing she wanted to discuss.

"So, Baine," the agent next to Kendall spoke up, his words loud and slurred. "I hear you were kidnapped."

Conversation around the crowded table stilled. Faces alive with curiosity swung toward her. The bar still echoed with noise, but the air around her seemed to stop moving.

"Do you know who it was?" the agent asked into the silence. "Did they catch the guy?"

Discomfort made her shrink in her seat. Why the hell would he ask her about that?

"Mind your own business," Kyle barked.

Evelyn turned, her arm brushing Kyle's as she discovered he'd shifted closer. There was a ring of darker blue around the outer edge of his deep blue eyes and a muscle bunching in his jaw.

Unsettled by his response, she hadn't found her voice before the agent said, "Damn, man, I was just asking."

With more effort than it should have taken, Evelyn yanked her gaze away from Kyle to find she was still the center of attention. She forced a shrug that felt stiff and unnatural. "No, I don't know who it was and he hasn't been caught."

"What happened? How did he manage to abduct you?" hulking HRT agent Jerry Halston asked eagerly.

An agent next to Jerry elbowed him hard.

"Ouch. What?"

"Dude," someone else whispered loudly. "Don't ask her about that."

"It's an active case, guys," Gabe said. "I doubt she wants to talk about it."

"Can't she speak for herself?" Kendall asked.

Fury tightened her ribs, making them throb. Fury at Kendall and his friends, for badgering her to talk about someone trying to rape, murder and mutilate her. Fury at the man— Justin Greene, as far as they knew—who'd made her live with constant fear that crawled on her skin, gave her nightmares, pulled her focus from work. At herself, for giving him that power.

She stood, her fists clenched at her sides. The words shot from her mouth like bullets. "How did he overpower me? He snuck up behind me like a fucking coward, hit me with a dart full of drugs so I couldn't fight back. *You* try fighting handcuffed. *You* try getting away from…"

She sucked in a deep breath. She'd almost told them her abductor was a serial killer. It could have compromised the investigation and made her friends follow her home every night to protect her. Not something that would improve her image.

In the calmest voice she could manage, she added, "I fought him off and got away." Actually, she had no idea how she'd gotten away. Hell, for all she knew, he'd tripped and knocked himself unconscious and she'd run screaming. But she wasn't about to tell them that.

Half the agents at the table were politely pretending they hadn't heard her outburst. The other half were staring, some with surprise, some with pity. She was afraid to look at Kyle and Gabe.

"Thanks for asking." She tried to undo her outburst by saying it lightheartedly, but the words dripped with venom. There was no salvaging her pride, so she mumbled to Kyle and Gabe, "I've got to go," then strode for the door. Better to run through the empty parking lot than stay and make an even bigger fool of herself.

This was going to come back and bite her in the ass. The Critical Incident Response Group was insular. They traveled together, constantly worked impossible situations under high stress. When anyone did anything stupid, it usually got around.

"Evelyn!"

She slowed her pace as she hit the parking lot, not needing to look to know it was Kyle. Trying to defuse the anger and hurt that had to be written all over her face, she turned. "This is why social gatherings aren't my thing." She tried to make it a joke, but she wasn't good at jokes.

"Evelyn." Kyle caught up with her, worry in his eyes. "Are you all right?"

She raised her chin. "I'm fine. Kendall hates me. I shouldn't have let him get to me."

"Kendall's an asshole."

She shuffled her feet. "I'm just going home."

Kyle put his hand on her arm. "Gabe's paying the bill. We're going to grab some food. Why don't you come with us?"

"I think I should head home and hope people have something better to talk about in the morning."

"That was nothing. Last week, Kendall got up on the table and recited a dirty limerick. At the rate he's been knocking back the beers, I'm betting on a repeat performance tonight."

Evelyn felt her lips stretch in a spontaneous smile as she tried to imagine Kendall, who looked as if he starched his shirt every morning while wearing it, standing on the table and yelling bawdy rhymes. "You're making that up."

Kyle gave her one of his dimpled grins. "Nope."

She stared, trying to figure out if he was putting her on.

Kyle stepped a little closer, invading her personal space.

She blinked up at him as her anger started to fade under the force of his penetrating gaze and those deep blue eyes.

"Evelyn—"

Whatever he was going to say was cut off by Gabe's arrival. "Where do you want—" Gabe looked back and forth between them, then said, "Uh, I think I forgot, uh, my wallet inside."

Evelyn flushed and took a step backward. "I'm going home. I'll see you guys at work."

Not giving them time to respond, she pivoted and speed-walked to her car, already dreading tomorrow.

Kyle watched until the taillights of Evelyn's car disappeared before he turned back to Gabe. "Shit, she's a mess."

"Yeah, she's got to be in worse shape than we thought to have shown up here tonight." Gabe sent Kyle a look that he interpreted to mean his opinion was expected.

His opinion was that Evelyn should have taken more time off work, given herself more time to heal, physically and emotionally. The abduction was a week ago; that should've been enough time to diminish the heavy moons under her eyes that told him she wasn't sleeping. They'd only gotten worse.

She'd always put in a crazy number of hours at the BAU office, but now instead of going home at night, she was coming to Quantico, using their firing range to practice with her new weapon. Her dedication to the job was something he admired, but she was taking it too far, using it as an excuse not to deal with her abduction.

Realizing that Gabe was still waiting for him to respond, Kyle just nodded. He wasn't going to share what he thought about her mental state and he definitely wasn't going to get into his feelings for her.

Gabe teased him about it mercilessly, but underneath the joking, Kyle knew Gabe wanted him to make a move. The problem was, Evelyn had made up her mind about him the day they'd met. He'd seen her do it with other agents, seen her profile them from a brief conversation. He'd been pegged as someone not to take seriously, someone who flirted with everyone, not just her.

It was Evelyn against the world. As long as he'd known her, that attitude had been plastered to her. It seemed to scare off a lot of people, but Kyle didn't scare easily. Still, he hadn't figured out how to breach her battle-ready defenses.

So, he focused on a problem he *could* solve. "Do you think Jerry was trying to be an asshole?" Anger simmered at all the agents inside who hadn't been able to see through her "I'm fine" act, who hadn't been able to resist asking about the one subject guaranteed to get her guard up.

He knew his anger was being fed by guilt. He'd been fifty feet away, inside the pub, oblivious, when she was abducted. Every night since, he'd wished he could go back to that moment when he'd decided to stay inside instead of walking her to her car. Wished he could make a different decision.

"You know Jerry." Gabe shrugged. "He says whatever the hell pops into his head."

Disappointment joined the anger. At least if Jerry had been rude on purpose, he'd have an excuse to be pissed. And if he had a reason to be mad at someone else, maybe it would eliminate some of his own guilt.

"What about Kendall White?" Kyle suggested hopefully. The guy had always gotten on his nerves, but it had worsened in the past year when Kendall had started bragging about how Evelyn kept asking him out and he wasn't interested. Especially since Kyle suspected it was the other way around.

"Oh, Kendall definitely should have kept his mouth shut," Gabe agreed, just as Kendall and his loose-lipped friend walked out of the bar.

Kyle felt a hard smile form as he turned to intercept them.

For the first time since she'd joined BAU, Greg beat her to work.

Evelyn saw his car in the parking lot when she pulled in, weighed down from exhaustion after spending most of the night tossing and turning, worrying about the BAKBURY case, worrying about the investigation into her abduction.

She ran her security card over the cipher lock, then quickened her pace and kept her head down as she rushed for the cocoon of her cubicle.

Greg came over immediately and Evelyn readied herself for his teasing about her lateness. Or worse, his concern.

What she got was an amused, "How was your evening?"

Damn it. He must've heard about her outburst. "It was okay," she mumbled, hoping he'd let it go.

The skin at the corners of his eyes crinkled. "There's a rumor going around that you went to the Den. Sounds like I missed all the fun."

Fun? What version of the story had he gotten? "Trust me, you didn't want to see that."

"Oh, I don't know. It's an incredibly juvenile way to deal with a problem, but..."

Embarrassment heated her face. The muffin she'd forced down for breakfast started doing somersaults in her stomach. Even her training officer was calling her juvenile. Had she tainted her reputation, her entire career, everything she'd worked for her whole life, with a few thoughtless words?

The muffin rose up in her throat.

"...black eye."

"What?" she croaked. Black eye? Had Greg still been talking?

The smile slid off his face. "Are you okay?"

Evelyn shook her head, trying to displace the fog that seemed to have filled it. "Did you say 'black eye'? Are you talking about my...outburst?"

The lines on Greg's face seemed to multiply. It was the look he got whenever he was worried about her. She'd seen it more in the past week than in the rest of the time she'd known him.

"I'm talking about the Den last night."

"Right. When I yelled at everyone."

The lines disappeared, replaced by comprehension. "I don't think anyone's going to remember your outburst considering what happened afterward. I thought you were there."

"There for what? *What* happened afterward?"

Greg suddenly looked less eager to talk. "They care about you, Evelyn. They were just trying to help."

Dread hit fast and hard. Kyle and Gabe. What had they done? "By doing something juvenile?" Oh, no. Greg had said… "Who has a black eye?"

Greg glanced out of the cubicle and Evelyn stood, spotting Kendall on the other side of the room. She dropped back down before he saw her.

Kendall, who came to work every day in a perfectly pressed suit, not a hair out of place, didn't look so perfect today. The black eye wasn't the only problem, either. There were two other bruises on his face and his gait toward the coffeepot had been faltering.

"I'm sorry. I thought you were there," Greg repeated, shaking his head. "I should've realized."

"I should've gone out for food with them," she mumbled, remembering with too much clarity the anger and worry mingling on the HRT agents' faces when she'd run for her car. She'd been so desperate to escape the scene she'd caused, she'd never considered what might happen after she left.

"It was my fight." How dared they do this? Not only had they put their own careers in jeopardy—God, they'd assaulted another FBI agent!—they'd jeopardized hers, too.

Greg put a hand on her shoulder as she squeezed her eyes shut. "None of them are going to admit what happened. This won't go in anyone's official file," he whispered. "No agent wants to say another agent got the better of him."

Relief was overtaken almost immediately by more dread. She opened her eyes and stared at Greg. "No one?"

Greg nodded slowly. "There was another agent with Kendall."

"Oh, no," she moaned.

"Gabe and Kyle were just trying to help," he said again.

"I can fight my own battles," Evelyn insisted, as if it were Greg's fault his cousin and friend had decided to protect her. "Everyone's going to see this as one more battle I lost and someone else had to fight for me." Like her abduction. She'd been attacked and it was up to some other agent to fix it.

"They'll see it that way—or you do?" Greg asked softly.

Evelyn's facial muscles tightened as she tried to hold back her frustration. "I can handle my own problems."

"Hey, Greg!" a familiar voice echoed through the room.

"Speaking of your problems…" Greg left her cubicle.

Evelyn had always been able to blank out the emotions on her face in an instant. It was a necessity in her job, especially when she went into an interrogation room and tried to get a serial killer to brag about his murders. But this time it took longer than usual before she could stand up without broadcasting everything she felt.

By then, Kyle was standing next to her desk. His cargo pants, T-shirt and combat boots were typical. Even the too-perceptive blue eyes looked the same. But the nasty bruise that shaded his cheekbone and spread over the left side of his face wasn't.

Her hand twitched upward, but she held it back before she could do something stupid, like touch his face. "Does Gabe look this bad, too, McKenzie?"

She didn't have to wait for the answer. Gabe strode over, wearing a gauze patch on his forehead.

The fear and fury that had been boiling inside her all week

mingled with shame and just a twinge of guilt. "Damn it, you guys." Her voice cracked, but she kept going. She couldn't let anyone else take on her troubles, get hurt for her mistakes. "You did *not* need to do that. If I was *that* angry at Kendall, I would have kicked his ass myself."

"Oh, yeah?" a new voice asked from behind her.

Evelyn turned to find Kendall standing there. He looked as if he'd been on the losing side of the fight, but there was really no other possible outcome. He was Bureau, but her friends were HRT. That unit was the gold standard of ass-kicking.

If she had to, she'd take on someone like Kendall. He was undoubtedly stronger than her, and they'd had the same training, but most people underestimated what sheer determination could do for a person. And *determined* had appeared on every Bureau evaluation she'd ever gotten.

But no one in his right mind would go up against an HRT agent. Conditioning and practicing close-quarters battle skills were part of their daily routine.

She took a calming breath, hoping she could smooth this over. Before she'd figured out what to say, she sensed movement behind her. When she glanced over her shoulder, she saw Kyle and Gabe standing a little too close. They had their arms folded over their chests, looking like her personal security detail. Farther back, Greg had plopped into his chair and was watching with glee.

She frowned at him. How could he possibly find any of this amusing?

Willing herself to control her emotions better than she had last night, she looked back at Kendall. "If you have a problem with me, let *me* know about it."

Kendall sidled closer. "So we can work it out ourselves?" He gave her a suggestive wink.

Evelyn wrinkled her nose. The guy sure had balls. She could actually feel the agents behind her tensing their over-developed muscles.

Apparently, it was Kendall's parting shot, though, because he turned to leave.

Before her friends said something stupid, she turned and hissed at them, "Don't you guys even *think* about it."

"What?" Gabe asked. But his tone was about as innocent as the dark look on Kyle's face.

"Let it go," Greg said.

Was he talking to her or them? Evelyn wondered.

She didn't get the chance to ask, because Dan stormed out of his office, intercepting Kendall before he was more than a few feet from her cubicle.

Dan's face was so tense it looked as if his skin was being sucked against the bone. He didn't say a word, just pointed at Kendall and back at her.

"Damn," Greg mumbled, rolling quickly into his cubicle.

Dan's voice was dangerously quiet when he and Kendall reached her. "I have half a mind to write all of you up."

Evelyn pressed her lips together as a hundred inappropriate "half a mind" retorts flooded her brain. What the hell was wrong with her? It was like her abduction had screwed up the wiring from her brain to her mouth.

"The only reason I'm not going to is because I don't have time to deal with your schoolyard bullshit right now." His voice rose in pitch with every word and Evelyn sensed ears pricking up all over the office.

"I want you two—" he looked at the HRT agents "—*out* of here."

When they didn't immediately move, his eyes narrowed.

Without another word, her friends were gone.

"Kendall, get back to work and just stay out of Evelyn's way."

With a meek nod, Kendall was gone, too.

Then it was just her and Dan. His nostrils flared, his lips flattened into a sharp line and she could actually see his chest rising and lowering as he breathed.

Panic hit her with a force stronger than when any of her mother's boyfriends had hit her. Was he going to tell her to hand over her badge?

"If you *ever* incite anything like this again, I *will* write *you* up." He strode back to his office, slamming the door behind him so hard that something crashed to the floor and shattered.

Evelyn hoped her career wasn't about to take the same fall.

Usually, the BAU office seemed silent, unless one listened carefully for the constant rustle of paper, the tapping of fingers on keyboards. Occasionally, the dull background noise gave way to the crescendo of an argument when two behavioral analysis experts disagreed on a perpetrator profile.

Now, it was so eerily quiet she almost screamed when the phone rang. The readout told her it was Ron Harding. Why was he calling her at the office after nine at night? Had they found Justin Greene?

"Evelyn Baine," she answered.

"Evelyn, it's Ron. I'm surprised I caught you. I was just going to leave you a message."

"I had to catch up on some paperwork. What do you need, Ron?"

"I thought you'd like to know we heard back from the agents in Boston."

The same hint of a memory that always appeared at the mention of Justin Greene flashed in her mind. Blue eyes glinting in the darkness, coming closer, filled with the intent to kill.

"What did they find out?" Her voice didn't sound quite like hers.

There was a brief pause. "Well, they located Justin Greene's parents. You're not going to believe this. Justin is dead."

"What?" Was it someone else who'd abducted her? Someone else raping, mutilating and murdering women in Bakersville?

"When? How?"

"Apparently, it happened not long after his grandfather lent him the car. No one reported it stolen, because when he went missing—his body wasn't discovered until the next month—the parents didn't even realize he had it. They said the grandfather brought it up a year later. By that time, the parents didn't feel it was worth their while to go to the police about the car. They said they just wanted to put their son's death behind them."

Questions swirled in her mind, mingling with the fuzzy memory of a man rushing toward her, a gun in his hand. A chill swept over her, leaving goose bumps behind.

"What about the grandfather? Why didn't he say anything?"

Ron made a noise Evelyn interpreted as frustrated laughter. "The grandfather doesn't know his grandson is dead."

"*What?*"

"Justin's parents said they never told him because his health's bad and they were afraid the news would do him in."

"So, he thinks his grandson is still alive and just hasn't returned his car?" Evelyn asked in disbelief. "Are you sure he's dead?"

She didn't know whether to hope he was or not. If he wasn't dead, they had a name. If he was dead, they had nothing.

"We're sure."

They had nothing.

"And that's not the end of it," Ron went on. "The locals had no strong suspects in Justin's case—and it's since gone cold. But Justin Greene was murdered."

By the BAKBURY killer.

"It's our guy." Ron actually sounded excited as he told her, "Justin was beaten to death and left in some woods off a moderately trafficked highway."

"So the killer could take his car," Evelyn mumbled, not even sure if she was talking or only thinking.

"Probably. So it would be untraceable."

Just like him. Untraceable.

"The agents there got a copy of the file," Ron said as Evelyn tried to focus. "They faxed it over and it included a picture of Justin. Whoever killed him was no weakling. Justin was six-two and two hundred and twenty pounds. And most of that seemed to be upper body strength."

When Evelyn offered no comment, Ron clarified, "It looks like the killer beat Justin over the head—maybe with a tire iron."

He paused again, like he was waiting for something, then said, "You're damn lucky to be alive, Evelyn."

A minute later, the dial tone blared in her ear and she realized he'd hung up.

A memory jolted through her, the feeling of the car she was driving speeding toward a tree. Her hands automatically went up to brace against the glass breaking all around her and she gagged on the air that caught in her throat.

Ron's words echoed in her head. *You're damn lucky to be alive. You're damn lucky to be alive.*

9

HIS WOMEN WERE GONE. THE COPS HAD PULLED them out, filled the holes he'd so carefully dug for them, ended their punishment early. And neither had deserved the reprieve.

He still visited the woods where their heads should have been. He still imagined adding new graves beside the old ones, but now the cops were watching, so he had to be careful, bide his time. And he'd tried.

He'd waited as long as he could, until even the jewelry couldn't satisfy him anymore. Until the rage churned in his gut, desperate for an outlet, demanding a new victim.

And then the anticipation surged forward, too, the desire to control whether someone lived or died. There was nothing else so powerful, nothing else that made *him* feel so alive.

His hands shook as he brought the contact to his eye, changing it from blue to brown, and he paused to take another gulp of whiskey. He hadn't been this nervous since his very first kill.

He studied his freshly shaven face, considering his options, then dipped his fingers in the putty. A pointier chin, a bulbous nose, fuller cheeks, he decided. He could reuse the stomach padding he'd worn when he visited the police station.

He hadn't found her yet—the next woman who deserved

his punishment—but when he did, she would know him like this. He'd get close, give himself the pleasure of talking to her.

Then, when the time came, he'd shed the disguise and show her his true self.

If Dan Moore thought of her as the office FNG now, he was really going to watch her every move once she told him a killer she was profiling had targeted her.

Reluctantly, Evelyn knocked on his office door.

"Come in," he called, sounding surprised.

He probably assumed no one was in yet. She'd arrived even earlier than usual so she could talk to him alone.

As the door opened, his expression changed from curious to tense. Anger emerged in his eyes, an instant tic developed in his jaw and his hand disappeared into his desk drawer. When it reappeared, he popped a handful of antacids in his mouth.

Evelyn walked inside and shut the door with slick hands, her pulse going too fast as she settled into the chair in front of his desk. "I have some information about my abduction."

His head jerked back. Slowly he nodded, but before she could tell him what it was, he said, "Maybe you should've taken more time off."

He was talking about the other day, implying she'd somehow provoked the fight. But when he heard she'd been abducted by someone she was profiling, he'd forget all about the fight.

"I'm almost caught up with my work," she said, as if that were a response to his suggestion. "And I came across some information that ties my abduction to an active case."

He leaned forward, the anger in his eyes fading as his interest grew. "Something from when you worked in Houston?"

"No. A case I'm profiling now. And I need your help."

Dan suddenly looked flustered and pleased. He flipped the

page on his ever-present legal pad, one of the holdovers from his days as a state's attorney. "Back before I was promoted, in the old unit, we worked a lot of profiles as a group."

Evelyn paused in the process of handing him her notepad, filled with important details she'd taken from the BAKBURY file, feeling rueful. Maybe she'd misjudged Dan. Maybe his insistence that she work with someone *wasn't* him trying to remind her she was the unseasoned newbie of the unit.

"I know you like to work alone. But there's no shame in asking for help when you're overwhelmed. You're still new to criminal investigative analysis, after all."

Evelyn pressed her lips together. It was the tune he always sang. They'd had two other profilers get initiated and then wash out in the time she'd been at BAU and he hadn't babysat either of them the way he did her. She'd wondered more than once if it was because both had been older and male.

He took the notepad. "This is the case? BAKBURY? How is it connected to your abduction?" His eyes filled with realization and what looked like worry. "Don't tell me you think—"

"The Bakersville serial killer abducted me? Yes." She explained to him what she'd found out about the bracelet.

The lines on Dan's forehead and bracketing his mouth deepened as he read through the BAKBURY details, jotting notes.

Finally he glanced up at her. "Tell me what you know about the investigation into your abduction."

She went through everything she knew, ending with, "I told Ron about the connection to Bakersville. He said he was going to ask for permission to take over the BAKBURY case, since he can claim jurisdiction now."

"Is Bakersville aware of that?"

"Not yet." Tanner was taking his time returning her calls. "But you think this is for the best?"

He actually seemed to want her opinion. Her heart rate

slowed back to normal. He wasn't upset that a perp she was profiling had somehow identified her and tagged her for death?

"Uh, yes. They were overwhelmed," she finally stammered. Plus, Ron wouldn't give up on her profile if it didn't yield instant results, the way Tanner had. She remained convinced that her profile was the key to catching the BAKBURY killer.

Dan tilted his head at her, obviously noticing her hesitation. She saw it on his face the second he realized why.

"It's a hazard of the job that someone you profile could turn on you, Evelyn. You go after the worst of the worst. I don't blame you for that—if it's even what happened here. And we can't be sure of that yet."

She nodded, lowering her head so he wouldn't see the relief that brought tears to her eyes.

When she looked up again, Dan was studying her the way Greg had been since she'd come back to work. Like he was worried about her. "If you decide you need some time off, it won't be a problem."

He didn't give her a chance to say no, just kept going, his tone shifting to a serious cadence—profiler mode. "We have two very different abduction styles, between the BAKBURY killings and your abduction. At least, according to your profile on the BAKBURY case and what you remember of your abduction."

Evelyn leaned forward. "I know. That's why I originally dismissed the BAKBURY killer as a suspect in my abduction."

"It's unlikely the UNSUB went from being a charmer to a blitz attacker," Dan said. "The other way around, maybe, as he gained more experience and confidence, became more convinced of his invincibility. So, in the BAKBURY case, he must have been knocking these women unconscious immediately."

"You think my profile is wrong."

"Given the methodology of your abduction—"

"You're right. That makes sense," she interrupted, even though the thought of such a big mistake caused tension to wrap around her lungs, pressing hard. Profiling mistakes could cost lives.

If she was making mistakes like that, did she have any business being a criminal investigative analyst?

She pushed back the doubt. "If he was using the same method on them as he did on me, why didn't he perfect it? Obviously, he didn't intend for me to wake up when I did."

Dan shrugged. "He could've mixed the solution wrong or given you less of the drugs. The Bakersville victims both weighed more than you. If he picked you out beforehand—which he probably did, since you're involved in the case—he might have used a lower concentration of drugs because of your size. Maybe that backfired on him."

It was the logical answer. That her profile was wrong and he'd always been a blitz attacker. "But the behavioral evidence in Bakersville suggested a charmer."

And the physical evidence suggested he was a sadist, someone who tortured his victims by beating them—for his own pleasure. But her gut told her that was wrong, too. Nausea surged at the possibility that she was screwing up, sending police in the wrong direction with her profile. That, thanks to her, the killer would claim more victims.

"Would chlordiazepoxide and buprenorphine show up in a toxicology screen during an autopsy? Could the Bakersville victims have had these in their systems?" Dan asked.

"I didn't see anything listed on the autopsy reports, but I don't know if the medical examiner would have needed to do a special test. It's not like anyone told him to look for those drugs."

"Your profile implies that the perp likes the thrill of abducting someone from a high-risk location. He probably didn't knock these women over the head. But you were abducted from the parking lot of a busy bar. The drugs in darts could have worked in a supermarket parking lot, too. That still meshes in some ways with your profile, even if he's a blitz attacker."

"I guess so," Evelyn said hesitantly.

One side of Dan's lips curved up, maybe because he could tell how much she disliked the idea of being wrong about any element of her profile, especially one this important.

"Okay, let's say you weren't wrong. If your abduction was an anomaly in terms of approach, let's consider whether it was because you're FBI. Maybe he did charm those other women, but wasn't going to risk it on a trained FBI agent."

"Maybe. But if he abducted me because I was on the case and he wanted me off, why did he drug me? He could just have shot me and been done with it. That would've been easier."

Dan nodded, looking at her too intently, with a profiler's eyes.

Before he could say what they both had to be thinking, she swallowed back a lump the size of the gun that had been stolen from her and said it herself. "Did he plan to rape, beat and mutilate me? Or just kill me and bury my body where no one would ever find it?"

Discomfort passed briefly over Dan's face. "You don't really fit his victim profile. If he picked you as a potential victim because he spotted you at the station, once he started stalking you, he would've realized you were Bureau. Wouldn't he have been scared off? Besides, you're not white."

"More and more psychopaths cross racial barriers these days. Serial killers don't necessarily want victims of the same race anymore," she said, even though she'd told the Bakersville cops that the victims' being white suggested their killer was, too.

"All right, let's look at this from another angle. Did you confirm that Mary Ann had her bracelet on the day she was abducted? Is it possible she lost it another day?"

Evelyn shrugged. "Her husband said she always wore it, when police asked for a list of items she would have had on her. I guess it's possible she lost it before she was abducted."

"Then let's consider that we're looking at two different killers. Victim choice and abduction style support that."

"What about the car?" Evelyn asked.

"Could be total coincidence, and Mary Ann Pollak was in both killers' cars at some point. Or both killers were in the same car."

"The BAKBURY killer murdered someone in Boston to get this car without any trail that led to him. It's not like he'd lend it to anyone."

"Maybe they're in cahoots," Dan said. "Was there anything at the crime scene to indicate a pairing?"

Was there? Had she missed something else? She considered the total quiet of the woods where Mary Ann and Barbara had been found, the type of personality who would go there to bury his victims, then return to stare at their decaying heads. "No."

There was certainty in her voice, but suddenly, Evelyn was doubting everything about her profile. The most logical explanation was that her abductor was the Bakersville killer. And that meant, one way or another, she'd missed something in her profile. Something important.

Was there any reason a killer would switch from a charmer to a blitz attacker? "What if…"

"What?"

"Maybe he tried to grab someone after Barbara, to use his old approach on her, and it didn't work. So he was afraid to try his normal method and relied on a blitz attack with me."

"And did he or didn't he figure out you were FBI?" Dan pressed.

"I don't know." There was suddenly a lot she didn't know.

"If he really did try again in between, this perp is moving fast."

"He was moving fast, anyway. We both know he's going to escalate." It was almost invariably true with serial killers.

"Unless your escape scared him into inaction," Dan said wistfully.

If only that were true. Except if he laid low now, how would she find him?

Greg hesitated before knocking on Dan's office door. He hated to go behind Evelyn's back, but he had to do something. And if he played this right, she'd never know.

"Come in," Dan called.

Greg pushed through the door, opening his mouth to tell Dan he wanted to take on some of Evelyn's caseload—and promptly shut it. He almost tripped on his own feet when he spotted Evelyn in the chair across from Dan.

They both stared at him.

"Uh—"

Evelyn angled her head, suspicion in her eyes.

"I didn't realize you were here," he covered. "I had a question about my vacation days. I can come back."

He was a good liar, but Evelyn's eyes narrowed. She didn't buy it.

What was she even doing in here? He'd sooner expect to see her sitting on Kyle McKenzie's lap than in Dan Moore's office. A laugh caught in his throat. Maybe that was stretching it.

And now they were staring at him as if he were nuts.

"Evelyn and I were discussing her abduction and how it's

connected to the BAKBURY case," Dan said. "Take a seat and share your thoughts with us."

Greg's gaze slid back to Evelyn. As usual, any emotion, any hint of what she was thinking, was shuttered behind impassive eyes.

Like every other profiler in BAU, Greg knew how to read people when they didn't want him to. It was a talent he'd developed as a kid. He'd noticed the "tells" people unconsciously gave off that revealed what they were thinking, even when they were saying something different.

Eight years as a regular special agent working violent crimes had honed his internal lie detector even further. When he'd first joined BAU, all the skills he'd been so cocky about had seemed useless standing next to his training agent.

Eight years of experience dealing with some of the worst sociopaths society could offer had made him one of the best. But Evelyn was better.

Right now, he suspected she could read every thought racing through his head. The only thing he could tell about her was that she wasn't sleeping at night.

Well, whether she wanted him there or not, he was going to try to help her. Because she might not ever admit it, but she needed help.

He shut the door and sat next to Evelyn. "I'll do my best to give you some input."

A hint of a smile lifted her lips, her way of reassuring him that he wasn't intruding. Still, discomfort radiated off her like ash from an erupting volcano.

He chose to believe it wasn't his presence, but the fact that she'd turned to Dan for advice. Although she was standoffish with most people, it was just her personality. She had to warm up to someone before she opened up even a little. With Dan, though—because he babied her—there was real dislike. And Greg was pretty sure Dan could tell.

"Great," Dan said, after summarizing what Evelyn had told him. "Do you have any other thoughts on the connection between Evelyn's abductor and the BAKBURY killer?"

"It seems likely to me that we're talking about the same offender. That this guy picked Evelyn in advance and, knowing her profession, didn't think he could manipulate her into his vehicle or stay in control. So he drugged her."

Evelyn's jaw was clamped tightly enough to crack her teeth. It was probably going to get worse when he added his other suspicion.

"I've been thinking about it since Evelyn told me the other day—"

"The other day?" Dan interrupted.

Shit. It had been two days ago, but Greg wasn't about to make his blunder worse.

"I wanted to confirm it was the same bracelet before I told you," Evelyn said, not too convincingly.

"Anyway," Greg continued, "I keep coming back to what a coincidence it is that for his next victim, the perp chose the woman who's actively working to identify him."

Evelyn's face went taut at the word *victim,* as he'd known it would. But there was no mincing words when they were talking about stopping a serial killer. Especially one who had an eye on his partner—because, although technically BAU agents didn't work in pairs, she *was* his partner.

"Frankly," he concluded, "I don't believe in coincidence."

Dan nodded. "We talked about the perp trying to kill her to get her off the case. But that's not what you mean, is it? You're talking about the killer trying to do to her what he did to his other victims not because she fit his victim profile, but as a *fuck you* to the investigators?"

Greg cringed. A serial killer who would rape and mutilate as part of some sick fantasy, he understood, at least on an intellectual level, as someone highly trained in psychology. But one who'd act out his deviant fantasies on a woman who *didn't* fit his victim choice just to make a point?

"That's not exactly what I had in mind," Greg hedged. "But Evelyn's profile tagged the perp as manipulative, and interested in police work to the extent that he could have applied to be one. Confusing the investigation like that might be enough of a turn-on for him."

He glanced at Evelyn, and saw more barriers going up. She didn't want to believe it.

But they had to consider everything. "We've seen the extent he'll go to send a message. Think about the heads."

"But who's that a message for?" Dan asked.

Greg shrugged, looking at Evelyn, who let out a long sigh.

"I still don't know what it means," she admitted. "Or if it *is* actually a message."

Dan looked as if he was going to start pondering it, so Greg got them back on track. "I'm wondering how the killer knew Evelyn was part of the case. Obviously, he'd be trying to keep an eye on its progress, so we can assume he'd know all the major players in Bakersville. But Evelyn's an outsider. Her participation hasn't been in the media accounts. He could be watching the police station, but that would only tell him she's been there a few times. From just observing, how would he know why?"

"You think he has an inside connection," Evelyn said with dread.

"Possibly." Greg wished he could keep his suspicions to himself. The last thing he wanted was to give Evelyn something else to keep her up at night. And a perp with police access who'd already made an attempt on her was definitely reason not to sleep.

"Yeah, it does," Evelyn said, her hands clutching the arms of her chair too tightly, but her voice even and thoughtful, the way he'd heard it a hundred times before as she dissected the actions of killers. "It's unlikely he picked me on the spot, because that would make me an unknown—my routine, who might miss me and how soon, if I had a weapon or if I'd fight."

"The choice of abduction time and place for the other victims, particularly the second one, does indicate he followed them beforehand," Dan said.

"The only reason he might have grabbed you without first acquainting himself with your routine is if he was so desperate for a victim he didn't have time. It's a theory," Greg added, mostly to make her feel better, "but unlikely, unless he had a really extreme precipitating stressor."

"So, we agree he was able to gain access to information on the case," Evelyn concluded, her voice only slightly strangled.

"Someone who can strike up conversations with a Bakersville cop without being suspicious," Dan suggested. "He'd need to have developed a relationship with one of them."

"Or he goes to a cop bar," Greg said. "Listens in. That's pretty standard for a killer with the kind of IQ this guy must have."

"He does seem to know a hell of a lot about how not to leave evidence. Evelyn thought he might have applied to be a cop but been rejected." Dan shrugged. "Maybe he actually got in."

Greg drew a quick breath, a heaviness settling in his gut. "You think he could be a cop?"

Dan looked at Evelyn. "It's not exactly unprecedented."

Evelyn's eyes were too wide. "No." She sounded as if she was trying to convince herself. "He wouldn't have been accepted. This guy has something in his past—dishonorable discharge from the military, minor criminal history, iffy psych evaluation. Something." She shook her head. "He wouldn't have gotten through."

Greg disagreed. "Depends on the department."

Evelyn turned a troubled gaze on him. "I've met the Bakersville cops, Greg. All of them."

"We're talking about a sociopath, Evelyn." They were master manipulators, able to hide all "tells" because they didn't think like normal people. They had absolutely no empathy for others, a completely screwed-up emotional system, so they didn't react like others. It was why, with almost every organized serial case, when they finally caught him, there was a confused outcry from the people closest to the killer. They'd never suspected.

"He may not react like normal people, Greg, but I don't see the world like other people do, either." Insistence vibrated in every word. "I know evil when I see it."

No, she didn't. Not always. Not if she was up against what he thought she was. And she might not admit it, but she knew it.

"Let's—" Dan started.

He was interrupted by a knock at the door.

Kendall White didn't wait for Dan to respond before he let himself in, already talking. "Dan, about this case in…" His voice trailed off when he noticed Greg, and when his eyes shifted to Evelyn, his lips bunched in distaste. "Anything I can help with?"

Evelyn jumped to her feet. "No, we're finished."

Greg stood, too. "I'll let you know if I have any other ideas," he said, addressing Dan.

He didn't think there was much more he could contribute. He'd looked at Evelyn's case file on the BAKBURY killer and even talked to Ron Harding about her abduction—God help him if she found out. Right now, staying in Dan's office was only going to add to Evelyn's ridiculously high stress level.

Glancing from Evelyn to Kendall with barely concealed annoyance, Dan made a shooing motion with one hand and reached for his coffee with the other. "Fine." Dismissing them, Dan turned to Kendall. "What can I do for you?"

Once Evelyn had preceded him out of Dan's office and he'd closed the door, Greg said quietly, "Even if the killer has an inside connection, it won't help him now. We'll find him."

Evelyn met his eyes briefly. "I plan to."

He grabbed her arm as she tried to leave, not about to let her shut him out. Not when he could—for once—read exactly what was going through her mind. "You're worried he knows where you live?"

The muscles under his hand tensed. "He might. I didn't have my license or my creds when he abducted me, but if he'd been stalking me beforehand, he could've followed me to my house. But it would be too much of a risk to come after me again."

Her words were measured, confident. Profilers worked hard to make others believe that tone. He didn't believe hers at all.

"Why don't you stay with us for a while? The kids would love it." Hell, he could easily get Gabe and Kyle to take turns playing security guard at his house. He knew they'd be up for it. And if there was anyone he trusted with his partner's life, it was them.

But she shook her head, as he'd feared she would. "I'll be fine where I am."

As she walked away, he prayed that was true.

10

"WERE YOU EVER PLANNING TO TELL ME YOU were abducted by my killer?" Tanner Caulfield demanded at a decibel level that made Evelyn hold the phone away from her ear. "Some self-important FBI agent called me this morning and told me he was stealing *my* investigation! This *Dragnet* jerk-off said because the killer abducted *you*, it's now a federal case."

As if it was her fault a serial killer had tried to murder her. Asshole.

"And you don't even have the fucking courtesy to tell me yourself!" Tanner ranted.

Her annoyance rose until she couldn't restrain it anymore. "I've been calling you for *days*," Evelyn yelled. "So let's talk about fucking courtesy."

Greg popped his head over the wall separating their cubicles, his eyebrows furrowed. His soft, fawn-colored eyes revealed his concern.

She put a hand over the mouthpiece and told Greg, "He thinks it's my fault the FBI is taking over, since I had the indecency to get myself abducted by *his* killer."

Greg shook his head, frowning, then disappeared again.

"That's not what I meant—" Tanner protested, his temper turning into remorse.

Apparently, she hadn't covered the phone well enough. Now that he was listening, she willed the anger out of her voice. "Let's put it behind us and work together." Thank goodness she'd be able to go to Ron now instead of this puffed-up, underqualified cop. "The agent who called you this morning was Jimmy Drescott. Not *Dragnet*. He and his partner, Ron Harding, will be in charge of the investigation."

"Not you?" Tanner's voice still rang with petulance.

She suspected it would be there through the rest of the investigation.

"No. My role is the same. The case agents have no intention of keeping you out of the loop. The fastest way to solve this is for all of us to work together, focusing on whatever each of us can contribute."

"And what are you suggesting *we* contribute?" Tanner asked. "Manpower?"

"You'll have to discuss that with Ron and Jimmy." If they planned to ask for the case file, and put Tanner's officers to work running down their leads—which she suspected they would—she wasn't going to be the one to tell him.

But since he was finally talking to her, she might as well learn what he and his officers were doing. "I've been wanting to talk to you about the proactive techniques you have in place. Have you looked through your old police applications?"

Was the killer in there? "Are there pictures with the applications?" she blurted before Tanner could reply.

"With the applications? No." The way he drew out the word suggested her question was stupid.

Wait until she told him she wanted to review all his active personnel files.

"I do have someone looking at those, but it's taking a back-seat to our other efforts," Tanner continued. "My officers are watching for anyone unfamiliar—especially outsiders approaching lone women. All my guys are on longer shifts until the killer's caught."

Had he paid any attention to her profile? She curbed her instant response. "That's a good start." She tried to sound positive, but could tell that her tone had come out patronizing.

She coughed and tried again. "There's more we can do, since the killer *isn't* a stranger. He lives in—or close to—Bakersville. Your officers know him. In fact, there's an excellent chance he's talked to one or more of them, digging for information on the case."

"My officers wouldn't talk to civilians about an open case."

"They wouldn't brag about how they're going to catch him? How they planned to stake out the victims' graves in case he showed up? Even at the local cop watering hole? Are you sure?"

"Well, they wouldn't mean to—"

"Exactly." She cut him off. "This UNSUB is a manipulator. He doesn't look like a threat. Not to your officers and not to his potential victims. Not even with the news coverage about Barbara and Mary Ann and how they died."

"Is this necessary? I mean, you didn't see him as a threat, either, right? But now, you can go through our books and identify him or work with a sketch artist. If we know what he looks like…"

"I *don't* know what he looks like," Evelyn said tightly. "Your killer didn't think he could trick me into trusting him, so he drugged me. It affected my memory."

"Shit. Well, maybe you getting away scared him into stopping."

"I wish I thought that was true. But this UNSUB is *com-*

pelled to commit murder. It's like an addiction. He's not stop-ping unless we lock him up. Me getting away might scare him into inactivity for a while—that might explain why there haven't been any more victims. But it isn't going to last."

"Chief!" Evelyn heard someone call.

Tanner must have put his hand over the phone more effec-tively than she had, because she didn't hear anything else until he told her, "I've got to go. One of my rookies just brought in a rowdy DUI."

"I also—" Before Evelyn could tell him about the possibil-ity that the killer was a cop, he'd hung up.

Swearing, she did the same.

Greg peered over the top of her cubicle. "Antagonizing the locals?"

"Greg," she began with a loud sigh. "I—"

"Take some time off, Evelyn. If you keep this up, it's going to come back to bite you in the ass."

She knew she was about to snap at Greg, so she turned her chair away from him and picked up the phone again.

"At least think about it," Greg said.

She heard him drop back into his own chair and instead of replying, she called the Fairfax Medical Examiner's Office.

"I read your autopsy reports for Mary Ann Pollak and Bar-bara Jensen and I had a question," she told the M.E. "Were drug tox screens done on the victims and, if so, did they come up with anything?"

"Let me grab the reports."

Evelyn tapped her fingertips nervously on her desk until finally, finally, he was back.

"In murder cases, we always do tox screens. No drugs were present in either case."

"Would…" Evelyn paused, digging through her notes to find the names of the drugs used on her. "Would chlordiazepoxide and buprenorphine have shown up if they were in either victim's system?"

"Chlordiazepoxide? Absolutely, depending on the amount ingested. With buprenorphine, after the amount of time that passed, it's a lot less likely. But everything is dependent on dose."

"If they were given enough of the drugs to render them unconscious almost immediately, would that be a strong enough dose? And it would be intravenous."

"Yes, if that was the case, those drugs would almost certainly have shown up, especially since the time between abduction and death wasn't more than a day."

"Thanks." As she hung up, Evelyn wondered what it all meant. The most logical explanation was that the killer had only drugged her because he knew she was FBI. Which meant he knew she was profiling him.

Which, in turn, meant he was connected to the police station somehow. Maybe that connection would ultimately be his undoing.

"Evelyn?"

Spinning her chair around, she discovered Dan waiting outside her cubicle. How long had he been there? "Yes?"

"Come to my office, please."

Her anxiety spiked at his too-serious tone, but she dutifully followed him to his office.

As soon as he'd shut the door, Dan stopped in front of her instead of going to his desk. "I don't think you should stay on the BAKBURY case."

"What?" Nausea rushed through her. "You're pulling me from the case?"

"Your personal involvement—"

"Doesn't matter," Evelyn broke in forcefully. "I'm a professional. It would be a waste of resources to make another agent learn the details of the case when I already know them."

Dan leaned against his desk, eyeing her as if he was looking for something, although she wasn't sure what.

"You don't even want to talk about the case in front of another agent." He was referring to Kendall. "Can you handle this? Or are you too close to the case to see it clearly?"

"My connection has no effect on my profiling."

"Doesn't it?" Dan's eyebrows jerked up. "Profilers are supposed to be detached. They're supposed to get inside the head of the killer, think like him. But you're still thinking like a victim."

Damn him. Her eyes stung with all the unshed tears that had been gathering since she'd woken in a stranger's car, drugged and handcuffed, helpless.

She slowly unclenched fists she hadn't even realized she'd made. She refused to be labeled a victim. She might have been one momentarily, but now she was the hunter. And her abductor was the prey.

She leaned closer, her gaze intense on Dan's, unblinking. "I know this killer. I *am* inside his head. And I'm going to get him."

Dan blinked first. "Okay. But remember you're a consultant," he said slowly. "Not a case agent. Understand?"

She nodded, but he kept going.

"If your personal involvement skews your ability to be effective, you'd better step aside and let someone else take over. If your pride costs a woman her life, you're going to be out of this program."

This time, she was the one to blink. "That won't happen," she said in a voice strangled by the distant fear that it could.

"Just as long as we're clear. I may regret this decision, but you're a fine profiler, Evelyn. I'd hate to lose you over something like this."

Was that a threat or Dan's odd way of being sympathetic? She wasn't sure so she merely nodded.

The phone rang and Dan glanced over at it, scowling. He waved in the general direction of the door as he scooted around his desk to answer it.

The first thing Evelyn saw as she left his office was Kyle and Gabe. She felt an absurd desire to turn back around; she was too short-fused to deal with them right now. She couldn't prevent a snort of laughter as she imagined Dan's expression if she were to take a seat in his office and start working.

Unfortunately, that noise, soft though it was, attracted Gabe's notice.

There was no escape now.

Especially when he called her name, alerting Kyle to her presence, too.

Evelyn managed a smile, but it felt forced. She hadn't seen them in three days—not since they'd appeared in the office sporting their bruises and bandages like medals.

Get your emotions in check, Evelyn. She brushed her hands over the Saint Michael's medallion she wore under her sleeveless turtleneck and navy pinstriped suit, but it didn't stop her from bristling at their constant overprotectiveness.

When she reached Greg's cubicle and took stock of the new bruise on Kyle's bare forearm jostling for space among the yellowing ones from the fight, she blurted, "Find someone else you didn't think I could handle myself?"

Shit. Way to sound as if she had it together. Greg's worried look returned and the others just seemed taken aback.

"I'm sorry. It's been a long day," she muttered, dropping into her seat. She hoped they'd let it go and leave her alone.

But Kyle maneuvered into her cubicle. It had to be her vulnerability from the case that made her want to slide closer, so instead she rolled her chair forward, putting distance between them.

He didn't seem annoyed by her rudeness as he told her, "No, I got a little banged up yesterday during CQB—close-quarters battle training. We're on active duty starting today, so my downtime will be filled with the fun stuff, like chopper rappelling." He shot her one of his killer smiles. "So, hopefully I'll be able to avoid any more injuries for at least the next few days."

Unless he was called to a real emergency. HRT's members were divided into two groups that rotated biweekly. One group trained, touching up their combat and firearms skills. The other was on active duty in case hostages needed rescuing, a dignitary needed protecting, there was an extremely dangerous raid regular law enforcement didn't want or something else came up that was too risky even for the Bureau's highly trained SWAT agents.

She knew the stats. The Bureau poured tons of money into making sure these agents were the best, so there were almost no HRT deaths in the line of duty. But still, worry hit her at his joke. "Be careful."

His gaze lingered on hers, his deep blue eyes penetrating, as if he was searching for signs that she was really okay and not going to fall apart any second.

"Have they made any progress on your case?" Gabe leaned over her cubicle wall.

"Not yet. But this guy isn't going to quit. We'll catch him eventually." If only she felt as certain of that as she sounded.

"Never had any doubt," Gabe responded.

"What do you mean, he isn't going to quit?" Kyle's gaze locked on hers again, suspicion in the sudden thrust of his jaw. "How many FBI agents has he abducted?"

Damn it. They didn't know her abductor was probably a serial killer. She should've been more careful with her words.

"It's possible he's attacked other women," she mumbled.

"Attacked?"

"Murdered," she clarified. There wasn't a lot that could shock these agents—they'd seen it all—but this did. "We'll catch him," she repeated, running the words together. *Please talk about something else,* she silently begged.

Greg seemed to catch her mental request, because he said, "It's an active case."

Meaning that, technically, she wasn't supposed to talk about it, even with them.

There was a long pause and Evelyn could sense Kyle's desire to know more. But then, in the most obvious subject change ever, he said, "So, what do you think of the Red Sox this season?"

She was kind of tempted to lean over and hug him for it. To prevent herself from actually doing it, she clutched the arms of her chair.

Gabe sent her a quick glance, then said, "So far, they're looking good."

As the three men started a heated discussion about baseball players whose names she didn't know, Evelyn tuned them out. She couldn't exactly get back to work, since Kyle was crowding her cubicle with his big body and his even bigger presence. She wished, not for the first time, that they weren't part of the same team. It had been years since she'd met anyone who made her want to take a chance.

But she wasn't risking her career for him. She just needed to keep reminding herself not to fall for his ocean-blue eyes and that dimpled grin.

"Evelyn?"

Kyle was staring at her expectantly, like he was waiting for an answer.

Hoping she'd just missed a sports question and hadn't said anything she was thinking out loud, she shrugged. "I don't really follow baseball."

A smile trembled on the edges of Kyle's lips. When it burst into a full-blown grin, Evelyn turned to Gabe and Greg, who both looked as if they were holding back laughter.

"That's okay. We don't have to go to a baseball game."

"What?" Evelyn shook her head. "Sorry. I wasn't paying attention."

Amusement sparkled in Kyle's eyes as he leaned down, wrapped an arm around her shoulders and squeezed her, bringing her toward him.

Heat blazed a fast path from his fingers down to her toes and she stiffened against it.

"We were trying to decide where I should take you for our date. I guess a baseball game is out," he added as she sputtered.

She looked over at Greg for assistance.

"I think you owe him," Greg said, deadpan. "He did get beat up for you."

They were definitely joking. Kyle hadn't really asked her out. Getting control of the unattractive noises she was making, she asked dryly, "Doesn't that mean I'd have to go out with both of them?"

Gabe snorted. He probably hadn't realized she knew how to make a joke. And he probably wasn't far off the mark. "Works for me."

"I'm not sharing," Kyle said, his arm still draped over her shoulders, which made her want to squirm.

Okay, time for a new subject. Before she could come up with one, Dan appeared.

He shot Kyle and Gabe a venomous look that would have

sent most agents scampering back to their desks, whimpering. But there was still curiosity in his eyes as he spotted Kyle's arm around her shoulders. "Can I see you in my office again, Evelyn?"

It was a reprieve from their teasing, but not the one she wanted. And she certainly didn't want him thinking there was anything between her and Kyle.

Once the door was shut behind them, Dan said, "Evelyn, I hate to do this after everything you've been through, but…" Turning to go back to his desk, he seemed to notice she was still standing. "Go ahead and sit."

"I'm fine." Her voice sounded far away. Dread climbed the walls of her stomach. What now?

"Okay. Look, I didn't want to have to do this, but it's policy. The report you filled out on your abduction has been reviewed by *my* boss and the fact that you lost control of your weapon is an issue. I'm going to have to give you a letter of censure."

The dread tangled with already twitchy nerves and, for the second time that day, tears stung her eyes. She'd never been in trouble with the Bureau before. Sure, a letter of censure was only a baby step up from a verbal warning, and plenty of agents had them. But it would go in her official file.

It would tarnish a close-to-perfect record. One she worked for seven days a week, often ten hours a day. One she'd planned for her whole life. Hell, it *was* her whole life.

Without it, how would she ever find Cassie?

The sting of tears intensified, though she'd never let them fall.

Between the damage her abduction had done to her reputation and this reprimand, the career she wanted was slipping away. And ironically, it was because someone else had fired a weapon she had never, in her six years with the FBI, discharged in the line of duty.

Dan was saying her name. Evelyn blinked and he came back into focus. "Sorry," she mumbled.

"I am, too." He actually sounded it. "I really didn't want to do this."

"I understand." She ducked out of his office before he could say anything else.

On autopilot, she returned to her cubicle, forgetting until she arrived about the HRT agents there.

Kyle turned away from whatever conversation they'd been having, his teasing grin in place. Until his eyes met hers. Then it faded away, replaced with the worried expression she was getting sick of seeing on everyone around her.

"What's the matter?" Greg asked as they all stared.

Evelyn tried to smooth the tension out of her face. She ran her hand over the side of her head, even though she knew her hair was still perfectly in place. "It's not a big deal," she lied, but her voice cracked. "I'll be right back." She pivoted quickly, not knowing where she was going, only that she had to leave.

She was a few seconds from escape—her hand was on the door to the ladies' room—when she heard Kyle's voice behind her. She closed her eyes, wanting to pretend she hadn't heard him, but there was no way he'd believe it. With a fortifying breath, she turned around, an "everything is fine" expression plastered on her face.

His long stride brought him beside her too fast until he was too close, with too much concern in his eyes. "What's wrong?"

"Just something about a case," she lied, then cringed. Kyle could always tell when she was lying. At least he didn't seem to realize that some small part of her wished he wasn't kidding when he flirted with her. "I'm fine, McKenzie."

"You know, you can tell me what's going on. I'm your friend. And it's Mac, remember?"

Evelyn felt her jaw tremble with the tension of trying to

keep her face impassive, with the strength it took not to lean in and take the comfort he was offering. "It's not a big deal."

"Then why don't you tell me so I won't have to wonder." He punctuated his request with one of his persuasive smiles.

Damn Kyle for his persistence, for his ability to see through her. Why *him?*

Sensing that it was the fastest way to get rid of him, she conceded. "Dan gave me a letter of censure. It caught me off guard."

"Well, you know what they say," Kyle told her. "If there's nothing bad in your personnel file, it means you're an ass kisser or just sitting on your ass."

Was that supposed to be a joke? Her lips twitched downward. This wasn't a joke; it was her life.

She cast another desperate look at the bathroom door, knowing she was about to fall apart and not wanting to do it in front of Kyle.

He squeezed her arm. "You really shouldn't worry about it."

As soon as he released her, she hurried into the bathroom, shut the door behind her and leaned against the wall. Closing her eyes tightly against the tears that threatened, she slid to the floor.

Without her job, what would she have?

Her head lolled to the side as the answer slammed through her. *Nothing.*

Evelyn waited until the office had cleared out for the evening before she made the phone call she'd been thinking about all afternoon.

Pick up, pick up, she silently chanted. If she had to leave a message, she'd probably get a callback during regular hours. And she didn't want anyone to overhear this request.

"Gilbert Havorth," he answered when she'd almost given up.

"Gilbert, this is Evelyn Baine."

"What do you need?" Gilbert asked cheerily, apparently not finding it odd that she was still working—or that she'd expected him to be doing the same.

"Did you get a match on that fingerprint found in the car from my case?"

"Not yet. I sent it, but haven't heard back."

She was surprised to feel a surge of disappointment. Wouldn't he have heard by now if there was a match? She knew the system was backlogged, but since an agent had been targeted, they should have rushed it.

Still, she didn't really think they'd find anything. The BAKBURY killer hadn't been caught for any of his crimes, except maybe as a juvenile. If he had, his signature would've been all over the crimes and they'd already have a name.

"Could you do me a favor?" She hoped he'd just help her and not go to Ron with questions. Especially since Ron had only taken over the Bakersville case yesterday.

"What is it?"

"Can you run the print through the FBI's database?"

Evelyn sensed Gilbert's confusion in the pause that followed.

"I sent it to Clarksburg. It'll go through IAFIS."

"I wasn't talking about IAFIS," Evelyn corrected. "I want you to check it against agents' prints."

"You think the killer is an *FBI agent?*" Gilbert squeaked incredulously.

"Can you just check for me? And keep it to yourself?"

The silence stretched out as she waited for Gilbert's answer.

The likelihood of the UNSUB being an agent was really slim, but the fact that he'd apparently connected her to the BAKBURY case meant he had an inside connection. That connection was most likely at the Bakersville Police Department, but Evelyn would deal with that possibility when she met with Tanner again.

It had occurred to her today that if her abductor could be a dirty cop, he could also be a dirty agent.

Organized killers like the man who'd abducted her tried to get as close to the investigations as possible. While FBI agents had to undergo extensive background checks, sociopaths were incredible liars. There was always the possibility that one had slipped through the cracks and made it into the Bureau.

"Evelyn," Gilbert finally said, sounding uncomfortable, "all the prints are in one location. If the print belongs to an agent—or a former agent, or even an applicant who got as far as the background check process—it will come up in IAFIS."

"Oh." She cursed herself for not having known that, but why would she? She'd never needed to look for a dirty agent before. "Okay. Thanks."

"Evelyn?"

"What?"

"You really think this killer is an FBI agent?"

Evelyn tried not to let him pick up on her fear. "I don't know. I hope not."

"Shit," he muttered not quite under his breath. "I'll call Clarksburg and get them to rush the print."

"Thanks."

He was still muttering curses when he hung up.

And so was she. But at least if the killer was FBI, they'd have a name they could track to an actual live person. She couldn't decide what to hope for—that the killer would be a trained FBI agent, someone who'd have the know-how to disappear if he wanted, or that the print wouldn't have a match.

★ ★ ★

A practiced serial killer had set his sights on her. And she couldn't find him.

There was only one person who could make her feel better right now.

Evelyn pushed open the door to her grandma's room, smiling at the thought of seeing her. But as soon as she walked in and her grandma's gaze lifted to hers, a heavy weight sank onto her chest, replacing her hopeful smile.

Mabel was sitting in her favorite chair, hair disheveled and eyes slightly unfocused. The TV was on mute in the background and a stack of discarded books lay on the floor beside her.

Evelyn forced the smile back in place, even though loneliness washed through her as she desperately missed the grandmother who was right in front of her. "How are you feeling today?"

Mabel's eyebrows furrowed, and she seemed to be looking at Evelyn from far away. "Are you…"

Her eyes dropped to Evelyn's hip and Evelyn realized her suit jacket was open and her gun was showing. She adjusted her jacket.

"You're with the FBI, aren't you?" Mabel's cheeks flushed bright red as she bent forward in her seat and her fingers began to dance nervously.

Evelyn's lips pursed. "That's right." She got ready to remind her grandma who she was, but she knew it wouldn't penetrate today. She could spend the rest of her visit trying to reach through her grandmother's fog of dementia, but she wouldn't get to her tonight.

Mabel preempted her. "Are you here because of my granddaughter?"

Evelyn's heart skipped. So, she remembered she had a granddaughter. Some days, the only person she could remember was Grandpa and Evelyn usually went home feeling wrecked after trying to explain why he couldn't come and see her.

"Someone needs to protect her." Mabel's voice turned fierce and she leveled an intense, determined stare at Evelyn, shaking a finger at her.

The heaviness in Evelyn's chest crept up her throat. Had her grandma heard what had happened? Had one of the nurses told her? How would they even know about the abduction?

"I'm— She's okay." Evelyn patted her grandma's hand, but she yanked it away.

"That madman threatened her life!" she shrieked. "My husband went out and bought a shotgun. You can't find this man and no one's protecting my granddaughter. It's your job!"

Evelyn shook her head, surprised at the fury in her grandma's voice and the fantasy she was creating. Grandpa had been dead for almost fifteen years. And who the hell had told her about the abduction?

"Grandma—"

"I saw the note." Her grandma's eyes narrowed. The gaze that locked on Evelyn, despite being not quite focused, was insistent.

What note? This wasn't about her abduction. Maybe her grandma had seen something horrible on the news and was projecting it into her life.

Sadness seeped through her, settling in her bones, and she tried not to let it show. Her grandma had never done this before; did it mean she was getting worse? Evelyn knew it was inevitable, but she always hoped for another good day. And another after that. Had her good days come to an end?

"I will *not* sit by—" Mabel pushed herself to her feet, leaning heavily on her undamaged leg and stepping into Evelyn's personal space. "No, I will not sit by and let him come back for my Evelyn. You people can't even find Cassie...."

Mabel kept ranting about the FBI's ineptitude, but Evelyn's ears were suddenly ringing and she swayed back. What if this *wasn't* her grandma's fantasy?

"What note did you see?" Seventeen years ago, Cassie's abductor had left a note behind. Evelyn knew that much. But why would her grandma think it had anything to do with her? The cops and FBI had been everywhere after Cassie's abduction, so why would her grandpa have bought a shotgun?

"I was at the Byers' house before you people arrived," Mabel said, her anger fading into exhaustion after her outburst. She gripped the arms of her chair and Evelyn helped her lower herself into it. "The note mentioned Evelyn, too. I'm not letting him come back for her."

A rush of poker-hot fire engulfed Evelyn, and ice chased it, the hot and cold sweeping through her in waves until she felt dizzy. She dropped onto the bed, memories from the days after Cassie's disappearance surging forward. Her grandparents, whispering about moving away when they thought she wasn't listening. An FBI agent promising her grandma they were safe.

Could it be true? Seventeen years ago, had she escaped Cassie's fate?

1

EVELYN PUSHED HER CHAIR UNDER HER DESK
and turned off her cubicle light. For once, she was going home
at a reasonable hour.

She'd waited until three in the morning last night to call
the police department in her grandma's hometown of Rose
Bay, South Carolina. She'd wanted the night shift so she'd get
a rookie officer, someone who wouldn't recognize her name,
wouldn't question why the FBI suddenly wanted copies of an
almost two-decades-old file.

She'd lucked out. Cassie's file was on its way. But she'd
spent the rest of the night tossing and turning. Tonight, she
was going to relax.

Then her phone rang.

"Ignore it," Greg said from his own cubicle.

Evelyn was tempted. But although she didn't recognize
the number, if the call had anything to do with her case, she
didn't want to miss it. "I can't." She grabbed the phone. "Evelyn Baine, BAU."

"Agent Baine, this is Marc Jensen." He sounded nervous.

The name wasn't familiar and Evelyn stifled a sigh, wishing she'd listened to Greg. "What can I do for you?"

"Uh, I got your number from the night desk sergeant at the Bakersville police station. I'm...I mean, I *was* Barbara Jensen's husband."

Evelyn fell back into her seat. She couldn't believe she hadn't recognized his name from the BAKBURY reports. "I'm so sorry for your loss."

"Thanks."

"Do you have information that would help the investigation?" She knew the cop should have given him Ron's number and not hers, but she wasn't going to pass on the opportunity to learn something new.

"Maybe. It's kind of hard to talk about. I mean, it's embarrassing. I only just found out or I would've told the police sooner." He made a sound somewhere between a laugh and a sob that came out resembling neither. "I thought she was at the grocery store when she disappeared."

Evelyn frowned. So had she. So had the police. Her car had been recovered there. They even had a receipt from the store placing her there a few hours before she was reported missing. "She wasn't?"

"Well, I guess she must have been. But that wasn't the only place she went that night."

This was new. "What do you mean?"

"She...she was having an affair. I never even suspected, but when I found out, it made sense. Everything she did—visiting her friends, getting her hair done, hell, even grocery shopping—took a lot longer than it should have. And sometimes she'd come home with nothing." He laughed in a self-deprecating way. "Yesterday, I overheard one of her friends. Apparently, she was going to meet this guy when she went missing."

And her friends hadn't bothered to tell the police? "Do you know his name?"

"Derek Couvaney. She went to high school with him. I found his number in her address book, of all places. Guess she didn't figure I'd ever notice." He let out another semilaugh, semisob and then read her the number.

Uncomfortable, Evelyn said, "Thank you for this. I'm going to follow up on it now. And I'm very sorry about… everything."

"Thanks." Marc sounded defeated as he hung up.

"What are you following up on?" Greg asked as she set her phone down. "I thought you were going home."

Evelyn wheeled her chair around and saw Greg standing behind her, hands on hips. The look he was giving her was the one she'd seen him use on Lucy when she was about to be grounded.

"I have some new information on a case I need to run down."

"It'll still be here tomorrow."

"Yeah, but I'm not great at pacing myself."

She was trying to be funny, but Greg just frowned, shook his head and went back to his cubicle.

She picked up the phone and called Derek Couvaney, who agreed to meet with her.

It wasn't until Evelyn was on her way to meet him that two things occurred to her. First, she should have handed the interview off to Jimmy or Ron. Second, if Derek Couvaney was the last person to see Barbara Jensen that night, it was possible he was her killer.

Evelyn loosened her knuckle-white grip on the steering wheel. She didn't remember much from her abduction, but the voice on the other end of the phone hadn't triggered any memories. Plus, if Derek *was* the killer, meeting with her would be risky.

They like to involve themselves in the investigation. The thought echoed in her head, even though she tried to deny the possibility.

If Derek had given her the runaround, he would have seemed suspicious. Disappearing or refusing to cooperate would make the FBI look closer. But if he was the killer, pretending to be helpful would give him another way to track the progress of the case. And play mind games with one of his victims.

"He's not the killer," she said aloud, then groaned at how crazy she was acting. Her profile pegged the killer as a stranger to the victims, so the fact that Derek was having an affair with Barbara made it unlikely he was the killer. And she needed to believe in her own profile. With a deep breath, Evelyn parked and strode into the coffee shop where she was meeting Derek.

It was packed, a line stretching to the door with commuters getting their last caffeine fix of the day, but Evelyn identified Derek immediately. He was sitting by himself, clutching a stack of photos in one hand while his other hand tapped rapidly against the table.

He had the compact build of a swimmer, with well-developed biceps that flexed with each tap of his fingers, but he wasn't as big as the BAKBURY killer had to be. He was at least forty pounds shy of two hundred. She couldn't accurately gauge his height while he was sitting, but there was no way he topped six feet.

His face was unshaven and haggard. If he was faking his grief, he was doing a good job. As his gaze swung in her direction, Evelyn took in deep chocolate-brown eyes. Not ice-blue. Not the killer.

Relief made her sway as she skirted the line for coffee and walked toward Derek.

Surprise flashed on his face when she sat across from him. "Agent Baine?"

"Thanks for meeting with me, Mr. Couvaney."

"Uh, sure." A puff of air burst from his lips. "I was expecting someone…" He floundered briefly, then settled on, "Sturdier."

Well, that figured. Instead of responding to the comment, she said, "You confirmed on the phone that you and Barbara were together the night she was killed."

"Yes."

"Why didn't you contact us when she went missing?"

"Uh…" Derek's eyes dropped to the photos he was holding. He fiddled with them, shaking his head. Finally, he looked back up at her. "I didn't want to hurt her husband any more. I didn't think he needed to know."

"You realize not telling the police makes you look suspicious." His brown eyes might have cleared him from her suspect list, but he wasn't off the hook.

Anger rushed into his eyes, darkening them quickly, as though it had been simmering under the surface for a long time. "You think *I'm* the Bakersville Burier?" His hands tightened, creasing the photographs. "I dropped her off at the grocery store. Ask her friend Susie. She's the one who called me that night, telling me Barbara was missing. She was pissed, said Barbara's husband had phoned looking for her."

"What did you tell her?"

"That Barbara wasn't with me. It was one in the morning! I'd dropped her off hours before. Barbara said she really needed to pick up some groceries this time or her husband was going to start noticing." He snorted. "A man who doesn't notice his wife is missing until one in the morning is *not* going to notice groceries."

"What time did you drop her off?"

"I brought her back to the grocery store around eight-thirty. We'd taken my car and left hers in the parking lot. We went to dinner in Jessup, because we didn't think we'd run into anyone we knew there."

Jessup, Virginia, was twenty miles from Bakersville. She jotted notes as Derek told her about his secret relationship with Barbara.

"I took some pictures that night," Derek finally said, sliding the stack he was holding across the table. His hand tightened around his coffee cup. "I wanted her to leave her husband."

Evelyn made a noncommittal noise as she straightened the edges and began flipping through the pictures. Most were of Barbara alone, looking the part of a cheating wife in oversize sunglasses and a wide-brimmed straw hat. She was smiling, apparently happy only a few hours before she'd been abducted and brutally murdered.

Evelyn paused, studying a shot of Barbara standing on a sidewalk, cars blurred behind her as they drove past. She squinted, peering more closely at a black Crown Victoria parallel parked directly behind her.

In itself, that wasn't unusual. It was a popular car, in a popular color, especially in an area flush with FBI agents. The partially ripped flag sticker in the right front window wasn't unusual, either. Patriotism was in style here.

Still, Evelyn held up the photo. "I'm going to need to keep this." It was evidence.

She handed back the rest of the stack and got to her feet. "Someone from the FBI may be in touch with more questions."

"That's it?"

"Thanks for your help. I'm sorry for your loss."

Derek nodded, his gaze on the photos he was clutching, and Evelyn rushed out the door, suddenly eager to get back to the office.

She had new insight into the killer's movements. Maybe it would finally lead her to him.

"What are you doing here?" Greg demanded as Evelyn nearly barreled into him in the BAU office stairwell.

He was on his way out, his suit jacket and tie draped over one arm and his briefcase in hand. She was on her way in. Too bad she hadn't been stuck in traffic for five more minutes.

"I found another connection between a victim of the Bakersville killer and the guy who abducted me—or at least his car." She held out the photo and he peered at it as she pointed to the sticker on the Crown Vic. When his eyes lifted to hers, she knew he remembered the last place he'd seen that same ripped sticker in another photo.

A photo that had shown the car hugging a tree off the highway.

"Where did you get this?"

"Apparently, Barbara Jensen was having an affair—and she saw the man right before she was abducted. I just met with him and he gave it to me. Now I can connect the car to both Mary Ann and Barbara." The chances of the bracelet being a coincidence were dwindling to almost none.

The number of lines raking across Greg's forehead seemed to double. "Isn't that the job of the case agents?"

It wasn't really a question. It was Greg reminding her not to wander into someone else's job. Taking the position as a criminal investigative analyst meant she was supposed to leave her life as a case agent behind.

Tension started to build at the base of her neck. "I know.

I wasn't thinking and then I was already on my way to meet him."

Greg rested his briefcase against the railing. "And what if this guy had been the killer?"

"He wasn't."

"But he could have been."

"No, he couldn't." She told herself that Greg worried about her because he cared, but she suddenly wished she hadn't said anything about where she'd been.

Greg nodded, but she realized her short temper was only making things worse. "Are you heading home now?" he asked.

"Soon," Evelyn promised. "I'm going to call Ron Harding and tell him what I discovered."

"He's going to be pissed you didn't hand the lead off to him."

"I know." She shrugged. "But it's too late now."

A hint of a smile tugged at Greg's lips, amusement peeking through his constant concern. "I guess so. I'll see you in the morning." He continued down the stairwell and Evelyn went to her cubicle.

She knew Ron's number from memory, but as the phone rang for the third time, she hoped he wouldn't answer. She'd prefer to tell his voice mail that she'd hijacked part of his case.

"Ron Harding."

Damn. "It's Evelyn."

He spoke before she could give him her news. "We had the print from your abductor's car checked against the police officers in Bakersville and there's no match. Jimmy and I spent most of yesterday there looking at the application files with Tanner Caulfield. No one stands out."

Relief mingled with uncertainty. Would the killer stand out to Tanner? Obviously he hadn't understood her profile. Would the killer stand out to Ron or Jimmy?

She'd wanted to be there when they'd gone through the files. Should she go down to the station herself and do it again? That would be a quick way to piss them off even more than Ron was about to be.

She took a breath and dove in. "I called because I have some news about the killer."

After she told him what she'd learned, he said excitedly, "Maybe this is the break we need." Then there was a pause and he added, "Wait. Why didn't you call me after you talked to Barbara's husband?"

"I'm sorry. I just ran out to interview Derek. I guess it's a holdover from my days as a regular special agent."

"Next time, call me first." The voice that had a moment ago been filled with happiness was now hard and flat. "If I want you involved in my investigation, I'll let you know. Is there anything else you haven't shared?"

Evelyn clenched her fists. "That's everything."

"Like I said, I'll let you know the next time we need you to work on the profile." He slammed the phone loudly in her ear.

She hung up, but before she could dwell on her misstep, the phone rang and she answered. "Evelyn, this is Gilbert Havorth." The workaholic agent's voice was more high-pitched than usual and his words ran together like he was too anxious to get the next word out to finish the last one.

It could only mean one thing. Her heart started beating faster.

"I don't know what made you suggest that the fingerprint might belong to an FBI agent," Gilbert said, "but it did."

When her vision dimmed a little around the edges, Evelyn reminded herself to breathe. Her attacker was an agent? "Who is he?" she croaked. "Does he work for one of the field offices near here?" More questions threatened to escape, so she clamped her mouth shut. A name. All she needed was a name. It probably wouldn't mean anything to her, but with it, she could find him and lock him away.

"It's not quite what you think. When I say FBI, I don't mean someone current. And—get this—the match was a woman."

"A woman?" she echoed. Her lungs deflated and she slumped forward in disappointment. There was no way a woman had committed the murders—or the rapes—and it definitely hadn't been a woman who'd abducted her. That much she remembered.

"A girlfriend?" Evelyn wondered aloud. "Another victim? An accomplice?" She frowned at that unlikely possibility. This killer worked alone. And even if he didn't, he was a misogynist. He'd never work with a woman.

Who else could she be? "Since the print was impressed into caulk, theoretically it could've been there when David Greene had the car," she pointed out. "This could be a complete coincidence."

"Actually," Gilbert said, "there's something even more unusual. Three years ago, this woman disappeared."

"What do you mean, disappeared?"

"Just what I said. She was an active agent at the time. When she didn't show up for work one morning and didn't answer her phone, her partner went to her place to check on her. He found no trace. No sign of a struggle or any other indication that she was the victim of violence. And no sign she'd packed up and left."

"Well, what happened? They must have looked into it."

"There was an extensive investigation," Gilbert confirmed. "But she was never found."

12

RON HARDING WAS STILL PISSED OFF.

She'd driven the hour out to the Washington field office in D.C. for a meeting on his turf and she'd been waiting for twenty minutes in an empty conference room. She craned forward to peer into the hallway, but still didn't see anyone. She reined in her annoyance because she knew she deserved the snub.

Finally, Ron and Jimmy strolled in together, carrying coffee cups that wafted steam, laughing about something. "Evelyn," Ron greeted her stiffly. He took a seat at the far end of the table, away from her, pulled out his notepad and started writing.

With a wide smile that showcased ridiculously straight white teeth, Jimmy slid into the seat next to her.

From the top of his dark gelled hair past a pressed blue suit to a pair of dark brown dress shoes, Jimmy screamed, *Look at me.* He scooted his chair just a little bit closer—enough that Evelyn itched to move over, but not so much that it wouldn't seem rude if she did.

"Evelyn." Jimmy rested his hand lightly on her upper arm. "How are you?"

"Fine, thanks." She shifted her arm away on the pretext of picking up her pen—and heard Ron snort, probably amused by Jimmy's lack of success.

Luckily, Jimmy didn't have time to make a less subtle move, because the door to the conference room opened and two more agents, who must have been the rest of Ron's team on the BAKBURY case, filed in.

One of them was a lanky guy with a head overflowing with blond curls who had to duck to get in the door. He stretched his Gumby arm across the table. "Miles Ferguson."

Evelyn smiled. "Evelyn Baine. I'm the criminal investigative analyst on the case."

"Nice to meet you, ma'am." Miles shook her hand carefully, as if his bony hand might hurt her.

His face was tinged with red as his gaze met hers and his eye contact was shaky. That was no surprise, since she'd already pegged him as an FNG. At least, he seemed like an eager FNG.

Miles glanced questioningly at Jimmy, maybe wondering why he was practically attached to her hip, and settled into the chair opposite hers. He put down a pen and notebook and took off his too-big, too-polyester suit coat to reveal an equally ill-fitting dress shirt.

The other agent walked around the table to introduce himself. "I'm Cory Fuller."

His handshake was firm, his eye contact solid and intense. Light blue eyes screamed intelligence, and his dark hair was cropped buzz-cut close. He was half a foot shorter than his partner, but a good fifty pounds heavier and Evelyn suspected it was all muscle. She pegged him to be around forty.

"Did you join the Bureau after being a military officer?" she guessed.

His eyelids dropped slightly as he assessed her. "Are you a profiler or a mind reader?"

"Do you tell fortunes, too?" Jimmy inquired.

Cory shot him a look of disbelief and sat next to his partner.

Ron briefly closed his eyes, then shook his head at Jimmy and stood. "Let's get started. You should all be familiar with Evelyn from the case file. Not only is she the victim who brought us into the case, she's also the profiler who was originally assigned in Bakersville."

Evelyn tensed at the introduction. What exactly had these agents seen in the case file? Her injuries had been photographed at the hospital for the investigation—mostly as evidence in the event that they found someone to take to court. She glanced over at the laptop in front of Ron, wondering how much of the information on his screen was about her.

"The reason we're here today," Ron continued, "is that Evelyn contacted Gilbert Havorth, who most of you probably know, about a fingerprint found in the trunk of the car from our case." Although he put no extra emphasis on the word *our,* he glanced at her meaningfully.

Yeah, she got it. She'd overstepped her bounds and he wasn't ready to forgive her.

"Evelyn requested a meeting with us because she came across some interesting information." Ron nodded at her once and sat.

Evelyn got to her feet. She didn't really need to, but at her height, standing when everyone else was sitting projected power. A good profiler used all the psychological tricks at her disposal.

"Gilbert ran the print from inside the trunk of our UNSUB's car." She purposely used the word *our,* just as Ron had.

He raised an eyebrow at her, catching the subtle cue.

"I called him back to make sure the database included FBI agents. It did, and that's who our print belonged to."

Miles blinked rapidly and looked over at Cory, as if he was wondering if he'd heard her correctly. His partner's jaw had gone rigid.

Apparently, Cory didn't like the idea that a fellow FBI agent might be a rapist and murderer. Neither did she.

"I did it on the outside chance the killer was Bureau, but the match was for a woman who used to work in the Boston field office. Her name was Diana Ballard."

Cory's head jerked back, but it was his partner who leaned forward. "A woman?" Miles asked, sounding confused.

"Yes. And from the crime scene, we can be pretty certain that the killer is male, and that he had no accomplice."

"Then what does the print mean?" Jimmy asked.

"It could mean several things. The first—though least likely—is that she has no connection. But here's what I know about the car—David Greene was the only legal owner, so theoretically, the car has only been in the possession of David and Justin Greene and our killer. Not a lot of coincidental reasons for Diana's print to be in the car."

"So how did it get there?" Jimmy asked.

"Because of the location of the print, we originally thought it was left by the killer. But the most likely alternative is that the person who left it did so from *inside* the trunk."

There was a long pause before Ron asked, "You suspect this agent was a victim of the BAKBURY killer?"

"Yes."

"Just like you," he mused.

The knots in her shoulders migrated toward her neck. "Not as lucky as me." She shared with them what she knew about Diana Ballard and her disappearance.

"*That's* why the name sounded familiar," Miles said. "I remember hearing about her...."

So had Evelyn, once she'd pulled a picture of Diana. It had been big news for a while, at least within the Bureau.

"So, why do we think she was targeted?" Jimmy asked.

"It's possible the killer trolled for a victim and chose Diana without knowing her profession, but I doubt it. It's more likely he picked her for the same reason he probably chose me."

"Earlier killings." Ron sat straighter, tapping the end of his pen on the table to click it open.

"Yes. I suspect she was working on a case involving his earlier murders." Seeing a blank look on Miles's face, she explained, "From the Bakersville crime scene, I concluded that he's killed before."

"So, after those first murders, he stole Greene's car and got out of town? Tried to outrun the investigation into Diana's disappearance?" Jimmy asked.

"No. The car was stolen *four* years ago. Diana went missing three years ago," Ron corrected.

"What about now?" Cory's gaze locked on hers with an intensity that must have scared new recruits when he was in the military. "Do you think there haven't been any more murders because he's skipped town again?"

"No." It came out forcefully, but doubt crept into her mind. Would he know the drugs had made her forget what he looked like? Or would he have run as fast as he could, regardless? "No," she repeated. "He's not finished here." Hoping it was her usually solid intuition telling her that and not just desperation to find him, she let her confident gaze sweep her captivated audience. It landed on Ron. "I think we should learn exactly what Diana Ballard was working on before her disappearance."

Ron leaned forward, interest in his eyes. "I'll put in a request to have the field agents who questioned David Greene look into this."

That was protocol, but it wasn't good enough. By the time the paperwork went through, the killer could have found another victim. "Maybe someone on your team could go to Boston. I can give them details on what to look for."

Ron shook his head. "I'm not going to waste a member of my team on something that can be handled by an agent already in Boston."

"Well, maybe I—" Evelyn started.

"You'll stay out of the investigation and stick to profiling."

Evelyn tried not to react to Ron's nasty tone. "Since the earlier murders didn't show up in ViCAP, they're not going to be easy to spot. We should have someone who knows the case files on this."

Ron shoved his chair back, got to his feet and shook a finger at her. "You're damn lucky you're still alive, so leave the rest of the investigation to us."

Evelyn instinctively braced herself on the arms of her chair, as if to fend off Ron's verbal blow. What was with him constantly reminding her that she'd barely escaped being brutally murdered?

Ron grabbed his notepad, pen and coffee cup and left without another word.

Apparently, the meeting was over.

Looking uncomfortable, Miles stood and buttoned himself back into his suit coat. "It was nice to meet you, ma'am. Thank you for the help." He hurried out the door after Ron.

Cory and Jimmy got up as Evelyn tried to regain her equilibrium.

"Evelyn." Cory took her hand again, shaking with a precision that had probably been drilled into him, his demeanor noticeably frostier.

As Cory marched out of the room, Jimmy gave her his default smile. "See you later, Evelyn. We'll get in touch when we hear back about Diana."

Alone in the conference room, Evelyn gathered her belongings. If Ron thought she was going to let them hand off something this important to an agent who could easily miss the connection, he hadn't learned much about her. Her job or not, she was going to find this killer.

"This crime scene has definitely been staged," Greg was telling Dan about his latest case when there was a knock on his boss's office door.

Dan slid his feet off the desk and called, "Come in."

To Greg's surprise, Evelyn walked in, a notebook clutched tightly in one hand. Nervous energy seemed to pulse from her.

Noticing Greg, she gave him a smile and then told Dan, "I can come back later."

"What is it, Evelyn?" Dan asked with a hint of impatience.

Evelyn took the seat next to Greg and her foot immediately started tapping a rapid beat. What had her so jittery? There was an excitement he only saw in her when she had an idea about a case, but lately nothing had been able to overcome her anxiety.

"Dan, I came across some new information on the BAK-BURY case."

Greg watched her face as she told them what she'd learned. And she was right. He could feel it in his gut as strongly as he could see it on her face. Diana Ballard was the key. But what would it cost Evelyn to unlock this case?

More and more, he worried it would be her job.

After yesterday, when she'd seemed contrite about overstepping her bounds, he'd thought she was going to leave the investigation to the case agents. But a day later, she was already throwing herself back into it.

Greg hoped Dan would stop whatever plan she had now, her need for closure be damned.

He'd assumed that as time went by, both her physical injuries and her emotional trauma would begin to heal. But the circles under her eyes just kept getting darker. And although she couldn't afford to lose any weight, her suits were starting to hang off her. She looked like hell—at least to him. He doubted anyone else could see past her rapidly shortening fuse.

If she didn't back off, *would* she end up like his old mentor? She was young for a heart attack, but there were endless other possibilities. She could get into a car accident because she was so exhausted she fell asleep at the wheel. Her involvement in the case could put her back in the killer's path. Or most likely, continuing to insert herself in someone else's investigation could destroy her career. For Evelyn, that might be worse than a heart attack.

If he voiced his concerns to Dan, his boss would see them as an excuse to remove Evelyn from the BAKBURY case entirely or make her take mandatory time off. Greg couldn't do that to her. So, he waited, praying Dan was smart enough to insist that she back away from playing case agent.

"I want your permission to go to Boston and review Diana Ballard's active cases from the time she went missing," Evelyn said.

Was she serious? How could she possibly justify going to Boston to look through cold case files?

Dan released a long, exasperated sigh. "You're no longer a field agent. That is *not* your job. If Ron Harding decides this lead is valid, he'll have someone in Boston check the cases."

Evelyn's foot tapping turned into shaking. "Yes, Ron was going to put in a request—"

"Fine. That's protocol. Get out of my office and do your own job."

Greg cringed, even though she deserved it.

But Evelyn plowed ahead. "I think a profiler's eyes are needed on these case files and on the evidence. I'm not sure a regular agent will know what to search for and I won't be able to access the details I need from here."

Dan looked as if he had to work to get his jaw unclenched. His words were clipped and angry. "So tell them to isolate any case where women are buried with only their heads sticking out and circles cut in their chests."

"I've already made a call to Diana's old partner. If it was that easy, we wouldn't need anyone to search the files. An agent who pulled that kind of case would remember it. He didn't."

"So what? Maybe it's not there," Greg said, wondering where she was going with this.

"More likely, the mutilation and manner of burial weren't evident for some reason. Maybe the burial site was disturbed."

Dan rested a hand under his chin. "And you think you'll spot his work, anyway?"

Damn it. Dan sounded less hostile, which meant Evelyn was getting to him. From a year of training her, he knew how persuasive she could be, but this was ridiculous.

Evelyn nodded rapidly. "Yes, I do. And if those were his *first* murders, it could lead me to his identity."

She was good, Greg would give her that. But it was in her best interest that he stop this.

He opened his mouth to suggest she consult with the Boston agents when she sent him a look.

It was full of warning, but that wasn't what made him close his mouth. It was the vulnerability lurking in her eyes.

If anyone could identify the killer from murders with no apparent signature—which was a profiler's best hope of connecting cases—it was Evelyn. And that might be the only way to make her vulnerability disappear.

"Get the paperwork to go to Boston on my desk and I'll coordinate it with Ron," Dan instructed.

When the phone rang for the third time in less than fifteen minutes, Evelyn just glared at it.

"Are you planning to answer that?" Greg called from his cubicle.

"Nope. It's Ron, pissed that Dan arranged for me to go to Boston. I don't feel like being yelled at again." She was getting really sick of everyone giving her grief about something all of them would be doing if they were in her position.

"You're going to have to deal with him at some point," Greg said. "And what if he actually needs to talk to you about the case?"

Cursing, she picked up. "Evelyn Baine, BAU."

"What the *hell* are you trying to pull, weaseling in on my case?" Ron yelled at a decibel level that made her ears ring.

"Nice talking to you, too, Ron."

"*We* were taking care of the Boston angle, Evelyn. Is this why you're a profiler, so you can work alone? Because you're not a team player?"

Evelyn ground her teeth and tried to rein in her temper. "Did you need something, Ron?"

"What I need is to work with professionals who don't overstep their boundaries. What I need is…"

Evelyn fanned her face, which was getting hotter with every insult. She kept her mouth shut, willing herself not to yell back. But she could feel her control slipping as Ron continued to rant.

Words she was going to regret clogged her throat as she

tried to hold them back. Just when she knew she couldn't, she slammed the phone down.

"Ron?" Greg asked.

Evelyn took a calming breath. "Yes."

"You do know he has every right—"

"Evelyn!"

Saved by Kyle's booming baritone. Go figure.

She and Greg stood at the same time and Kyle came running from across the office.

"What's going on?" she asked him.

"I heard you're going to Boston."

"How did you hear that?" Evelyn shot a pointed glance at Greg.

"I mentioned it to him yesterday."

She frowned. Why was Greg talking to Kyle about her active cases? She took their confidentiality requirements seriously.

Shifting his weight impatiently, Kyle jumped in before she could say anything. "A group of us from HRT are heading there, pretty close to where you need to be. It's not a triple eight beep situation—" he referred to the call-out code that would appear on his pager if they had to leave immediately "—but we go wheels up at 23:30. I got permission for you to join us on the flight there. We don't know how long we'll be gone, though, so you'd have to find your own way back."

"Sounds good." Evelyn's sour mood started to evaporate. She'd asked the travel agent BAU used to book her a flight, but this evening was much earlier than she'd expected to get to Boston. And the sooner she could look at the old cases, the faster she might uncover the connection that would lead to the killer.

"You'll need to meet us at Andrews Air Force Base by

23:00." Kyle gave her and Greg a parting wave as he dashed back the way he'd come.

"Thanks!" Evelyn yelled after him.

Greg seemed ready to dive right back into his earlier reprimand, so Evelyn dropped into her chair.

She picked up the phone and called Diana Ballard's old partner, Terry Kincaid. She'd already questioned him once.

"Is this about the serial killer again?"

"Sort of." She hadn't mentioned the BAKBURY case connection to Diana's old partner before, because she hadn't wanted to get bogged down talking about Diana when she couldn't tell him anything. "I'm coming to Boston to look at your old case files."

"Excuse me?" He sounded insulted, probably assuming she doubted his memory.

"I know the killer is connected to one of your cases and I need to figure out which one it is."

"How do you know he's connected if we had no cases with your M.O.?"

"Signature," Evelyn corrected. A lot of law enforcement agents didn't know the difference between signature and modus operandi and it always made her want to give them a lecture on Serial Killers 101. Instead, she told him, "I found a print from your old partner in his trunk."

Terry was silent for so long she almost asked if he was still there.

"*In* the trunk?"

"Yes."

There was a string of cursing. "When are you coming?"

"Can you pick me up from the Hanscom Air Force Base tonight?"

"I'll be there."

13

"WHERE IS SHE?" GABE ASKED AS HE AND KYLE stood outside the C-17 transport taking HRT to Boston.

Kyle stared toward the entrance of the base. "She's late."

HRT's gear had already been loaded into the jet for tonight's mount-out. Normally, he'd be on board by now, along with twenty-one other HRT agents and a negotiator. Instead, he was twiddling his thumbs, waiting for Evelyn.

As soon as he'd learned she needed to go to Boston when HRT was going, anyway, he'd run straight to his boss. He'd practically begged, but he'd gotten his way. Which meant that at least he could keep an eye on Evelyn for an hour or two.

Since the moment he'd rushed to the hospital after her abduction, he'd had to fight the constant urge to watch over her. Logically, he knew she could take care of herself; after all, she'd escaped from a serial killer. But emotionally, all his protective instincts had gone into overdrive and he couldn't seem to shut them off.

Feeling helpless came with his job. He'd spent enough time on missions waiting for headquarters to give the green light when every minute's delay meant more deaths. But on missions, once he got the go-ahead, he could count on his training and his teammates. He'd run practice operations with just about every spec ops team in the U.S. He could take out a terrorist without hitting the hostage three inches away. He could bring down an armed target with his bare hands. But what he couldn't do was shield Evelyn from a threat when he couldn't even identify who the threat was.

It was a totally different type of helpless.

"There she is." Gabe jerked his thumb at the base entrance, where Evelyn was running toward them in one of her typical dark suits, a briefcase in hand and an overnight bag slung over one shoulder.

"Sorry I'm late," she said as she skidded to a stop, a hand clutching her rib cage. "The cab got stuck behind an overturned semi on the beltway."

"No problem." Kyle reached for her belongings. "Let me stow these."

"I can do it," she responded predictably. "Hi, Gabe."

"Glad you got here," Gabe said, and stepped into the plane.

"I've got to secure it." Kyle took her briefcase and bag.

She relented, following him up into the plane where most of the agents were already strapped into their seats. "Okay, thanks."

Several waved at her, but she didn't seem to notice as she looked around, her eyes widening.

He remembered his awe during his own first ride—the inside of the windowless jet had reminded him of a cave. Despite the hundreds of rides he'd taken in it since, sometimes it still did. The four-wheel-drive van, box truck, ambulance and helicopter they'd loaded earlier were all secured in the center with the agents' gear. There wasn't even walking room now that the seats running along both sides of the cavernous fuselage were folded open.

He gestured to the two available seats on the end and she strapped herself in next to Gabe.

"The ride's a little bumpy," Kyle warned as he belted himself into the seat next to her, his knees pressed against the equipment in the middle. "The military gets the choppy air no one else wants, but the pilots are the best."

"I promise not to puke on you."

Evelyn, making a joke? He must have done something right. "Oh, good."

He handed her a pair of earplugs. "Trust me. Put them in now and don't take them out until we land. Did you bring anything to read?"

"No."

From the longing look she sent her briefcase, he suspected she'd brought work.

He resisted an eye roll and offered her his book, *War of the Worlds,* which he'd just cracked open yesterday. "Here."

"What are you going to do?"

"Review the mission details." He stuck in a pair of earplugs as the jet door closed and took the mission briefing out of his bag. He'd read through it once, but it wouldn't hurt to go through it again.

"Thanks," she mouthed, putting in her own earplugs and opening the book.

From the other side of Evelyn, Gabe leaned forward and gave him a pointed glance.

Kyle ignored it, resting his head against the wall of the fuselage. He tried to focus on the coming mission as the jet started to move, the dull hum of the engine edging past his earplugs.

But Evelyn's knee bounced against his leg with every bump, which made it hard to concentrate. Instead of the clean scent he was used to—presumably shampoo, since she didn't seem like the perfume type—she smelled like gunpowder again.

He snuck a look at her. She was staring at the book, but he didn't think she was reading. She was probably thinking about the same thing he spent too many hours focusing on. The man who'd abducted her. Every time he saw her, her "nothing fazes me" facade slipped a little more.

She was a far cry from the woman he'd met a year ago who held her shoulders a little too straight, jutted out her chin a little too far and gazed at the world with those too-intense eyes, daring anyone to mess with her. The minute he'd met her in Greg's office, he hadn't been able to resist taking that dare.

But the joke had been on him, because he'd fallen hard and she had no clue. He wasn't even sure if he'd been able to inch past "colleague" and onto her "friend" list.

As the plane rode over conflicting air currents, her knee rocked against him and the hand not holding his book gripped the side of her seat—toward the back, probably so no one would notice.

He hid a smile. It figured she wouldn't like plane rides. Or anything else where she couldn't be in total control. Like relationships.

For all he knew, he just wasn't her type. But he'd never gotten the feeling there was anyone else, so he kept hoping. Maybe one day he'd actually work up the courage to flat-out tell her how he felt.

As the plane began its descent, his fear shifted forward, fear of watching her walk away and never seeing her again. Fear that wouldn't go away until her abductor was caught.

One glance at her holding her earplugs, moving her jaw around to pop her ears, reminded him of how tiny she was, how fragile she'd looked covered in bruises and hooked up to an IV in the hospital.

"Be careful," he blurted before he could stop himself. He stepped around her quickly and grabbed her luggage before it got lost among HRT's extensive gear.

He hopped down and she jumped out after him, taking her bag and briefcase.

"You have a ride?" He shuffled his feet, not wanting to let her go. How the hell was he going to concentrate on protecting foreign dignitaries with an image of Evelyn unconscious and bandaged in his head?

"An agent from the Boston field office is picking me up." She checked her watch. "I'm sure he's already here, so you can get back to work, McKenzie."

"It's Mac," he said automatically, pulling her out of the way as Gabe drove the box truck off the jet.

She looked around at the other agents unloading equipment and weapons, and drew a hand through her hair.

He knew her discomfort had nothing to do with leaving him, though, and probably everything to do with the fact that she'd actually accepted an offer of help—which in her mind was a sign of weakness.

"Thanks for the ride." She offered him a wobbly smile and still seemed a little off balance.

He wanted the old take-no-prisoners Evelyn back.

At least he could erase the lost look from her eyes. So, he winked and gave her a wide grin. She'd think it was meaningless flirting as usual. He'd get an eye roll in response—as usual. "No problem."

She didn't disappoint him. She even added a head shake to the quick eye roll. But the off-kilter look was gone. He thought she might have been smiling as she headed off to meet her ride.

"Agent Kincaid?"

The big man standing beside a Buick LaCrosse wasn't wearing a typical Bureau polyester-blend suit and he didn't have the typical agent's cropped haircut. The fact that it was after hours could explain the ratty jeans and Yankees T-shirt, but not the long hair pulled back in a ponytail.

A tired smile lifted one side of his mouth as he offered her a beefy hand. "That's me. Call me Terry."

She'd barely shaken his hand before he tossed her belongings in the back and opened her door, then stood beside it waiting.

"Uh, thanks." Evelyn got in and he slammed the door after her.

He slid into the driver's seat, which was adjusted practically into the backseat to make room for his huge frame. "So, Evelyn, where are you staying?"

"The Holiday Inn a few blocks from the field office. But if you don't mind, I'd like to go straight to the office and look at case files."

Terry raised an eyebrow as he got onto the I-95. "You don't want to get some sleep first?"

"No, that's okay. I'm not tired." She tried not to punctuate her lie with a yawn.

The glance he sent her said he didn't believe her as he drove at a slow and steady pace in the right lane. "The cases you'd be interested in are all from my time in the VC division."

The Violent Crimes Major Offenders squad—VCMO—in Houston was where Evelyn had been, before she moved to BAU.

"Now I'm working white-collar crimes." Terry shrugged enormous shoulders. "It's not as interesting, but I sleep better at night."

When he shot her another probing glance, she realized he expected conversation. She smiled and nodded. "I bet."

"Anyway," he blabbered on, "I've had a lot of partners over the years. I chased bank robbers in Detroit and Seattle before coming here. But Diana was the best." Wistfulness crept into his tone. "Probably her only fault was her Red Sox loyalty."

"Huh?"

"I'm from New York. Yankees all the way."

"Oh." Sensing that Terry was getting tired of her one-syllable responses, she added, "I don't follow sports."

"It was the only thing Diana and I ever argued about."

Evelyn waited, but Terry had lapsed into silence. "So, tell me about her disappearance."

Terry's whole profile hardened. "One day she was there, the next she wasn't. We went out to dinner the night before. Me, my wife, Diana and her sister. I dropped Diana off at her house afterward, told her I'd see her in the morning. I never saw her again."

"You were the last person to see her?"

"Yes. As far as we know."

"Then what?"

"When she didn't show for work the next morning, I called her. Diana was never late. She didn't answer, so I went to her place. I had a key, and I let myself in. She wasn't there."

Terry let out a weighted sigh. "Her purse was sitting on the counter, cell phone, creds and weapon inside. The Evidence Response Team went over the house and found nothing. No sign of a struggle, no sign of forced entry, nothing missing. None of her friends had any idea where she might've gone and she had no enemies, at least not personal ones. It was like she vanished without a trace."

As Terry pulled off the freeway, Evelyn said, "I'll probably want to talk to any friends or relatives who might know something."

"Look, Evelyn, I wasn't the only one on this case." Terry's jovial tone from the beginning of the ride had grown solemn at the mention of Diana; it was now laced with bitterness and anger. "There was a team put together—the case was called ABFED, for the suspected abduction of a federal agent. It was taken pretty damn seriously. One of our own disappears and the Bureau isn't going to sit on its hands. It caught a lot of news coverage, too."

"I remember." The national news had even picked it up, because Evelyn remembered seeing Diana's face flashed on the screen and thinking that when they did find her, it wasn't going to be pretty.

"Eventually, though, the media lost interest. And the Bureau ran out of resources. But our team spent five months just on her case. After that, I kept following leads on my own up until the one-year mark after she went missing."

He flashed his security card and pulled into the Boston field office parking lot. "Believe me, if there'd been anything, any evidence at all, I would've found it."

When his troubled gaze met hers, Evelyn nodded. "Maybe now it'll be different."

Terry shook his head. "Because of a print in a trunk?" He opened his car door. "I hope you're right, Evelyn, but whoever did this doesn't make mistakes. He didn't make a single one when he took Diana."

He stepped out and shut his door before Evelyn could tell him the killer had made one this time.

This time, he'd tried to take her. And she wasn't stopping until she found him.

"Tell me about CAPEKIL," Evelyn requested.

She and Terry had been digging through his old case files in a conference room at the Boston field office for so long, the sun was coming up. Evelyn had been fighting exhaustion and frustration for most of that time. But when she'd opened the CAPEKIL file, her blood pressure had spiked.

This was it. It had to be.

"CAPEKIL?" Terry leaned forward to look at her computer. "Oh, yeah. It was nasty. We got jurisdiction because the bodies were dumped on the Cape Cod National Seashore. By the time they were found, there wasn't a lot left. We never found the killer." He looked up. "Is this connected to Diana?"

"Maybe." Instincts honed by a hard year of profiling told her the cases were connected to BAKBURY. Which meant they were also connected to Diana. And to her. "What do you remember about it?"

"It's all in here. We caught the case probably seven months before Diana went missing."

"There were only two victims. Is that right?"

"Yes." Terry opened the victim photos attached to the case file. "Angela Mason and Debra Chin. This one—" he pointed at Angela Mason "—reminded Diana of her sister. Not that they looked that much alike, other than the red hair and blue eyes. But there's something about the picture. I can't really put my finger on it, but even now, seeing this shot of Angela Mason makes me think of Kate Ballard."

"There was no actual connection to Diana's sister, though, was there?"

"No. Just that Diana was really invested in this case and I'm sure it was because seeing the picture of this victim always made her think of her sister." Terry's forehead creased. "I haven't talked to Kate in a long time."

Evelyn nodded, waiting. She had to remember Terry wasn't just a case agent. Talking to the family and friends of victims had never been easy for her. Not because she empathized with them—although she did—but because she never knew the right thing to say.

Greg was better at that part. She'd hoped some of his quiet supportiveness would rub off on her when she'd trained with him, but she didn't think it had. She was better with the paper trail of an investigation than with the people involved.

She supposed when you spent most of your life avoiding people, it became difficult to talk to them. Early on, she'd learned that she was safer if she stayed out of the way of her mom, out of the way of her mom's many boyfriends. And by the time she'd moved in with her grandparents, it had become a habit that was hard to break.

"We always thought there'd be more," Terry mused.

"More?"

"More victims."

"But there weren't?"

"Not that we ever found out. But these two women didn't know each other. They didn't have much in common, other than where they were last seen. Dance clubs," he answered before she could ask. "So, Diana and I figured a wacko. A serial killer. As I said, we thought there'd be more. Except…"

"Except what?"

"The victims looked nothing alike. That bothered me." He gazed up at her, fire in his eyes fueled by six cups of coffee and a still-burning desire to find out what had happened to his old partner. "Don't serial killers like the same type of victim?"

"If it's the same guy and he's what I think he is, not this guy. He's after something, but it's not physical similarity." Evelyn studied the shots of Debra Chin and Angela Mason attached to the file. The only similarity seemed to be age. Compared to Angela's pale skin and average build, Debra had been tiny, with long dark hair and dusky skin.

She stared at Debra for another minute or two. If this was the same killer—the BAKBURY killer—she'd been wrong about him only going after victims of the same race. Evelyn and Diana didn't count, since he'd probably just wanted them off the cases that involved him. They wouldn't have to fit his victim choice. But what *was* the common denominator between his victims? "What about lifestyle?"

"Similarities?" Terry shrugged. "They were both married. From middle-class families. Otherwise, there wasn't much. They didn't even live near each other. Debra was a stay-at-home mom. Her husband said she was shy, only went out to the club to meet some old friends who were in town. Angela was a textbook editor, no kids. Friends said she was really outgoing."

"Tell me about their abductions."

"They were both leaving dance clubs. Debra's friends said she'd gotten tired and left early. She never made it home and we never found anyone who saw her in between. Angela was meeting friends, too, but she left partway through the night for another club with a mutual friend. Can't remember his name, but it's in the report."

Evelyn scrolled down until she found it. "Tony DelMarco?"

"Yep, that's it. Anyway, her friends told us they thought running into Tony was planned. They thought Angela and Tony were having an affair."

"What did Tony say?"

"He denied it. He said he walked Angela partway home later on and then she insisted on walking the rest of the way herself. He said she didn't want her husband to see them together."

"Did you rule him out?"

"Yeah. Witnesses said Tony met up with them at another bar not long after he left the club with Angela. Not enough time to abduct her and stash her anywhere. And he had a solid alibi for when Debra was taken."

"Okay. What about other suspects?"

"Apparently, Debra drank too much that night, danced with a lot of men she didn't know. She didn't leave with anyone, but we did try to track them all down."

"Anyone promising?"

Terry sighed. "None of those guys. We did find someone else we liked for it, but we never came up with anything substantial on him."

"Who was he? Did he have ice-blue eyes?"

"His name was Edward Krup. I don't remember his eye color. We never found enough evidence to arrest. Two years later, he was picked up for assault."

"Sexual?"

"Yes. He spent time in jail for it."

"When did he get out?"

"I don't know if he has. You'd have to check."

"Okay." Evelyn opened the crime scene photos. They showed a wooded area of the Cape Cod National Seashore that looked eerily similar to the woods in Bakersville. Different trees, different victims, but the same sense of solitude. The same appeal to a killer who wanted privacy.

The bodies had been discovered way off a trail that was in the process of being rerouted. It was an area with little foot traffic, totally inaccessible by car. Just like Bakersville.

Debra's and Angela's bodies had been found in the summer by two park workers. Unlike the Bakersville victims, Debra and Angela had been fully dressed. They'd also been out in the open, but they'd definitely been dragged by animals. Their original drop spot had never been determined.

Angela had been dead for more than a month and Debra for somewhere between two and three weeks. Most of the physical evidence had been destroyed by then.

Autopsies had concluded that ligature strangulation had been the cause of both deaths, but many of the other details were a mystery. Rape was suspected, but impossible to tell for certain.

Animals had done a lot of damage. The medical examiner

had been able to reconstruct the bodies pretty well, but Angela Mason had been missing her left ring finger. It was never determined whether the killer or the animals had taken it. But no body parts had been taken in Bakersville, and judging by the length of time these bodies had spent out in the open, Evelyn would guess animals were the culprit.

"Do you have any close-ups?" Evelyn asked.

Terry sighed and got to his feet. "Yeah. They're not in the system yet. Let me go grab the evidence box."

When he returned a few minutes later and popped a DVD into his computer, Evelyn took a deep breath and leaned closer, studying shot after shot of the victims at the crime scene. But her trained eyes couldn't tell her more than the medical examiner had discerned. If there were circular knife wounds on the women's chests, she couldn't see them on what remained of the breastbones.

She swallowed hard and looked away.

Sympathy shone in the curve of Terry's lips, the slant of his eyebrows. "Hard to look at, huh? You probably see a lot of this shit, don't you?"

Evelyn nodded and tried to conceal whatever he saw on her face that had made him ask. "Worse."

The sympathy intensified. "How many years have you been a profiler?"

"Only a year."

"Most profilers last very long?"

Evelyn raised one shoulder in a tight shrug. "My boss has been doing it for decades. We have another one who's been around almost as long. Since I've been there, we've had two join and transfer out pretty quickly."

"What about you?" He studied her as though he was seeking an explanation—why would someone be willing to stare at that kind of crime scene on a regular basis? "You in it for the long run?"

"Yes."

Terry nodded, as though he'd read her reasoning in that one word. "It's a hell of a job. I couldn't do it."

It's my life. Instead of saying it, she told him, "The autopsy reports listed cranial wounds."

"Yeah. The medical examiner never determined if they were inflicted before or after death. But if they were beforehand, they weren't severe enough to cause death on their own. Diana thought maybe the killer knocked the women out."

Evelyn nodded. "Blitz attack. Could be. What about bruising on the body?"

Terry lifted bushy eyebrows. "We had mostly skeletons, Evelyn. If there was bruising, it wasn't deep enough to damage what was left of the bodies."

"What about burials? Was there any reason to suspect the bodies were buried before animals pulled them out?"

Terry pursed his lips and opened another set of photos on the DVD, these taken at the morgue. "Maybe. We never found the drop spot, but you can see from the autopsy photos that the lower half of each body was better preserved. The medical examiner said partial burial was a possible reason." He frowned. "That never made much sense to me, though. Why would you only bury someone up to the waist when they're dead? What's the point of that?"

"Just up to the waist? Not the head?"

"No."

Some vague thought niggled in the back of Evelyn's mind, telling her both burial styles should mean something to her. But what? Frustration shot through her. "Anything else you can tell me about the case?"

Terry gestured at his computer. "It's all in there. We never really got anywhere. Any suspects we had were eliminated—well, except for Krup. There was no useful physical evidence. And we never found any other murders to connect to it."

Evelyn looked up from the screen. "What about Diana? Can I see her file, anything I won't be able to access from home?"

The muscles in Terry's jaw clenched and pulsed. "Sure. I can get you Kate's number, too, if you want to talk to her. I think she's still in the same apartment."

"Thanks."

Terry glanced up from staring at his coffee. "When your boss arranged with mine for you to come here, he said you were one of the best."

Evelyn blinked in surprise. *Dan* had said that? Had he just been trying to smooth her way with an uncooperative ASAC or had he meant it?

"Please find her." Terry's plea was little more than a whisper, filled with the same pain she'd heard from the loved ones of other victims.

She felt a responsibility to do what thousands of hours of solid detective work by agents before her hadn't accomplished. She never made promises. Sometimes there wasn't even a body left to find.

But she knew what it was like to wonder. To lose someone and never know what had happened, never know for sure if that person was dead or alive. She'd spent years wondering that about Cassie.

She met his desperate gaze and made a promise she might not be able to keep. "I'll find her."

14

KATE BALLARD'S APARTMENT WAS CROWDED with memories of a sister who was probably never coming home.

When Diana's little sister had let her in and showed her to the living room, Evelyn had immediately noticed the pictures of Diana covering almost every horizontal surface. The mismatched furniture, Kate had told her, was a mix of hers and Diana's. The rest of Diana's belongings were in storage, waiting for her to return.

Fidgeting on the couch, Evelyn glanced at the kitchen, where Kate had disappeared to brew herself some tea. She'd heard the teakettle whistle a minute ago, but Kate hadn't reappeared.

Getting restless, Evelyn stood and took a closer look at one of the pictures of Diana and Kate tucked among the novels on the bookshelf. The shot had been taken in front of Quantico. Tall, muscular, brunette Diana had a huge, proud smile, her arm around the shorter, red-haired Kate. The younger woman was smiling, too, but her eyes weren't on the camera. They were on Diana.

In the photo, Kate and Diana looked vibrant, full of life. Now, Diana was more likely dead than alive and Kate looked a decade older than the thirty-five Evelyn knew her to be.

"That was taken right after Diana graduated from the FBI Academy," Kate said as she reentered the room, clutching tea Evelyn knew instantly was spiked.

Back before her mother stopped trying to hide her addictions, she'd put liquor in everything. But Evelyn could always smell it.

"You look very proud of her in this photograph," Evelyn said gently, trying not to cringe as Kate sipped her tea.

Kate seemed brittle, ready to break, as if Diana had disappeared three weeks ago instead of three years.

Kate smiled, a shadow of the smile in the picture—form but no substance. "There was never a reason *not* to be proud of Diana. She was perfect. I mean, of course she had her flaws, but she was as close to perfect as you could get. As far as my parents were concerned, Diana could do no wrong."

The smile slipped and her face went back to the flat expression that had clearly become habitual. "Growing up, I resented her for it, because I was the screwup."

"You didn't get along when you were younger?"

"No. I mean, Diana tried. She'd make time for me, even though we were four years apart. She used to pick me up from school in her car. My friends were so jealous. I thought she was sucking up to our parents. But she actually wanted to be friends, even then."

When her words had trailed off, Evelyn prompted, "Obviously you became friends later."

"When I finished college, Diana had just been transferred to Boston. She said I could live with her while I figured out what I wanted to do with my life. It was better than staying home with my parents, so I did. And Diana helped me find a marketing position with a good company. When I'd been working for a while, I got my own place."

Kate released a long, shaky sigh. "I sold her house last year. I couldn't swing the payments anymore and it felt too…weird to move into her house." Tears gathered in the corners of her eyes and she wiped them away, taking a loud gulp of tea.

Evelyn struggled to come up with a response, but before she could, Kate was talking again.

"My parents always thought Diana would be a social worker, because she could never turn away anyone she believed she could help."

"That's why she joined the Bureau?"

"Yeah. I used to think it was because it sounded cool. You know, because she got to carry a gun and chase bad guys. I remember joking about it one day and she said her job probably wasn't anything like I imagined. She said she spent most of her days at a desk and the only time she'd ever shot her gun was for practice."

Me, too, Evelyn thought. The only time it had been shot in the field had been by her abductor.

"I asked why she liked it, then, and she said it was about keeping people safe, that she liked helping people and this was how she wanted to do it." For a second or two, a hint of a smile raised the corners of Kate's mouth.

"I'm sorry to make you relive this." Evelyn expected this sense of devastation immediately after someone went missing, but seeing the shell of a life Kate was still living was something of a shock. Was this what people saw when they looked at her? More than once, on her grandma's good days, she'd made comments about Evelyn spending her whole life chasing closure after Cassie's disappearance.

"That's okay." Kate's voice wobbled. She drank the last of her tea and added, "It's just that it's been years since anyone looked into her disappearance. I mean, I know Terry tried to find her for a long time. I think it almost cost him his marriage."

She stared vacantly for a minute, then said, "I don't mind talking about her. But it's hard to—to hope," she finished in a whisper. "Officially, the FBI still says Diana is missing, but I know they think she's dead. I just…" She twisted the hem of her T-shirt.

"You don't want to believe it."

"Yeah."

Evelyn forced herself to look Kate in the eye. The hope trying to bloom through the despair brought her back to the way she'd felt years ago. "I understand."

She glanced again at the picture of Diana as a proud new academy graduate. This time, something in the shot reminded her of herself.

Sharing personal details wasn't in her nature, but she sensed that it could help Kate. "When I was ten, I moved in with my grandparents."

Kate seemed surprised by the change of topic.

"My mother wasn't really fit for that title." Evelyn stared down at the fire-engine-red throw pillow totally at odds with the blue plaid couch. "Before that, I'd spent so much time moving from one place to the next, it was hard to make friends."

Evelyn looked back at Kate. "But the girl who lived next door to my grandparents became my best friend."

Kate was watching expectantly, her expression tense, as though she knew the story wasn't going to end well.

"Cassie was abducted out of her own house by the same person who took two other girls that summer." Evelyn blinked back tears she thought she'd long ago cried out. "None of them were ever found. There's a good chance they never will be."

Kate wrapped cold hands around hers. "I'm sorry."

Surprised that this woman, so lost in her own grief, would try to comfort her, Evelyn felt guilty. She wasn't here for Diana. She was here for herself. "Thank you."

The furrows in Kate's forehead got deeper. "You're telling me this because it's the same with Diana, right?"

Evelyn locked her gaze on Kate's. Now the hope and despair were hidden behind a stoic expression Evelyn knew others often saw in her. "I'm telling you because I understand what it's like to hope. But the truth is that after this much time, even if I do find out what happened, it's unlikely I'll have good news."

"I know." Kate's voice was watery as she let go of Evelyn's hand and grabbed her mug. "I'll be right back." She hurried out of the room as tears began tracking down her face.

"Shit," Evelyn muttered. Why had she shared that with a stranger? Not even Greg knew about Cassie.

She hadn't talked about it with anyone but her grandma in years—not since she'd finally told Jo and Audrey.

For a long time, she'd let herself dream that Cassie might one day be found. That, somehow, she'd beaten the odds and was still alive.

That same hope flared to life now and she tried to snuff it out.

What was she doing to Kate by coming here? Guilt warred with her need to learn more about Diana so she could get to her own abductor.

"It was something in her job, wasn't it?" Kate asked as she returned, surrounded by alcohol fumes. "Diana's, I mean."

Evelyn shoved the guilt back. "Probably."

Kate nodded as she settled into her well-worn chair. "When

we were growing up, I made fun of her for always collecting stray people."

"What?"

Kate let out a burst of laughter, short and harsh, like machine-gun fire. It died out just as quickly. "You know, like some people collect abandoned animals? Diana was like that with people. Me, included. Not that I was abandoned, but let's just say I was…lost. Most people would've given up on me. I think my parents did. We get along okay now, but back then…"

When she didn't continue, staring off into space, into the past, Evelyn said, "Diana didn't give up on you?"

"Diana always saw the possibilities in people. No matter how hopeless they seemed, she tried to help. She had this case shortly before she disappeared and it was like that, too. The case was going nowhere—Terry wanted to consider it inactive and move on—but she wouldn't give up."

She had to be talking about CAPEKIL. Evelyn leaned forward. "She persisted?"

"I think so."

Could she have stumbled across the killer and not even realized it? "Do you know if she documented anything somewhere other than the case file?"

Kate shook her head. "Diana did everything by the book. She was never in trouble. Never. Not at work, not growing up. Well, except for when she'd get in trouble because of her stray people. Like this guy we grew up with—Harley was his name, like the motorcycle. His mom was gone and his brother was in a mental institution, and Harley was a little off, too. But Diana didn't care. She took him under her wing, the hell with what my parents thought."

A wistful expression flitted across Kate's face. "Practically every one of those messed-up kids she tried to help when we were growing up in Connecticut kept in touch with her until the day she..."

Kate grabbed her teacup, clutching it too tightly. "I can't say it. I know I should accept that she's dead. But I can't. Until someone finds her, she's just missing."

Evelyn waited until Kate's short, jerky breaths evened out before she asked, "What did she tell you about the murder case she was so dedicated to figuring out?"

"It was in the news. Two women were found at Cape Cod. Terry thought she was taking the case too personally." Kate sipped her alcohol. "It was probably true, but Diana took all her cases personally. It's the way she worked."

Evelyn nodded. An image of Diana, working late at night from home, popped into her mind with such clarity it was as if she was there. She shook her head to dispel it. It reminded her too much of her own evenings.

Kate sighed. "I don't know any more about Diana's disappearance than I told Terry three years ago."

"That's okay. I didn't expect you to. I just wanted to hear about her from you, see if anything struck me as a possible connection to the case I'm working."

"Did it?" Kate asked hopefully.

This woman deserved the truth, so Evelyn gave it to her. "I'm not sure yet, but I think your sister's disappearance is connected. And your sister and I have something in common. I'm dedicated to my job, too. I won't give up."

Kate leaned over and clutched Evelyn's hand. Tears welled up in her eyes. "Please find my sister."

It was a plea Evelyn knew she'd hear in her head for years. Over the lump in her throat, she gave the same promise she'd made Terry. "I'll find her."

The first thing Evelyn did after taking a red-eye back to Virginia was stop by the nursing home. Her grandma was having a typical day; she recognized Evelyn, but thought they were living sometime in the past.

As soon as Evelyn walked into her room, grandmother Mabel took her hand and commented, "What a beautiful ring. It looks just like the one my husband gave me."

Evelyn smiled down at the worn gold with the small diamond. "This *is* your engagement ring, Grandma. Remember, you gave it to me a few years ago?"

It had actually been more than a decade now, about a year after her grandmother's stroke. She'd been recovering, but had an uncertain future ahead of her, between hitting the limits of what physical therapy could do and her worsening dementia. Besides a small cross, her wedding and engagement rings had been the only jewelry she wore, and she'd wanted Evelyn to have one of them.

Mabel frowned, and Evelyn knew she didn't remember.

"That was a good idea," she finally said.

Evelyn smiled, looking down at the ring she never took off, until memories she hardly ever revisited rushed through her mind.

An image of her father, tall and stoic, before he'd had his heart attack when she was six. Evelyn only had a few memories of him. But her grandparents had told her stories. So had her mother—on the increasingly rare days when she was sober.

Evelyn knew her mother had always been wild; she'd left home and hitchhiked across the country after graduating from high school. That was when she'd met Evelyn's father and brought him home. Her grandma had admitted to Evelyn that they hadn't approved at first. But soon they'd realized he was good for her. And by then, Evelyn had been on the way.

Her grandparents had thought her mother was finally going to kick her alcohol addiction. But after her dad died, she'd pulled out the vodka bottle and never put it away. Most of the memories Evelyn had from the time of his death until she was ten were pervaded by the medicinal scent of vodka and a steady stream of her mother's boyfriends.

None lasted long. Every few weeks, her mother would lock herself in her bedroom with a new man and a lot of liquor. Usually, around the time the cupboards started going bare, the relationship ended. Her mother would reappear briefly and then the cycle would begin again. Most of her boyfriends ignored Evelyn, if they even knew she was there. There was only one whose face still showed up in her nightmares.

They'd just moved back to South Carolina, back to their old apartment. During the whole trip from Florida, Evelyn had daydreamed about how her life would change. She'd get to see her grandparents again. And maybe her mother would stop drinking, stop bringing home new boyfriends more often than she brought home paychecks.

Instead, her return to Rose Bay had been a blur of heartaches. Her mother hadn't let her see her grandparents. And she'd met a new man, one who'd moved right in.

Evelyn shivered, and goose bumps prickled her arms and legs.

As a profiler, Evelyn knew how lucky she'd been. A single mother who regularly drank until she passed out was a beacon for a skilled pedophile. The one who'd targeted her had been thwarted by the bathroom lock that held long enough for Evelyn to get out the window. She'd made it to a pay phone down the street and called her grandparents, who'd taken her in and changed her life.

As the memories faded, her grandma's ring came back into focus and Evelyn realized she'd been twirling it as she thought.

Mabel reached over and turned the ring so the diamond was facing up. "Your ring's on the wrong hand."

"It's not my engagement ring," Evelyn reminded her absently.

Her grandma smiled a little, her lips stretching farther on the right than the left from her stroke. "I guess you don't want to discourage a potential suitor."

Evelyn started to roll her eyes, then suddenly jerked forward. Could it be?

She tried to remember the autopsy reports from the CAPE-KIL case, but all she could come up with were the details of the violence, the things that told her about the perpetrator's pathology. As hard as she tried, she couldn't remember what she needed.

Maybe Terry would know. "Grandma, I need to make a phone call. I'll be right back, okay?"

She kissed her grandma on the cheek and rushed into the hallway to dial Terry.

She felt guilty calling him instead of waiting to see if she had the information in her notes, but this could be the key to the case. The excitement running in her veins, probably more potent than her mother's liquor, told her it was.

"Terry Kincaid," he answered, sounding bored and tired. The latter was surely because she'd kept him up going through old files; the former, she guessed, was because he'd gone from violent crimes to white-collar investigations.

"Terry, this is Evelyn Baine."

The boredom was gone when he asked, "Did you find something?"

Evelyn grimaced at the hopeful note in his voice. "I'm sorry. Not about Diana."

"Oh." There was a world of disappointment in the word.

"I may have found the connection between my case and Diana, but I don't have what I need to confirm it."

"Okay." Now Terry just sounded weary. "What do you need?"

"It's about CAPEKIL. The victims were both married, right?"

"Yes."

"Did you recover either of their wedding rings?"

"No, we didn't."

"Are you sure?"

"Positive. I remember because we found Debra Chin's engagement ring, but not her wedding ring, and her husband was really upset about it. But it wasn't surprising we never found them, given the condition of the bodies. Angela Mason was missing her ring finger entirely."

"Is it possible her finger was cut off?"

A nurse walking down the hall did a startled double take, but Evelyn visited often enough that all the staff knew what she did for a living.

"I guess so," Terry said, "but I doubt it. You saw what animals did to those bodies. That's probably why her finger was missing."

"Then the autopsy didn't uncover any indication that a knife was used?"

"The autopsy didn't find incisions from a blade, but you saw the report. If there was any mutilation before the bodies were dumped, the decay combined with the bite marks could have hidden it. Isn't that partly why you were interested in the case? Because the decay could have hidden those circular marks you were looking for?"

"Yes." So, it was possible. An image of the Bakersville victims flashed through her mind.

"Why?" Terry asked. "Do you have a reason to suspect the killer cut off Angela's finger?"

"Maybe." Evelyn twisted her ring around with her thumb, considering.

Finally, Terry said, "Is there anything else?"

"No. Thanks."

"Good luck." He hung up.

Evelyn was slower to put her phone back as she thought about the BAKBURY case. Neither Mary Ann Pollak's nor Barbara Jensen's wedding rings had been recovered from the crime scene. She'd figured that was because the victims hadn't been found with any personal effects, even clothing. Now she wondered if the missing rings were more significant.

A familiar thrill ran through her, telling her she was on the right track.

She'd been struggling to find a common denominator between the BAKBURY victims, some specific characteristic that had drawn the killer to these young women. Usually, serial killers wanted a certain hairstyle or body type. Not this one.

Evelyn remembered moving her grandma's ring to her left hand the day she was abducted, because her fingers had been swollen. She'd flipped the diamond over, so it wouldn't look like an engagement ring, but it hadn't occurred to her that the plain gold band would make her look married.

Since her abduction, she'd been assuming the logical thing: that the killer had targeted her because she was part of the team investigating him. But maybe she'd been wrong. Maybe he'd picked her for the same reason he chose all his victims.

He'd believed she was married.

1
5

EDWARD KRUP'S CRIMINAL RÉSUMÉ INCLUDED attempted rape. The question was, did it also include murder?

Terry said Krup had been their main suspect in CAPEKIL and it was one hell of a coincidence to discover he'd moved to Virginia shortly before Mary Ann and Barbara had gone missing. As Greg liked to say, if someone claimed coincidence, check for a lazy investigator.

Evelyn had asked Ron and Jimmy to pick him up. It had taken them almost a week, but they'd finally done it. Now, Evelyn stared through a one-way mirror at the Washington field office into the interrogation room where Ron and Jimmy were questioning him.

As Ron strode toward him, Evelyn studied the twenty-nine-year-old. He looked strong enough to have pulled off the recent murders. At nearly six feet, he had the kind of muscle tone that suggested he spent a lot of time with free weights at the gym. But his baby face lent him a certain innocence.

That innocence had fooled the woman he'd gone to jail for assaulting. At the trial, she'd testified that Edward had offered to help her change a flat tire and she'd been relieved, since her car had broken down in a bad area of town. She'd thought he would keep anyone unsavory from approaching. She'd never expected *him* to turn on her.

Right now, it was Edward who looked afraid. When Ron clapped a hand on his shoulder, he jumped halfway out of his chair.

An odd reaction if he was the practiced serial killer they were hunting. But maybe he was faking.

"Eddie, what have you been up to since you moved to Virginia?"

Across the table, Jimmy stared expectantly at him.

"It's Ed, man." Ed's gaze darted from one special agent to the other. "And I haven't done anything wrong."

Ron raised his eyebrows in obvious disbelief. "That's what you said after you were charged with assault in Boston."

Shit. It figured Ron would take the antagonistic route.

"If you're charging me with something, I want a lawyer."

Apparently, Ed had learned at least one thing in jail.

Jimmy leaned forward. His tone calm and friendly, he said, "You're not under arrest. Just answer some quick questions for us and we won't have to bother looking more closely at your activities."

Evelyn smiled in amusement. So, Jimmy was the good cop, was he? She supposed it fit. She didn't think many criminals would be intimidated by the pretty boy playing a badass.

"Help us out," Jimmy wheedled. "We know you've been working part-time as an assistant at the library in Kensington, right?"

At the mention of the town where she'd been abducted, Evelyn's whole body tensed. She moved closer to the glass.

"Yeah," Ed admitted, sounding less than thrilled.

She supposed it was because prior to his arrest he'd worked

as a teacher at a community college in Boston. Probably no schools in Virginia had wanted an ex-con on the faculty, especially one with a history of assaulting a woman.

"You work pretty odd hours," Ron said. "It seems like you have a lot of time off. What do you do when you're not working?"

"I work whenever they tell me to work," Ed barked. "Anyway, I'm applying for new faculty positions. This is just for now. And it's none of your damn business what I do in my free time."

Not exactly words to inspire confidence. Evelyn squinted, trying to get a better look at the eyes hidden behind smudged lenses.

"Eddie, Eddie," Ron mocked. "If you haven't done anything wrong, there's no reason not to help us out. It only makes you look guilty if you refuse to talk to us."

"It's Ed!" Bolting out of his chair, Ed stomped over to the glass, stopping directly in front of her.

He glared through the glass as if he knew she was there, and Evelyn took an involuntary step back. This close, she could see past the smudged lenses. His eyes were definitely blue.

"Why don't you sit down, Ed?" Jimmy said. "Tell me how you like Virginia."

Ed's lips puckered in the middle, like there was a snarl trying to break free, but he held it back and returned to his chair. "Virginia's fine. I figured if I got out of Boston, the cops would hassle me less."

Jimmy laughed as though that was a joke. "So, you live alone?"

"Yeah." He glanced quickly at Ron, who'd settled into the seat next to Jimmy. "But, uh, I have a lady friend in town, so why don't you tell me why I'm here?" His leg started jiggling under the table. "Then maybe I can tell you if she was with me during whatever time you want to know about."

Ron smirked. "How long have you been seeing this woman, Eddie? And what's her name?"

"Well, it's not just *one* woman," he backpedaled. "I'm a popular guy." He gave them a wolfish smile.

Ron looked unconvinced. "I see. So, what are the names of these *several* women?"

"None of your business. Anyway, one of them's married, so I doubt she wants me spilling her infidelities all over town."

Evelyn stepped forward again, close to the glass. If she was right, the BAKBURY killer was targeting married women, probably because a married woman—either his wife or another important woman in his life—had betrayed him in some way.

"Let's begin with your secrets, then," Ron said. "Do your lady friends know you were in jail for attempted rape?"

"I wasn't going to rape her." Ed banged his oversize fists on the table.

"No?" Ron asked. "If that man hadn't stopped his car, you would've just untied her?"

"Look, man—"

Ron cut him off. "I know the police pulled a rape kit from your van."

It was another reason Evelyn had wanted him questioned. A rape kit—police slang for items like rope, duct tape and even condoms that rapists would use in the commission of their crimes—told the police two things. That the crime was premeditated. And that it almost certainly wasn't the first offense.

"I have no idea what that means," Ed denied, blinking as he looked anywhere but at Ron or Jimmy.

"We know what happened in Boston, Eddie," Ron said. "So, you might as well tell us the truth."

"I *am* telling the truth!" Ed jumped from his chair with such violence that Ron's chair squeaked as he shifted backward.

"I don't know what you want, but I didn't rape anyone! I wouldn't do that!" He shook his head. "I'd never do that."

"All right, Ed," Jimmy said, inclining forward, one hand out in a "calm down" gesture. "We don't have to talk about Boston anymore. Okay?"

"Fine." His expression sullen, Ed hunched lower in his seat, staring down at the table.

Damn. The protective posture was a sure sign Ed was cutting himself off from the investigators.

"We want to ask you about something else," Jimmy said. "Something maybe you can help us with. You see, we've been wondering why someone might cut another person after that person's dead."

"What?" Ed's eyes widened, then his lips curled in disgust.

Evelyn studied him closely, trying to decide if it was a facade.

"After someone's dead," Jimmy said, "her killer cuts a circle in her chest. Why do you think he'd cut her?"

It had been Evelyn's idea for Jimmy and Ron to try to get Ed to "theorize" on the BAKBURY killer's signature. Sometimes serial killers, wanting to brag about their crimes without admitting to them, would offer investigators their "speculations" on a crime. Except they'd know too many details.

Evelyn had seen it work more than once. Brilliant as many of the serial killers she'd chased had been, they were also egotistical. They didn't want to go to jail, but they sure as hell wanted to brag.

Ed didn't fall for it.

"What are you talking about?" he demanded. "Who's cut up? How the hell would I know? What kind of sicko are you, man?"

"Okay," Jimmy said, seeming unperturbed. "What about burying someone up to their head?"

"What?" Ed jumped out of his seat again, glancing back and forth between Jimmy and Ron. "I'm out of here. You want to ask me anything else, arrest me." He rushed for the door.

Jimmy looked into the one-way mirror and shrugged. Then both agents joined her in the viewing room on the other side.

"He fits the profile," Jimmy said, sidling too close to her. He ticked off points on his fingers, as if he'd get extra credit for knowing the answers. "He's the right size, he's employed in a position below his abilities, he's single, he's white, he's the right age—"

"I don't think it's him," Evelyn interrupted.

"What?" Ron's surprise mirrored Jimmy's. "He fits the profile. And he's attacked a woman in the past. He's smart and he was definitely spooked that we were on to him. Plus, check out the timing!" He crossed his arms over his rumpled suit jacket.

Evelyn shook her head, taking a step away from Jimmy. She'd thought, at the beginning of the interrogation, that they might have found their killer. But he hadn't reacted the right way.

"He fits the profile superficially, yes, but so do a lot of men. I thought he might be the one, too, since the timing was just so perfect. But too many things are off."

"Like what?" Jimmy sounded bewildered.

"Well, first of all, his job may be below his skill level, but he's trying to get back into his previous field. If he's looking for regular work, he'd have less time to stalk his victims."

"Maybe he's lying about that," Ron said.

"Okay, but—"

"He's obviously good at approaching women without looking suspicious," Ron broke in. "*And* he was really nervous about being questioned."

"That's not surprising, with his history, and I *do* think he's on the lookout for another victim—another woman to rape, not to kill. He's definitely someone the police should watch, but I don't think he's the BAKBURY killer."

"The Boston police assumed he was going to rape that woman he assaulted. But maybe he planned to abduct and kill her." Jimmy agreed with Ron. "He did freak out when I asked about the mutilation and the heads."

Evelyn sighed. "Yeah, and that's the problem. Sure, the guy we're after is a good actor, but Ed was so worried about going back to jail he made himself look suspicious. And he got defensive about the attempted rape in Boston, which we *know* he did, but not when you asked about the mutilations and the burial style."

Ron seemed ready to argue, so Evelyn said, "You should check his whereabouts at the time of the murders, in case I'm wrong, but I really don't believe it's him." She almost wished it was. At least then they could watch him, wait for him to slip up. Instead, they were back where they'd started. With no suspect.

Ron's chin jutted up. "Well, I do. And since you can't identify the killer, we'll go with *my* gut. I'm the one in charge."

He headed for the door and, when Jimmy didn't immediately follow, barked, "Let's go."

Jimmy gave her an apologetic grimace and trailed after his partner.

"Dammit," Evelyn muttered. How long would the case agents spend tracking that dead end? And what would the killer do while they were busy looking in the wrong direction?

He had to be careful.

Too many things had gone wrong lately, so he had to go slowly, bide his time. The cops weren't a real threat, but they were learning. They'd been driving by his woods more often, denying him the pleasure of lingering there with the memories of his victims, in the place he best heard their screams.

He had the darts full of drugs with him now, although he wouldn't use them tonight. The fact that he needed them at all made fury boil in his gut. He missed the thrill of the chase, the way his lips wanted to smile when one of them got in his car. The way he had to restrain himself until later, until he could show them their mistake.

But now he couldn't risk it. Now he was reduced to drugging them.

His fingers started to tingle and he looked down, realized they'd gone bone white around the steering wheel. He loosened his grip, refocused on the woman counting her cash as she stepped away from the ATM.

"Sarah." He whispered her name, liking how it sounded on his tongue. She looked around and got into her SUV. She never noticed him.

As she pulled into traffic, he settled in a few cars back. He didn't have to think about the drive. He'd done it so many times with her during the past week.

When she got to her house and the garage door rose, his heart rate began a happy climb. Her husband was out.

Adrenaline shot through him, but somehow he forced his hands to turn the wheel left, to continue past her house. Just a few more days, he promised himself.

Another woman came forward in his memory, a bloody fight replaying, heating his anger. The cops would never find her body, never know she'd been his.

And then the next one, the one who'd lied to him. Who'd made him believe she was someone else. His hands still twitched with the urge to wrap around her neck, to punish her for her lies, then display her like the whore she was. But it was too risky.

No, he had a different plan for her. She'd get the message when she found Sarah's body.

Serial killers get pleasure from outsmarting their victims.

Evelyn snorted as she read a well-known psychologist's deductions from interviewing a dozen incarcerated serial killers. She'd been trying to read the book all week and couldn't get into it. As she debated whether to give up on it entirely, the doorbell rang.

She debated ignoring it, because it was after midnight and she was in her pajamas. But something told her it was important, so she pushed herself out of the sole chair in her living room and stood.

She started for the door, then swiveled and grabbed her weapon from the crevice of the chair. That was the farthest it had been from her since the abduction.

The bell chimed again before she got to the door.

"Good grief, I'm coming." Evelyn peered through the peephole, her gun clutched reassuringly by her hip like a child holding a security blanket.

A grin stretched wide as she opened the door to a friend she hadn't seen in a long time.

"What are you doing here?" She ushered him inside and turned to shut the door.

She was about to bolt it when a strong hand clamped over her mouth from behind, jerking her head backward.

Panicked, Evelyn tried to point her gun behind her, but his other hand gripped her wrist with abnormal strength and snapped it like a twig. Her gun clattered uselessly to the floor.

She tried to scream, but too fast, the hand that had broken her wrist snaked up to her neck and squeezed.

Evelyn's good hand grappled with his, trying to pry it away from her neck. Her vision blurred and dots danced past her eyeballs. He was too strong.

Giving up on that tactic, Evelyn twisted, swinging her elbow hard and low into his stomach.

Her attacker grunted and his hold on her neck and mouth loosened.

Evelyn screamed.

Kyle grabbed Evelyn's wrists as she lurched toward him.

If he hadn't, he suspected he'd have been flat on his back with a black eye. He wasn't fool enough to think she couldn't hold her own in a fight. Her escape from the serial killer was proof of that.

"Evelyn!"

She wrenched her hands free, her eyes still closed. Her right hand was twisted at an odd angle, but she held it up to block her face as her left hand drew back again, her fingers curled into a fist.

"Evelyn!" He jumped backward, raising his arms protectively in front of him. Trying to restrain her now might hurt her. If she decked him—well, he could handle the embarrassment. And he supposed it would mean she'd owe him.

But instead of attacking, Evelyn dropped her arms to her sides, blinking rapidly. Her gaze darted around the room and then settled on him. Her breath still came in short jerks, but she was awake.

He lowered his arms.

Evelyn looked at her right arm, frowning. She grasped her wrist and bent it forward and backward, then looked up at him, seeming completely lost.

"It's almost eleven," he told her. "I was working late, finishing some paperwork, and when I drove past the BAU office, I noticed your car was still here." She wouldn't know Aquia wasn't on his way home. "I thought I'd come in and make sure everything was all right."

He frowned at the tension in every line of her body, still not clear on what had made her attack when he'd leaned over and tried to shake her awake. "You must have fallen asleep while you were working."

"I'm at work," Evelyn said inanely.

"Yes." Kyle glanced at her desk. The open file on her computer was labeled BAKBURY. Worry gnawed at the lining of his stomach like termites eating through wood. "Nightmare?"

Embarrassment flooded Evelyn's features as though the single word had broken a levee. She slumped back in her chair, spinning it to face her desk. She quickly closed the file and shut down her computer.

When she finally turned back to him, her mask of composure was almost in place. "I'm sorry." She frowned apologetically. "Did I hit you?"

"No. Don't worry. It's not a big deal."

Now she looked mortified. "Oh, shit. I tried to hit you, didn't I? I was, uh…"

Maybe she didn't want to tell him about her nightmare. "It's okay. Really. I've taken plenty of accidental hits from guys on the team over the years. One more wouldn't kill me." He smiled, but she wasn't paying attention to him anymore.

She whipped her chair around and yanked her desk drawer open, pulling out a notebook. He saw the label "ABFED and CAPEKIL" on the front before she flipped through several pages.

"Is it possible?" she murmured, but Kyle didn't think she was talking to him.

Yet when he didn't answer, she whirled the chair around

again, almost slamming into his knees. She didn't seem to notice.

"What?"

"I...I was dreaming that I was at home and I opened the door and someone attacked me."

"Well, it's probably because of your abduction. I'm sure the nightmares will go away once you catch this asshole." Maybe his would, too.

Evelyn jumped to her feet. "No. That's not..." There was frustration in every word. "When I opened the door, I let him in. I *knew* him."

Confused, Kyle asked, "Who was it?"

"I don't know." Evelyn breathed out a heavy sigh, as though she shouldn't have to explain it to him. "But in my dream, I knew him, whoever he was. And I think..."

"What?"

"I think there was no evidence of a struggle at Diana's house because she knew her killer."

16

WHEN KYLE PULLED HIS BUCAR INTO HER driveway, instead of hopping out, Evelyn sat frozen in the passenger seat, her heart racing. Was she really going to ask him in?

After a moment of silence, he said, "Call me in the morning and I'll pick you up."

After she'd fallen asleep on her desk and been woken by her nightmare, she'd been jittery. So jittery that she'd left her car at the office and taken the ride home Kyle had offered.

"Okay." Evelyn nodded, still debating.

When she didn't get out of his SUV, he said, "Nice house," speaking slowly, like he was searching for conversation.

He didn't say anything about the exclusive neighborhood in Aston, Virginia, with its large wooded lots dotted with a few houses like hers but mostly mansions. He must have noticed, though, and probably wondered how she could afford to live here on her salary.

"Uh, thanks." She turned to face him, gulped back her nerves and asked, "Will you come in?"

He blinked his surprise away. "Sure."

It wasn't until she'd walked up the driveway and stepped inside the entry that she remembered the state of her house. She stopped abruptly and felt Kyle halt just before he could walk into her.

She turned around and found her nose practically pressed against his chest. He smelled like gunpowder and aftershave and she had the urge to take a deep breath. Instead, she backed away and looked up. "I don't really have...furniture. Sorry."

He was trying hard not to react to her strange behavior, but since she was trained at reading people, she knew she'd thrown him totally off balance. He wasn't even flirting.

"You've been here awhile, haven't you?"

"Almost a year." She was too nervous to come up with excuses, so she told him the truth. "I work too much."

He gave her a dimpled half smile. "No kidding."

Since there was only one chair in the living room and no furniture in the dining room, she led him into her kitchen. She wanted to walk through her house with her weapon out, checking all points of entry, but showing fear wasn't her way, so she sat straight-backed in a chair and gestured for him to do the same.

"I need to bounce ideas off someone and it's too late to call Greg."

Emotions flitted across Kyle's face too quickly to absorb.

Evelyn felt her own face heat up. Why had he thought she'd asked him in?

When she was silent, he prompted, "About the Bakersville killer?"

Her heart rate slowed down. They worked together. He might be attracted to her—and vice versa—but he cared about his job, too.

"Yes." She slipped out of her suit jacket, but left her gun

holstered. It had been weeks since she'd taken it off. Even when she slept, she nestled it between the mattress and the headboard. "But I'm not really supposed to—"

"I'm not going to talk about it with anyone."

He looked sincere, but… "It could be my job," she muttered.

"Evelyn." He leaned across the table toward her, and she could tell he'd already cataloged every fading bruise on her bare arms and the still-raw skin on her wrists. "You've got my word."

She didn't trust many people, but her gut—or maybe it was his eyes—told her she could trust Kyle.

So, she gave him a brief sketch of what she knew about the killer's movements, ending with his abduction of her. "I originally assumed he grabbed both me and Diana because we were investigating him. But if he grabbed me because he thought I was married, he must have seen me with my ring flipped around." She showed him her grandmother's ring. "And I'm pretty sure I only flipped it over that day."

Kyle's jaw had grown noticeably tense the second she mentioned her abduction. It looked as if he had to forcibly pry it open when he asked, "Where did you go that day?"

She thought backward from that moment in the darkened parking lot. "Before Haggarty's, I was in Bakersville. Tanner—the police chief—was giving a news conference about the killer. Before that, I was at a funeral for one of the victims. Before that, work."

"When did you flip your ring over?"

"In the morning."

"Before you left for work?"

Panic sizzled through her like lightning. Until she remembered it had been at Aquia. The killer hadn't followed her from her house. "No. At work."

"Okay. He wouldn't have seen you in the BAU office, right? There were no nonBureau guests, were there?"

"No." She didn't have to think about that one. They never had nonBureau guests. Dan didn't even like nonBAU personnel. Particularly not the one sitting across from her, tension etched into every line of his face.

"Well, then there are three possibilities, right? He spotted you at Haggarty's, in Bakersville or at the funeral."

"Right." Evelyn frowned.

"What?"

"I profiled the BAKBURY killer as organized, as someone who picks his...victims carefully. They're random in that he didn't know them personally, but specific in that they had to meet definite requirements."

"Like being married."

"Yes." She sighed in frustration. "But he's not the kind of killer who spots a potential victim on the street and abducts her immediately. He stalks her first, learns her routines, her personality. He figures out how long it would take after she went missing before anyone would notice. He knows her relationship with her husband."

"But he didn't know you don't have one."

"Right." Evelyn stood and started pacing from the kitchen doorway to the edge of the counter near Kyle and back again. "So why? He wouldn't have had time to learn anything about me. If he had, he would've realized I didn't fit his victim profile."

"But he drugged you. Are you *sure* he didn't know your profession? If he didn't drug the other women, why you?"

A memory appeared in her mind with such clarity it almost made her stumble—the surprise and anger in her abductor's eyes when he'd tried to pull her out of the car and she'd fought him. The fury when she'd struck a blow hard enough to make him bleed. "He didn't know."

"Why do you say that?"

"He was stunned when I fought him. He didn't expect the drugs to wear off, so that was part of it, but I don't think he expected to find handcuffs and a gun on me, either."

Kyle's intense gaze followed her as she kept pacing. "What reasons are there for a killer to deviate from his normal methods?"

The memory teasing at the edge of her consciousness got stronger. The pain exploding in her head when her abductor dragged her out of the car. His eyes as he leaned toward her. She sucked in air.

"Evelyn." Kyle's hand closed around hers, pulling her to a stop.

She blinked the memory clear, her breathing growing even at the comfort of Kyle's touch. "What?"

Now it was Kyle's gaze boring into her, but his was full of compassion. Worry.

Tears rushed to her eyes. She pulled her hand free and tried to remember what he'd asked.

"Why would he deviate?" When she didn't immediately answer, Kyle said, "Any killer. Why would any killer deviate from his pattern?"

Evelyn sank back into her seat and smoothed her hair. "Greg suggested maybe a stressor he couldn't handle. So, he'd just gone trolling for the first potential victim he could find who fit his basic needs."

Kyle nodded. "That makes sense."

"It would explain why he didn't know I'm not married or that I'm FBI."

"What else?"

"Um, an easy victim. He spotted someone he thought he

could just grab without stalking first." She glanced up at Kyle. "I'm not an easy victim."

"No," Kyle agreed. "But you're small. You might have looked like one."

She scowled.

A smile flitted across Kyle's lips and then it was gone, buried beneath layers of other emotions Evelyn was afraid to study too closely.

"Come on. You can't tell me it hasn't worked to your advantage before to have people underestimate your strength."

"Fine," Evelyn conceded. "I was alone in a bar parking lot and I had a bad headache. I wasn't paying as much attention as I normally would to my surroundings."

"Is there anything else? To explain why serial killers might deviate from their patterns, I mean."

"Ego. Sometimes, when murderers have been doing it a while and don't get caught, they start feeling invincible. It can make them overconfident, less careful. They need a bigger challenge to get the same thrill. Sometimes it turns serial killers into spree killers."

"So, instead of weeks between victims, they go after several at once?"

Evelyn nodded. "Or within a really short period of time. Hours instead of weeks, with no cooling-off period in between. But when that happens, they usually get caught."

A whisper of hope fluttered inside her and Evelyn quashed it almost before the guilt that came directly after. She refused to wish for mass murder to lock up her abductor. Besides, he hadn't struck again for weeks, so obviously he was in still in control.

"Are there any other reasons?" Kyle prompted when she fell silent.

She shrugged. "Not really."

"Well, let's go back to where he could have spotted you."

"Why?" Evelyn slumped. This was useless. She still had no answers, just questions only the UNSUB could answer.

"Killers like this tend to follow the investigation, right?"

"Yes." She met his gaze. "I'm looking into the possibility that he knows someone at the police station."

Kyle leaned back in his seat. "I was thinking about the news conference."

"Huh?"

"You said you were at a news conference in Bakersville before you went to Haggarty's."

"So?"

"So, if he was in the crowd—"

"He might've been caught on camera." Evelyn vaulted out of her chair. "I might recognize him."

Kyle's gaze followed her every movement, as if he didn't want her out of his sight. "Let's talk to the news stations. Get copies of their tapes."

He said it as though it was something they'd do together. He probably would help if she asked. But she couldn't bear to admit that she—the ultimate loner—didn't want to work alone. Being afraid to do her job wasn't a reputation she wanted with anyone, least of all a man who ran into situations everyone else ran out of. A man whose respect she craved too much.

"I'll call tomorrow." Some of her tension eased. Having a plan made her feel less powerless.

Kyle nodded, staring at her as if he expected something, although she wasn't sure what.

The silence stretched, turned awkward, until finally he asked, "Why are you still here?"

"What?"

"In this house, by yourself."

She bristled. "We just decided he doesn't know where I live."

"Right. We *just* decided. Does that mean you'll be getting some sleep tonight?"

He could tell she wasn't sleeping? "Um, yes, I'll get some sleep."

"Well, you should. I've done so many protection details I could do them in *my* sleep." He grinned. "No one's getting past me."

"Huh?" What was he talking about? Did he think *he* was staying here?

Some cowardly part of her wanted him to. Not even a serial killer stood a chance against an HRT agent. And something told her that was especially true with *this* HRT agent, if she asked him to protect *her*.

She gave him a shaky smile. "I don't own a couch."

He stood and suddenly her kitchen felt way too small, as if there wasn't enough oxygen for both of them. "That's fine. I don't need one."

Her face flushed, her heart picking up speed, until he continued. "Believe me, I've slept on a hell of a lot more uncomfortable places than your floor." The dimples came back out. "And unlike some of the HRT guys, you probably don't sound like a rhinoceros about to charge when you sleep."

She opened her mouth, not sure whether she should go with her pride and demand he leave, or with her emotions and beg him to stay.

She didn't know which one of them was more surprised when she nodded and said, "I'll grab you a blanket."

Maybe she *would* actually get some sleep tonight. If she could sleep at all with Kyle under the same roof.

Was her grandma right?

Evelyn turned over in bed, trying to get comfortable. But

between thinking about the HRT agent downstairs and what her grandma had told her about Cassie, sleep was elusive.

Cassie's file was in a box beside her bed. It had arrived two days ago, but Evelyn hadn't been able to bring herself to open it yet. She turned over again, flicked on her bedside lamp and, with a deep breath, reached into the box.

The first page of the file just had a title: The Nursery Rhyme Killer. Cassie had been the third girl abducted, but the only one from Rose Bay. She'd also been the last known victim. None of the girls had been found, but the media had dubbed their abductor the Nursery Rhyme Killer because of the macabre versions of nursery rhymes he left at his crime scenes.

Evelyn's eyes felt gritty as she skipped past the details of the abduction until she found a photocopy of the note he'd left after Cassie's abduction. She scanned it, searching for her name, praying she wouldn't find it.

Then her heart gave a painful thud, and her fingers and toes started to tingle, as though her blood supply had been cut off. Her grandma was right.

She and Cassie were supposed to have died together.

Evelyn's hands jerked, crumpling the note, and she dropped it. Moisture rushed to her eyes as she slapped the file shut and threw it back in the box, her breath coming too fast.

The Nursery Rhyme Killer's note said he'd taken both her and Cassie. Only he'd never come for her. What had happened? Why had she lived, while Cassie had—presumably—died?

The room blurred… She and Cassie had spent the day together, unsupervised in the huge lot behind the Byers's house. The profiler in her knew that a killer who'd gotten away with abducting three young girls was a stalker, too. He would have watched them first, maybe for weeks.

Chills danced over her skin as she remembered the game of hide-and-seek they'd played shortly before Cassie disappeared. She thought of all the opportunities they'd given him to strike.

But he hadn't. He'd waited until night, when the whole town was sleeping, and slipped into Cassie's bedroom.

Evelyn had lived next door. In the summer, she'd slept with the window open and there was a sturdy live oak right outside.

She'd been an easy target—probably easier than Cassie. But he'd only taken Cassie.

Was that why she was so desperate to find Cassie? Why she'd joined the FBI and worked nonstop to get into the BAU? Subconsciously, had she known all along that she was supposed to have died seventeen years ago?

A sob broke in her throat. Taking a breath, she pushed back the covers and stood.

The wood felt too cold on her bare feet and Evelyn realized she was freezing. As she threw a robe over her nightgown, the groaning of the wood made her jumpy. Just the house settling, she reminded herself. There was an HRT agent in her living room guarding the doors.

Her eyes darted to the bedroom window. No trees anywhere near these windows. Still, she grabbed her weapon and stuffed it in the pocket of her robe.

Maybe some tea would warm her up and calm her down—and while she was downstairs, she'd check the house like she had every night since her abduction.

Avoiding the unfinished part of her stairs, Evelyn crept slowly down. At the bottom, she hesitated. Right toward her kitchen and tea? Or left toward her living room and Kyle? Even as she told herself to go right, her feet moved left.

When she rounded the corner, he was sitting up, the blanket pooled in his lap. His steady, alert gaze told her she hadn't been quiet enough.

Warmth rushed to her face as she stared at his bare chest. Considering his job, he had to be fit, but with a body like that, Kyle probably didn't even need a weapon. She forced herself to look up at his face, glad it was dark so he wouldn't see how hard it was to fight her attraction to him. Or so she hoped...

There was heat in his eyes, but his tone was calm as he asked, "Couldn't sleep?"

She crossed her arms, tugging her robe more tightly closed. "No." Her voice sounded scratchy, as if she hadn't slept in weeks.

"Want me to do a walk-through?"

A smile raised one corner of her mouth. If he'd heard her, as silent as she'd been, there was no way anyone had gotten into her house. Some of the tension at her shoulders loosened and a surge of affection rushed through her. "That's okay."

He scrubbed a hand over his eyes, braced his arms on the floor behind him and asked, "Want to talk?"

She couldn't help staring at his shifting muscles and forced herself to look back up. She must have seemed uncomfortable, because he reached for the T-shirt balled up beside him and put it on.

An unexpected desire to tear it away from him made her hands twitch. She clenched them instead. She was tempted to forget about Cassie and the Bakersville killer by indulging in a few hours with Kyle, but she pushed the temptation aside. *He'd just break your heart or ruin your career,* she reminded herself.

"Okay." She nodded, then hurried to the chair a few feet away and sat stiffly. He just waited, and she didn't know what to talk about, so she was surprised when she heard herself asking, "Do you have anything in your past that you can't let go?"

He looked surprised, too. When she thought he wasn't going to answer, his expression turned serious and he said, "Yeah, I do. When I was new to HRT, we got a call..." He shook his head, reached for the cross around his neck. "Pretty typical hostage situation, really, but it was at a middle school. I pulled out a kid who'd been shot and she didn't even make it to the ambulance." His voice cracked. "She died in my arms."

Kyle frowned down at the floor, and Evelyn felt guilty about making him remember that day.

She'd always known his job was dangerous, but she usually thought about him kicking down doors and taking out terrorists with his MP-5. Not holding young hostages while they bled out.

"Despite everything I'd done to get on the team, I almost left HRT that day. I was a cop before I joined the Bureau, but I'd never had anyone die on me. Not like that. Not a kid." He let out a heavy sigh. "It made me take a close look at why I picked this job and how much I wanted it."

Kyle still had one hand on his cross. Her grandma wore one, too; all her life she'd wanted Evelyn to find something to believe in.

She'd never seen this side of Kyle before. Never tried to look deeper than his easy flirting and hotshot position with HRT.

After tonight, she was never going to see him the same way again.

He met her eyes. "There was nothing I could've done differently. It was already too late by the time HRT arrived on scene. But it doesn't stop me from wanting to change the past."

"I'm sorry." She couldn't hold his gaze, because she somehow knew his last words were directed at her, too.

"You have a victim from one of your cases like that?"

She shook her head, even as she answered, "Sort of."

He nodded, as though he understood. But maybe it was just that, on some level, he understood *her*.

"It wasn't a case. It was my best friend when I was a kid. Cassie. She…" Evelyn sucked in a deep breath as the insides of her eyelids started to sting. "She was abducted by a serial predator. She was never found."

Evelyn blinked rapidly, trying to keep the tears at bay.

After a moment, she resumed her story. "Cassie was the first real friend I had. I still don't know what happened to her. I joined the FBI to find out. And now, with this case..." Would she ever get the chance? Or had being abducted by the Bakersville killer completely derailed her career?

Kyle said softly, "There's no case that's unsolvable. Not the one you're working now and not your friend's disappearance." His intense eyes met hers again and she knew he believed it when he told her, "Someday you'll find the person who took her."

Evelyn's eyes watered at his unquestioning belief in her. Maybe he was right. Maybe she could actually track down Cassie's abductor, find out whether Cassie was dead or alive. Maybe that was why she'd been spared seventeen years ago.

"You have a gift, Evelyn. I don't have to be in BAU to see that. Don't lose faith now."

Maybe it was the low, soothing rumble of his voice, or the earnestness in his tone, but all the tension seeped out of her. Her whole body sagged, her eyes too heavy to keep open. She curled her feet up and twisted so her head was resting on the corner of the chair.

"Thanks," she mumbled. Somehow, just looking at Kyle, she felt safer than she had since her abduction.

Before she drifted off, she felt him tuck his blanket around her. When she was little, her grandma had done that.

She smiled as visions of Cassie filled her head. Visions of the two of them running through the field full of flowers beside Rose Bay's cemetery. A hand holding hers as Cassie whispered, *"We'll be friends forever, Evie."*

★ ★ ★

The tape of the news conference was useless.

She pressed Rewind again, then decided not to bother. She'd watched the tape five times since she'd arrived at the Bakersville police station. The killer wasn't on it.

Grabbing the tape, she left the tiny office she'd been in for the past hour and handed it back to Tanner.

"Anything?" he asked hopefully. His eyes were rimmed with red and underscored with deep circles. Just because the killer hadn't struck in his town again, that didn't mean Tanner was sleeping.

"Sorry."

Tanner sighed. "Guess you could've slept in."

She shrugged and headed for the door. She'd actually slept better than she had in weeks, despite the crick in her neck from curling up in her living room chair. Six o'clock in the morning had felt like sleeping in.

After an awkward drive to BAU—with Kyle's small talk and her trying to hide her discomfort over letting down her guard with him—she'd found the office empty. Relief that no one was around to see her get out of Kyle's SUV had been quickly overtaken by anxiety at being at the office alone. So she'd gone back out to her car and driven to Bakersville.

And oddly, during the whole ride over, she'd missed Kyle's deep voice. She'd always thought of him as having the kind of voice that would make criminals drop to the floor as soon as he yelled, "FBI!" But somehow, that same lazy baritone in conversation reminded her of the calming rush of the ocean tide, powerful yet constant.

Shit. Her plan to bury her attraction to him wasn't working at all. With every minute they spent together, it just seemed to get stronger.

She hurried through the parking lot, and came to a stop

as she noticed the old man standing next to her car. "Can I help you?"

He looked up from her legs, and piercing, almost-shamrock-green eyes stared at her. In a face full of folds and lines, they seemed oddly young and faintly familiar. As he stepped out from between the cars, Evelyn saw that he was leaning heavily on a cane.

"I'm Roger Pendleton. I stopped by the station to see my nephew Craig. I was only inside a few minutes, because he wasn't there, but..." Bushy eyebrows shifted inward as he glanced around the parking lot. "I can't remember where I parked." His sheepish smile revealed a glimpse of what had to be capped teeth, and Evelyn figured him for a real charmer fifty years ago. "I thought it was this one." He gestured to the car next to hers. "But I guess not."

As he gazed around, Evelyn took pity on him. "Can I help you find it?"

"That's okay, miss." He pointed to a car just outside the lot, similar to the one beside hers. "I think I see it." He flashed her one more smile and started slowly for the other blue sedan.

Evelyn waited until he stopped near the other car and waved before she headed back to Aquia.

The minute she'd settled at her desk, she called Kate Ballard. "Kate, it's Evelyn Baine."

"Did you find anything?" Kate's voice was squeaky with nervous hope. "About Diana, I mean."

More guilt. She'd made promises—to both Kate and Terry—that she shouldn't have. "Not yet."

She could hear Kate's disappointment in the faint sound of her breathing.

"But I have a few more questions."

"Okay." The disappointment was still there, but not surprise. "What do you want to know?"

"Is there anyone in Diana's personal life who'd be familiar with her cases for the Bureau?"

"Well, I knew she was working that one case I mentioned—the women who went missing."

"What about specifics? Is there anyone Diana would have given specifics about her cases?"

"Not outside of work. If anyone asked, she'd say she wasn't supposed to talk about it."

Evelyn felt a heavy sigh build in her chest. "Are you sure?"

"Pretty sure. Diana liked to do things by the book, especially when it came to work."

She was about to thank Kate and move on when she realized the killer wouldn't need specifics. Maybe the problem wasn't that he thought she'd gotten too close to the truth in her investigation. Maybe he was afraid he'd left a clue to his identity that she'd eventually pick up on because she knew him.

Excitement started drumming through her veins. If that was the case, all he'd need to know was that Diana was the investigator.

"Who else might have realized she was working on the Cape Cod case?"

"Besides Terry and his wife? I don't know."

"You can't think of anyone else?" Evelyn pressed. "A boyfriend, maybe?"

"I don't know," Kate said again. She sounded upset. "Diana didn't have a lot of close friends. Friends, yes. *Close* friends, who might've known what cases she was investigating, no. I mean, maybe Kim or Becky. She met them through work, but neither was FBI."

"What about a man?"

"I doubt it. Most of Diana's friends were women. She didn't date much, I think because her job got in the way."

That was the excuse Evelyn used, too. Maybe in Diana's case, it had actually been true.

"What about Kim and Becky? Or one of their husbands?"

"Kim's divorced and Diana disliked Becky's husband, so I doubt it."

A dead end. It had to be someone who knew Diana well enough that she could have seen *him* in his crime scenes. Then, something Kate had mentioned in Boston popped into her head. "What about Diana's stray people?"

"Oh, maybe," Kate mused. "She didn't really collect them in Boston the way she did when she was younger, but there were a few. One of them—Freddie—had been in trouble with the law a few times."

Evelyn lifted her pen. "What's his last name?"

"Her," Kate corrected. "It was short for Fredericka. I don't remember her last name, but I can find it if it's important."

"Probably not," Evelyn admitted. "I'm looking for a man who might've known about your sister's cases."

"Oh." There was a pause and just when Evelyn thought Kate was going to tell her she was out of luck, she said, "Well, maybe Harley."

At first it seemed that Kate was just desperate to give her a name, but this one sounded familiar. "Harley?"

"Yeah. He's the one I told you about who we knew growing up. Harley lived next door to us. He was about ten when Diana went to college. But she kept in touch with him. And he moved here. I think it was five years ago now." Wistfulness filled her voice. "That seems so long ago. I can't believe it's been three years since Diana…since she's been gone."

Evelyn wrote down the name. "He still lives in Boston?"

"What? Oh, Harley. No, not anymore. He moved back to Connecticut maybe two years ago, because his father was sick."

Was he still in Connecticut? Or could he be the one she

was looking for? "What can you tell me about Harley? What's his last name?"

"Harley Keegan. When he was a kid, everyone knew he was screwed up, but Diana felt sorry for him. She thought she could help him. See, his family was a mess, too. I guess that's why Harley was the way he was."

"Which is what?" Evelyn asked.

"Well, just weird, really. His mother ran off when Harley was five. Harley didn't remember her very well and his dad got rid of all her pictures. I heard that Harley's dad told him she'd been cheating on him and that she'd left him for her lover, but everyone in town seemed to think she'd taken off to get away from Harley's father."

It must have been a small town. The kind where people liked to know everyone else's business. Her grandparents had lived in one of those. Being half Zimbabwean in a town that was otherwise all white had made her a prime source of interest. And some hostility. Too much hostility for a ten-year-old. Evelyn felt a burst of sympathy for Harley. "Why? What was Harley's dad like?"

"He was a real jerk. That's why I couldn't believe it when Harley said he was going back home to look after him. Diana said Harley's dad beat him and his brother after his mom left because he blamed them for her leaving."

"His brother?"

"Mason. He was a lot older than Harley. And when Harley was ten, Mason went mental."

"How so?" Her investigative instincts clamoring to life, Evelyn scribbled notes rapidly. An absent mother, an abusive father and a mentally ill brother. Definitely a recipe for problems. The question was: Had Harley come out of that situation fantasizing about hurting others?

"I never heard many details. Just that his dad put Mason in one of those state institutions. I believe he's still there."

"Do you know anything else about the abuse?" Serial killers came from all walks of life, but many of them had faced abuse as children. If Harley's father had started abusing him after his mother left, he might have blamed his mother for abandoning him. It was a possible starting point for the kind of hatred of women the BAKBURY killer displayed.

"Not really," Kate said, sounding uncomfortable.

"What else can you tell me about Harley?"

"Um, well, he had small parts in a couple of local shows when we all lived in Connecticut. I saw him a few times when I came home on breaks from college. He was a decent actor, but he was amazing with costume design and makeup. In one of those plays, I saw a friend from school. He'd made her look ten years older and like a man! I had no idea it was her until the show ended. Even Hollywood came calling."

"Really? Did he go?"

"Nah. He wasn't interested. Crazy, isn't it? I would've gone. He said costume design was for women and sissies."

"So, what did he do in Boston? More theater?"

Kate snorted. "Just on the side, as a hobby. He gave up Hollywood to be a security officer at the mall."

Evelyn's clamoring instincts turned into a shrill alarm. "What else can you tell me about him?"

"Well, he told Diana his mom didn't really leave."

"What do you mean?"

"I guess his dad kept his mom's wedding ring. I used to see him wearing it on a chain around his neck sometimes. Maybe she threw it at him when she took off—that's what I would've done. Anyway, maybe because his dad had her ring, Harley thought she hadn't left, that his dad had killed her. He told Diana he used to try to find her."

"How could he find her if he thought she was dead?"

"Harley said his dad buried her in their backyard."

Her mind conjured up images of Mary Ann and Barbara, mutilated and naked, their decaying heads displayed in the dirt.

Kate made a sound that could have been laughter. "I told you he was weird. I guess he tried to dig her up. He never found her, obviously, since the truth is she did just leave. My mom kept in touch with her. The last I heard, she'd moved overseas."

"And she never contacted her children?"

"I guess not."

Pity stabbed briefly through her excitement, but only for Mason. If Harley had turned into a killer, she had no sympathy for him. Maybe for the child he'd once been, but not for the man he'd become. "What else? Was Harley ever married?"

"Yes. He joined the army out of high school, and when he got out, he married a girl from our hometown—Kelly—and moved to Boston with her. She was younger than him, about nineteen when they got married. She was quiet, depressed all the time."

"Because of Harley?"

"No. I remember her growing up. She was always like that."

Evelyn jotted the name Kelly Keegan on her notepad. The BAKBURY killer was socially intelligent and a good profiler himself. Choosing a younger, mentally vulnerable woman as his wife made sense for someone who'd been planning to abduct and kill women and needed a wife to believe any explanations he came up with for suspicious behavior or unusual absences.

When Evelyn was quiet for a minute, Kate added, "But Kelly killed herself."

"What?" The word came out as a screech. "When? Are you sure it was suicide?"

"Um, yeah. It was the year before Diana went missing, so four years ago now."

Four years ago was when Justin Greene had been murdered—for his car. A wife's suicide was a hell of a precipitating stressor for a first kill. Evelyn's pen moved faster.

"Is there anything else you can tell me about him, Kate?"

"Not really. Like I said, he was just weird. If you didn't know him, you might think he was a little creepy. But other than Terry, there was no one more helpful than Harley when Diana disappeared. He even lent me money to go to California when some guy called saying he had information about where Diana might be. But it turned out to be nothing."

"Thank—"

"You don't suspect *Harley,* do you?" Kate interrupted. "Terry and the FBI investigated everyone Diana knew when she went missing. And Harley might've been strange, but he would never have hurt Diana. He adored her."

"Right now, I'm just looking for information," Evelyn lied. Harley might be a dead end, too, but unlike Ed Krup, he fit the profile.

"Okay." The word was filled with disbelief. Before Kate hung up, she added, "But I'm telling you, he had nothing to do with it."

As Evelyn hung up her phone, she debated calling Ron. Harley Keegan was a solid lead. But Ron was still set on Ed Krup as the killer. Would he look into Harley or would he put it off until someone else turned up dead?

It was possible that a single phone call would eliminate Harley. If he was still in Connecticut, he wasn't the killer; if he wasn't there, she'd hand the lead off to Ron.

Before she could make that call, Greg wheeled over to her cubicle. "Want to see the newest addition to the Ibsen household?"

Evelyn grinned. "Let me guess. Another cat?"

"Not this time." He held out a picture. "Lucy brought home a parakeet yesterday."

Evelyn felt a laugh crawl up her throat. Greg's fourteen-year-old daughter periodically sent new pictures to work with him. She was an animal-lover and her father was a sucker for her pleading dark eyes, so if Lucy found an animal that needed a home, it came to the Ibsens'. "How many is that now?"

"Just four. The dog, the cats and now the bird. The real problem is Lucy's discovered boys."

The tension that had been building in Evelyn's chest all morning was released in a whoosh of air at Greg's disgruntled expression. "So, she wants to date now?"

"Oh, no. She's not dating until she's at least eighteen. Maybe thirty."

"Good luck with that."

Greg scooted back to his cubicle and Evelyn walked down the hall to see Walt.

When she approached, he looked at her with his typical expressionless stare, waiting.

"Hi, Walt."

He nodded his greeting. If there was anyone in the office who made her seem social, it was Walt.

"I need you to access the NCIC for me." The National Crime Information Center was the FBI database that contained criminal history. "The name is Harley Keegan. I need to know if he has a criminal record. The Harley Keegan I want was born in Connecticut and would be in his early thirties."

Walt swiveled back to his computer, his short, stubby fingers stabbing frantically at the keyboard. "Nope. Nothing for a Harley Keegan in that age range."

"Thanks." It wasn't surprising. If he was the BAKBURY

killer, he would've had brushes with the law, but not serious ones. Probably nothing to put him in NCIC.

Back in her cubicle, she opened the file on Diana and came up with the name of the town where the Ballards—and Harley Keegan—had grown up. Two minutes later, she was on the phone with Chief Paul Janey, who'd been with the police force there for almost forty years.

She rattled off her job title, then asked, "Can you tell me if Harley Keegan still lives there?" Kate had said he'd moved back few years ago to take care of his father. If the town was as small as Kate had indicated, Paul should know. She drummed her fingertips on her desk in a nervous *thump, thump, thump* she hoped Greg wouldn't hear.

"He left a long time ago."

"Didn't he come home a few years back?"

"If he did, he didn't stay long. Why?"

Evelyn ignored the question. "What about his father? Does he still live there?"

"No, Phil Keegan left a couple of years ago."

"With his son?"

"I couldn't say," Paul said with a meant-to-be-heard sigh. "Is this why you're calling?"

"Actually, I want to know if Harley ever got into trouble with the law when he was younger."

"Juvenile records are sealed, Agent Baine. You know that."

Words jammed in her mouth, reasons for him to tell her, but she didn't need them.

"Foolish idea, I always thought. Especially these days, with kids killing kids, then getting out of juvie with no record. Harley's not one of *those.* But he did come from a pretty ugly situation and I don't think he was completely right in the head."

"So, he was in trouble with the law? He had a record?"

"No. The woman never pressed charges. Harley was sixteen at the time and it was petty burglary. He returned what he'd stolen and the woman felt sorry for him. To tell you the truth, his father probably punished him worse than the law would have."

"His father abused him?" She already knew from Kate that he had, but she wanted Paul's take on it.

There was a long pause. Finally Paul replied in a weary voice, "Did I think Harley and Mason were abused? Yes. Could I prove it? No. Believe me, we gave it a shot, but those kids were terrified of their father after their mother took off. Nowadays, we'd be able to get social workers involved, but back then..."

When Paul didn't continue, Evelyn asked, "Do you remember what Harley stole?"

"I do. The woman was in her front yard. This was a middle-of-the-day burglary. She'd left her doors unlocked, and he just walked right into her house. But all he took was her wedding ring. She'd taken it off to do some gardening."

"A fetish burglary," Evelyn breathed.

She hadn't intended to say it out loud, but Paul heard her. "Fetish? Wouldn't that be more like if he'd stolen her panties?"

"Not if he's who I think he is." Before Paul could ask her more, she quickly thanked him and hung up.

Then she started searching. But half an hour later, she hadn't found any information on Harley Keegan. No titles for anything—not a house, not a car, nothing in the past two years at all. Not even a new driver's license since his Massachusetts license had expired.

Could Harley have gone underground? And if so, why? If he'd waited a year after Diana went missing to disappear, it would effectively thwart suspicion. But it would mean he hadn't been worried about being caught. So why go underground later?

Evelyn frowned. If Harley's dad had left Connecticut a few years ago, maybe Harley had picked him up, taken him somewhere else. After that, maybe he'd moved on to live with some other person who'd provided things like a house and a car. But it seemed unlikely.

She called the Massachusetts DMV. After a brief argument, the clerk promised to email her a copy of Harley's old license.

It took twenty long minutes. When she opened the attachment, Evelyn stared at it. Harley Keegan's driver's license listed him as being six feet and a hundred and ninety-five pounds.

The picture showed an unremarkable man. He had dark brown hair, stringy and dirty, that hung just below his ears. Oval-shaped and evenly proportioned, Harley's face wouldn't stand out in a crowd.

He didn't look familiar.

Until Evelyn peered past the wire-rimmed glasses to his ice-blue eyes. Even in the photo, they were unnerving, and they looked exactly the same as the day he'd abducted her. The oxygen rushed out of her lungs.

Harley Keegan was her abductor.

17

SHE DESERVED TO DIE.

She knelt before him now, her hands and feet bound, swaying from the effect of the drugs, blinking up at him, confused. There was fear in her eyes, but she didn't really know what she was afraid of yet.

"You deserve this," he spat, his fury getting stronger and stronger.

It wasn't a single transgression. Her evil would grow. Maybe one day, she'd have kids. And he knew what would happen to them. Insanity, if they were lucky. His brother had been lucky.

He'd gone the other way. The Bakersville Burier. The moniker the press had given him was ridiculous, but he didn't give a fuck. They helped him spread fear. Maybe fear would make these women reconsider their sins before he had to punish them.

He stepped closer to her, and the ring he wore on a chain around his neck seemed to burn through his skin. It had been his wife's, but she hadn't deserved to take it with her. She should've needed him more than anyone, but she'd left him, just like his mother. So the ring was his now.

He gazed down at Sarah's ring, felt himself snarling, and she whimpered.

"Please," she begged.

She was no one's temptation now. She had blood on her face from when she'd fallen seconds after the dart hit her. Her dress was dirty, wrinkled and smelled of urine; she'd actually wet herself when she'd seen him. Fear oozed from her. But she'd brought it on herself.

He was a vigilante. In his country, they didn't understand, but other cultures knew. Other cultures made these tainted women pay, buried them up to their waists or their necks so there was no escape when they were stoned. They had their trial, their chance to be proven innocent. But if they were guilty, they were punished by their own relatives, their own community. And the price was high. The price was their lives.

As it would be for her.

He couldn't do it exactly the right way, of course. The woods were perfect for the burial, but they were too risky for the kill. It galled him that he couldn't properly emulate what he'd helped them do that one time in Iraq.

But he'd been unwanted there, anyway. Here, he was in charge.

He'd spent considerable effort making sure his cabin was soundproofed, and he carefully lined it with plastic each time. The stones were ready, waiting, and he couldn't help glancing at them now.

He walked through most of his days emotionless, but the thought of punishing her made him feel powerful, excited. He smiled and reached for his belt buckle. "Sorry, Sarah."

Her eyes went wide, her mouth opening and closing without words, and she tried to back up on her knees, but there was nowhere to go.

She was his now.

The urge to kill was in him, anyway, the need to have power over life and death. It always had been. He knew he was different. But he wasn't indiscriminate.

She deserved to die. And she would.

"Evelyn! You have visitors."

Startled by Dan's announcement, Evelyn turned her chair to face him. "What? Who?"

"Ron Harding and his team. They're waiting in the inter-agency coordination room."

"They're *here?*" It was a stupid question, but she had a con-ference call planned with the agents in ten minutes. Why were they at BAU? Could they have found Harley?

She shoved out of her seat, sending the chair wheeling backward into her desk with a thud and raced down the hall.

The case agents all looked up from their gas station coffee when she opened the door with enough force to dent the wall.

Ron glanced from her to the wall and back again. "Evelyn." He tilted his head with a "what's wrong with you?" expres-sion. "We were on our way back from Bakersville and figured we'd just do the meeting here."

Evelyn's lungs instantly deflated.

Ron shrugged. "I've never been to the BAU offices. I ex-pected to see more pictures of serial killers."

Seriously? He thought BAU agents put pictures of violent killers on the walls and stared at them all day? "Why were you in Bakersville?"

"Going over leads from tips and those pictures you had us release to the public," Jimmy said, giving her his typically wide smile.

"Did you get anything useful?" She'd called Ron immediately after seeing Harley's picture, suggesting he release it to the public in Bakersville. They'd even had the photos altered to show what a good makeup artist could do to hide identity.

"No. But we did set the cops straight on their role," Cory replied as he stepped into her personal space and shook her hand with slightly too much force.

Evelyn winced—both at the rough handshake and the idea that the agents were pissing the cops off even more—and nodded.

She was disappointed but not surprised. To have a background in stage makeup and costuming and not use it would've been plain stupid. And even if Harley Keegan's records hadn't included ridiculously high IQ tests, she knew he wasn't stupid.

"Hi, Evelyn." Miles greeted her from his perch at the conference table. He had a notebook and pen already out and his face was its usual shade of just-ripened tomato.

Before she could return the greeting, Jimmy told her, "Now that we're pretty sure Diana Ballard's connected, we have an interesting coincidence."

Evelyn turned her gaze his way.

Jimmy's chest seemed to inflate at her attention. "Cory met Diana."

"What?" Shocked, she gaped at Cory.

Cory's features hardened. "I worked in the Boston field office before transferring to D.C." His tone warned her not to make anything of it.

But Evelyn hadn't succeeded at the Bureau by letting anyone push her around. "When did you transfer here?"

"About three years ago," he bit out in an "it's none of your business" tone.

"Right when Diana went missing?" Her voice sounded

higher than she would have liked, but none of the other agents looked as though Cory's announcement was news to them.

"A few months before." The edge in Cory's voice reminded Evelyn of talking to Dan.

"Why did you move away?"

"Why does it matter?" Ron broke in, joining Miles at the conference table. "Let's get started."

"Why?" Evelyn asked again.

Cory's eyes narrowed; he seemed to be debating whether to answer or tell her to go to hell. Finally, he shrugged and said, "The Bureau sent me to D.C. on a ninety-day TDY for a case that ended up lasting two years." TDY was Bureau-speak for *temporary duty*. "After that, my supervisor fixed it so I could stay. Which worked out for me, because by then, my divorce was finalized and my ex-wife got the house."

"Where did you meet Diana?"

Cory let out a long sigh and sat down next to Miles. "At the office. I worked counterintelligence, so we never actually worked together. But when she went missing, it was big news, even here. I bet you remember the stories."

She did, which was part of the reason she couldn't believe Cory had never mentioned it.

"It's not important," Ron snapped. "Let's talk about Harley Keegan."

"Good idea," Cory muttered.

Ron hit some keys on his laptop. "Evelyn and I have been looking into Harley Keegan's past since she got his name yesterday. We haven't been able to locate Harley's father, but I found his older brother. Mason Keegan has been in an institution in Connecticut since he was seventeen. He's been diagnosed with a multitude of disorders. We sent an agent in Connecticut to speak with him and he got back to me about an hour ago. That lead is useless. Mason's barely aware of his own surroundings, let alone his brother's whereabouts. The agent said all Mason wanted to do was talk about the past."

Evelyn's head jerked up. "What did he say about it?"

Ron frowned at his notes. "Mostly he babbled about his father. The agent couldn't understand a lot of it, but he got the impression that the father made Harley and Mason beat each other with belts."

"What?" Miles's eyes widened.

"Mason is institutionalized, remember, so who knows if this is reality or fantasy? But he claimed their father gave them a choice—hit each other or be hit by him. He said the father promised they wouldn't have to be punished anymore when they started behaving well enough for their mother to leave her lover and come home."

"No wonder Harley has a mother complex," Cory mumbled under his breath.

"And why Mason's in an institution," Miles added. "You'd have to shut down emotionally to beat up your own brother or watch your father beat him."

"When did Mason last see Harley?" Jimmy asked.

"According to the state facility where Mason lives, Harley and his father last signed in for a visit thirteen years ago. Not long after, Harley moved to Washington, D.C., and worked part-time as a cashier at a convenience store. He spent most of his free time working on local shows, again winning accolades from the community for his talent with makeup and costumes. He was even written up in the local papers, there and, later, in Boston."

Ron held up one of those papers, a five-year-old copy of the Boston *Globe*. And there was Harley Keegan, bearded and unsmiling in a small photo in one corner. The other pictures were his work.

Evelyn reached for the paper and looked more closely. Kate

hadn't been kidding. There were elves and fairies in the picture above him that hardly looked human.

Suddenly she was terrified that he was too good. That they'd never find him.

She sat up straighter, pushed the fear back and handed Miles the paper.

"Wow." Miles jotted something in his notebook.

"No wonder no one came forward after we released the pictures," Jimmy said.

"Why? Because he knows how to dress like an elf?" Cory snorted. "Maybe he's just not here."

Ignoring Cory, Evelyn said, "Maybe he's using less charm than I originally thought in his abductions."

An image of the elderly man leaning heavily on his cane at the Bakersville police station floated through her mind. Years of investigating serial crimes had taught Evelyn that plenty of insecure criminals preyed on the elderly, because they were viewed as easy victims. Maybe Harley had turned the idea on its head.

"Instead of putting these women at ease by feigning an injury or laying on the charm, he might be using his talent with disguises to make himself look like an old man," she said slowly. "A woman with a flat tire probably wouldn't think twice about accepting a ride from an eighty-year-old."

"Should we warn the women in Bakersville to beware of old men in wheelchairs?" Jimmy joked.

Ron didn't lift his head, but his pupils darted up, his annoyed gaze locking on Jimmy. "Apparently, while he was in D.C., Harley had been writing to his future wife, Kelly. He kept writing her when he joined the army."

"He was in the army?" Miles shot a look at her.

"For two years, before he was discharged. We got his file, but it just mentions that he had problems following orders.

Some of the details on his discharge are a little vague. I'm waiting for a callback from his superior there."

Jimmy made an appreciative noise in the back of his throat. "It sounds like Evelyn's hypothesis on the UNSUB was right on the money."

He flashed his ultrawhite teeth at her, as if he would earn points for referring to her professional profile as a *hypothesis*.

"How about we stay away from the guesswork and focus on what we actually know?" Cory suggested.

Insulted, Evelyn frowned at him, but Cory didn't look hostile. In fact, he was aiming the jibe at Jimmy, not her. Either he didn't realize calling her profile *guesswork* was offensive or he was sneaky with his insults. She suspected the latter. When Cory's eyes darted her way and his lips stretched just a millimeter, she was sure of it.

Annoyance at the belittling of her profile turned into anger at his childish response. "You're an only child, Cory."

He jerked back slightly. "Excuse me?"

"You have an old-fashioned father, also military, and your mother didn't work outside the home."

He thrust out his jaw. "Have you read my personnel file?"

She forced a tight smile. "No. It's my *guesswork*."

He stared at her and Jimmy's eyes widened. Miles glanced back and forth between her and Cory as though he was waiting for Cory to dispute her conclusions.

But she was right. The one positive thing about not having a life outside the office was that she was damn good at her job.

And this trick—spouting off details of someone's life that were easy to figure out from his behavior—had worked before on agents who didn't believe in profiling.

As Cory scowled at her, Ron said, "Let's get back on track." He resumed looking at his computer. "Harley married Kelly after he got out of the army and both of them moved to Boston, possibly to be near Diana. In Boston, Harley trained to be a police officer, but he was eventually denied a position. Instead, he worked as a security guard. Work records show him quitting about a year after Diana went missing, which is also when he left town, at least as far as we know. There's no information on him from that point forward."

"That's fishy." Miles stated the obvious.

Ron closed his folder. He lifted his hand and pointed at her.

Evelyn took that as her cue to give the agents a different timeline—of Harley's possible progression to a serial killer.

"When Harley was twenty-seven, his wife killed herself. Shortly after that, I believe Harley killed Justin Greene and stole his vehicle. He's been using that vehicle ever since. Well, until I crashed it." When Jimmy and Miles laughed, she managed a self-deprecating smile.

"You're saying his wife's death was the stressor?" Miles asked.

"Yes. And he must've known Justin's car wouldn't be reported stolen."

"How?" Cory demanded.

"Maybe Justin hadn't planned to return it and told this hitchhiker—Harley—that his grandfather would never report him or that he wouldn't remember lending it to him. The reason I say that is because I have to believe this was a murder of opportunity."

"Why?" Jimmy asked. "I thought you said the serial killer would've been dreaming about committing murder for a long time."

Evelyn fought back frustration. If everyone at the Bureau understood profiling, she'd be out of a job. "Yes, the killer had been fantasizing about murder, but it was the type of sexually based murders we're seeing in Bakersville, not murdering a teenager for his car. But then this kid comes along with a car he says will never be missed and a lightbulb goes off for Harley. It was an opportunity and he took it."

"And then what?"

Evelyn wondered if Jimmy's excitement was feigned for her benefit. "It was his first murder. He was afraid of getting caught. But he got away with it, which gave him the courage to go after what he really wanted. So, he started trolling for victims—the sort of victims he'd fantasized about. He found Debra Chin and Angela Mason."

"And then Diana Ballard," Jimmy inserted, giving her the quick grin that seemed to be his default flirting expression.

He needs to take lessons from Kyle McKenzie. Evelyn shook off the errant thought and leaned back, trying to focus. "Right. And he didn't even have to charm her into going with him. She knew him, so she probably just invited him into her house."

"And then what, she hopped into the trunk of his car?" Cory scoffed.

Evelyn ignored him. "He could have knocked her out after she let him in, maybe as soon as she turned her back to shut the door."

"And then he carried her out to the trunk?" Miles asked skeptically. "Wouldn't it have been easier to convince her to get in his car and then knock her out once he got to wherever he killed his other victims?"

"Except he felt guilty about Diana." Evelyn realized it had to be true as soon as she said it. "I don't think he raped her. Not only did she not fit his requirements, he knew her personally. They were friends and she'd always watched out for him. He probably didn't want to look at her, because then he'd feel even guiltier. So he knocked her out and stuffed her in the trunk right away."

"And she was rolling around in the trunk and her print

happened to hit the one place where wiping down the car wouldn't make a difference," Miles said, his voice curious.

"That wasn't chance." Evelyn imagined the victim regaining consciousness and finding herself locked in a trunk. After the initial flood of panic, she'd felt around for anything to use as a weapon when the chance came, but found nothing. Then her fingers grazed a patch of wet caulk that had been used to fill the hole that went all the way through from the outside. She'd pressed her print into it, knowing it would connect her to Harley, even after death. Except in Diana's place, she saw herself.

A shudder racked her so hard Ron sent her a questioning look.

She forced the image out of her mind. "Harley hadn't originally intended or even wanted to kill Diana. He did it out of fear. Maybe he discovered she was on the CAPEKIL case and thought that because she knew him, she'd connect the murders to him. Or maybe he realized there was something at the crime scene that would incriminate him—and she'd eventually figure it out. I don't know and Diana can't tell us. Whatever the case, it would explain why Diana doesn't fit the normal victim profile."

"Which is what?" Cory asked. "Just being a married woman?"

"That's vital to him, so yes, it's the main reason I say she doesn't fit. Kate said Harley didn't remember his mother well, because she left when he was young. But his obsession with wedding rings is obviously connected to his mother leaving and his father keeping her ring. Based on that, it's probable that Harley is looking for more than just a woman with a ring on her left hand. He could also be picking them because of some element they share with what he remembers of his mother."

Miles glanced up from his rapidly filling notepad. "Like what? Someone who smiles like his mom or has her eye color?"

"Given the victims we've seen, we know it's not eye color," Evelyn answered, "but it could be a smile." She shrugged. "It could be any resemblance, from how she walks to how she talks to strangers. But he sees *something* in them that reminds him of his mother."

Miles nodded and went back to his copious note taking.

"The connection to his mother also explains his choice in drop sites. He believed his father buried his mother in their backyard—a large wooded lot—and that's what he's doing with his victims. Harris's property is ideal not just because the bodies wouldn't be found quickly, but also because he's playing out the scenario that supposedly happened with his mother."

"What about the circles?" Miles asked. "What's with the mutilation?" His gaze darted from Evelyn to Ron, as though he wasn't sure whom he should be asking.

Evelyn leaned toward him. "Kate Ballard told me Harley's father started wearing his mother's wedding ring on a chain around his neck after she left. My guess is it's connected to that image. He's essentially punishing his mother over and over again for leaving them. For abandoning him and his brother. He—"

"I thought you said Harley believes his father killed her?" Ron interrupted.

"Yes, he does. But he still blames her. His father told Harley she left him for her lover. What exactly he thinks the sequence of events is, if he thinks she never really left or if he believes his father tracked her down to kill her, I don't know. But he blames her. He thinks his father had to kill her because she betrayed him."

"Okay. How do the displayed heads fit in?" Jimmy interjected.

Frustration nipped at her. She shook her head. "I don't know that, either."

"What about the recent murders?" Cory asked, sounding unconcerned about Harley's psychology. "What happened between the time he killed Diana and he started stalking Mary Ann Pollak? Did he just stop killing for three years?"

Was he actually interested in her opinion? "Well, Diana's murder got national attention. It's possible he tried to lie low for a while. But I'd bet he's killed between Boston and here. Where, we may never know. Nothing promising came up when we ran the M.O. and signature through ViCAP—"

The ringing of Ron's government-issued BlackBerry cut her off. Ron frowned, but as soon as he looked at the readout, he sat straighter and answered it. "Special Agent Ron Harding. Thanks for returning my call, sir."

Could it be Harley's superior in the army? "Speakerphone," Evelyn whispered.

Ron frowned at her, but did it.

"You wanted to know about Harley Keegan?" a voice boomed.

"Anything you can tell us that wouldn't be in the file the army sent over," Ron said.

The silence stretched out until Evelyn started feeling jittery. Leaning closer to Ron's phone, she said, "Special Agent Evelyn Baine. Can you tell me about Harley's behavioral problems? He was dishonorably discharged?"

Ron scowled at her, but the lieutenant colonel answered, "Yes, ma'am. He had a problem following orders."

"Can you be more specific?"

"It's in his file. He'd refuse orders. Discipline didn't fix it, and we don't need that kind of problem in a firefight, especially in a country as volatile as Iraq."

"Any problems with women in the unit?" she asked.

"No women in Harley's unit then. But…"

"What?"

He made a sound that might have been a sigh, might have been a snarl. "There was a rumor. I can't confirm it and the officers who reported it retracted it the next day, claimed they'd made it up."

"You suspect Harley convinced them to cover for him?"

"Wouldn't surprise me. He was a manipulative son of a bitch. Couldn't get the locals to confirm, either, but shit, if it was true, what's more surprising is that they didn't kill him."

"What happened?" Ron asked.

"*Might have happened.* There was a rumor Harley tried to participate in the stoning of a woman who'd been found guilty of adultery."

Realization jolted through Evelyn. The bruises the medical examiner hadn't been able to identify on the bodies. They'd been from stones. "It happened."

Everyone's eyes locked on her, but no one said anything until the lieutenant colonel asked, "Any other questions?"

Ron raised an eyebrow and, when she shook her head, said, "No. Thank you."

"He stoned them," she said as soon as Ron hung up. "It explains the bruising. It even explains the burial style, although Harley is changing the order. He stones them to death *first,* and then buries them up to their heads."

"How does it explain the burial?" Miles asked, looking confused.

"The cultures that still participate in stoning as a punishment for adultery often bury the woman up to her waist or head first."

Miles's lips puckered with distaste. "But why would Harley do that?"

"Just like the circles he's carving on his victims, it ties back to the fact that he thought his mother cheated on his father. Harley's picking women that he's decided need to be punished."

"Only one of the victims was cheating on her husband," Ron said.

"But there were rumors about one of the Boston victims. It doesn't matter if they're true. He's decided they are. He's using it as an excuse to kill."

This was it; this was the thing that compelled him to search for victims. He wanted someone to punish.

"Well, what about you?" Cory asked, his eyes shifting to hers. "You said he abducted you because he thought you were married and, presumably, cheating. But doesn't it make more sense that he saw you working with the Bakersville cops and grabbed you for the same reason he grabbed Diana? It would explain why he drugged you, wouldn't it?"

Cory's questions felt like a challenge. Before she could rise to it, Miles asked, "How did he even know what drugs to use?"

"I can answer that," Ron cut in. "The agents in Connecticut dug into the Keegan family history. They learned that besides being a head case, Mason also struggled with alcoholism and addiction. He was in and out of rehab before being committed. At different points in his life, two of the drugs Mason was on were Librium—the brand name of chlordiazepoxide—and buprenorphine. The Librium was an attempt to treat his bipolar disorder and the buprenorphine was because he got hooked on heroin."

"So, Harley could have gotten those drugs from his brother's prescriptions?" Miles asked, scribbling furiously.

"No. Mason was on those drugs more than twenty years ago and they were controlled substances, so they were administered in a hospital. It's probably where he learned about them, though."

"Then where did he get them?" Miles persisted.

Ron shrugged. "Probably on the street. Or he found a doctor willing to prescribe anything for the right price."

"And there's no reason he'd use them on Evelyn unless he knew she was FBI," Cory insisted.

She started to argue, but Ron held up a hand as his Black-Berry rang again.

While Ron talked on the phone, Cory stared at her with an expression that told her he wouldn't back down.

Well, neither would she.

"Shit!" Ron jumped up, knocking his chair to the floor. He had the look of a bloodhound on the scent of something good.

Could it be about Harley again?

Ron turned off his cell phone and shoved the chair out of his way, instead of picking it up. "Let's go!"

"What?" Miles frantically gathered his belongings. Jimmy and Cory were a little slower getting to their feet.

"That was Tanner Caulfield. We have to get back to Bakersville *now*."

Evelyn swayed in her seat as queasiness hit hard. "Why?"

Ron glanced back from the door. "They think there's another victim."

18

EVELYN RAN HER THIRD RED LIGHT AND SPED
onto the freeway. She called Tanner while waiting for an opportunity to pass the tractor trailer in front of her.

"Tanner Caulfield."

"It's Evelyn Baine. You just talked to Ron Harding about
the location of a possible body or a suspicious person." Her
words tumbled over one another as her anxiety increased. The
longer it took to get to the crime scene, the longer the killer
had to get away. "Can you tell me where to go?"

"I thought you were off this case, Agent Baine."

"No. I'm still consulting as the criminal investigative analyst."

The hell with Ron, telling her the crime scene wasn't her
concern and racing off without her. The hell with the rest
of them, for following him even as she'd tried to chase them
down the hall.

When they were talking about the man who'd abducted
and nearly killed her, she didn't give a damn about protocol.

It was her responsibility as much as theirs—no, more than theirs—to make sure he was locked up.

"Oh." Tanner sounded as if he didn't believe her, but said, "Harris reported a suspicious character on his property. Normally, we wouldn't be too concerned. Harris calls all the time to tell us *someone* is trespassing, even if they just put a foot on his lawn. But considering recent events and the fact that he said this guy was carrying something big, I decided we'd better call Ron."

Evelyn finally had an opening to get over and punched down on her accelerator. "Do you know where Harris saw this person?"

"I don't. He wasn't too specific. And the officer who took the call couldn't get any more detail. He was too busy trying to convince Harris not to go after the trespasser himself with a shotgun."

Dammit. So, during her search for the serial killer who'd already gotten the upper hand against her once, she'd have to worry about an overzealous landowner shooting her in the back.

"You might want to watch out for him," Tanner added. "He's not a half-bad shot."

"Get an officer—" Evelyn started, but the click of Tanner hanging up cut her off.

"Shit!" she hissed, weaving around the car that was keeping her at eighty-five miles an hour and then punching the accelerator again.

As her exit came into sight, she flipped her blinker, then raced across all four lanes and onto the exit ramp. The blare of horns followed.

She sped into Bakersville. Bypassing Harris's driveway at a speed that was probably dangerous, she slowed for the unmarked, unpaved road Tanner had taken her to that first day in

Bakersville. Swinging onto it, she slowed even more, watching for the trail into Harris's woods.

Calling Jimmy—her best bet for information—Evelyn maneuvered her Bucar onto the trail at the fastest speed she dared, which was barely thirty miles an hour. The car bounced along the uneven ground with teeth-chattering intensity. Her call went to voice mail.

Up ahead, she saw Ron's Ford Explorer and parked next to it, looking around. No other vehicles. Was the killer already gone?

The trill of her BlackBerry made her grab for it. "Hello?"

"Evelyn?" Jimmy's voice was so low she could hardly hear him.

"Jimmy, I just parked next to Ron's car. Where are you?"

There was a pause, maybe while Jimmy marveled that she'd disobeyed his partner's orders. And Ron had certainly made it sound like an order when he'd barked, "Stay here!" at her in the office.

"We're on Harris's property. We haven't spotted the killer, but he's here."

Evelyn's breath seemed to catch in her lungs. "Are you sure?"

"Well, there's a body."

Another victim. Could she have prevented this? If she'd been able to subdue him that night, instead of running away...

Jimmy interrupted her thoughts. "I have to go. Ron says to stay where you are."

Tension spiraled through her as Jimmy hung up. Forget that! She pulled her replacement weapon from her holster, stepped out of her LaCrosse and hunched down near the front tire of Ron's vehicle to scan the area.

Just like the last time she'd been here, all she saw were evergreens, hickory and oak trees stretching high and vying for sunlight. A few resilient weeds and flowers sprouted below, but mostly the ground was carpeted by dead leaves that should reveal footsteps. All she heard were birds chirping and a squirrel scurrying from one tree to another. And the roar of her heartbeat thudding in her ears.

Was the killer still here or were they too late?

Unease left goose bumps on her skin, made her nerve endings tingle. If he *was* still here, was he close?

She swiveled her head to check behind her in a panic, losing her balance and catching her weight with her free hand. There was no one behind her. *Get a grip, Evelyn.*

Where was he? If he was still in the woods, he hadn't come this way, because there was no other vehicle. Tanner had said this was the closest trail, but he hadn't said it was the *only* trail.

She reached for her cell phone to call him, but then put it away. The killer had her weapon. If he heard her, there was too good a chance he'd be armed. She'd have to figure it out herself.

From a distance, off to her right, twigs snapped and undergrowth rustled. It could've been a deer, but there was an equal chance that the sound was made by a man. Her Glock ready, Evelyn crept in that direction.

Heart racing as if she'd run here instead of driving, Evelyn wished for the training Kyle had. HRT agents learned how to be invisible, something she could really use at the moment.

A hundred feet from her car, she saw a flash of dark blue in a distinctly human shape. Sucking in a breath, Evelyn pressed herself against the sturdy oak beside her and carefully peered around it, her finger tense against the trigger of her Glock. As she tried to shrink into the tree in her cream pinstriped suit—in retrospect, a horrible choice—the person reappeared on the other side of the evergreen he'd just passed.

Evelyn lowered her weapon and let out a shuddering breath.

It was Ron, followed by Jimmy, walking closely enough to be his shadow. Evelyn started to head toward them, but changed her mind. Ron was already annoyed with her. And the idea of becoming Jimmy's shadow made a lump of distaste rise in her throat.

When they were out of sight, Evelyn considered which direction to take. Toward the spot where the other bodies had been found—which was likely the site of the new victim—didn't make sense. The killer was probably fleeing *from* that direction. But where, then?

Unless the killer was one of Harris's neighbors, and that was doubtful since they'd all been checked out, he had to have a vehicle nearby. Which meant there had to be another trail.

The most likely place for a trail no one knew about was farther down the same unmarked road that forked from the trail where she'd parked. Evelyn turned and began walking parallel to the unmarked road.

In her cream-colored suit she was an all-too-visible target, so she kept close to the trees. The tree roots were a liability with her heels, but she couldn't afford to watch the ground when she needed to be watching for an armed killer.

The rustling of dead leaves made her sink against the nearest tree. She held her breath, straining to hear. Scanning the area ahead of her didn't reveal anyone, but then came the crunch of more dead leaves.

And again. The distinctive beat of walking. It sounded like two legs, not four.

Evelyn stepped away from the tree, longing for someone at her back in case she was tracking an FBI agent instead of the killer, who could be anywhere. The steps ahead of her were faster than hers, the stride probably longer, so Evelyn increased her pace. It was a risk. The faster she walked, the more noise she made, and the more chance he'd hear her. But she had no choice, or she'd never catch up.

As hard as she peered into the thick woods, she couldn't see anyone. She had to pause periodically to listen for his steps. If she got careless, he might hear her, veer off course and flank her.

But every time she paused, he sounded farther away, like he was increasing his own pace, and she couldn't match his stride. Forcing herself to adopt the breathing she used when she ran—in through her nose, out through her mouth in long, controlled breaths—Evelyn quickened her pace to a near-jog. Every dozen steps, she stopped and listened.

Her heartbeat still roared in her ears, not from exertion, but fear of facing her abductor. That made it hard to hear anything else, but the snap of another twig told her he was still in front of her and she was finally gaining!

Leaping away from another oak tree, Evelyn started jogging again. Shock pulsed through her as she caught sight of someone in the distance—just before he disappeared around a thick evergreen. She sucked in a sharp breath and stumbled on something in her path.

Righting herself before she hit the ground, Evelyn ducked behind the nearest tree and listened. Nothing. *Shit.* He must have heard her. And if he hadn't called out, she had to assume it was the killer, and not another agent. He was probably listening for *her,* maybe trying to get a bead on her with her own weapon.

Afraid to breathe, Evelyn adjusted her grip on the Glock, cursing at the sweat she couldn't afford to wipe from the palms of her hands. She pressed tighter against the scraggly pine, which must have been the thinnest trunk in the whole forest. Rough bark dug into her back; she hardly noticed because of the pain radiating from ribs she'd thought were finally healing.

Evelyn arched forward, darting a careful glance around the poor shield of the pine tree. *Show yourself, dammit.* She felt like shouting it, running out into the forest screaming and shooting.

Sweat slicked her forehead, and she heard her own out-of-control breathing. He had to be close. But she didn't see a single spot of color that didn't blend with the greens and browns of the forest. No movement anywhere. *Nothing!*

She evened out her breathing, calmed her raging anger, and tried to think like the killer. He'd planned to be in the woods today. He'd be dressed to blend in. And he had military training, which meant he knew how to move without attracting attention. It was a lot of advantages.

But she had the best advantage of all. This time, she wasn't the hunted. He was.

The longer he stayed in the woods, the higher the chances one of the agents would find his vehicle. He needed to get back to it or he'd risk losing his getaway. Since she'd crashed his last car, this one had to be new. Whether purchased with his current identity or stolen, there would be a trail. Maybe even fingerprints if they got to the car before he did. Fibers. Something. There had to be.

So, she could wait him out as long as it took, but he needed to move. On that reasoning, Evelyn stayed plastered against the tree, straining for any glimpse of activity.

It felt like an hour, with her veins pumping blood too fast and her breath catching at every imagined sound, but finally she heard him. It was a tiny rustling at first, hesitant, as though he wasn't sure if there was someone behind him or it had been his imagination. Then a figure appeared, bent low as he darted from one tree to the next.

And it was definitely a *he*. Someone muscular and fit. He was dressed in brown, with dark hair. That was all she could tell as she dashed from her own hiding spot, trying to close the distance between them.

She knew there was a chance she wasn't chasing the killer at all, but Cory. He, too, was dark-haired, wearing a brown suit a bit too snug on his wide shoulders. But she'd worry about the potential embarrassment of chasing another agent later, after she caught up to him.

She raced through the rustling leaves, a heel occasionally sinking just enough to make her lose momentum. He was going faster, too, either because he knew she was behind him or in desperation to get out.

Not going to happen, Evelyn vowed. Suddenly her left foot, just lifting off the ground, slammed into a thick tree root her right foot had cleared. Her left hand, not burdened with her weapon, flew out automatically to catch herself, but the damage was done. He'd definitely heard her.

She straightened just as a rush of air whizzed over her scalp. Then the loud report of a bullet rang out, its supersonic nature preventing it from sounding a warning in time had the shooter aimed better.

Evelyn jumped to the right, pressing herself against the nearest tree, an evergreen with needles that poked through her suit into her skin. She touched her head to be sure it was only air she'd felt. It came back clean. No blood.

No question she was chasing the killer—since he was shooting at her.

Another bullet sailed past, probably imbedding itself in one of the trees behind her. Footsteps pounded away from her, the killer fleeing fast, no longer trying to be quiet.

Evelyn dragged in heavy breaths, checking the back of her head for blood. *Move,* she screamed to herself, but she felt paralyzed, remembering the last time she'd gone up against this killer.

There was a loud thud from behind her, somewhere to the left, and Jimmy yelled, "Who's shooting?"

His voice shook her out of her stupor and she pushed herself away from the tree, panting, her ribs throbbing, warning her something wasn't right. She tried to yell a response as she took off, but what came out was a breathless, "Over here," she doubted anyone would've heard.

The killer disappeared behind a thick wall of pine trees and Evelyn stretched out her strides. Intense pain ripped through her abdomen, racing up to her lungs, but she didn't slow.

He was still faster. She caught sight of him periodically through the trees as he outpaced her, little by little increasing the distance between them. She wanted to use her Glock, but knew she couldn't hit him while running. And if she stopped, she'd lose him.

Then she saw it. Directly ahead and well-concealed behind a group of trees was a dark green vehicle. The killer's getaway.

Too soon, he reached it. He ducked down next to the door as he opened it, minimizing the target he'd make, but Evelyn had to try.

She jerked to a stop, kneeling down and cradling her gun hand with her left one, trying to steady it. Sighting on the back of his head as he stepped up into the vehicle, she squeezed the trigger.

The door slammed shut. She'd missed him. *Shit!*

Her hands shook, and she tried to still them. She aimed at him through the side window and squeezed off another shot. The window shattered, but the truck thundered to life, so if her shot had hit him, it hadn't done enough damage.

She'd probably only get one more try before he was gone. She took a deep, shuddering breath, wasted precious seconds steadying her aim, lining up perfectly with his brain stem. This was it.

Another shot rang out from her left, way too close.

Instinct made her flatten against the ground, then her training kicked in and she recognized the sound. It had come from a shotgun, not a pistol.

It had to be Harris. "FBI!" Evelyn yelled. "Don't shoot!"

The truck was already squealing to life, spitting a cloud of dirt as it spun away from her.

Desperately, Evelyn pushed to her knees and tried to line up another shot. But she didn't have one. Not anymore. The truck was gone.

The loud crack of the shotgun came two more times, even though there was nothing left to shoot.

Bracing an unsteady hand in the dirt, Evelyn pushed to her feet. Her ribs throbbed with an intensity that darkened her vision, but she blinked and steadied herself on the nearest tree. "Stop shooting now, sir, and stand up so I can see you! I'm with the FBI!" Her voice sounded ragged.

From slightly closer than she'd expected, the old man climbed clumsily to his feet. He looked as if he'd have a hard time walking out of the woods by himself, but he held the shotgun like a man used to weapons.

"That's some damn poor aim you have, young lady," he grumbled.

Then Cory burst into the clearing beside them, from the opposite direction Jimmy had called. His face and clothing were damp with perspiration. "Where is he?"

"Gone," Harris volunteered bitterly.

Evelyn squinted behind Cory, then back at him. "Where's everyone else?"

Cory lowered his weapon. "I outran them." He grabbed the shotgun out of Harris's hands. "Stay here." He turned back to Evelyn. "Which way did he go?"

"He's gone," Evelyn agreed. "He got into a vehicle. We won't catch up to him now."

"Not if we don't try!"

Evelyn flinched at his anger and then Miles appeared from the opposite direction.

"Where did you come from?" she asked him.

"Back there." Miles gestured vaguely behind him. "We lost the bastard?"

"We lost him," Cory confirmed, eyes narrowed as he glanced at her.

"What happened to you?" Miles asked his partner.

"I thought I heard the killer." Cory shrugged. "Sorry. Didn't mean to lose you."

Miles nodded and then Ron and Jimmy arrived. Ron was panting, a sheen of perspiration in the lines of his face. Jimmy's perfectly pressed suit was wrinkled and dirty.

"What the hell happened?" Ron demanded. "I heard gunshots. A lot of them." He looked pointedly at the shotgun in Cory's hand and then at the old man slumped against the base of the nearest tree.

"The killer shot at me," Evelyn explained, trying to pitch her voice above her pain. "I returned fire and Mr. Harris also fired at the killer as he got into his vehicle." She gestured to the small clearing ahead that led to a barely visible trail. "He was parked over there."

"Fuck!" Ron blurted. "Did you get a license plate?"

When she shook her head, he turned to Harris. "Sir, while we appreciate you trying to protect Agent Baine, you can't just go around shooting at people."

Evelyn bristled, but kept quiet as Ron turned back to her. "You'd better go and have a doctor look at you."

Evelyn stared at him, baffled, until she realized she'd

wrapped her left arm protectively around her ribs and hunched forward to ease the pain.

She dropped her arm to her side, trying not to flinch as she uncurled her body. "I'm fine," she insisted in a voice that proved her a liar. "We might as well go look at the body."

Ron studied her for a moment, then shook his head. "Go see a doctor. You don't need to be at the crime scene, anyway. It's a case agent's job." He nodded at Miles. "Help her back to her car." He looked at Evelyn "We'll handle the body and call you with an update."

Embarrassment heated her cheeks and she was about to protest when pain so strong she thought she might pass out sliced through her ribs. So she swallowed her shame at letting the killer get away and started slowly back to her car, Miles on her heels.

Nausea churned with every step, but she didn't think her reinjured ribs were causing it. Her pursuit of the killer, and her escape from him, would have left him enraged, determined to be back in control. Whoever this victim was, she probably wouldn't have eliminated that rage. The BAKBURY killer had to be deteriorating. Which meant no cooling-off period. He'd want another victim. And soon.

19

AS SOON AS SHE WALKED INTO THE BAKERSVILLE police station conference room the next day, Ron gestured to his open laptop. "The latest victims."

Victims? There'd been more than one?

She looked at the four case agents, plus Tanner, crowded around the conference table. Tanner seemed petulant, probably because he'd been reduced to following the FBI's lead. Miles had his pen ready and was watching her with anticipation, as though she'd be able to give them more profiling details just from standing near the case file. Ron, Jimmy and Cory were watching her as if she might need a doctor at any second.

Evelyn sank into the sole empty chair, careful of her bandaged ribs, and started up her laptop. She was pretty sure the invitation to today's meeting had been coerced—by Dan. Oddly, he'd applied pressure to get her invited. Even though he wasn't too happy with her, especially since she'd forgotten about the report he'd asked her to prepare for the new ADIC. He'd had to get another agent to rush something right before his meeting.

But Dan knew her involvement was necessary. With Tanner getting ready to go on the national news tomorrow to answer questions about the BAKBURY killer, they needed her. Ron hadn't wanted an FBI media rep to stand with Tanner and field the trickier questions, no doubt because there was nothing good to say. The killer was still out there, trolling for more victims.

There was a fine line between reassuring terrified members of the public that they were safe in their own town and scaring the killer into running across the country and starting up somewhere else. There was an even finer line between scaring the killer off and prompting him to prove himself with more murders. She was here to tell Tanner how to walk that line.

Time to get to it. Her hand, poised to open the new file in her email, froze. She dreaded seeing what had been done to the latest victim.

She clenched her jaw and opened it, anyway. The crime scene photo was the first attachment.

In life, Sarah Murphy had been too emaciated to be called pretty. In death, she was hideous. Pain and terror had etched themselves onto her face so clearly she'd died with them.

Like the other victims, she was nude, but the deep circle carved into her chest was smeared with coagulated blood and dark residue circled her ankles and wrists. Round bruises covered almost every inch of her skin. A small rectangular object rested on her stomach. Evelyn peered more closely, trying to identify it.

"Driver's license," Ron said.

"Whose?"

"Carla Bridgemoor's."

Regret slammed into her. "The woman who went missing right before I was called on to the case," Evelyn remembered. "Did you find her body?"

"No. But this has to be a message that he killed her, too."

"It is." She closed the photo with Sarah Murphy's lifeless stare and opened the report that had come with it.

Before she could read it, Tanner gave her the highlights. "She was thirty-eight, married. We know she stopped at an ATM just after 11:00 p.m. Her car was found around the corner three hours later, after her husband called police, worried because she hadn't come home. There was no sign of a struggle at the ATM or near her car."

"Which isn't surprising," Ron broke in. "He drugged Sarah with the same drugs he used on you, only more."

"More?" Evelyn glanced back at Sarah's personal information in the file. She'd been struggling with anorexia and hadn't even weighed a hundred pounds.

"The autopsy said she wasn't killed until close to when we found her, thanks to that call from Harris. That was almost twenty-four hours after she was abducted." Miles spoke up, still watching her expectantly.

"Twenty-four hours? Are we sure?" Twenty-four hours was a long time to be in the hands of a killer. Especially one whose ice-blue eyes promised that death wouldn't be easy.

"The rape was more violent than the others," Cory said, studying her with more neutrality than she'd expected. "The M.E. took swabs, of course, but she was washed like the others. I doubt we'll get any foreign DNA. And the circle on her chest was carved while she was still alive."

How long would Sarah have survived before she bled out? Evelyn tried not to think about it. She put on her best professional voice, but it still vibrated with something more than empathy, because this had almost happened to her. "The murders are getting more brutal. He's escalating."

"Does that mean he'll make mistakes?" Hope quivered in Tanner's voice.

"He already has. The fact that he only left Carla's ID and not her body means he probably made the kind of mistake that can identify him. So he's hidden the body instead of displaying it."

"But we don't *have* the body," Jimmy said. "How does a mistake help us if we can't use it?"

"It explains the things we've been wondering about, like how my abduction fits in." Adrenaline rushed through her, like it always used to when she had an insight about a profile.

"Carla was more difficult to subdue than the killer expected. They fought and she must have injured him—enough to get his DNA on her. It's the one thing he'd fear, the one thing that might give away his identity. He thinks he's superior to us. He's trying to reassert that by displaying Sarah's body in the woods. But he's afraid of leaving DNA behind. We know that because of how carefully he washes the bodies before dumping them. So he got rid of Carla's body more carefully, probably fully buried her so there'd be no chance of its being spotted. He left her ID because he still wants to brag. He—"

"Wait," Miles interrupted. "I thought you said this killer wasn't looking for attention."

"Initially, he wasn't," Evelyn agreed. "The game has changed. Now that he's seen himself in the news, he likes it. He wants credit for his kills. That's why he left the ID."

"But what about your abduction?" Jimmy pressed. "Didn't you say his mistake explains your abduction? How?"

They all stared at her eagerly, waiting for the facts, the details, they needed.

"Almost losing control of Carla scared him. It made him afraid to rely on a simple ruse with his next victim. So, he resorted to a blitz attack with me. Something that would instantly render me unable to fight back."

"But you did," Miles said.

"Right. He *still* lost control once I started recovering from the drugs. So he waited longer before his next abduction. There were twenty days between my abduction and Sarah's, instead of two weeks. And he took even *fewer* risks when he abducted Sarah. More drugs. And the residue on her wrists and ankles in the picture looks like duct tape." She glanced at Tanner for confirmation.

He nodded.

"So, again, the killer's limiting the risks he's taking during the abductions. The media coverage probably contributes to that, too."

"Well, that's good. We're making it harder for him to get victims, right?" Jimmy asked.

"It's good and bad," Evelyn replied. "The news coverage means it'll make the abduction stage more difficult for him. The bad thing is that taking away the challenge of convincing a new victim to trust him, to go with him voluntarily, is making him compensate with more violence."

The words tangled on her tongue. Could she have prevented it? A narcissistic personality like his would blame her for getting away, thinking she'd tricked him into choosing her as a victim. And he'd take it out on others. Maybe even use it as a way to keep hurting *her*. Because by now he surely knew she was with the FBI, consulting on the case. And he'd know she'd see his handiwork.

Everyone was watching her, so she cleared her face and told them, "Until we catch him, the violence will continue to escalate."

The last thing Evelyn wanted to do after looking at photos of Sarah Murphy's lifeless body was go out to dinner with her friends. But it was too late to cancel. She should've been at the restaurant twenty minutes ago.

She knew she was frowning as she strode toward the table in back where Audrey and Jo were waiting, half-finished cocktails in front of them. She sat in one of the two remaining chairs and mumbled, "Sorry I'm late."

Audrey shoved a wayward strand of hair out of her face, her lips puckered with concern. "Everything okay?"

"It's been a long month."

"Maybe you should take a vacation," Jo suggested.

Evelyn sighed. "I can't just run away from this. I have to track down this guy."

Jo looked as if she was going to argue, but the waiter's arrival cut her off.

After they'd placed their orders, silence settled over the table. Jo and Audrey shared a glance and Evelyn knew it was about her. She wanted to snap at them to leave her alone. But it wasn't their fault a serial killer had decided she looked like an easy target.

It wasn't their fault that even with a name, he was untraceable. That, more and more, she worried he was uncatchable.

Finally, Jo, in her typically cheerful voice, asked, "Did I tell you about the new guy I met?"

A wide grin appeared on Audrey's delicate face. "How do you meet all these guys?"

Jo shrugged. "Meeting men is a cinch. It's finding one you want to keep that's tough."

"Not if you give them a chance," Audrey advised.

Jo made a face, but she didn't reply.

Evelyn and Audrey both realized that Jo wasn't looking for long-term. Jo's parents hadn't been happy and hadn't hidden it, which had made her reluctant when it came to relationships.

After her mother's string of violent boyfriends and her own

ill-fated relationship with Jo's brother—the one guy she'd thought was a safe bet—Evelyn knew the feeling.

But lately she'd had to remind herself more often of her reasons for not dating. Especially since Kyle, with his rock-hard body and soft blue eyes, had slept on her floor and tucked a blanket around her. And with his job, he was about as far from safe as she could get.

"Anyway," Jo continued, "I met this guy the other night at the grocery store, of all places. He's a little weird, but seriously hot."

Audrey made a face. "What do you mean by weird?"

"I'm not sure, exactly. He seemed really outgoing—*he* approached *me*—but once I started talking to him, he got shy."

A smile twitched Audrey's lips. "Maybe you make him nervous."

"What do you know about this guy?" Evelyn asked, attempting to join the conversation. "And what does he look like?" she added in a sudden, paranoid fear that it could be the BAKBURY killer venturing outside his comfort zone.

"Well, he works at a hospital, doing what I didn't quite catch. He's a couple of years older than me and a few inches shorter, but he seems nice enough." Jo shrugged. "We're going to dinner tomorrow night. I guess I'll find out more then."

Shorter than Jo meant too short to be the BAKBURY killer. But that didn't mean he was safe. "Ask him about his past," Evelyn insisted. "All sorts of psychopaths can seem perfectly normal at first. Some of them are actually charming." Just like Harley had probably seemed to his victims. And even to a trained federal agent like Diana Ballard. Tension shot down the back of her neck.

Jo made her best "give me a break" face. "I think I have better taste in men than *that*."

Six years in law enforcement had shown her how many

women figured some internal radar would warn them a man was dangerous. The files that were sent to her every day proved how wrong they could be.

A long time ago, she'd given Jo and Audrey a crash course in self-defense, but the best defense was never get to a point where it was needed. "Ask him about his relationship with his parents. Ask about pets, friendships, that sort of thing."

Jo raised her eyebrows. "Well, that sounds like a fun inquisition."

"Psychopaths lack empathy, but they can fake it. And a lot of them had poor relationships with one or both parents and started out with cruelty to animals or smaller children. That's why you want details. It'll help you evaluate if he's lying."

Jo and Audrey shared another look. This one was full of worry—but not about the possibility that Jo's date could be dangerous. About her.

She frowned, ready to lecture them about taking their safety seriously. She'd already lost one friend to a psychopath. She couldn't go through that again.

Then Jo said, "I think I made a bad decision."

Evelyn's hands curled into fists. A lot had changed since Cassie's disappearance. These days, she carried a gun and a badge. These days, she *could* protect her friends.

You can't even protect yourself. She ruthlessly pushed back the cruel voice in her head. "You think this guy is dangerous? Give me his name."

Jo waved a dismissive hand. "No. It's just that I told Marty I was meeting you and Audrey here tonight."

"So?" Evelyn glanced at Audrey, who'd swung her head toward the entrance.

Evelyn twisted in her chair, causing a twinge in her ribs. The man entering the restaurant caused a much bigger twinge in her heart.

He had the same hazel eyes she remembered, almost the exact shade of his sister's. The same chestnut-colored hair, still chopped short because of its tendency to curl. She turned away before he noticed her, calling on all her FBI training to paste a neutral expression on her face.

"I'm sorry," Jo said, her voice barely above a whisper. "I suggested he drop by tonight. I thought…"

Evelyn took a calming breath. It had been eight years, but her quick glance told her time had been good to Marty Carlyle.

Hearing him approach, Evelyn straightened and turned to face him, offering him a stiff nod. But it was only herself she was mad at, for letting him affect her after all these years.

"Hi, Evelyn." Marty put his hand on her shoulder. "How have you been?"

He said it as if they were old friends getting together to catch up. Not like he'd dropped her one day, then two weeks later moved on to the woman he would eventually marry.

"Fine," she muttered, shifting away from him.

Instead of taking the hint, he settled into the empty chair next to her, greeting Audrey and Jo with an oblivious smile.

"Have you ordered yet?" Marty asked his sister. "I'm starving."

Seriously? Jo wanted her to spend the rest of the evening pretending it didn't bother her to sit beside the man who'd once broken her heart? She was too busy pretending it didn't bother her that a serial killer had chosen her as his intended victim. There was only so much pretending she could do.

Her throat swelled with emotions she didn't want to study too closely and she pushed back her chair.

"I'm going home," she snapped. She knew she was being ridiculous, but she couldn't stop herself.

"Whoa." Marty stood, too, lifting his hands in a "calm

down" gesture that only pissed her off more. "If you don't want me here, I can leave."

Jo stood, too, misery all over her face. "I'm sorry, Evelyn. I should have—"

"Forget it." On the verge of saying something she knew she'd regret, Evelyn turned and strode for the door.

Her friends were smart enough not to follow.

Tanner had gotten ambushed.

Some ambitious reporter had found a source inside the police station, because as soon as that reporter got close enough, she'd started barking questions about the victims, mentioning facts she shouldn't have known. Which had made Tanner release information he shouldn't have shared.

Right now, Ron had to be regretting not bringing the media rep. And Evelyn regretted being involved in the news conference at all.

She rushed out of the cramped room where she'd been watching it with a few of the cops on a fourteen-inch television and onto the steps of the police station. It looked as if all of Bakersville had come out for the news conference. Men and women in suits sipped their lattes and nervously checked their watches. Moms clutched their kids close and huddled in groups. Police barricades kept all but the reporters below the steps of the station.

At the top of the steps, Tanner stood, his face a blotchy red as he moved away from the microphone, deliberately ignoring the persistent reporter who had screamed questions at him. The other crews had all eventually shut up and started filming their colleague instead.

The only good news was that although the reporter had known one victim had gotten away, she didn't know who. And Tanner had actually dodged that question.

As Evelyn made her way down the steps toward the audience, she avoided all of them, not wanting to get caught on camera. She paused partway down to scan the crowd.

The pictures of Harley that had been plastered all over the news should have scared him from coming today. But a killer who could make actors look like elves could probably disguise himself convincingly as an old woman or a sixteen-year-old boy. Even if he was right in front of her, she might not know it. Shivers crawled in slow motion down her spine.

She studied the crowd, searching for a feature she recognized. All she saw were terrified residents trying to hide their fear and curious residents convinced that murder only happened to other people. And overworked cops standing guard.

Disappointment mingled with a tiny, cowardly hint of relief. She took another step, then something caught her eye and she whipped her head to the left.

Ice-blue eyes.

Memories mingled. Someone muscular and too strong, slamming his palm into her face, murder in his eyes. A civilian, bearded and overweight, talking about ViCAP on the very first day she'd come to the Bakersville station.

The same man. And he was here. Talking to one of the cops.

Evelyn stumbled forward just as officers picked up the barricade and moved it aside, letting the crowd swarm around it. Evelyn started running.

With every step, her ribs throbbed, ricocheting pain into her lungs, making each breath a struggle. She ran faster, panting by the time she reached the officer who'd been talking to the killer in front of the crowd.

"Where did he go?" she asked in a breathless whisper.

"Who?" The officer flushed, glancing around curiously, and Evelyn realized she knew him, too.

The day she'd first seen the killer, he'd been disguised as he was today, and he'd been talking to the same officer.

"The man you were talking to. Where is he?" Evelyn pushed up onto her toes, trying to spot him through the crowd dispersing in all directions, some toward the station, others the parking lot, and more to the sidewalk.

"I have no idea. Probably home."

Evelyn grabbed his sleeve. "Do you know where that is?"

He frowned, moving away from her. "No."

He was a waste of her time. The killer was getting away.

She took off through the crowd, toward the sidewalk. She'd seen him too briefly to know what he was wearing, but she'd seen his face, with the glasses and a beard and mustache. And he hadn't disguised his eyes.

The mass of people was thinning out, making room for her to run. She glanced back every time she passed a man who might have been Harley. Several looked back at her questioningly, but none had the cold blue eyes that haunted her sleep.

When she'd passed the entire crowd, she stopped, letting them walk around her as she stared at each man. He wasn't there. Shit! Where had he gone?

Back to the police station? Was he really that cocky?

He probably was. Evelyn swallowed something that tasted like fear and slipped off the sidewalk and into the shade of years-old elms. Behind the station were dense woods, the kind where this killer liked to bring his victims after he'd stoned them and carved them up.

She took her Glock from its holster. The closer she got to the back of the station, the more the trees formed a canopy overhead, blocking the sun. And the more icy fingers danced across the back of her neck. He was nearby. She shifted her trigger finger inside the guard of her gun.

"Evelyn!"

Her heart rate rocketed and her trigger finger instantly tensed, almost too far. It only took three pounds of pressure to shoot. How close had she come to taking off her own foot?

She pivoted to see Tanner framed in an open window, peering at her curiously.

"What the hell are you doing?" he yelled.

She whipped her head back toward the woods when she heard a slight rustle of leaves somewhere in the distance. Her imagination? An animal? The killer getting away? It was too late to find out now.

"Nothing," she called back, holstering her weapon and heading for the station, her ribs throbbing in protest as her adrenaline rush slowed.

Inside, she went straight to his office and pointed out the rookie who'd been talking to the BAKBURY killer.

"Devlin, get in here!" Tanner barked into the bullpen.

Other cops' curious glances followed as the young officer joined them.

"Craig Devlin, meet Evelyn Baine, the profiler from the FBI. Craig finished the academy two months ago and joined the force."

Craig nodded at her, swallowing hard. He knew he was in trouble; he just didn't know why.

"Evelyn says she saw you talking to the killer after the news conference," Tanner told Craig.

"Huh?" Craig's pudgy cheeks flushed. Then his face contorted, his eyebrows forming a V at his nose. "Roger?" he asked in disbelief.

Before she could demand a last name, he huffed out a breath of laughter. "*Roger* is the Bakersville Burier? No way. The guy is the definition of average. Besides, he doesn't look anything like the pictures of that Keegan guy."

"Roger what?" Evelyn asked.

Craig's gaze flicked over to Tanner, as if to question whether or not he was supposed to answer. The fury on Tanner's face made him stand straighter. Words tumbled out. "Pendleton. Roger Pendleton. He's a car mechanic nearby. I forget where. But he can't be a killer. He looks nothing like any of the pictures," he repeated desperately.

Roger Pendleton. Why did that name sound familiar? Evelyn searched for it in her memory, but couldn't find it. Had she heard it the day she'd seen Craig talking to the killer at the station? She was pretty sure she hadn't. So where?

"How do you know this guy?" Tanner asked.

Craig jammed his hands in his pockets and shuffled his feet. "Uh, well, sometimes I go to the Flying Pig. Just to get a bite to eat. Never on duty."

When she'd asked about cop hangouts in town, Tanner had mentioned the Flying Pig, saying it had questionable entertainment. She'd taken that to mean strippers.

Tanner rolled his eyes and opened his mouth, but Evelyn interrupted whatever he'd been about to say as realization hit.

"I met a Roger Pendleton here a few days ago."

Tanner sent her a sharp glance and Craig looked back and forth between them, as if he was still trying to catch up. She had a feeling he never would.

"But…he said he was Craig's uncle. And he was an old man. Older than the guy I saw today." She felt the blood drain from her face as she remembered how his appearance had made her wonder if the killer could be posing as an old man to abduct his victims. She'd never thought he *was* the killer in disguise.

Craig's head continued to pivot as Tanner frowned at her.

Before Craig got whiplash, Evelyn demanded, "Tell me about Pendleton."

He looked at Tanner again, his eyebrows raised, like he was waiting for the police chief to declare her nuts and send her home. When he didn't, Craig shrugged and said, "I met him at the bar maybe three months ago. I told him I was going through police training and he said he was a mechanic."

"What else?" Evelyn asked sharply. "Did he ask about the investigation? What else did you talk about?"

Craig's foot-shuffling got faster. "I, uh…"

"Dammit, Devlin," Tanner said. "What did you tell him?"

"Nothing big," Craig insisted. "He said he'd seen news coverage on the case and wanted to know how close we were to catching the killer. The sort of thing everyone wanted to know."

"*What did you tell him?*" Tanner asked, his right eye starting to twitch.

"Uh, well, first I just said we were working on it."

"So he knew we weren't on to him," Evelyn summarized. But what else? Had Craig been the killer's inside connection? Her hands folded into fists, her fingernails digging into her palms. "Did you ever mention me? That I was profiling him?"

Craig's forehead creased and his lips twisted, broadcasting his belief that she had an inflated opinion of her own importance. "No. Why would I?"

Her gut said he was telling the truth. Which was probably good, because she was in enough trouble with Dan for forgetting about his report; decking a rookie cop wouldn't improve her standing.

From the way Tanner's lips quirked, she suspected he could tell exactly what she was thinking. He coughed and asked Craig, "What did you tell him today?"

Craig chewed his lip. "I said we knew the guy's name, but the name Keegan was in the news, anyway, as a possible connection. I said we couldn't find him," he added more quietly. "I, uh, might've said that a lot of us figured we never would."

Tanner's scowl deepened so much, she thought it might leave dents in his forehead. "For God's sa—"

"What about the spot where the bodies were dumped?" Evelyn cut in. "Did you ever discuss that?"

Craig shot another apologetic look at Tanner, but his boss's fury made him step back and quickly redirect his gaze at her. "I, uh, I guess I said something about how the FBI told us to monitor it."

"What else?" Evelyn pressed.

Craig shrugged again, a quick, anxious jerk of his shoulders. "Nothing. I didn't tell him anything he wasn't supposed to…I mean, nothing that—"

"Have Craig talk to the sketch artist," Evelyn told Tanner. "I'll do the same and describe the old man I saw. We'll release new pictures along with the old ones."

"I'm sorry." Craig's voice was watery.

"Go talk to the sketch artist," Tanner snapped. "Now."

"Let's do a search on Roger Pendleton," Evelyn suggested as Craig shuffled off, head down. "See if we get any hits."

"Come on." Tanner hurried over to the front desk, where he had a sergeant try to access the name Roger Pendleton. But nothing came up when they searched for anywhere he might work as a car mechanic. Property and title searches came up empty on homes and cars.

After an hour of searching, Tanner and the sergeant looked at her with matching questions in their eyes.

"He must have another alias," she said over the lump in her throat.

Tanner's chest slumped with his heavy sigh. His eyes met hers. "He's too good. We're not going to get him, are we?"

"We'll catch him," Evelyn insisted. But even to her, the promise sounded empty.

20

IT WAS TIME TO GET MORE AGGRESSIVE IN THE
search for Harley Keegan. That's what Dan had told Greg
when he was ordered to an emergency meeting with the BAK-
BURY case agents and Evelyn. Apparently, Ron had gone
over Evelyn's head and complained about her continuing involvement in aspects of the case that weren't hers to investi-
gate. Somehow, by the end of the phone call, Ron had been
asking for even more profilers to help them.

When Greg pushed open the door to the interagency coordination room, he found Dan talking to an older agent he
assumed was Ron. Three other men sat on the same side of
the table as the lead agent. Evelyn was across from them, an
unreadable expression on her face.

He sat beside her, but didn't even get to say hello before
Ron stood.

"You must be Agent Ibsen." When Greg nodded, the man
went on. "Ron Harding. I'm the agent in charge." He gestured to the man on his right with too much gel in his hair

and a suit nicer than most agents liked to wear in the field. "My partner, Jimmy Drescott."

The younger agent stretched his hand across the table, but Ron plowed on. "Next to him is Miles Ferguson and on the end is Cory Fuller."

Miles flushed and Cory nodded and Ron kept talking. "Let's get started. I assume you've been briefed on the case?" He didn't wait for a response. "The Bakersville police have been overwhelmed with tips since yesterday's news conference. They've had dozens of callers claim they were the killer." A sudden smile pushed his droopy skin upward. "We all know how that goes."

Jimmy snorted. "All the crazies have come out."

"Because that news conference was such a disaster," Ron continued, "it's been hard to rule people out. Meanwhile, the killer's gotten more violent. That's why I've asked Evelyn's supervisor and the head of BAU here today."

Her supervisor? Greg raised an eyebrow, assuming that meant him. He didn't dare look at Evelyn; he didn't have to. He could feel her tension increase at the implication that she wasn't getting the job done.

"We have to get this killer off the streets *now*," Ron was saying. "I'm worried that all the media attention he's getting might send him packing and he'll just pick up somewhere else."

Had Evelyn suggested that possibility? If she had, Greg was pretty sure she was wrong. He suspected the killer was enjoying his newfound notoriety too much to leave. Plus, his ego would be big enough that he'd believe he could keep outwitting them.

It was their job to prove him wrong. And they needed to do it fast. Not just for the women in Bakersville the killer was targeting, but also for Evelyn. If they didn't, he worried he'd be training a new profiler soon. And BAU couldn't afford to lose Evelyn any more than she could handle losing them.

Ron finally sat down, gesturing toward Dan. "Dan Moore has been with the Bureau for more than two decades and he spent twelve years of that time as a profiler. He's currently the ASAC of BAU."

Jimmy, Cory and Miles looked suitably impressed as Ron said, "I'll let him lead today's meeting."

When Greg dared a glance at Evelyn, he saw that her jaw had tensed at the snub, but she kept her mouth shut.

So did Dan. He was obviously trying to placate Ron. Which told Greg that Ron was even more annoyed than he'd thought about Evelyn running down leads on her own. And that Dan knew it.

Dan strode over to one of the dry erase boards lining the conference room walls and wrote in his trademark cramped handwriting: *set up surveillance teams near the drop site for the bodies.*

"Leaving the latest victim so close to the others, when he knew we could be monitoring the site, means this UNSUB is arrogant," Dan said. "It also suggests he may continue to go back. Especially since one of the cops may have told him police could be watching the site."

"He thinks he's invincible." Ron frowned, looking at Evelyn. "Evelyn already mentioned that to the cops. I'll make sure they're on it."

Jimmy leaned forward. "What about luring Harley—if it really is Harley—out of hiding by using his brother?" He gave a shiny grin, with a lot of teeth but not a lot of substance, and glanced at Evelyn.

Greg's lips trembled. If Jimmy was trying to impress Evelyn, he was going to have to do better than that.

Dan dutifully wrote down the idea, probably out of politeness, but Greg felt compelled to ask, "How would we use the brother to bring Harley out of hiding?"

Jimmy shrugged. "I don't know. Maybe we tell the press he's in some kind of trouble." His eyes widened. "Oh! Let's tell them he's dying. See if Harley goes to visit him one last time. We can stake it out."

Patience wasn't Evelyn's strong suit, but Greg could tell she was trying as she said, "Harley hasn't seen Mason in more than a decade. And if he did fall for it, we'd be sending him to Connecticut. He could do a lot of damage between here and there."

"What? You mean, kill people along the way?" Cory sounded skeptical.

Evelyn nodded. "Remember what I've said about serial killers who get away with it for a while? How they can turn into spree killers? They start needing more victims to fulfill their needs and they care less about who those victims are."

"We can't push this guy too far," Greg said, supporting her. "It could lead to a bloodbath."

The folds in Ron's face creased more and more until he seemed about to speak.

"Using the brother in some way is a possibility," Dan said quickly, probably sensing an argument. "But let's see what else we've got."

"The most recent victim was just released for burial," Greg noted. "And the first two are buried in the same cemetery. Evelyn and I attended one of the early funerals, thinking he might show. He still could, especially if we make a big deal of it. If he doesn't, there's a good chance he'll go to her grave site. The police should plan on some surveillance at the cemetery."

Miles and Jimmy bobbed their heads as Dan wrote it down.

"What about the victims' relatives?" As Miles spoke, crimson slowly spread from his cheeks to his neck, but he spoke confidently. "Don't some serial killers like to taunt relatives? Maybe we should see whether any of them have been contacted. If they have, we could set up phone taps, see if we can trace him."

Dan was poised to write down that idea when Evelyn prompted, "Ron?"

Ron shook his head. "I checked, back when you suggested it. None of them had been contacted. I gave them all my number, but I haven't heard from anyone."

Dan tapped the marker against the board, leaving behind a circle of red dots. "I'm surprised he hasn't, especially after he had trouble controlling Evelyn. I'd think he'd want to reassert his power by bragging."

"I doubt that he feels the need to taunt the relatives at this point," Evelyn said. "Why bother with the families when he can taunt the whole town? And the control issue is just making him angry. It's why we're seeing more violence."

Dan nodded thoughtfully. "And with more violence, his appetite is increasing. His trophies aren't going to satisfy him for long. He's going to go after a new victim. Soon."

Evelyn nodded, too, a sharp tilt to her lips that said she'd already been singing that tune.

Greg saw the muscles in Cory's massive arms flex and sensed the anger to come, but he wasn't fast enough to preempt it.

"What do *you* suggest?" he asked Evelyn. "You sit here shooting down everyone else's ideas." His gaze flashed to Greg. "Except your *supervisor's*. But you haven't had any of your own."

Greg studied Cory, wondering what the emphasis on *supervisor* was about. Did Cory know he wasn't Evelyn's supervisor and just wanted to harass her about how, intentionally or not, Ron had snubbed her today? Or was he implying they had some other kind of relationship?

Cory's eyes were tense at the corners, and his jaw was tight even though he wasn't scowling. The muscles in his arms were outlined. The expression and the body language told Greg he was trying to antagonize Evelyn. But why? Was he simply a misogynist who didn't like women in roles of power? Or was there more?

Before she could rise to the bait, Greg said, "I know Evelyn already suggested some of the things we're talking about, like monitoring the drop site. If that had been done in the first place, we probably wouldn't need to be brainstorming now."

Cory and Ron both leaned forward, but Dan held up a hand. "That's irrelevant. We need ideas, not arguments." He made another bullet on the wall, ready to write something else, but Ron jumped in.

"What about, instead of finding his brother, we try to locate Harley's dad? If Harley hates the guy so much—and it sounds like he should—maybe he'll come out of hiding for his father."

"You mean if we set him up as a target?" Jimmy asked. "Do we know where he is?" He looked at Evelyn, not Ron.

Evelyn was silent until, slowly, everyone turned to her, and she was where she should have been, leading the discussion.

The irony of it was that finding out where Harley's dad lived was the job of a case agent, not a profiler.

"He disappeared two years ago, around the time Harley left Boston," Evelyn said. "Harley told Diana's sister he was going to Connecticut to take care of his father, but if he did show up there, no one seemed to know."

"So where did his dad go?" Miles asked.

"There's no record of him showing up anywhere else. Eventually, the bank foreclosed on his house and used the sale of his belongings to pay some of his debt. He's never returned to complain."

"Like father, like son?" Jimmy wondered. "Does being a serial killer run in the family?"

"Could they have gone underground together?" Miles asked. "Could they be accomplices?"

Greg shook his head as Dan tried to answer Miles, but Jimmy was excited and loud, convinced there could be another Keegan murdering women somewhere in the country.

"Even if we *could* find his father," Cory said, "Harley might realize it's a setup."

"We're not going to find him," Evelyn announced. She wasn't loud, but the finality in her voice silenced them. "Harley's dad is probably dead."

There were several beats of silence, then the agents started arguing again.

Greg turned to Evelyn. "You think Harley killed him?"

She nodded. "The timing fits. Phil Keegan seems to have disappeared like Diana did, without a trace. Plus, by then, Harley had killed a few times and gotten away with it. He might have figured, why not detour to Connecticut and take care of his father. It's likely he disposed of the body where he thinks Phil buried his mother, in the woods behind his house."

"Like his drop site now," Greg mused.

Cory swiveled toward them. "Why didn't you mention this earlier? You gave us a timeline of who you thought Harley killed and when. You never mentioned his father."

"Enough!" Dan bit out. "This is counterproductive."

"Harley's dad isn't going to help us now." Evelyn looked at Miles. "And no, Harley isn't working with any accomplice."

"What about his mother?" Ron asked. "She's still alive, isn't she? What about finding her?"

Greg gaped at him. What was with the case agents wanting to set up Harley's family as bait? It was dangerous to the family, a liability for the Bureau and unlikely to work.

"She is alive," Evelyn confirmed. "She's overseas. But we don't—"

"If Harley is so brilliant, why hasn't *he* found his mother?" Jimmy asked. "Why does he still think she's dead? When you profiled the killer, you said his IQ would be high, right?"

"Harley is intelligent," Evelyn replied. "But he's believed his mother was dead since he was young. He's probably never thought of verifying it. For him, it's just fact."

Discarding that route, Jimmy offered, "What about looking for the rings Harley took from his victims? Maybe he pawned them. One of them had an engraving on her ring that would make it easier to identify."

Evelyn's sigh was full of frustration. "He didn't pawn the rings. He kept them. He uses them to relive the experiences. When that doesn't work anymore, he'll troll for a new victim."

Cory snorted. "When you say 'relive,' you mean masturbate, don't you?"

When she nodded, Miles muttered, "Gross."

"What about their clothes?" Jimmy asked, either not willing to let go of his idea, or desperate for one that would impress Evelyn. "Maybe he donated them."

"I'm sure he burned them," Evelyn contradicted. "He's smart enough not to make that kind of mistake."

Cory tapped his fingers against the table, a heavy *thud, thud, thud* meant to attract attention. "Aren't you going to write any of this down?" He looked pointedly at Dan. "What's the point of the rest of us being here if Evelyn just shoots down everyone's ideas?" he asked again.

Greg leaned forward, ready to leap to Evelyn's defense, but Dan jumped in. "Evelyn is your criminal investigative analyst." When Cory opened his mouth, Dan barked in his "I've hunted serial killers for decades, so don't mess with me" voice, "If she tells you something won't work, it won't work."

Evelyn blinked a few times, but that was the only outward sign she was surprised by Dan's support.

Cory's eyes narrowed, but he looked dutifully at Evelyn and suggested, "How about we give a news conference where we say we doubt the validity of his claim that he killed Carla? Make him prove it."

Evelyn frowned. "A challenge like that could send him in the other direction. Though—"

"Let's go back to Harley himself," Ron interrupted. "He exists. We know his name. And Evelyn has been to his house."

Evelyn seemed to sink against her chair as everyone focused on her, but she hid her discomfort fast. "I wish I could, but I don't remember where I was."

"But we know where you were when you crashed," Jimmy said enthusiastically. "We can work from there. You were driving north, so Harley's place must've been south of there."

"What we don't know is how far south," Miles reminded him. "We have no idea how long she'd been driving before she crashed or if she'd been going east or west first. Heck, she could actually have been coming from the north and then turned around on the highway."

The expression on Dan's face was the same one he'd probably worn to scare uncooperative witnesses back in his prosecuting days. "Evelyn doesn't remember it. The cabin is a dead end."

"Not necessarily," Ron argued. "She may not remember it, but it *happened*. So, subconsciously, she must know something."

Evelyn smoothed back her hair with a slightly shaky hand. That nervous habit was the only body language she was bad at hiding. Ironically, the self-preening action was a sign that she was looking for acceptance. Usually, Greg was saddened that she didn't think she had it. Today, it just pissed him off with the case agents.

Anger crept into Dan's voice as his gaze swiveled from Evelyn to Ron. "What are you suggesting?"

Greg knew Dan frowned on hypnosis, called it garbage science and a waste of time. He might have chosen a field that went hand in hand with psychology, but there were still aspects of it the lawyer in him didn't trust.

In this case, Greg agreed. "She was drugged. I don't think hypnosis is going to tell us anything. Often, with cases of anterograde amnesia brought on by drugs, the memory is never recovered." He'd been reading up on it since her abduction.

Evelyn looked sharply at him.

"What about one of those truth serum drugs?" Jimmy asked eagerly.

"Pentathol?" Cory returned.

"They can use some related drug—Sodium Amytal maybe— to retrieve regressed memories," Ron contributed.

Obviously he'd been reading up on it, too.

Greg scowled. "Evelyn's memories aren't regressed. She has amnesia *because* she was drugged. She doesn't need more! Why would we want to drug her to make her relive the experience?"

As soon as he blurted the words, he realized they were a mistake. He'd talked about Evelyn as if she wasn't there *and* he'd implied there was something she couldn't handle. He knew more than anyone how hard she worked to prove she belonged in the unit; he didn't want her to think he doubted her.

Dan seemed ready to support him, but Evelyn spoke, using a clipped tone, too loud for the small room. "Let's start with something else we know." She held up a finger. "One. He has trophies from his victims, and when they fail to satisfy him, he'll look for a new victim." Another finger went up. "Two. He's getting more arrogant. The excessive media coverage is going to inflate his ego even more. He's begun to enjoy the notoriety. So, we know he's following it."

She had their attention. When she went silent, Miles looked around, then pressed, "And?"

"We use it," Evelyn concluded, the thrill of the hunt rushing into her features, putting life back into her eyes.

"How?" Ron asked.

"We use that news coverage to our advantage." Her voice grew in volume, getting more vibrant with every word. The pallor slowly faded from her face, replaced with a flush that matched the intensity in her voice. "We use the media to bring him into the open. We taunt him."

What the hell was she thinking? Evelyn's plan was just as bad as the case agents' ideas to lure Harley out by using his family.

"That's dangerous," Greg said. "We don't want to incite him into grabbing a new victim. That's what we're going to do by taunting him."

Evelyn smiled, a tight, closed-lipped, triumphant smile. "Exactly."

She folded her arms across her chest and leaned back in her seat. "We taunt the killer about the victim who got away. Me. And we give him another chance."

21

"WE HAVE BREAKING NEWS IN THE SEARCH FOR
the Bakersville Burier."

The words had been blasted all afternoon on the local chan-
nels and they'd drawn a huge crowd to the Bakersville police
station. Reporters were crammed onto the steps, their camera operators jockeying for the best positions. Behind them,
past a bright orange barricade, Bakersville locals huddled together, speculating.

Tanner stood at the podium, in full uniform, beads of sweat
above his upper lip.

Standing off to the side, Evelyn tried to hide any hint of
fury, triumph or fear. Inside, the emotions tumbled over one
another.

This was her chance to catch the killer. One slipup and he
could disappear forever. But she had him in check. She just
had to turn it into a checkmate.

Cameras swung toward Tanner as he introduced himself.
"For the past several months, Bakersville has been terrorized
by a killer targeting the wives, mothers and daughters in our

town. Tonight, we have new information on the search for the killer."

Tanner's tone was stilted as he read the script in front of him. "A few days ago, we released photographs of a man wanted in connection with the killings. Today, we're asking for your assistance in finding these men—" Tanner held up the sketches she and Craig Devlin, the rookie cop, had helped make "—and any information leading to the whereabouts of a Roger Pendleton, who might work as a mechanic in the area."

As Tanner spoke, Evelyn tried to scan the crowd, but the lights from the cameras were too bright and she couldn't see anything past the first row of reporters shoving their microphones at Tanner.

"Today, I have an expert in serial murder from the FBI with me." Tanner let a long pause go by before he added, "She's also the only victim to escape from the Bakersville Burier."

The reporters suddenly stilled, before there was a sudden flurry of questions and an explosion of flashbulbs. Over them, Tanner said loudly, "Evelyn?" and gestured for her to step forward.

Evelyn raised her head to disguise her nerves as she moved to the podium. She'd worn one of her most professional suits, even gone to the trouble of slipping pearls into her earlobes and dabbing on a generous amount of makeup to conceal the evidence of too much stress, too little sleep and the fading scar near her left eye. Today, more than ever, she needed to look unfazed by her abduction.

Questions were shouted at her, so many that she couldn't make any of them out. She waited silently until they stopped.

"As an expert in serial murder," she began, "and as an intended victim of this killer, I can tell you that the man we're looking for preys on lone women. Like most serial killers, he's looking for a specific type of victim—and his type is married women."

As she said it, she lifted her left hand and placed it on top of the podium, gripping the stand as she positioned her grandmother's ring, worn on her left ring finger, upside down, in full view of the cameras.

If indeed the old man who'd called himself Roger Pendleton was actually Harley Keegan—and she was almost certain he was—the reason he'd been staring at her in the parking lot was because he'd noticed the lack of a ring. Realizing she wasn't married would have enraged him, made him think she'd led him on.

Taunting him with her ring now would rekindle that anger. And she wanted him furious.

Evelyn looked past the reporters, into the crowd she couldn't really see, where she suspected the killer was lurking, disguised. A shiver slid up her spine, gaining intensity, and she stiffened.

"This killer is a master of disguise and deceit. He moved to this area in the past few months, and if you talked to him, he probably seemed overly interested in this case. He fits easily into groups, but if you think about it, you'll realize you don't know anyone who really knows him. The killer also talks to his victims before he abducts them. It's part of his power trip to fool them into believing he's harmless before he ultimately comes after them. If you saw any of the victims talking to a man who fits his description, you need to contact the police."

She glanced back at Tanner, his cue to stand directly behind her. She wanted to use Tanner—the more than six feet and two hundred pounds of him—to emphasize her own size. She'd skipped the heels today, because for the first time in her life, she wanted to look small, weak, an easy target.

"When this killer abducted me..." Evelyn had to force herself to keep going. "He drugged me because he was afraid he wouldn't be able to control me."

Evelyn felt her shoulders stiffen as she imagined the killer's fury growing. *That's right, asshole, I'm telling everyone. Taking away what's most important to you: the ability to dominate and control. I'm telling everyone you can't do it.*

"Since I got away from him, he's made drugging his victims part of his abduction style. He's more afraid of getting caught now. And we *will* catch him. This man is *not* invincible." She paused, looked over the sea of reporters. "He's making mistakes. He made a mistake when he abducted me—he couldn't control me, so I got away. And he'll keep making mistakes until we get *him.*"

So no one would have time to question her, Evelyn stepped back, almost bumping into Tanner as he took her place.

"Tomorrow, I'll be giving another press conference on the status of the case," Tanner said. "I hope you'll join me here again."

The reporters yelled questions as he stepped away from the podium, but Tanner ignored them all until most of the camera operators gave up and lowered their cameras. Only one, the husband of Bakersville's female cop who'd been asked to cooperate, swung back to Evelyn and Tanner, ready to capture a conversation as though it were an accident.

"I'll meet with you tomorrow right after I finish the news conference," Tanner told Evelyn, just loudly enough for the camera to capture.

Hoping she'd done enough to lure the killer, Evelyn nodded and walked out of the shot.

Kyle positioned himself, his stance wide, near the BAU office coffee machine. Gabe joined him, arms crossed over his chest. His back to them, Dan dumped spoonful after heaping spoonful of sugar into his coffee, too preoccupied to notice the trap. With his escape route blocked, Dan would have no choice but to hear them out.

And Kyle wasn't leaving until Dan agreed to his plan.

When Dan finally finished turning his coffee into a diabetic's nightmare, he started turning. Seeing Gabe put an instant scowl on his face. "Don't you have your own coffee at Quantico?"

Then he turned the rest of the way. When he saw Kyle situated like a linebacker determined not to let an opposing quarterback through, the scowl changed into a heavy sigh. "What is it?" he growled.

"We watched Evelyn's news conference this morning."

The live feed from Bakersville had been running when he'd walked out of HRT's daily intel briefing. The instant dread he'd felt at seeing Evelyn on the news had quickly turned into confusion. She wasn't a media rep. She had no business being on TV. He'd been furious, thinking she'd unintentionally put herself in more danger.

And then he'd understood. Evelyn never did anything unintentionally. She was using herself as bait.

His first instinct had been to rush to Dan, convince him Evelyn was too emotionally involved in the case to make a safe decision. But sanity had returned even before he'd herded Gabe into his Ford Escape. Evelyn would never forgive him if he did that. Besides, a frantic phone call to Greg told him Dan hadn't given in to Greg's pressure to stop the scheme. And Dan actually *liked* Greg.

Dan was already glaring at him as if Kyle were one of the scum he profiled, instead of a fellow agent. "And you've come to tell me what you thought of the news conference?"

Kyle's temper was ready to flare, but Gabe answered first. "Not exactly."

"We know what she's doing." Kyle tried to imitate Gabe's easygoing tone and not sound as worried as he felt.

Dan sipped his coffee. "She's just helping the cops."

"Yeah, right." Gabe shook his head. "We know Evelyn better than that."

"Really?" Dan glanced at Kyle, curiosity gleaming in his eyes.

With sudden clarity, Kyle remembered the day he'd jokingly put his arm around Evelyn's shoulders and the odd look Dan had given them when he'd emerged from his office. Well, shit. No wonder Evelyn had tried to shrug him off like he had the plague.

"We're all friends," he explained tightly. "Gabe is Greg's cousin."

"Hmm. Well, he's in his cubicle if you were heading over there to say hello."

Kyle ignored the ruse, but when he didn't move, he saw that Dan hadn't expected him to give up that easily. "We actually came to talk to you."

"We realize Evelyn's speech had a purpose," Gabe said.

"And we'd like to offer our assistance," Kyle finished.

Dan's eyes narrowed. "The case agents have everything under control. But thanks." He tried to walk away, but stopped abruptly when Kyle didn't move.

"We know Evelyn's trying to get this guy to come after her again." Even saying the words made Kyle's muscles tighten with the desire to use some of the more painful takedown techniques HRT had taught him on Evelyn's abductor. Beating him to a bloody pulp was pretty damn appealing, too. "I'm sure you have plenty of backup for her, and I think that's wise," he continued, trying to sound calm.

"That's where we'd like to help," Gabe added.

"I think we can convince our boss to lend us out to your

team for one evening," Kyle said, jumping back in. "We've run plenty of protection details for HRT. We have a lot of experience blending into the background."

Dan was starting to shake his head, but Gabe didn't let Kyle raise his voice. "If your killer is as intelligent as he's made out to be, he'll spot a regular SA."

He referred to normal special agents, most of whom had little or no experience working undercover or securing perimeters. But HRT did that kind of work regularly.

"If you need more than just the two of us," Kyle said quickly, "we can probably get some of the other guys to help." Hell, if he had it his way, there'd be a damn army of agents guarding Evelyn.

Dan sighed. "I'm not involved. I may be Evelyn's boss, but I'm not in charge of the BAKBURY case. I had no say in this." Under his breath, he muttered, "If I had, I would've vetoed it before she went on the news."

His gaze moved over them thoughtfully. "Go and talk to the agent in charge. His name is Ron Harding, over at the Washington field office. You can tell him I recommended you." With that, Dan walked past—with no resistance.

Kyle shared a congratulatory smile with Gabe and they headed for Greg's cubicle to give him the good news.

They hadn't made it far before a furious voice from behind a partition being used as a corkboard stopped them. "What do you think you're doing?"

Kyle felt his shoulders tense as he exchanged a glance with Gabe. When they rounded the partition, there was Evelyn, arms crossed and a look on her face that could make serial killers beg forgiveness.

The damn partition had completely hidden her. He frowned, trying to figure out why she looked shorter than usual when he realized. No heels. That extra inch or two would have given him a little warning.

"We're just trying to help. You're our friend," Kyle said.

"It can't hurt to have a couple of friends watching your back, right?" Gabe gave her one of his most charming smiles.

But Evelyn had always been immune to charm. She was immune to damn near everything.

"*Watching* my back?" Evelyn demanded. "Don't you mean going *behind* my back?" Her lips pursed and Kyle could see her trying to control her anger. "I don't care what Dan told you— I'm already having trouble working with Ron. I know you're trying to help, but I don't want you making things worse."

Frustration rose inside him. It had been there for too long, ever since he'd seen her lying in that hospital bed. He'd felt helpless. But not anymore. He opened his mouth, ready to lay it out for her. It didn't matter what she wanted. He was getting on that protection detail.

Gabe intervened, a half smile indicating he was going to try charming again.

Instead, he pointed to a sketch of Dan underneath the words *Predator Still at Large*. "Did you catch the guy?" Gabe joked. "He looks dangerous."

Evelyn didn't seem amused, but Kyle laughed. How had Gabe managed to post that without anyone noticing? And why was it still on the board?

Deciding not to ask, Kyle got back on topic. "Your plan's risky—"

"My plan makes perfect sense," Evelyn broke in, sounding insulted. "How do you even know about it? Did you talk to Greg?"

"No," Gabe said, not too convincingly.

"Yes, they did," Greg said.

Kyle almost jumped as the agent appeared from behind him

without warning. Shit. He'd better get his act together fast if he wanted to be any kind of protection.

"I agree with them that the plan's unsafe and unnecessary," Greg told Evelyn. "You can catch this guy without putting yourself in danger."

The combined pressure of the three of them should've made Evelyn back down. But Kyle supposed anyone who could interview serial killers didn't back down easily.

Instead, she narrowed her eyes. "It's only unnecessary if I'm willing to risk him finding more victims. I'm not. He'll come for me and we'll catch him." She jabbed a finger at Kyle and he saw the vulnerability lurking underneath her anger. "It *will* work. And I want you to stay out of it."

She didn't give them a chance to argue, just whirled around and strode back to her desk.

"Shit." Kyle sighed. "She's really going to be mad when we get involved, anyway."

"I don't think *mad* is a strong enough word," Greg warned. He glanced at the drawing on the partition, then over at his cousin. "And one of these days, Dan *is* going to figure out that's him."

As Greg headed for his own desk, Gabe said, "Let's go talk to Ron?"

Kyle nodded. "Let's go talk to Ron."

Evelyn tried to focus on her computer screen, but it kept blurring. She couldn't get her mind off Harley Keegan. And she'd been unfocused for too long now, just going through the motions. Meanwhile, he was still out there, still killing.

And the knowledge that she could've stopped him was taking over her life, destroying her career.

She had to quit sitting around, compiling profiles of the killer and his victims. She had to lure him in, get rid of the constant threat hanging over her head. It didn't matter what Greg wanted or what Kyle and Gabe thought of her plan.

It would work. It had to.

The chime of her telephone startled her, but it was a welcome distraction from the thoughts she couldn't block.

"Evelyn Baine, BAU," she answered.

"It's Ron Harding."

The tone of his voice was hard, and it made Evelyn wish she hadn't picked up the phone.

"I just got a visit from your HRT friends."

Evelyn squeezed her eyes shut and choked out, "I'm sorry."

Ron's voice shook with fury. "This may have been your plan, Evelyn, but it's still our case. It's insulting that you think we can't handle a simple protection detail."

"I don't—"

"I turned them down. We don't need their help. We're doing this on our own." He ended the call abruptly.

Evelyn regretted not handling her friends more tactfully, not handling everything about this case more tactfully.

Nerves tore at her stomach lining, making her long for some of Dan's antacids. If her backup agents hadn't been peeved with her before, they sure were now. And she needed them, because alone, with her injuries, she'd be useless in a real fight. Was her plan a huge mistake?

She clutched her rioting stomach. It was too late to back out.

22

EVELYN TOOK A DEEP BREATH AND TRIED TO relax. It didn't work.

She was crammed into the back of a specially outfitted surveillance van borrowed from one of the FBI's undercover units, with Ron, Jimmy, Cory and Miles, waiting for Tanner's news conference to begin. The ten-inch TV screen built into the back of the van crackled with static through one commercial after another. The other agents ignored it as they chatted about the plans they'd canceled to be here.

Evelyn couldn't take her eyes off the screen.

She swiped sweaty hands on her jeans, part of tonight's casual dress. The gym shoes and short-sleeved button-up shirt worn over a tank top completed the outfit of a woman who was supposedly off duty and meeting with Tanner to solicit information on the progress of her case.

Or maybe the ruse was that Tanner wanted to go over the particulars of her abduction one more time. Evelyn wasn't certain what had been decided, since most of the details of tonight's trap had been planned by the BAKBURY case agents.

After all, she was just the bait.

As the TV went to yet another commercial, Jimmy leaned too close, his cologne making her nose twitch. "Are you worried the killer won't show?" He pitched his voice low, as though it was a private conversation, but suddenly everyone went quiet and stared at her.

She forced a confidence she didn't feel into her voice. "He'll show. Tonight's his only definite chance to follow me. And it's his legacy we're talking about."

Evelyn slid her hand over the comforting shape of the Glock hidden under her shapeless button-down. "Let's make sure he takes that chance."

Cory looked at the hand resting on her weapon, then back at her face.

Could he read her fear?

Normally, she kept herself in peak physical condition. Joining the FBI had forced her to get into ridiculously good shape and she'd kept it up. But now, her bruised ribs throbbed with every quick movement. The doctor said she'd reinjured them by chasing the killer in the woods. He'd told her to rest and she hadn't.

So, tonight, if the killer got close, all she had for protection was her gun and the agents around her. Putting her life in the hands of agents she barely knew suddenly made her wish for Greg's calming presence. God help her, it even made her wish for Kyle and Gabe, with their swagger and attitude. Especially since all their big talk came with big muscles and even bigger guns.

"Okay," Ron said, "here's the plan. We're going back to Haggarty's, the bar where Evelyn was abducted. The killer might try to grab her in the parking lot right away, like last time. We want him to try. So, let's make him feel welcome."

A huge smile enlivened Ron's face, knocking a solid decade off his appearance.

Apparently, he'd had fun planning today's setup. Evelyn wasn't sure if that made her feel better or worse.

"Cory and Miles will stay in the van," Ron continued. "Out of sight. Jimmy and I will go inside ahead of Evelyn." He looked at her. "If you can, wait until the parking lot's deserted before you walk through it."

"Right," Jimmy agreed. "Make him think you're ripe for the picking."

Disgust flashed on Cory's face. "You're talking about a rapist, asshole."

"S-sorry, Evelyn," Jimmy stuttered, his face turning red.

"Anyway," Ron continued, glaring at Jimmy, "Miles and Cory will stay in contact with Evelyn during the drive. They'll park in the spot we designated so they can see both the entrance to the bar and the whole parking lot. We've got a cop holding the spot and he'll leave when Miles and Cory pull in. If you see anything suspicious, contact me. Evelyn, you'll pause outside the bar long enough to give the killer his second chance. If he doesn't take it, go inside to the meeting with Tanner."

Ron's gaze swept the circle of agents. "Any questions?"

Jimmy was still flushed, his fingers plucking at imaginary lint on his khakis. Miles shook his head, serious and eager, like a freshman on his first day at college. Cory's blue eyes had turned hard and intense, as though he were back in the military and ready to go into battle.

"Good," Ron said just as, on the television, Tanner strode up to the podium.

The police chief spent ten minutes stressing how close they were to finding the killer, ignoring the questions screamed at him by reporters, while Evelyn's leg started shaking faster and faster and wouldn't stop.

Finally, Tanner raised his hand and told the reporters, "I have to conclude now. I've got another meeting." He said that as if it were merely an offhand comment, not the purpose of the entire news conference.

The reporter who'd been asked to assist the FBI yelled out, "Is the surviving victim giving you information to help catch the killer?"

Tanner smiled and, three streets away, inside the van, Evelyn felt herself smile, too, at the irony.

"She'll be going over the details of her abduction with me."

Somewhere, she thought—probably hidden in the crowd at the police station—the killer was thinking he'd get to listen to her relive the terror of her abduction. Thinking he'd get the chance to repeat it.

When the reporter asked where they were meeting, Tanner replied, "At the abduction scene." He said it as if no one would know what he was talking about, but he'd just told the killer how to find her.

Reporters continued to yell questions, but Tanner stepped back from the podium.

Ron stood and turned off the TV. Jimmy stood, too, adjusting his carefully creased baseball cap.

"See you there," Ron said, stepping out of the van and into his Bucar.

Evelyn followed, getting into her own car, parked right behind Ron's. She locked herself inside, her heart thudding a loud, frantic beat in her eardrums as she watched Ron and Jimmy drive away.

Tonight's plans had been made on her terms and her timeline, but it was the killer's move. If she had it her way, he'd be behind bars by the end of the night. If he had it his way, she'd be in a body bag.

The lot at Haggarty's was full.

Evelyn drove through once more, looking for somewhere to park, looking for the killer, looking for the surveillance van. She spotted the van, parked near the front, but that was it.

Shit! She wasn't parking on the street and walking, because she doubted Cory and Miles would see her. And the federal agent in her just wouldn't let her double-park.

Finally, a man exited Haggarty's, hopped in a truck and took off.

Evelyn whipped into his spot. It was near the back of the lot, under a burned-out light Haggarty's hadn't bothered to fix, even after her abduction. The other lamps were dim, creating shadows more than they actually provided light.

The sun was low on the horizon, intensifying the shadows in the lot crammed with vehicles but empty of people. Unless someone was skulking behind the SUV two spots over. Or lurking in the back of the dark van three rows closer to the door. Or hiding somewhere else in the dingy lot, waiting for the right time to attack.

Her pulse instantly spiked, and her skin dampened with sweat. Fear anchored her to her seat, even though she knew the dark, empty lot was the perfect backdrop for her plan. But it was also the perfect backdrop for his.

She *knew* this guy. She'd been inside his head. And he was here.

The ringing of her BlackBerry made her jerk so hard in her seat that she bumped her head. She yanked the cell out of her pocket. "Hello?" she panted.

"Evelyn, what the hell are you doing?" Cory growled. "Get out of your car!"

She tried to control her breathing. "I'm going in now. Watch for him." She ended the call, hoping she could trust Cory with her life.

She patted her Glock, dried her palms on her jeans and took the keys out of the ignition. Stepping out of her car and shutting the door behind her felt like déjà vu, only backward.

Goose bumps suddenly prickled her arms and danced up to her neck, her internal warning system alerting her to danger.

She whipped around, leaping sideways in case a dart was flying toward her. Her fists shot in front of her face to protect her from a blow, but no one was there.

Evelyn let out a whoosh of breath, lowering her arms, but the tingling at the back of her neck persisted. Was he close?

She needed to get moving. She tucked her keys in her pocket and took slow, even steps toward the door. Her calves ached as she tensed her muscles against the need to walk faster, to race for the safety of the pub. Instead, she sucked in a deep breath and raised her chin.

Was this what Cassie had felt before she was abducted? Had she known the end was coming, sensed someone watching before he grabbed her? Or had she been oblivious until it was too late?

Not the time to think about that, Evelyn knew as she neared the door of the pub. Still, images rose in her mind, images she'd never seen, images that didn't exist, of Cassie lying in an open body bag. Her blond ringlets matted with blood, her pale skin even whiter, her limbs twisted and bruised, a circle carved in her chest.

Haggarty's door opened and a lone man stepped out. A dark baseball cap was pulled low over his brow, shadowing his eyes. He was dressed in black, from the work boots to the pants and long shirt.

Evelyn felt her nostrils flare as she angled her right foot back and her left hip forward so she was in a fighting stance. Her hand shifted toward her Glock.

He looked up. Muddy brown eyes locked on hers.

Her gaze raked over his face, searching for signs that it might be a disguise. Appearances meant nothing, especially tonight.

She stepped backward as he moved toward her. Were Cory and Miles watching? They'd damn well better have their guns out and their hands on the door handles.

The man held out a hand. "Jasper Evans." He smiled, revealing slightly crooked teeth. "You here alone? 'Cause if you're looking for company, I'll change my mind about leaving."

Evelyn squinted, studying the edges of his face for creases where he might have used makeup. But her gut told her it wasn't Harley. "Sorry. I'm meeting someone."

His shoulders jerked. "Figures. The pretty ones always are." He sighed and walked past.

She watched until he got into a beat-up Chevy and drove away. Then she scanned the parking lot, but she didn't see anyone, despite her gut screaming that someone was too close.

Maybe it was just anxiety making her paranoid. She wished she could believe that was it.

Now was the best time for the BAKBURY killer to make a grab for her, but the longer she stood at the door, the more suspicious *she'd* look. It was time to go inside.

She was reaching for the door when her BlackBerry rang. "Evelyn," she answered. Had one of the other agents spotted him?

"It's Ron."

"What is it?"

"We're all in place, waiting for you. We haven't seen anything."

She swallowed her disappointment. "Okay." That meant either the killer hadn't shown or he was in a solid disguise. If he planned to grab her from inside the pub, he'd need a much more elaborate plan than she'd expected. Or maybe he wanted to wait until she left, when it was even later, even darker.

Because as she stepped inside, the feeling of being watched didn't diminish. It grew stronger.

23

IT WAS SHOWTIME.

Evelyn shoved open the door to Haggarty's and walked inside. The acrid scent of beer instantly invaded her nostrils, mingling with the odor of too many people in too little space.

She tried to stride into the room the way Jo always did, as if she owned it. But her limbs felt disconnected and clumsy, too attuned to the fact that someone was probably watching her, waiting for an opportunity to strike.

Pushing through the crowd at the bar, she ordered a bottle of water and then scanned the room. She was looking for Tanner, but she was also looking for the killer. For any sign of the icy blue eyes that haunted her dreams. Or the shamrock green eyes of "Roger Pendleton." She saw neither.

But that would've been too easy. The killer knew the Roger Pendleton cover was blown. And his real image had been plastered on TV. He'd be in a new disguise.

She glanced around again, anyway, still not seeing Tanner. Then she froze.

At a table near one of the windows, so darkened with dirt

it was impossible to see through, were Kyle and Gabe. They were dressed casually, like her, in jeans and button-up shirts just oversized enough to conceal weapons. On the table in front of them were half-finished drinks.

They seemed to be deep in conversation, and they gave no sign they'd noticed her. Apparently, their acting was as good as the killer's. If she walked over to their table, they'd probably act surprised to see her, feign innocence about why they were there.

She felt hot, then cold. Kyle and Gabe meant well, but they didn't have any briefing on the case. Their very presence could jeopardize everything. But affection pushed through; she'd lost her temper with them and they still cared enough to look out for her.

Don't focus on it, she told herself. Now that they were here, she couldn't afford to draw attention to them. She sure as hell didn't want the killer to see them. She didn't want Ron to see them, either.

So she continued to maneuver through the packed pub. She saw Tanner near the back of the room and, to get to him, she had to walk within touching distance of Ron and Jimmy, who sat at a table near the bar.

As she walked past, she ignored them both, pretending not to know them. Ron just kept drinking. Jimmy gave her a quick up-and-down, but he'd probably done that to every woman who walked past.

Finally, she made it to Tanner, who was sitting at a raised table meant for four, but occupied only by him. Judging by the glares he was getting from the group of intoxicated men at the next table, he'd taken flak for it. Since glares were all he was getting, he'd obviously played his trump card and flashed his badge.

A nervous smile trembled on her lips. Tanner drawing attention to himself could work in her favor.

She climbed up onto the stool next to him.

"Evelyn." Tanner offered his hand over the table.

She put her hand in his and shook it perfunctorily. "Tanner. How's your evening going?" She raised her eyebrows meaningfully so he'd understand she was really asking if he'd noticed anything unusual.

"Just your average night. So, should we discuss the specifics of your abduction?"

"That's why we're here." Evelyn filled her suddenly dry throat with a large sip of water from the bottle she'd grabbed as she passed the bar. The thought of reliving even the few moments of her abduction she could remember made the pasta she'd forced down for dinner tumble in her stomach. Sweat gathered at her pores, and the room felt even hotter, more stifling.

Was the killer here, listening, waiting for his second chance?

"Right." Tanner shifted his bulk on the small stool.

Evelyn took a deep breath. "Let's get started." She wanted to be done with this. Her nerves were humming, her whole body twitchy and tense. Every second that passed without a phone call from Ron and Jimmy or Cory and Miles made her dinner do another flip in her stomach.

Someone see him, she prayed. But her phone stayed silent, so Evelyn forced herself to talk. Her tongue felt too thick, nervousness making her mouth dry despite another gulp of water. She pitched her voice a little too loud and said, "The killer waited until I had my back turned to sneak up behind me and hit me with the dart."

She needed to talk about her abduction in a way that made the killer seem cowardly. He was also a misogynist, so having people hear a woman talk about how she'd bested him should infuriate him. Evelyn hoped her acting was up to par. She'd had a lot of practice, sitting across the interrogation table from serial killers, but never when she'd been the intended victim.

"And the drugs wore off before he got you to his cabin, right?" Tanner prompted.

"Enough for me to fight back." Evelyn tried to vanquish the chill that ran through her as she remembered how the killer had chased her, her own gun in his hands.

She shook the image away and continued in a voice that almost didn't quaver. "After I got away, he tied up his next victim."

Tanner's eyebrows drew together and he nodded, delivering his practiced line perfectly. "That makes sense. He couldn't handle you, so he became worried about controlling anyone."

Evelyn shot a quick glance around the room, hoping to spot someone who was paying too much attention to their conversation. But no one seemed to care. She didn't even see anyone who appeared to be alone.

She squeezed her hands together under the table. Where was he? Dammit! Why hadn't someone spotted him?

The ringing of her phone shocked her so much she actually had to grab the table to keep her stool from tipping. She closed her eyes briefly. *Way to look nonchalant.* Cursing herself, she fumbled to answer the phone without even checking the readout, and cupped her hand over her other ear. "Hello?"

She dropped her feet off the rung of the stool, ready to jump down and race outside if Miles or Cory had seen him.

"Evelyn?"

She forced herself not to look at Ron. Was he looking at the killer? "What is it?"

"What the hell are your friends doing here?" Ron's voice was low, but his tone was furious. "I told you we didn't need help. It's bad enough that you invited them despite my refusal, but it stops there. Your friends better not follow us. Understand me?"

What was he doing, calling her to argue? He was going to make the killer suspicious, maybe even back off. She'd taken a huge gamble assuming that Keegan wouldn't be able to resist the first opportunity to come after her again. If he realized this was a trap, if he *did* resist, then she'd just set herself up for a whole new crisis.

One crisis at a time, she reminded herself, taking a deep breath to calm down. Now was not the time to have second thoughts.

She had to trust herself, had to trust that her profile of the killer was accurate. It was a hell of a thing to bank her career on, when she was as unsure of herself as she'd ever been, but her career was everything to her. She wouldn't risk losing it.

"This isn't the time—"

"I just wanted to make that clear," Ron broke in. "And you can damn well believe I'll be talking to your supervisor."

He hung up before she could reply, but she knew she had to act before he made things worse.

Evelyn leaned toward Tanner and improvised loudly. "Sorry. That was my boyfriend. I already told him I'd be late tonight, but I think I'll just call him back and tell him I'll see him tomorrow instead."

Tanner looked perplexed at first, but then he seemed to realize she needed his help. He leaned over and asked one of the drunks at the next table, "Any of you know what time this place closes?" Faster than she'd expected, he struck up a conversation, loud enough to cover the conversation she was about to have.

She dialed Gabe's number, figuring he'd be easier to reason with than Kyle. When he answered, she whispered, "You guys are pissing Ron off and causing problems for me. I need you to stay there." The words came out in a flurry, slowing only at the end to emphasize *stay there*.

Out of the corner of her eye, she glanced at them just as Kyle's gaze skipped over her. It moved past her as though he was simply looking around the room, but the force of that glance seemed to push her back in her seat. She suddenly wished he was the one watching her back instead of Ron.

But she couldn't mess this up. "Gabe?"

Gabe sounded contrite when he said, "We're concerned about you." He looked at Kyle before promising, "We'll back off."

"I have your word?"

He sounded reluctant, but said, "I promise."

In the background, she heard Kyle arguing, but she wasn't worried. He wouldn't break a promise, even if it was Gabe's.

She couldn't give him a chance to talk Gabe into backing out of it. So she said a quick "thanks" and hung up.

And felt a twinge of regret at losing the only backup she really trusted.

The FBI agents were laughable. To amuse himself while she talked to the cop, he'd asked the pretty boy agent for the time while he waited for the bartender to pour him a drink. That was reckless, but it had filled him with power, mended his frayed nerves, when the agents investigating his murders hadn't recognized him.

But he'd kept his distance with her. Unlike the rest of them, she was his equal.

He'd underestimated her the first time. And she'd almost overridden his control when she'd taunted him on TV. It had taken everything he had not to go for her in the parking lot, not to fall right in with her plan.

No, tonight, she was going to fall for *his* plan.

He pretended to laugh at a joke one of the engineers at his table told. He'd charmed his way into their group so he wouldn't stand out, but it was a challenge to pay attention to their idiotic conversation when she was across the room, a mere gunshot away.

His whole body was tense, his muscles pressed against the skin, shaking with the need to touch her. But that would come later, once he'd shed the disguise. Once the agents trying to blend into the crowd near the bar were taken care of and the cop had left. Once she was alone.

Evelyn. The name whispered in his mind, the name he'd wanted to know for so long.

She'd worn the ring for him tonight and he closed his eyes for just a moment, let himself imagine taking it from her.

When he opened them again, she was looking at him. He felt a jolt, then realized she was looking behind him, toward the windows. Slowly, he exhaled, sipped his whiskey and waited.

Soon, very soon, he would slide that ring from her finger, slip his blade into her skin and carve his mark on her. He imagined her head displayed in his woods…

A smile trembled and he hid it, stroked the gun in his pocket, the gun he'd taken from her before. He wouldn't have to be patient much longer.

An hour later, Evelyn knew it was time to go. The killer—if he was here—wasn't making his move in the pub.

She lifted her hands over her head, ostensibly stretching, but actually giving Ron and Jimmy their cue to leave. They chatted for another minute, then stood. Their table was immediately taken over by a group of men standing nearby. The agents didn't look back as they headed for the door.

She watched their progress out of the corner of her eye,

her breath catching as they neared Kyle and Gabe. But they passed by without acknowledging the HRT agents. Kyle and Gabe didn't even look up.

Across from her, Tanner seemed anxious for her to leave. Initially, he'd been thrilled at his inclusion in the plan. Now he sat slumped forward, both hands wrapped around his empty beer mug.

Evelyn spent another minute detailing the way she'd pushed the killer away from his own car and driven off, then said, "I don't know what else I can tell you about it."

"I think we have what we need." Tanner stood, shaking her hand once more. "You get a good night's sleep now."

She pushed herself off the stool. "I will. That's where I'm going now."

"Should I walk you out?"

"Nah." She waved off his offer with one hand. "I'll be fine."

Her legs wobbled when she started for the door, threading her way through a room that had become even more crowded since she'd arrived. As she maneuvered around a couple in the middle of the bar, she shot a glance back at Tanner.

He'd resumed sitting and struck up a conversation with another patron. If appearances could be believed, he wasn't paying attention to her at all. That probably wasn't true. But she hoped the killer would think she was on her own.

As she walked past the bar and over to the door, she felt Kyle and Gabe staring at her. She had a strong, sudden urge to call Kyle, but she ignored it and stepped outside, into the near-darkness of the parking lot.

A sudden flashback made her stumble. Images of herself, desperately grabbing for her car to stay upright as the whole world slid into oblivion. A gloved hand pressed hard against her mouth…

She sucked in air and forced her mind back to the present.

At the far end of the parking lot, Miles and Cory were feigning drunkenness, arguing loudly and occasionally shoving each other. They didn't seem to notice her.

Evelyn mentally applauded their performance, but her hand trembled as she positioned it near her hip, near her weapon. What if they were too far away to get to her in time? What if the killer wasn't waiting with a dart but with her gun?

Fear flooded in and she tried to dispel the panic. This killer didn't want her dead. Not immediately at any rate. And he wasn't going to use a gun unless it was his last resort. He liked to drain the life from his victims with his own hands.

She forced her feet to keep moving. Out of the corner of her eye, she spotted Ron's SUV and knew he and Jimmy were inside, watching her.

Although she didn't look back, she sensed that Kyle and Gabe were watching her, too, through the dirty window. An image of Kyle sitting in her living room, awake and alert when she'd come in, popped into her head. It calmed her nerves just a little, put slightly more confidence in her steps.

As she approached her vehicle, Evelyn pretended to stumble in the worst possible place. It was directly in front of her car, and when she went down, she was hidden from the view of Miles and Cory, the supposedly drunken men, by several large trucks and an SUV. The lightbulb directly overhead was burned out.

She'd planned it ahead of time, but with her hands on the pavement, in the place most suited for someone to attack, Evelyn's instinct was to jump right back to her feet. Instead, her trembling hands reached for the shoelace she'd loosened while sitting in the bar.

She lingered over retying it, her ears perked for the shuffle of footsteps. She heard nothing other than Cory and Miles, so finally she stood, resigned. A glance around the parking lot confirmed it.

He wasn't coming. Not here.

Feeling equally disappointed and relieved, she got into her car and locked the doors. Time for the next stage of her plan. Time to head home.

24

THE ROADS WERE DARK, BUT JUST AFTER TEN, there were enough vehicles to hide a tail. Evelyn's fingers moved nervously on the steering wheel as she checked her rearview mirror, looking for the agents. Looking for the killer.

The closer she got to her neighborhood, the more her foot unintentionally lifted off the gas. She stuck in her earpiece and called Ron on her BlackBerry. "I'm five minutes out. Are you in place?"

Some tiny, cowardly piece of her willed him to say he wasn't, to tell her he wanted to call the whole thing off.

"We're here," Ron said. "Your friends went home, right?" There was a demand behind the question.

"Yes." She'd have to talk him out of complaining to Dan about it, but later, when she didn't have to worry about a killer on her tail.

"Great. We're ready."

If only she felt as confident as Ron sounded. But it was *her* plan. And it was too late to back out now. "You'll see me soon."

Evelyn ended the call as she turned into her street. Here was where it could get tricky for the killer, because it would be a lot harder for him to follow her without being noticed.

She flicked on her brights to make it easier as she drove slowly toward her house. She noticed Ron and Jimmy's SUV on the street near her neighbor's place as she pulled into her driveway. Instead of going into her garage, she put the car in park, a beacon to the killer in case he'd lost her.

She reached for the door handle three times before she found the courage to open it. Locking the door behind her, she walked toward the front door, trying to look around inconspicuously for Ron and Jimmy.

She knew they were in the front yard and there were limited places to hide. The hedges separating her property from her neighbor's were dense, too dense to wade into. Massive fir trees dotted the yard, the best place for the agents to conceal themselves, but if they were there, she couldn't see them.

Fear made it hard to swallow. She comforted herself with the reminder that she wasn't supposed to see them. Neither would the killer.

But Ron and Jimmy would be watching her. She'd be illuminated by the accent lights lining her drive and the porch lights that came on automatically at nine. As she climbed the steps to her wraparound porch, Evelyn slowed her steps. Since her abduction, every shadow seemed to hide a potential threat.

Hypersensitive to the weight of the Glock at her hip, Evelyn strained for any sound that seemed out of place, especially a vehicle. She heard nothing. Either the killer hadn't taken the bait or he was talented at tailing potential victims. The tingling at the back of her neck told her it was the latter.

She reached the door and paused. It wasn't part of the plan for her to go inside like this.

Where the *hell* was he?

The tingling sensation at her neck grew more intense, made her shoulder blades tense against a blow and her feet prepare to run. She whipped around, but saw no one.

Trying to calm her pulse, she pulled out her keys. Every instinct told her not to go in alone, but what choice did she have? She couldn't stand on her front porch forever.

When a car pulled into her driveway, her eyes actually watered with gratitude. Then Cory jumped out. Where was Miles? *He* was supposed to walk her in.

In a voice that projected loudly enough to wake half the neighborhood, Cory called, "Evelyn! I'm glad you're still up. I need to talk to you. I promise I'll only stay a minute."

Even though they hadn't stuck to the plan, Evelyn stuck to the script. But her vocal cords felt strangled when she called back, "Sure. But just for a minute."

Cory's quick, efficient stride brought him to her side in seconds. The hair on the back of Evelyn's neck jumped to attention.

"Where's Miles?" she whispered tersely.

"I told him I'd do this," Cory whispered back, his warm breath brushing her ear, the scent of whiskey sliding into her nostrils.

Had he been drinking? Disgust and anger rolled over her. Evelyn took a step back.

"He's a rookie. I did a stint in the marines." Cory's gaze darkened. "And I'm a crack shot."

Evelyn pushed back the unease curling through her and opened the door.

When she started inside, Cory gripped her upper arm hard and shoved her aside so he could go in first.

Evelyn clenched her teeth at his bullying tactic. By the time she had the door shut and locked and the security system reset, Cory had his weapon in hand. He held it out in front of him, as if he was standing at the firing range, his eyes focused and assessing, his profile hard and uncompromising.

It should've made her feel secure. Instead, something about the glint in his eyes made her grab her own weapon.

She shifted the Glock in her hand until it felt more natural. The grip was different from her SIG Sauer, but a bullet from this weapon would be no less effective.

Her legs felt as weak as they had the day she'd been drugged as she waited for Cory to move. But he just looked back at her, raising his eyebrows expectantly.

Of course. He wanted her to go first because he didn't know the house.

She forced her legs to move, walking toward the living room and flipping on the light. The muscles in her back tightened, too attuned to Cory's closeness, and she had to fight the urge to check ahead of her *and* behind her. It was a hell of a time to realize how much she didn't trust him.

She flinched at the sound of his voice. "Whoa, Baine, you just move in?"

"No. It's a work in progress." The upside was that there were few places to hide, so she continued through to her study.

Cory followed so close behind that she occasionally felt his puffs of breath against the top of her head.

She looked under the massive desk, then turned to find Cory eyeing the books lining her shelves. Books on antisocial personalities, crime scene staging and signatures.

Giving him a wide berth, she headed back through the living room. She made short work of the dining room, which was completely devoid of furniture. Nowhere to hide and no one there.

The rest of the first floor didn't take long. They descended into the basement. The wide-open space, filled only with tools for fixing up the house and a few unpacked boxes, had never felt sinister. But today, it was an instant reminder of all the criminals she'd profiled who'd used their basements as burial sites. Images of crime scenes flashed through her head in vivid color, the smell of decay and death so strong in her memory she gagged.

"No one here." Cory's eyes narrowed as he watched her try to pull it together. "This is one hell of a house. You live with a boyfriend?"

Evelyn drew in a deep breath, tried to dismiss the images. "No." She kept her voice terse, an unspoken request for no more questions.

"What do you need such a big house for, then?"

Instead of answering, Evelyn went back up the stairs.

"And how can you afford this on Bureau pay?"

"None of your business" rushed to her lips, but she managed to restrain it as she climbed up to the second floor, avoiding the stairs she'd started to fix but never finished. Instead of replying, she warned, "Watch your step."

Cory made a guttural sound in response.

Two of the three bedrooms were totally empty and easy to sweep. After a quick peek into the closets, they moved toward her room. She didn't want him in there, but she didn't have a choice.

When she opened the door, he walked past her. She watched him assess the antique bed with the covers still thrown back and the over-the-counter sleeping pills on her side table. She'd finally decided to try them last night and forgotten to put them away.

As he checked under her bed and in her closet, Evelyn made a fast sweep of her bathroom. "Nothing," she told him as she returned to the room.

Cory stepped quickly away from her side table, but not

quickly enough to hide that he'd been snooping. Her sleeping pills were turned so the label was facing front.

Evelyn scowled, but Cory's hard, grim expression didn't change, and he didn't apologize. "Let's go."

She gestured for him to precede her down the stairs, wanting him out of her house so badly her whole body was tense.

He walked slowly toward the front door, turning back at the last second as if he were going to say something. Instead, he pressed his lips into a tight line as he studied her. Then he shook his head and opened the door, making a big show of leaving her house and driving away.

Evelyn's shoulders slumped with relief, but her fingers shook as she fumbled with the lock. Now there was nothing to do but sit here alone and wait for the killer.

Once before, a practiced predator had set his sights on her and she'd lived. Back then, someone else had died. Would it happen this time, too? Or was it finally her turn?

Where was he? Why hadn't the case agents called to tell her he was in handcuffs? To tell her he was no longer a threat? That she could sleep at night again, that she could go back to work with her head up, that she could stop being so afraid. *Dammit, where was he?*

The more time that passed, the more she feared the killer *wouldn't* come. That he'd followed her, figured out where she lived, but recognized the trap and had the willpower to wait however long it took for the case agents to give up.

She clutched the arms of the chair in her living room, where she'd been positioned for hours. She got up only to do periodic sweeps of her house when she felt too anxious to sit still and paranoia insisted he was in the house. She was feeling anxious right now. And paranoid.

Evelyn pulled her weapon from her holster and bracketed

the grip with cold hands. Stepping from room to room, she saw the house as Cory must have.

Moving from one apartment to the next with her mother and an endless stream of boyfriends had made Evelyn long for her own space. She'd craved the brief span of security she'd experienced at her grandparents' home. The old house, surrounded by live oaks, too large for just the three of them, had always been filled with friends and neighbors. With the smell of the strawberry pie her grandmother used to make. With love. It was the only place that had ever felt like home to her.

So, she'd tried to recreate it.

In Houston, she hadn't even tried to put down roots, knowing she wouldn't be there for more than a few years. She'd been putting in her time, filling her personnel file with a record of long hours and fierce dedication, waiting for a spot to open up at BAU.

And here she was, in her dream house, a near-replica of her grandparents' home. It had plenty of space, not just for her, but for the people she loved. But for the first time, instead of the comforting haven she'd craved for so many years, it just felt like an advertisement that she was all alone.

Moisture stung her eyes as she climbed up from the basement.

She wanted her grandma's voice in her ear, telling her everything would be all right, the way she had when Evelyn had first gone to live with her. She wanted her grandpa's arms, weathered from age but somehow strong enough to make her feel safe, wrapped around her.

Whenever she doubted herself, whenever she felt lonely, those memories rushed forward to sustain her. Tonight, they were absent.

Evelyn slid her weapon back into its holster and lowered herself into the chair in her living room. She was calling Ron every half hour and her watch said it was time to check in, so she hit redial.

Ron picked up immediately and whispered, "Everything's quiet."

Evelyn let out a sigh shaky with disappointment. "Here, too." She'd been so sure the killer wouldn't be able to resist.

"It's after midnight," Ron continued, and Evelyn had to punch up the volume on her phone to hear him. "This was a good idea, but it looks like our guy isn't going to bite. Maybe we should move you to a safe house for the night and regroup in the morning."

No! The word screamed through her head as panic squeezed tight. What would the killer do while she was holed up in some safe house? Scout out her place, breach her security while no one was watching and lie in wait until she returned? "The team's supposed to stay all night."

Ron sighed. Branches rustled as he shifted around, probably uncomfortable as hell inside a fir tree.

Surveillance was a thankless job, especially when nothing was happening.

"Don't you think if he was going to come after you, he would have done it already?" Ron asked. "We need to re-strategize."

Anger rushed after the panic and Evelyn grabbed on to it hard. Better to be mad than afraid.

In the background, Jimmy whispered something and Ron said, "Hold on." A minute later, he came back on the line and said, "I'll call you back." Before she could argue, he'd hung up.

It felt like hours, but only two minutes passed before her BlackBerry rang again. "I've been talking to Cory and Miles," Ron said when she picked up. "We can continue what we're doing, but it seems pointless."

The anger intensified, rushed forward like the surge of the

ocean, and Evelyn clamped her lips together, trying to keep it in.

"I told the others you were scared of being alone, but it didn't sound like you wanted to go to a safe house," Ron continued, "and Cory volunteered to stay. You could set him up in one of your spare bedrooms. Cory said you have a couple."

Like hell.

Evelyn closed her eyes and tried to rein in her temper.

"Evelyn?"

"It's not pointless," she said when she thought she had control of her anger. But it seeped into her voice, vibrating in every word. "If the killer's going to take the bait, it'll be tonight." She said it as much to reassure herself as to convince him. "But he might wait until he thinks I'm in bed."

Ron sighed again, but beneath the exasperation was acceptance.

She'd won. Relief rushed through her.

"Fine, we'll all stay," he muttered. "Why don't you pretend to do that?"

She was so focused on his first words that it took her a minute to catch up. "Do what?"

"Pretend to go to bed. We'll see if he makes his move." Ron didn't give her time to agree before adding, "You know, turn off the lights downstairs and turn them on in your room. If the curtains are open, leave them that way when you go to bed. Make sure he gets the picture."

Ugh. Evelyn's lips puckered in disgust. Now he sounded like Jimmy. She glanced at the window beside her, covered with opaque shades, wondering where the agents were positioned.

She'd turn off the lights down here and turn on the ones upstairs, like a trail of bread crumbs leading to her location, but she wasn't giving anyone a peep show!

Before Ron could offer any more advice, she said, "I'll head upstairs now," and hung up.

With one last look around her empty living room, she stood. She flipped off the light, then walked to the kitchen, checked the lock on the back door and turned that light off, too.

Then she maneuvered blindly up the steps, avoiding the dangerous spots.

In her bedroom, Evelyn hit the switch and flipped on her lamp, flooding the large room with light. Even with the curtains closed, anyone watching would see that only the lights in this room were on. It was like a beacon, screaming, "Come and get me."

That thought made her reach for her gun. So she'd have quicker access to it, she took off the shirt covering her tank top and tossed it aside. She hadn't slept well in weeks, but she felt a sudden, intense desire to bury herself under the covers, pretend this was all a nightmare and wake up to a new day.

She flipped off the overhead light. She began to turn off the lamp, too, but her hand tensed, unwilling to move the last inch, even though the moon was full enough to send slivers of light through her drapes. Instead, she lowered it to the floor beside Cassie's case file, where it wouldn't shine through the window.

She sat on the bed and leaned against the headboard, knowing it could be a long wait. But her anxiety spiked, and she had to sit up again, had to rest her palm against the grip of her gun.

She looked from one window to the other, then to the bathroom door, then the door to the hall. If he got past the agents, he'd most likely come in through either a downstairs or basement window.

He won't get past them. She tried chanting it out loud, but paranoia pushed through.

This killer would do whatever it took to get to her. After she'd gone on TV and mocked his inability to control her, it would be all he thought about, all he planned for. That kind of obsession was hard to beat.

A tremor shot through her body.

Call in, Evelyn willed Ron. *Tell me you caught him.*

But her phone was silent.

She glanced at her watch, but it wasn't time to call Ron yet. Unable to stay still, she got to her feet and started pacing, trying to work off her nerves. Every time she neared the door to her bedroom, she peered into the darkened hallway, looking for shapes that shouldn't have been there. She saw nothing.

On her fifth pass, she veered into the bathroom and reached under the bottom of the blinds to test the window latch. It was definitely locked.

Her gaze traveled to the smoked-glass shower door and her heartbeat thundered in her ears. Glad no one could see her, she pulled her weapon before wrenching the door open.

No one. She gasped out a relieved breath. Of course not. She'd checked the shower when she and Cory had gone through the house together. If someone had broken in since then, her alarm would've gone off. Plus, it wouldn't make sense for the killer to crouch in the shower waiting. He would have just come after her.

A violent shiver went through her, and her finger jerked against the trigger guard. She holstered her weapon and looked at her watch. Time to call Ron.

Walking back into her bedroom, she pressed redial. As she peered into the dark, motionless hallway, the phone rang and rang, finally sending her to voice mail.

Hope and terror twisted together. Could Ron have spotted the killer? Was that why he hadn't answered?

Just in case, Evelyn slipped her gun out of its holster. She hit redial a second time and walked into the bathroom, which had the only window facing the street. The blind was drawn, but when Ron still didn't answer, she flicked two slats apart with her fingers and pressed her eye into the space. She saw nothing.

She was about to drop the blind and call again when she glanced past the lights lining her driveway and into the street. The van that had been parked at the curb by her neighbor's property was gone. Ron's van was gone!

Fury overtook her fear. It was one thing to decide a stake-out was worthless and call it off, but to leave without warning the bait? To abandon her here without protection, letting her think they were keeping her safe?

"Dammit," Evelyn cursed.

She hit redial yet again and punched the send button with her gun hand as she pulled apart the same two slats, hoping she'd imagined it and the van was there. Or that someone had moved it. But she looked in both directions and didn't see it. As she got Ron's voice mail again, she let the blind fall back into place.

"You bastard—" she started, her voice trembling as she turned back into her bedroom.

Then her internal warning system went on high alert, the back of her neck prickling with sudden intensity. She wrenched her weapon up, but not fast enough.

A hand snaked around and clamped down hard over her mouth.

2 5

WITH FRIGHTENING SPEED, EVELYN WAS YANKED backward, crushed against someone bigger, stronger. His body felt as if it were made of steel instead of flesh and bone. His fingers clamped over her lips, making it hard to breathe, making it impossible to yell for help.

Her BlackBerry slipped and hit the floor. It split into two pieces and skidded across the bathroom. Using all her strength, she tried to push away from him, tried to move her gun.

His other arm slid around her waist, trapping her arms against her.

Her gym shoes fought for purchase on the floor as she tried to yank her arms free, but he squeezed tighter.

Her ribs creaked at the pressure and she wheezed in a frantic breath filled with whiskey, some kind of spicy cologne and her own sweat. He started dragging her backward, toward her bedroom, and Evelyn stomped down, hard, on his foot. Her gym shoe made contact with a heavy boot and just made him grunt.

He kept dragging her, lifting her slightly off the ground, his bicep bulging against her stomach.

She tried again, this time slamming her foot back toward his knee. Her ribs made an unnatural cracking sound and then his leg slipped out from under him, knocking them both off balance.

Her head smacked the floor, and then his weight came down half on top of her. Somehow, she still had her gun. And he'd shifted to brace his fall. She squirmed, twisting to aim her gun at him, her fingers straining to put pressure on the trigger.

He was faster, slamming an oversize fist into her hand, pounding it into the floor.

She managed to keep her grip on the gun. She tried to curl her finger back around the trigger, but it wouldn't bend.

He pushed himself up and a blur of dark green shirt and thick facial hair moved out of her vision as he yanked a needle from his pocket. Then his hand was hurtling toward her.

Her left hand was trapped between her body and the door frame, so she lifted her right hand, gun and all, to block the needle. The drugs had worked too fast before. And today, drugged meant dead.

She swung hard, slamming into the needle with enough force to send it skittering across the bathroom floor. In the process, she lost her grip on her gun and it, too, flew out of reach.

There was no time to go for it, because the hand she'd batted away came at her again, this time clenched in a fist with knuckles the size of bricks.

Evelyn moved fast, rolling back toward him, flipping her body on top of his in a gut-rocking motion that made her insides churn and spots form in front of her eyes. It knocked him back to the floor, and before he could move, she dug her elbow into his chest, propelling herself upward.

With every gasped breath, pain skipped over her ribs. She

saw her Glock across the bathroom, and her legs tensed to run for it, but she knew she wouldn't make it.

Abandoning her weapon, she spun to face her attacker. For the first time, as he pushed to his feet, his gaze locked on hers. The same ice-blue eyes, the same desire to kill. But first, to rape, torture and mutilate.

Fear froze her just long enough for him to land a solid punch to her chin. Her head went backward, and her body followed. Her vision blurred as she hit the floor.

He moved in for another quick hit. Bolting upright, Evelyn used all her strength to hurl the fist of her uninjured hand into his groin.

He hunched forward with a howl that echoed off the walls and should have sent the case agents storming the house had they not left her all alone. While he was still bent over, she jackknifed her right foot into the side of his leg, and he slammed sideways against the sink with a loud thud and the heavy clang of porcelain.

She pushed herself to her feet and lurched toward her bedroom. Unsteady, she banged into the door frame on the way, but she barely felt it.

She was almost there when a vicious yank on her ponytail sent her feet flying out from under her. She landed on her back, knocking all the air from her lungs.

She gasped for breath over and over, getting nothing.

Then he was straddling her chest, his knees crushing her arms, as he grabbed her tank top and ripped it down the middle.

Terror tore through her, the memory of her mother's boyfriend attacking her as a child rushing to the surface. She panicked, started thrashing. She tried to scream, but she could barely even take a breath.

Her hands flailed uselessly, her arms trapped. Her fingers began to go numb.

Then his hand closed around her neck and started squeezing, making her eyes water as she choked. But he wasn't squeezing hard enough to kill, she realized as he leaned closer, still smiling. He was playing with her.

Repulsion mingled with a sudden surge of fury. With strength she didn't think she had left, she yanked her legs up and out, hooking her feet around his chest. Then she pulled back and kicked.

He shot backward, landing several feet away with a thud that shook the floorboards.

Evelyn wheezed, trying to get air. Her throat felt bruised and swollen. Her arms shook as they tried to support her weight, tried to push her to her feet. He was standing over her again before Evelyn could get up, so she kicked and somehow managed to make contact with the same knee she'd gotten before.

He toppled down on her, bracing his fall with his hands. She tried to shove him off her, but he was too heavy. His chest was oddly flat and hard as it pressed into her. She could barely breathe, but a strangled yell ripped free.

She wasn't going to die this way.

Sucking air into her lungs, she slammed her hands as hard as she could into his chest. It felt like hitting a steel door. Pain radiated up her right hand as her little finger twisted unnaturally to the side, but she ignored it as he slid off her. She scrambled to her feet, made a desperate grab for the bedside phone, for help.

She jammed her finger onto nine and one, then realized there was no dial tone. Before she could turn, he crashed into her with enough force to propel her upper body into the wall over her side table. The table bruised her hips and her sleeping pills flew off.

Evelyn shoved herself off the wall, directly into him.

He hadn't expected it and they both stumbled backward.

He hit the lamp, and it toppled over and shattered, plunging the room into darkness.

Catching herself on the bed, she spun around, ready to dash past her attacker to the door, but he was back on his feet, closing the distance between them.

Cupping her left hand into a C shape, she drove it forward into his neck, using his own momentum against him. He made a gurgling noise as she tilted her hand upward and jammed it toward his chin. His head snapped toward his spine, and the strike knocked him into the box holding Cassie's case file and the mattress behind it. His disturbingly intense eyes widened with pain as he slid slowly to the ground, taking frenzied gasps of air.

Trapped between the killer on the floor and the wall behind her, Evelyn froze, looking for options as her eyes adjusted to the darkness. The only escape was out her bedroom door, so she leaped over him.

He managed to shoot his leg up, catching her hard on her shin.

She tripped, nearly falling flat on her face. Her right hip slammed into the floor with bone-jarring intensity, but she barely noticed as her left leg came down on top of the shattered lamp, ripping through her jeans and into her skin from ankle to knee.

Her leg throbbed, but she put her hands on the floor. It was slick with her blood and she slipped in it as she struggled to her feet.

The killer was still dragging in loud, labored breaths, but he was getting up.

She pulled back her fist, aiming for his head, intense fury almost blinding her.

He blocked her punch with his arm, but as he turned away to avoid the blow, Evelyn had her chance to escape.

She ran for the door.

They should've followed Evelyn from Haggarty's. But Kyle had been too afraid of being spotted, of angering Ron enough to jeopardize Evelyn. Kyle didn't want Ron thinking about anything besides protecting her tonight.

But that didn't mean he was going home. He'd done that the last time she'd left Haggarty's and he'd woken to the call telling him she was unconscious and hospitalized.

So he'd phoned Greg, demanded to know about the rest of their plan. Greg claimed he didn't know, and Gabe had decided that was the end of it.

"The other agents can handle it," Gabe had said, then raised an eyebrow and added, "If Evelyn doesn't handle it herself. He's not going to sneak up on her with a dart full of drugs this time. She'll be waiting for him with a loaded gun."

Gabe had gone home, probably assuming Kyle would, too. But a bad feeling had settled in Kyle's gut and refused to leave. The plan to catch the killer had seemed risky from the start. Gabe was right that Evelyn could normally take care of herself. But against the killer who'd gotten the jump on her before? The man who'd put fear in her eyes?

He couldn't chance it. He had to be there, watching her back. He didn't trust anyone else to do it.

The plan had been set up hastily, so he'd figured the most logical routine for Evelyn would be to go home. With no time to set up a false place of residence, they'd use her house.

So, here he was, feeling like a fool as he crept up to the edge of her yard. He didn't see the other agents' vehicles, but the smart thing to do would be to park on another street. Still, everything seemed quiet and the yard looked empty.

Had he been wrong about their destination?

He kept watching, searching for signs that she was inside. The lights were all off, except for porch lights that could have been set on an automatic timer. The yard had several huge fir trees the agents could have concealed themselves in.

He squinted, but didn't spot them. Deciding he could sweep the yard without getting caught by the other agents or the killer—if any of them were even here—Kyle pushed his way into the hedges separating Evelyn's property from her neighbor's. They seemed too dense to get into, but Kyle knew the branches would be bare near the center, giving him space to crawl forward, toward the house.

He'd done it before, in other locations, on actual missions, although he'd been better dressed for it. Now, branches tore at his arms and dirt caked on his knees. If the other agents *were* here and they did see him, he'd look like an idiot.

Still, he'd rather look like an idiot than have something happen to Evelyn. This was easier than sitting at Haggarty's had been, avoiding Ron's death stare and the nervous energy radiating off Evelyn.

But it was probably useless. He didn't see anyone and the most likely explanation wasn't that the agents were well hidden. It was that they weren't here.

Evelyn almost made it.

She had her hand on the door frame when the killer grabbed the back of her shirt, wrenching her arms behind her. But he'd already ripped it down the front, so it slid off her arms and left her free.

She kept going, getting a foot in the hallway before he

grabbed her again, this time by the hair, pulling her backward into the room.

Instinctively, Evelyn raised her right hand in an arc over her head, stretching ribs she'd definitely cracked again, and got hold of her ponytail right behind his hand. Her broken fingers throbbed, but she gripped harder, loosening his leverage. Regaining her footing, she shot her left, uninjured hand straight back and punched hard into his groin.

He yelped and dropped her hair.

Evelyn lurched forward, and he shoved her into the door frame. Her forehead and nose absorbed the brunt of the shock and her vision, already fuzzy, split everything in two.

Sensing that he was reaching for her again, she whipped around, only to discover that she was wrong.

He wasn't reaching for her. He was reaching behind him, and when his hand came back around, he was holding a switchblade. With a quick, practiced flick of his hand, it opened, revealing blood on the blade.

A shudder ripped through her. The blood was still wet. There'd been another woman and her death had been recent.

Son of a bitch. Rage coursed through her, gaining strength until it almost overpowered her fear.

His lips curled with predatory glee as he swung the weapon back and forth, stepping toward her.

She moved back slowly, sliding on her own blood, still dripping from her leg.

She hadn't regained her balance before the knife was shooting toward her face.

Evelyn darted sideways and the knife flashed past, close enough that she felt the tip graze her ear.

He leaned into the strike, and Evelyn flung both hands out, seizing his wrist. With strength she didn't think she had left, she twisted her hands in opposite directions. Pain reverberated from her broken fingers up her wrist, but she held on until his grip failed and the knife clattered to the floor. She kicked it out of the way.

Ignoring the knife as it skidded into the hallway, he reached behind him again. This time, when his hand reappeared, he was holding a gun. *Her* gun, the SIG Sauer he'd taken from her before.

Terror swelled as he raised the weapon.

Kyle didn't see anyone.

Still, he kept thrusting through the bushes, scanning the yard for possible hiding spots. There weren't many and he'd chosen the best one.

Just as he was calling himself all kinds of foolish, he heard a gurgling noise ahead. Kyle froze, straining to hear, then crept closer.

Realizing the source of the sound, he felt panic slam through him with the force of a sledgehammer. He bolted out of the bushes toward the fir tree closest to the house.

Jimmy was inside it, clutching the T-shirt he'd taken off to hold against his neck. Blood dripped between his fingers, streaking his chest with red.

When Kyle landed beside him, Jimmy whimpered and fell backward, dropping the shirt.

Kyle grabbed it, pressing it more effectively against the wound slashed from the left side of Jimmy's neck toward his chin. It looked shallow, but it had barely missed the jugular, and it could definitely still kill him. Given the ashen shade of Jimmy's face, whoever had slashed him had probably thought him dead when he'd moved on.

And he'd moved on to Ron.

Farther inside the tree, the senior agent lay unmoving, his

eyes open, unseeing. Kyle knew before he pressed his fingers to Ron's neck that he was dead.

"What happened?" Kyle asked Jimmy. He hadn't seen the killer, so the attack must've taken place several minutes earlier, before he'd arrived.

He stared up at the house, his blood racing way too fast in his veins. Several minutes was plenty of time to make another kill. Where was Evelyn?

The desire to rush inside was so intense he grabbed the closest tree branch to keep himself from moving. He'd learned the hard way that going anywhere without the right intel could get the hostage killed.

Jimmy's gaze was unfocused as he pulled his cell phone from his pocket. Tears streaked his face as he stabbed at the BlackBerry with shaking hands.

Kyle took it, saw that 9-1-1 had been dialed and requested police and an ambulance.

"Where's Evelyn?" he asked Jimmy, his dread intensifying with every second he didn't race for her.

"Inside," Jimmy croaked. His eyes darted back to Ron, then more tears dripped down his cheeks. "He's dead."

"Where's the killer?"

Jimmy's lips moved, but no words came out as he shook his head.

Kyle's hands tensed with the need to shake the young agent out of his shock. "Was there only one?"

"I—I just saw one," Jimmy managed.

Kyle pulled his Glock and checked the yard once more, desperate to move, desperate to get to Evelyn as fast as he could. But terrified of what he'd find.

"The other agents?" Kyle asked, not wanting to accidentally shoot any friendlies.

"They're not—they're not here," Jimmy said, taking one hand off his neck to clutch Kyle's arm. "Am I going to die?"

"You'll be okay. Help is coming." He forced Jimmy's hand back to his neck. "Keep pressure on this." It was all either of them could do for him.

"Don't leave me alone," Jimmy whispered, but Kyle was already dashing for the front door. He had no choice.

He'd been trained to assess the injured and keep moving, had done it dozens of times before. Usually, he could shift instantly into battle mode and do his job, no matter the chaos and casualties around him. But today, the terror coiling in his chest was like nothing he'd ever felt before. Evelyn was in there.

He stayed low as he rushed the door, in case the killer had brought something more suitable for long-distance killing than a knife.

As he lifted his foot to kick in the door, a gunshot cracked through the air.

Evelyn slapped both hands into the side of the gun as it exploded, making her ears ring. But the bullet went past her.

He growled and swung it back for another try.

She caught his wrist, forcing her broken fingers to bend, and yanked the gun past her side and down.

In the same motion, she jerked her good knee toward his face. Pain wrenched through her ribs, slowed her down, but she made contact with his nose.

There was a satisfying crack, then he gave a strangled cry and the gun clattered to the floor.

As he grabbed for his broken nose and stumbled backward, Evelyn threw herself to the ground. She landed hard, her hips absorbing most of the impact, and grabbed the gun. She flipped onto her back.

He was coming toward her again, rage and a touch of insanity in his eyes.

She pulled the trigger.

The shot was dead center in his chest. It propelled him backward into the middle of her bedroom. He hit the floor so hard that she felt it vibrate. Then he was still.

Sucking in a raspy breath, her heart pumping so fast her chest hurt, Evelyn pushed herself to her feet. Every step toward him hurt, and an even stronger pain wrapped around her chest. The pain of betrayal.

Where had the case agents gone? Why had they left her alone? Pushing the thought out of her mind, she followed FBI protocol and stepped forward, reaching for her handcuffs.

She was about to check his pulse to make sure he was dead, when there was a huge crash downstairs, the sound of wood splintering.

She almost lost her balance as another crash followed—someone falling on her unfinished stairs. She raised her weapon toward her bedroom door, toward the new threat, whatever it was.

Then the body at her feet leaped up, knocking her weapon from her mangled grasp as he threw her backward into the wall.

Realization spiraled through her as his body pressed hard against hers. *A vest.* The bastard was wearing a Kevlar vest.

She thrust her left fist into the bridge of his already broken nose and, twisting her body for leverage, she kicked his injured knee with all her strength.

His head snapped back, then his leg buckled. He hit the floor, blood streaming from his nose. His eyelids flickered, as though trying to stay open.

Evelyn dropped to her knees. She didn't have the strength to flip him. So, hands shaking, she cuffed him in front.

Then, she went for her gun. She gasped for air, her bruised throat burning as if it were on fire as she swung her weapon back and forth between the unmoving killer and the unknown danger heading for her door.

Her finger tensed on the trigger as Kyle raced through the door, his own weapon held out, arms corded with tension, murder in his eyes.

A shaky breath escaped as she loosened her grip on the gun and swung it back toward the man she'd finally defeated.

As his eyelids closed over eyes still fixed eerily on her, Evelyn's body gave out and she fell to the floor beside him.

2 6

"GET MY OTHER GUN," EVELYN WHEEZED, NOT taking her gaze off Harley Keegan.

Instead, Kyle knelt beside her, pressed his hand to her chin and tilted her head upward.

Too exhausted to argue, she let him study her pupil reaction, let him reassure himself that she was okay. Tears threatened to spill over and she gulped in deep breaths, hoping to keep them in.

Finally, he nodded, his face taut with too much emotion, his own eyes watery. He slid his hand around her head to probe at the various bumps.

She hardly felt his careful inspection as she watched for any sign that Harley was conscious. But he lay unmoving, his right leg bent at an unnatural angle, blood streaming from his nose.

Kyle finally finished poking at her head and followed her gaze. His eyes narrowed and he stood, strode over to Harley and grabbed a fistful of his shirt, lifting the killer partway off the ground.

When Harley didn't react, he muttered something Evelyn

could barely make out over the ringing in her ears. But he sounded disappointed and she finally understood what he'd said. "Out cold."

Kyle reholstered his weapon, unbuttoned his shirt and pulled it off.

It wasn't until he slipped the sleeve over one of her arms that Evelyn noticed she was only wearing jeans and a bra. She was too busy fighting tears to worry about the embarrassment as she let him cover her up.

As he pulled off his undershirt, ripped it down the middle and wrapped it carefully over the shredded skin on her calf, she leaned forward until her forehead was resting against his shoulder. She shuddered, squeezing her eyes tightly shut.

He knotted the undershirt around her calf, then slid closer, placing his arms around her.

She slumped against him, her heart rate slowing. For the first time since she'd been abducted, she felt safe again.

Her next gulped breath sounded like a sob. She didn't know she was crying until she turned her head and felt her tears on Kyle's neck. And then they wouldn't stop. As sobs racked her, she soaked his bare shoulder with seventeen years of pent-up grief.

His arms tightened around her until she could almost forget there was a killer lying on her bedroom floor.

As her sobs came to an end, the ringing in her ears got louder. It wasn't the after-effects of the gunshot, she realized, but an ambulance, getting closer.

She pulled back from his embrace and scrubbed her hand over her damp face, wiping away the rest of the tears on the shirt he'd put on her. As her breathing evened out, a different tension settled in her stomach.

Kyle was still close beside her, so much worry in his eyes.

He'd cared enough to follow her, to risk his career by butting into another agent's case, to risk his life by coming after her.

Right now, only one thing mattered—that he was here for her.

Before she could change her mind, she leaned forward again. He was very still as she brushed her lips over his, either afraid to hurt her or unwilling to take advantage.

So she pressed a little harder, until he was kissing her back, softly, carefully.

Too soon, footsteps were pounding toward them and Kyle pulled back, something new in the blue heat of his gaze.

"Thanks, Mac," she whispered as Cory rushed into the room, weapon raised.

"Front door was broken in," Cory said, sounding winded, his eyes wide as he surveyed the room.

Evelyn followed his gaze, from the broken lamp to the blood on the floor, to the unconscious killer. His face paled as he looked at her. "Jimmy sent me inside to help you. Miles is with him, but he's in bad shape."

Evelyn wanted to ask about Jimmy and Ron, but what came out was a broken, "Where were you?"

Cory's mouth opened and closed until he finally said, "Miles and I went to get coffee for the team." His voice became lower, unsteady. "Jimmy said the killer snuck up on them. He was good. Neither of them heard him." His voice shook when he added, "Ron didn't make it."

Evelyn felt herself sway.

"Help Miles with Jimmy," Kyle ordered. "Keep pressure on his wound until the paramedics get here."

The ringing sound suddenly stopped and Cory said, "They're here." When his eyes went back to the killer, then to Kyle, the shock on his face changed into grudging appreciation. "At least you got him."

There was an edge to Kyle's voice when he corrected him. "Not me. Evelyn took him down."

Cory's gaze came back to her. The worry and dislike fighting in his eyes mingled with something else. Something like respect. He gave her a curt nod, then hurried out of her room.

A moment later, four police officers and two paramedics pushed their way in. Someone checked her pulse, someone else checked Harley's and then the paramedics lifted Harley onto a backboard.

As they began to carry him downstairs, his eyes flickered open.

His eyes darted frantically around the room, then latched on to her. They still held evil, but this time, she wasn't afraid.

Before the paramedics carried him away, she met his ice-blue eyes and raised her chin in victory.

The cops still in her room shuffled their feet, looking around the crime scene, apparently uncertain what to do now.

"Please get my gun," she croaked at them. "My other gun. In the bathroom."

One of the cops nodded jerkily and went into the bathroom and then he was back, handing her the Glock. Trembling, she wrapped her broken fingers around the butt of the gun.

She heard an ambulance roar to life outside and the other cop told her, "Agent Drescott's on his way to the hospital. Medics said he's going to live."

His partner added, "There's another ambulance for you. The medics will be up with a stretcher in a minute."

Evelyn looked at Kyle and shook her head.

Somehow, he knew what she wanted. "I'll carry you."

"No." Even through her raw throat, she sounded sure. "I can walk." She glanced down at the blood already seeping through the undershirt tied around her calf and cringed, but she was *not* getting carried out like a victim.

She holstered her SIG and moved her finger outside the trigger guard on her Glock, then reached her hands out toward him.

He got it. Somehow, she'd known he would.

Instead of taking her hands, he lifted her from her hips, letting her brace herself against him as he pulled her up. He helped her turn, looping one of her hands around his waist.

Even as she clung to him, Evelyn glanced back at the spilled box by her bed, the one the killer had fallen into, the one containing Cassie's file. The contents of the file were scattered by her bed, an instant reminder of the first time she'd escaped death.

For seventeen years, she'd felt like a piece of her was missing along with Cassie. She'd chased that missing piece, chased Cassie, chased her career, for so long now.

But maybe it was finally time to move forward.

Evelyn took a deep breath and turned back to Kyle, letting him take most of her weight.

"Ready?" Kyle asked.

"I'm ready."

EPILOGUE

One week later

"FIDELITY. BRAVERY. INTEGRITY. THE MEN AND women we honor today exemplify the FBI's motto." The FBI director spoke solemnly from the front of the room at headquarters in Washington, D.C.

Against the back wall, Evelyn leaned more heavily on her crutch to take the weight off her aching leg. Hundreds of agents filled the room to capacity. Beside her, Kyle stood stoically in a dark blue suit.

Technically, she was still on mandatory sick leave and would be for another three weeks. But although she needed time to heal, she already missed having real purpose to each day; she'd be badgering Dan to let her come back early. And there'd been no way she was missing the annual FBI memorial service.

"Today we recognize their sacrifice and we mourn the addition of two more names to our list of Service Martyrs." The director nodded at someone in the background and the screen at the front of the room showed the image of the very first FBI agent killed in the line of duty, back in 1925.

By the time Ron Harding's picture came up, Evelyn thought

she was ready for it. But regret rose in her chest, guilt that Harley had come for her and Ron had paid the ultimate price.

Kyle's fingers laced through hers and she latched on to them. At least Harley was in custody. It would probably be a year before his trial, but he wasn't going to see the outside of a cell ever again. Evelyn hoped Ron's family could take some small comfort in that.

Then Diana Ballard's smiling face lit up the screen. It was the shot from Kate's house, the day Diana had graduated from the FBI Academy. For three years, the FBI had considered including Diana in the annual ceremony and decided against it. No one had wanted to admit she was gone.

Evelyn understood the desire to keep that hope alive, but she also knew how it could destroy those left behind, left to always wonder. So, when she'd heard that Harley had asked to talk to her, she'd been adamant about going.

She'd stared into his ice-blue eyes, intent on using every trick she'd ever learned about getting information from a killer in order to find out about Diana. But ultimately, Harley had wanted to tell her.

She was right that he'd never intended to kill Diana, that he'd felt guilty about it. And ironically, even though he'd wanted to kill *her,* he would talk to no one else about Diana because he'd viewed her as a worthy opponent. He'd told her she'd earned it.

And then he'd actually cried when he'd admitted the truth, told her how he'd buried Diana in his basement, then moved her to Connecticut two years later. FBI agents had gone to Harley's childhood home and, in the woods, they'd uncovered the bodies of Harley's father and Diana.

Evelyn had called Terry and Kate personally, had cried with Kate in a bond she'd never wanted to share with anyone before. Cassie hadn't been her sister, but she might as well have been. One day, Evelyn wanted closure for herself. But for now, giving Diana's family that closure had healed something inside her, something she'd thought would always be broken.

She drew strength from the knowledge of what she'd managed to accomplish where thousands of hours of investigation had failed. If she could solve this case, then maybe, someday, Cassie's case would come to her desk and she'd be able to find answers for herself, too.

But for now, Kate would finally be able to move on. And all the doubts that had begun to creep into Evelyn's mind about where she belonged had disappeared.

As Diana's picture faded to black and the lights came up, Evelyn turned to Kyle, surprised to find she was still clutching his hand. Her eyes felt watery, but she smiled at him, a strange lightness in her heart she'd never felt before. If Kate could move forward, then so could she.

It was time.

★ ★ ★ ★ ★

Author's Note

I'm so glad you picked up my debut novel, *Hunted*. It's the first book in The Profiler series and it follows dedicated FBI profiler Evelyn Baine as she discovers just how deadly it can be to get inside the head of a killer.

I've long been fascinated by profiling—looking at a crime scene and seeing pieces of a killer's personality he doesn't know he's left behind. Evelyn picked this job when she was twelve years old and her best friend disappeared. She was never found and now Evelyn spends her days trying to give other families the closure she didn't get.

Evelyn will be back in January 2015 in *Vanished,* when she may finally get the chance to uncover what really happened to her best friend. After *Vanished,* I hope you'll check out my romantic suspense trilogy with Harlequin Intrigue, also featuring FBI agents (can you tell they make some of my favorite characters?).

Visit me at www.elizabethheiter.com for more information about upcoming releases!

Elizabeth Heiter

Acknowledgments

Writing can be a solitary process, but I have been blessed with unfaltering support from my family and friends along this journey. I hope you all know how much I appreciate you.

Special, heartfelt thanks to:

My mom, Chris Heiter, and my writing partner, Robbie Terman, for reading every single book, sometimes more than once, and always pushing me onward.

My sisters, Kathryn Merhar and Caroline Heiter; my uncle, Tom Dunikowski; my friends, Charlie Schaldenbrand, Ian Anderson, Kristen Kobet, Christy Piangozza, Alea Gale, Drew Knofski, Steve Bennett and Julie Lepsetz; my pixie pal, Rachel Grant; and my mystery writers' group, Ann Forsaith, Charles Shipps, Sasha Orr and Nora Smith. Thank you for all the feedback over the years. I'm so grateful to each of you for your love and support!

My friends Ian Anderson and Chris Kobet for sharing their knowledge. Thank you for helping me get the details right!

My graphics gurus Jason Tastevin and Mark Nalbach for creating my fantastic website.

My agent, Kevan Lyon, for guiding me through this process. My editor, Paula Eykelhof, for pointing me in new and fascinating directions. I'd also like to thank the entire team at MIRA for all their work behind the scenes (with special thanks to the Art Department for giving me a cover I adore!).

Finally, I'd like to thank Allison Brennan, Suzanne Brockmann, Laura Griffin, Hank Phillippi Ryan and Zoë Sharp for agreeing to read *Hunted*—it's thrilling to have such incredible authors endorse my debut.